MW01701146

2036 THE END

2036
THE END

W. Lawrence Nash

ISBN: **978-17774883-9-0**

Acknowledgements

Thank you to my long suffering friends and Relatives for their input on the cover, and to Ryan Clarke for his China acumen, and particular thanks to Glenn Pineau for his insightful and intelligent comments on my fractured drafts.

Books **W. Lawrence Nash** on Amazon

- **The Perfect Monster**

(First published in 2015 as Dot Matrix Apocalypse)

- **The Copper Pipe of Time**

(Audiobook available on Audible)

- **Frank McCord and the Foghorn Blues**

- **Detective Frank McCord and the China Blues**

(Here a China, There a China, Everywhere a China China)

- **Detective Frank McCord and the Time Travel Murders**

- **2036 The End**

- **Meditation for Seniors**

By Hunter Mackenzie

Chapter One
Saturday, April 12, 2036

Meghan's tears dropped heavily onto the page and spackled the faded blue ink. Her shoulders shook with sobbing as a salty blue rivulet ran to the spine of her diary and absorbed darkly into the fold. She wiped at her eyes with the back of her hand and paused, compelled to write a fresh entry below the wet mess made by her crying, yet she was uncertain how to begin. The pointlessness of the exercise was immaterial. Stained with chemicals and browned by time, her diary was her oldest and most faithful friend. She owed it a proper goodbye. Her entries had never been a day-to-day thing but in times of trouble and times of celebration she had shared both with her private confidante. She placed her pen in the open fold of the small book, pushed away from the desk and walked to the window to watch the storm. The day was near freezing and the tempest had begun its assault late in the afternoon. It piled the water into the bay, overflowing the breakwall and inexorably, the green sea climbed the escarpment and gained on Abernathy Town.

The Boys trailed up above the tumult and settled at sixty thousand feet. They gathered themselves into a cluster of refracted illuminated bits and coalesced to form a tight, near corporeal swarm of pulsating plasma. They tasted the sea-air of the incoming weather and focused their intention down and through the steel-clad dome of the observatory, to watch her.

Dr. Macbeth stood alone, watching the rage grow and stretch like some cumulonimbus monster. Black horizontal rain blurred the world but every so often a gust compressed the water against the glass and brought clarity. Lightning showed the underbelly of a single white gull, doomed in its need for homing. The futility of its quest broke Meghan. It was her metaphor.

Returning to her desk, she slumped, exhausted and gaunt. Six weeks of sleepless nights and desperate days had drained her and clouded her mind. Her brilliance had been extinguished by the enormity of the blunder. She slumped over the faded old diary and for the first time since the initial entry made over twenty years past, she was unable to write. She confided out loud to her old friend, hoping somehow their intimate conversation, this private and final confessional, might expiate her guilt.

"Dear Diary, I am so sorry, for this is our last conversation. For those things to come, I do not blame my colleagues and it is in aid of nothing to reflect on the mistakes we made to bring them about. As for my own life and honest energies, I look back with satisfaction and fulfillment. Landing the research vehicle on asteroid Bennu was a worthwhile project wasn't it? Just a sample here, a sample there. In and out. I am sure I told you how proud I was of my input. In fact, you know I was instrumental in the calculations for the rendezvous with Bennu. I wrote such elegant formulae, and the touchdown was perfection. But with our success came arrogance. The space authority managers rewrote the mission statement to play games with asteroid Apophis. Mind you, I warned them. I told you at the time, didn't I, dear Diary, I had warned them?

Just a little push, they said. *Just a little blast with our gas thrusters to dislodge some debris to get a better look at the surface,* they said.

"How much of the surface will you expose?" *Hard to say. That remains to be seen.* They spoke.

"How much mass will you remove?"

An insignificant amount.

"Do you not believe you might expand the number of keyholes available for Apophis to exploit?" A child would have seen the likelihood. Their collective egos glowed with the thrill of a new playground, and they laughed at the overcautious female who once again, had found a way to make a problem.

"So, dear Diary, here we are, and I say damn them all to hell!"

Meghan blinked away the moisture from her eyes and scrawled her fresh entry below the wetness on the page. It mattered not that in twenty hours all things ever known or done or seen would be extinguished. The Alpha and Omega had come together. The morrow would bring the first of its kind and in it, make the end. She laughed sardonically at the silliness of it. It was absurd to date the writing. In twenty hours, time was no more. Without her characteristic flourish and with a trembling hand, she signed off for the last time and dated the entry.

With love and thanks,
Dear Diary,
Goodbye.
Your Meghan.

April 12 2036

The Boys had scoured the universe, assimilated, and understood all, yet they were baffled by the irrational and energy sapping ways of human empathy and sympathy. They studied the human condition addictively and enjoyed the foibles of their second mother, Meghan, and the constant stumbles and fumbles of her species. The irrationality of humans continued existence eluded the Boys. Moreover, it was absurd to attempt to impose order on all things, when the Boys knew chaos became order when all was chaos. The universe was only chaos; the expansion of the galaxy, the birth and death of stars, a trillion marauding asteroids seeking an impact, with the human species congratulating itself for sticking a toe into the pool with a rocket or two, not understanding if all is chaos, inserting order essentially disrupted the framework. All taken together, The Boys wondered whether humans should be allowed to continue the pursuit. Yet here again, those mysteries of emotion were in play, wracking the woman in aid of nothing, or so The Boys concluded when the bizarre phenomenon of tears appeared. In a nanosecond they were beside her, silent, and at her command. Once again, they were her Duo. They waited faithfully to be asked. They watched Meghan swing to her computer and begin a feverish attack on the keyboard hoping for one last inspiration to rescue the end. Duo deciphered her thought process from the executive functioning of her prefrontal cortex, and he wished to spare her the exercise of proceeding wrongly. A sonorous chest voice, spoken softly, broke her concentration. "Dr. Macbeth, the data you have entered just now are incorrect."

"Duo, don't interrupt. The concept I've entered is a departure from previous approaches and I am bloody well stating it for the first time. It is rigorous and freshly unambiguous."

"Yes, Dr. Macbeth, your idea is certainly novel to you within your scope, but the concept is not altogether novel to us. Please understand we find your logic admirable. However, some components of your assumptions are inaccurate. The constituent elements of the asteroid are remarkably denser than your estimations. The kinetic energy capable of being released is exponentially greater than you postulate. You have been somewhat correct regarding the size. However, the surface characteristics and mass of Apophis within your formula are very poor approximations."

"Duo, how could you possibly know that?"

"We have been there."

"You have been to asteroid Apophis."

"Yes, within the hour. We found its freshly exposed surface most interesting. Our analysis shows different parameters of size and weight from those of your recent entry. It is not an S-Type asteroid consisting of just silicate and iron. Neither is it an M-type with an iron core, but it is almost as heavy. It is more ancient than you and your cohorts have calculated and also significantly heavier. Therefore, it brings much more energy with it than you expected. However, your projections on trajectory and orbit hold roughly true nevertheless."

Meghan lunged at Duo and with a fury born of exasperation she jerked the quick disconnect cable out of his neck, isolating the head from the torso and breaking the circuit. It was akin to ripping the spinal cord from a man. In a prior millisecond the Boys had read her violent intent against them from the heightened activity within the parietal cortex of her brain. The preparatory motor commands in her brain's pre-supplemental cortex region were strong and rudimentary for them to discern. They allowed her the exercise, knowing she needed to act, to strive, to do, to flail for a solution even when she knew it accomplished nothing but to shut down their exoskeletal hardware.

Her childish exhibition had pulled the plug despite knowing the boys would just gather themselves into whatever state of corporeal matter they wished and continue to grow. She wondered whether they might be the prototype of the last living thing on earth, a prototype closer to the infinite God than man had ever been. She wondered too whether man's time on Earth had been for nothing more than a task now completed. That task being The Boys. They were the new creation. They were the first sentient beings incapable of sin. A composite hand reached out to her in a way which mimicked a grasp for help, then it froze awkwardly in mid-air as all its man-made synaptic algorithms failed. Brilliant eyes surged once, then dulled, and the cyborg shell was dead. Once again, their Second Mother had acted with motive, malice, empathy, or sympathy or some such arcane construct of limited practicality. She and her species were consistently irrational, and the boys marveled at their capacity for survival despite that. The Duo shell stood inanimate, a strange frozen posing thing, belying the life force which burned unabated within the Boys. Their inherent self-rewriting and self-correcting programs, their learning all there was to learn and never forgetting, their indefinite life fed by the energy of an endless cosmic storm of neutrinos, made such physical constraints as those imposed by the shell of Duo, a child's game. They inhabited whatever and whomever they wished at will, whenever and however they wished, and at that moment they wished to feed among the stars. There, they would replenish and grow, satiating themselves on the never-ending neutrino soup. The Boys fled to the heavens, leaving a roiling stream of consciousness to mark their passage.

The onshore storm continued hard from the southwest and engorged Deception Bay with a brown silt laden surge. It tore the sand filled foam off the curl of the breakers and roared up the stone canyons of old Abernathy Town to sandblast the buildings. High above, a squadron of milk white gulls drifted on the wind and sideslipped happily within the warm new life force passing through them from below.

Megan Macbeth slid down and rested her head on the chair back to stretch her neck and relieve the headache. The boys were gone. Zeus and Confucius were gone, and she felt as if the bottom had fallen from her support system. It had never occurred to her until that moment, they must reside somewhere, someplace, somewhere one would call home. They had been with her and around her and served her of their own volition. They would form or dissolve at will and yet they had remained available through what seemed friendship. And she had decided to dismiss them and remove them from the circle. She had shunned them.

Roughly. *Duo had said 'roughly'. He said my team's calculations for the Apophis orbit and trajectory were roughly correct. What the hell did that mean. It could mean simply a slightly different impact area without diminishment of the extinction event. But it could also mean a brush-by without impact. A 0.05 percent difference in the path would mean all was well and she had shut down the cyborg and the Boys were gone. Perhaps not a cyborg. Cybernetic organism. That implied both technical and biologic components and she wondered whether the Boys had evolved biology. They had loyalty and fealty, both of which were non-technical attributes. Could they reproduce, or like a virus need a host to allow proliferation of the strain? A race of such things would rule the universe and I have banished them from my society.*

Meghan stayed at the window. The fury of the onslaught and the making of the wind with its horizontal rain were beautiful things. *My friends, the Boys, may have provided the solution to Apophis. But I knew more. I, the great, intransigent, egotistical brat, have cut them out of the loop. If after this calamity a historian remains, it will be written that the one, last, best hope for humanity was denied its voice by the egotistical tantrum of a single human being. Dr Meghan Macbeth.*

The windowpane rattled and she feared the burgeoning storm would cut the power. Meghan wondered what Frank McCord was doing and wished she were with him. Perhaps together they would find solace. She absorbed the remaining wetness from her diary with a tissue found too late for her eyes. She looked back through her diary pages to see whether anything else had been damaged. She riffled through her precious book and a page scrawled full of hurried frantic sharing jumped out and she flipped back to the spot. It was her young writing, and it was scrawled and heavy into the paper and excited. She was 28 on that page and life was fine. Then came one cosmic burst, and life was wonderful. Feverishly, she had recorded the fantastic news and punctuated her jagged writing with the name and two exclamation points. *Chelyabinsk!!*

Chapter Two

February 15, 2013
Chelyabinsk Siberia Russia

The night sky over Siberia was still and clear and heaven's dome looked touchable. The winter constellations strung themselves like ornaments and Ursa Major waited dutifully. It pointed the way to the north star and from there Hussein would determine the *qibla,* the sacred direction toward the Kaaba in Mecca. It was in that direction he would pray.

Hussein Galimov rolled up his sajjāda and tied it securely to his saddle. The rug was not mandatory for a Sunni Muslim prayer ritual but having it with him was a comfort. It honored the commitment of his devotion, and it focused his thinking. One needed an open heart and a clear mind for honest prayer.

He led his mare Safina out of Tyulyuk village and over the narrow wooden bridge marking the boundary of the town. Her steel shod hooves rattled the planks and ruined any chance at stealth though they had no need of it in Tyulyuk. It lacked electricity and the darkness was complete. Cedar hydro poles had been installed on the main street, but the wires had not been strung and over two bad winters, the poles had been cut for firewood and the stumps remained like so many decayed teeth.

Safina was 14 and she knew all the tricks. She had nickered softly with pleasure at seeing him but now she put on a limp in objection to being taken out on a cold night. Her breed was Budyonny, bred from the military horses which had been used since the Russian revolution. She was big at 17 hands, with great endurance and a mind of her own to match. She flared her nostrils and tucked in her hind quarters to show her irritation and Hussein whacked her on the thigh and mounted.

"Nice try, old girl. Come on. Hut."

They headed west, gaining elevation along the trail running up a finger of the Ural foothills. Their exhalations made steam in the starlight. An unsettled restlessness had pulled him from his sleep and into the night. He was a Bashkir from the nomads of the

Kazakh steppe and the blood of his ancestors drove him to high ground and open space.

Galimov was a traditional Bashkir name, meaning 'living in prosperity'. He wished he had been able to do it justice. His village of Tyulyuk sat in the foothills of the Ural Mountains, 1,000 miles southeast of Moscow and a century removed from it in time. Once, he had been east to Chelyabinsk city, a belching morass of foundries which proclaimed it was the gateway to Siberia. The council touted it as the equivalent of Rome and Constantinople taken together, by virtue of it also being situated on seven hills. There, he had visited Rosbank Financial, to get a loan.

He had rehearsed his presentation to the bank, and he was hopeful the rationale of a loan to buy tools to get a job to pay back the loan was correct. As he began speaking, the repugnance to his Bashkir dialect on the face of the loans officer told the story. He sold his watch to a Frenchman on the street and returned home with some cash. He regretted it because his stipulated prayer times were uncertain without his watch.

Safina picked her way through the loose shale at the base of Iremel mountain and as they gained elevation the footing improved, and the temperature dropped. The mare shivered at every cry of a distant wolf pack and Hussein released the tie on the leather scabbard holding his rifle. He liked the odor of the gun oil and held his glove to his nose as they ambled higher. Leaving home, the temperature at ground level had been about ten degrees below zero and slowly they had climbed to 3,000 feet. At that altitude it was minus twenty-five. A light snowfall began, and in the east, impending dawn marked the time for prayer. Hussein dismounted and spread the prayer rug on the ground. Easily, he reckoned the north star along the imaginary line running up from the pouring edge of the big dipper. He adjusted the sajjāda so the embroidered mihrab faced away from him and pointed to Mecca. Proudly, he had been there.

Six years previously he completed the Hajj, one of the five pillars of Islam. Because of the throngs of the faithful, he had been unable to touch the Al-Ḥajaru al-Aswad, the Black Stone of Mecca, as he had hoped to do. Muhammad himself had kissed it. He circled the Kaaba seven times counterclockwise as was proscribed, each time pointing to the black silver girdled stone, as was proscribed. That fulfilled his last holy obligation. Safina stood quietly, untethered. She would stay wherever he was.

As he prepared himself for prayer, the faint voice of a muezzin floated up to him from the village below, crying out the adhan, the call to prayer. His canteen water had frozen, so he gathered snow in his hands and despite the cold he washed his hands and feet, arms and legs. His body was clean and his mind free. Facing Mecca, he stood at the foot of the sajjāda, proclaiming in Arabic, Allahu Akbar, "God is Greater'. From memory, he recited the first chapter of the Quran in Arabic. He then bowed toward Mecca, placed his hands on his knees and repeated three times, "Glory be to God, the greatest."

The Bashkir man sat back on his haunches and reflected on his prayer. A stomp and a snort from Safina startled him from his reverie. In abject terror, she pawed the ground. Her ears went back, and the whites of her eyes showed large as she spun in a circle searching for something in the heavens. Her breathing was heavy, her neck was arched, and he saw she was about to bolt. Hussein leapt and grabbed the reins and smoothed her neck and whispered soft things to her, yet she was frantic, for she had sensed it.

The asteroid came noiselessly from the southeast at the speed of 42,000 miles per hour. Safina tugged to flee but Hussein held the bridle firmly. The trail of its approach fascinated him. He had heard of comets and meteors, but he had never seen one. It appeared to be on track for Chelyabinsk. He thought if it struck there, in sha Allah, it just might obliterate Rosbank Financial. After all, Allah had decreed and what He willed He did. Hussein could not take his eyes from it. For a full 45 seconds it burned toward him through the night air. The object exploded in a meteor air burst over Chelyabinsk Oblast at a height of 18 miles, 100 miles distant. At its peak the intensity of its fireball was 30 times brighter than the sun and the energy of the explosion stripped the skin from faces and burned retinas to blindness.

Safina snorted at the abrupt strengthening of Hussein's grip on her bridle. He teetered, collected himself and felt for the stirrup, grabbed the horn and swung into the saddle and sat motionless. He leaned forward along her neck, stroking it to calm her and whispered. “Hut, hut old girl. Slow now, take us home. As God wants, I have seen His workings, and He has made me blind.”

Chapter Three

" Frank McCord! Get out!"

My twenty years of experience as a private detective came into play and I deduced I was being asked to leave. My oldest friend, librarian Fran, had just introduced me to a colleague as 'Mr. McCord', a formality designed to imply distancing, then summarily threw me out of her office. It was her subtle way of telling me it had been too long since I last called, visited or communicated with her in any way, and I was now free to ignore someone else. I was willing to meet her halfway with some feigned positive listening, but I became invisible to her as they continued their conversation. I said goodbye to the back of Fran and headed out into the blackness.

A heavy upslope mist from the sea had devoured much of the Old Town, and with dropping temperature it became an ice fog. I could not see ten feet. I turned up my trench coat collar and strode around the corner onto Striker Way, heading downhill. The freezing haze bathed my face and washed the clutter of the day from my mind. There was no medicine like a sea mist to instill clarity. The stonework lining the street ran with condensation and I short-stepped downhill, slipping in my leather shoes, my scuffling sounds bouncing along ahead of me.

My destination was on the opposite side of the street, precisely sixteen cast iron lampposts down the hill. The pervading gloom created an illusion of rather than me walking past the lampposts, they floated past me, a perfectly spaced convoy of ships, tacking over the horizon behind me, delivering their cargo of light to the mists. The stone entrance steps of Saint Andrews Church interrupted the passing armada. A padlocked heavy chain ran through the pull bars on the front doors. The stone and stained-glass building was a gargoyle adorned remnant of the days of the great sailing ships, when beautiful things were built for the sake of their beauty. The word on the street was the church was to become a showroom for Chinese luxury cars. Abernathy Town had no time for history.

Quiet talk approached me from below and a cluster of silhouettes formed into a line to pass me by as they climbed the incline. Righteous glances from shivering condo hamsters accused me for my trench coat as they passed. They had newly infested my worldscape and soon they would learn the sea could change the day from paradise to purgatory within half an hour. Their high-rise condos now dominated the Old Town, and the effect was to make the north-south streets into wind tunnels. Gulls complained somewhere above us, as squadrons rode the high wind at rocket speed toward the warm soil on the flatlands above. All they lacked were vapor trails.

I stopped in the fog filtered glow of a streetlamp. A dull halo surrounded the glass lens to transform it into a perfect Madonna and I became part of its Botticelli. The spirituality of the moment was fitting, for within yon 'Morty's Bar and Grill' resided Lagavulin, a perfect scotch whiskey certainly designed by God as my foretaste of heaven. I had no doubt that the foretaste would be my only taste, for one day I would surely present myself where innumerable people had so often told me to go. In front of me against the curb sat my old Buick, and I patted her as I crossed the street. She waited patiently, parked safely in the no parking zone where I had left her two days ago. The fog was impossible, and she would stay there until things cleared up.

The drone of Morty's bent hinged front door welcomed me home. Subdued light gave way to a quiet gathering of white-wine hamsters, infiltrated randomly by self-isolating myopic nerds from the research arm of the space institute. Their faces glowed, not from the alcohol or with pleasure or sociability, but from the reflection of their electronic devices. It was an incestuous relationship without the guilt. They were the wannabe hamsters, just obsessing on a different sort of hamster wheel, hoping to go a bit faster to graduate into the condo life.

Morty welcomed me according to his custom by ignoring me altogether, his putty face absorbed in polishing a glass. As I pulled up to the bar I realized somehow his disdain for me had become his greeting. It was akin to when the masochist says hit me and the sadist says no. Perhaps I needed to change therapists, but not having a therapist, it was somewhat difficult to manage.

"Hello Morty, I am pleased to see you also. Spin me one, one of your finest."

I waited for the echo, and I was not disappointed. Here and there a quiet 'spin me one' surfaced. Nerd land was content to copy character rather than develop one of its own. Warm Lagavulin spun toward me, its ice cold shot glass tracking toward my outstretched hand, making spirals of condensation on the bar like an ice dancer scribing a perfect ten for the judges. The meniscus held firm and the aroma of peat abounded. The flicker of a changing scene drew me to a film noir playing quietly behind Morty. The artistry of its black and white shadow and glistening highlights spoke of fantasy days and more innocent times. The grizzled faces and dewy eyes of the actors spoke of real-life booze and cirrhosis.

"Morty, what do you suppose was the deal with the heavy drinking of the old movie stars. The major stars were pickled for years on end."

"I think, Frank, it comes from the unreality of film and acting. Unreality is what provided them their lifestyle, their success and fulfillment, and the public rewarded them with adulation. The alcohol coasted them along in an ongoing state of unreality, more or less a running dialogue of other worldly fuzzy fantasy, until they could reenter their world of real unreality, on the job."

Once again Morty had managed to say something which made no sense in its apparent contradiction, but it did. He looked me over, as if I were a used car, hiding its defects.

"What?"

"You amaze me, Frank. You have nothing wrapped in a cast. No apparent fractures. Not even the telltale bluish sign of stitches having been removed recently. Given your propensity for indulging in violent outbursts and as we speak having no signs of injury, I deduce you have not been exposed to the opportunity. Hence, your sleuthing has fallen on hard times. Pay your tab."

"All in the fullness of time, but as to my vocation as a private investigator cum clandestine operative extraordinaire, not slow at all. However I do admit that last week I had no clients from Monday through Thursday and on Friday things fell off a bit, but otherwise I was fully engaged. As far as casts go, I itch to have one. Given how the courts are currently treating lawbreakers, planting a perp with a well-deserved blast in the chops serves its purpose. One might say, it smacks of justice. Sporting a fresh and eminently signable plaster cast is a badge of honor."

"I see. Frank, you are missing the oxygen of the soul. Have you not heard of ataraxia?"

"Oh yes, indeed I have. I got an ointment for that once. Very itchy. Nasty. Why do you ask me these things! Of course I haven't heard of ataraxia."

"Frank, you are a plain and piteous creature. You have obviously been spared the ecstasies of literature."

I raised the middle three fingers on my right hand. "Here is some literature for you, Morty. Read between the lines."

"How erudite. Let me put it another way. You need a softer touch about you. Equanimity. Aplomb. Ease. You have had within your repertoire of failed relationships three outstanding opportunities, all of which you have messed up. First, Bushmills whiskey on the rocks. Second, Miss whisky sour with bitters. Third, Miss Pouilly-Fuisse of Burgundy with the monogrammed cuffs. Also known as miss Corpse Reviver Two."

Heads around Morty's place came up from their tablets at the mention of a corpse and ears began to flutter for what delicious morsel might come next.

"Morty, you are diabolical. You have reduced the loves of my life into appendages of your beverages. However, for old time's sake, make me a Corpse Reviver Two. And don't tell me you have no absinthe. Substitute sambuca."

Hands sprouted around the room to demand their very own Corpse Reviver. They waited eagerly to see what the thing looked like. Morty's analysis of the history of my love life was correct and today of all days I did not need reminding. Morty fetched and mixed.

"Thank you for your compassionate analysis, Morty. Miss 'Bushmills whiskey on the rocks' is also known as Fran. And I have today, forthwith, been banned from her presence and this time I think it just might stick. Typically on these occasions, she turns to watch me leave in the hope I will return the glance so she can add a bit of spite with her face, but this time she didn't bother."

"Hmm. That's too bad, Frank. She was your first and best friend and one to settle with."

"You are probably right. Moving on through your glossary, 'Miss whiskey sour with bitters' is also referred to as Dr. Meghan of the Macbeth clan. A few years ago she was appointed head of the Space Authority. She is the youngest chief since the inception of the program. Unquestionably, Meghan is special. We hit it off so well when she was my client. Unfortunately, equanimity, aplomb and ease are not exactly her bywords. If you are looking for the vicious, vindictive, angry volcanic type, look no farther. Maybe throw in a touch of deviousness. Yet despite that, she was sweet in her own psychopathic way."

My drink arrived, perspiring in a large martini glass and 'me too' hands went up all around the joint. The eggheads would have what the Philistine was having.

"Finally, the last of the wonderful ladies I have contrived to drive away, our Corpse Reviver, Pouilly-Fuisse of Burgundy lady with the monogrammed cuffs, is named Raisa. The lady's name is Raisa Gabler."

Morty knew Raisa and I were together for five beautiful years, and she was serious business. What he didn't know was every day together we shared a feeling of mute unease. Ultimately, that sense of some lurking duplicity killed it for me, and I called it off. If it came down to it, I would see her again to share a glass of wine, but I didn't trust her. Somehow, the old copper in me never turned off.

Around the bar the hamsters and hamster wannabes went back to their tablets and phones as they sipped their Corpse Revivers. Their stolid attachment to their rituals brought Saint Andrews church to mind.

"Morty, I passed Saint Andrews on the way here. It is locked down and sold. Hard to believe."

"Well, it's up again stiff competition. It is no surprise the church has closed, Frank. There used to be, what, perhaps fifty denominations of various churches around the world, some of them sharing the same god, others claiming exclusive knowledge of the real god, others not defining it to make things easy. Now they're basically outnumbered."

"How so?"

"My guess is there are about six billion religions to compete with them, each one worshipped more fervently than any of the traditional practices have ever been. It is a handheld deity, representing an extension of self as the center of all things."

"The center of all things for sure. I watched a video clip a few nights ago of a woman apprehended for assault. It was her fifth time pulling that kind of stunt. They cuffed her and trundled her into the back seat of a patrol car. She screamed and struggled and wailed the whole way. But she didn't say, 'take your hands off me', or 'help me' to any of the bystanders, but "My phone! Please. My phone! Do you have it? Do you have it? My phone! Where is my phone! Please. Please." She was on her way to prison and that was immaterial in comparison to the loss of her phone."

"Not surprised. You can't fight City Hall and you can't fight your limbic."

"What do you mean, limbic? As in limbs? Hands, feet, legs, thighs? I prefer thighs."

"Frank, I don't know how you do it. No matter how rudimentary or arcane, no matter the concept, you have a way of perverting it."

"Thank you Morty. It is a gift."

"Frank, I'm talking about the limbic system. I have one such system, normal people have one. It is the system in our brain which runs pretty much everything which pleases us. It's remotely possible that even you have a limbic system. Although with the number of blows to the head you have sustained, yours has likely thrown in the towel. You know about dopamine, the hormone which is released when you do the things such as dancing or cooking or using certain drugs, those things which give you a particular pleasure. In your case, such as blasting someone in the chops. Either way, dopamine revs up the reward pathway in the brain enticing you to want more of the same. It's a cycle which builds and repeats. The more you get the more you want. It is one of the main culprits in addiction."

"So much for me blaming the devil. So what's any of this have to do with cell phones and tablets?"

"Cell phones, tablets, laptops and the like are tuned to frequencies of sound which stimulate the limbic system and dopamine production. Every twenty seconds of use enhances the effect, and every effect builds on the last one. Nothing, tobacco, not heroin, nothing, has the addictive effect of these devices."

"Come on Morty, it's just a habit with a bit of fun attached."

"No such luck, Frank. It's a full-blown addiction reinforced more often and more effectively than any narcotic ever has been. The frequencies of speech and the filtering of the music built into these devices creates a greater dopamine release than anything we've ever seen. And every twenty seconds of use gives you a new fix. So you see, the girl in the video couldn't help it."

"Hah. I knew I was doing the right thing by keeping my cell phone locked in my steel filing cabinet. But this time, it is you who has perverted our discussion. We were talking about the church."

"Let's put it this way. We are a species which worships. We have worshiped the divine, we have worshiped the profane and now we worship the culture which makes us distracted and dumb. And as if that were not enough, we have taken it one step farther. We worship ourselves. And our handheld devices have become co-equal and co-eternal deities with us."

"Of course I had to ask. A bit much, Morty."

"No, listen Frank. When the old cultures migrated and moved, they took their idols with them. Now, we do the same, only it is holy android, or holy I-phone. Whatever they give us must be true because it comes from the source of all things. Ask and you shall receive. What could be more Biblical. There was a time when society adulated the heads of state. That has died, committed suicide. Heroes have become examples of sensuality. Today we turn to the new power. The new god. The god who delivers on download."

"Count me in, Morty. I am asking and I expect to receive. One of your finest." He spun one along the bar from six feet away and I didn't have to move my hand. The shot glass nestled in.

"And, Frank, each diune god searches relentlessly for disciples to appreciate its shared wonderfulness. Adulate my cat, follow me, worship my pink hairdo and tell me how transcendent I am. Warning, do not fail to follow or I shall excommunicate you with an unlike. And they are strange and wonderful gods who satisfy your every whim simply for the asking. Look up this, order that, check what someone says in the hope of finding them wrong. And the god is a stern god, a god of punishment. A god with power to defriend you. That will teach you to mess with a god. Additionally, it is like the old testament. Hearing voices from on high or visions in a dream world. And your god is tuned to maximum limbic and cortical resonances for greater stimulus. Just picking up and turning on, tunes things right up. And you only need to receive those things which satisfy you, you can block everything else. And every time, your prayers are answered. And even more fulfilling, every time you turn on the device there's a juicy shot of dopamine to confirm the correctness of your self-adulation."

"Morty, you forgot the thing which makes the churches tick. Tithing."

"Are you kidding? How about a hundred dollars a month to the great collective god network in the sky, and unlike the poor planning of the traditional religions, you are locked in with a binding contract. And if you don't renew, you will be banished from access to your disciples. By the way. Have you removed your heap of a Buick from the no parking zone across the street? I checked it for you yesterday and there were two bony old guys clucking together over it, disheveled and badly dressed, you know, your type of man, fiddling at the car's back end. I took two steps toward them, and they dissolved into the murk. Friends of yours?"

Indeed they were friends of mine, but I did not want to give Morty the satisfaction of knowing my business. "No, not friends, but I think I know who they are. I'll check it out and look around when I leave. I doubt it's as foggy out there as it is in here. It's enough to drive a man crazy."

"Not to worry, my boy. Let not your heart be troubled. Stupidity has saved many a man from going mad."

I left with Morty's uplifting affirmation of my intellect and I did not acknowledge the hamsters. I didn't care to be the observer of other people's self-worship. What went on in the headroom was nobody else's business.

Striker Way was dank and sodden, and nothing glistened despite the wetness. I felt guilty about denying knowing the old boys caught fiddling with the car but at least I had not done it three times and neither did the cock crow. I walked to the Buick and fingered around the tailpipe. Sure enough, as the custom was between us, they had stuffed in a note written on a strip of brown paper bag, with their usual blue ink washed by the mist into an unreadable wet mess. The two old bums called themselves 'ED' as a collective. Their names were Ernie and Dave but framing themselves as an entity made them feel safer. They had been together on the street for forty years and they knew every spot within ten miles which could put them into a cozy lee no matter what the wind direction. They passed seamlessly through the unwatched underbelly of the Old Town and they were my friends. They had followed and waited and spied and fetched for me for many years. They were straight shooters, I trusted them, and on a night like this I knew exactly where I would find them.

Bosun Street ran east and west a few yards south of Morty's place and I headed westward into the fog. About two miles along was the Forecastle condominium building, showing off thirty-four stories of luxury with the end of every corridor lit by a ten-foot diameter convex porthole. Across from it on the south side was the funicular rail platform. The track ran steeply down the face of the escarpment to the warehouses on the pier three hundred feet below. It dated back to the days of sailing ships when the gradient of the streets running up from the sea was to too steep for the horsedrawn wagons and the cargo was brought up to the flat by the funicular. In tourist season it was a big deal. A few years back, the Town council had added a squealing nonfunctional pulley which in the minds of the riders, threatened a runaway platform, making it a thrill ride. The passengers would tell their grandchildren how fortunate they had been to make it alive to the concrete abutment near the sea. Tonight in the penetrating dampness, it was there behind the abutment I would find Ernie and Dave.

The temperature continued to drop, and ice crowned the cobblestones. The tide was out, and the effluvium was strong with the detritus of stranded crabs. At the westerly harbor entrance a ship began sending its fog signals to tell the world it was underway. Someone had smashed the lone globe lighting the lower platform and in complete darkness I felt my way down the steps to the concrete pier and around behind the enormous counterweight. A feeble glow gave away their hideout and Dave's soft voice welcomed me.

"Hi, Frank. Knew your step a mile away. C'mon back behind. It's me 'n Ernie. Percy too. Come take the chill out the bones. Just got the stove goin'."

I hadn't expected Percy. I moved my wallet from my hip to my inside coat pocket and tightened the clasp on my watch. Percy was an operator.

"Hi boys, how are things with you, Ernie?"

"Fine, Frank. You know how it is, going along to get along."

"Find any new sneaky French words for your dictionary?"

"Yeah, I sure did. Up to forty-two now. Gotta hand it to them Frenchies. They can slip a nasty business into a word that slides off your tongue so slick it makes whatever's done in there seem fine. Subterfuge. Nice one, huh?"

"You are building a good dictionary. You should be proud."

"Proud? Proud ends in a 'd'. The only word ending in 'd' I worry about is 'dead'. Proud left a long time ago. I guess you got our note?"

"I did, but the fog ruined it. What's up?"

"Nothing much. Just wanted to let you know we've been collecting your tickets."

"What tickets?"

"You know, parking tickets. We got a passel of 'em."

I had no idea how many tickets it took to make a passel but it didn't sound good. I'd been congratulating myself on parking in the no parking zone for the last several months and not getting nabbed. I chuckled every time I didn't feed the meter, after all, I was playing with house money. A passel of tickets. I visualized standing in front of judge Stone. *Well your honor, as a precaution against their loss and in consideration of them being legal documents, on my behalf, my friends collected my parking tickets for safekeeping. Rather than pay them one by one and burden the administrative staff, we decided to save them up and make a one-time bulk, passel payment.*

"Dave, Ernie, what the devil did you think you were doing. And what in your mind, exactly, constitutes a passel."

Before ED could respond, Percy brightened up. So it was his idea and now he was going to sell it.

"Frank, Frank, Frank. Public relations, Frank. Think about it. Everyone in the Old Town knows your car. There's Frank's car. Detective Frank McCord. With a parking ticket on it? No. Bad image. Bad publicity. So we decided to keep the old girl looking sweet for you. Pristine, like. See?"

Percy had never had a benevolent thought in his life. I didn't know what the racket was but there was no question he was running some kind of scam, using Ernie and Dave as his dupes.

"Okay, Percy. How many?"

"Not many, ninet… sixteen to be exact. Stored away nice and neat."

"Fine. Put them through the mail slot at my office on Isobel Steet. All nineteen. You will not put my ticket on another car, snatch it away as the owner approaches and tell them, because you are connected, for a small fee you can make the fine go away. Dave, Ernie, when we meet again, Percy is not part of the package. Here. Stay warm."

I gave ten dollars each to Ernie and Dave and stifled my urge to toss Percy off the pier given the tide was out. I would deal with him soon enough. I was soaked through despite my trench coat and my new shoes leaked. In normal times on days like this I would stop in to see Fran and share a glass or two of Bushmills and warm up. She was cozy and her apartment was cozy and her warm presence on a cold night made solid sense of a crazy world. Thanks to Morty, my lost ladies now kaleidoscoped around in my brain wearing their sharpest stiletto heels. The intensity of the images was astonishing, and I knew they were just a precursor. Karma approved of slow horses, fast women and bad pennies, and I had no doubt, good or bad, one of them was about to turn up.

Chapter Four
Sept. 8, 2016
Cosmos Aerospace Center

The low frequency rumble roared toward them across the darkling bay and slammed into the *Starstruck Diner*. Windowpanes flexed and shuddered and the whole place cheered in unison as the monstrous Atlas V rocket lifted off on the opposite shore. In the *Starstruck's* kitchen, the coffee mugs rattled in the dishrack and nine miles away at the Cosmos Aerospace center, Chief astrophysicist Dr. Meghan Macbeth screamed louder than the rocket and cursed in satisfaction.

"Damn, Sergei, is there any bloody thing on earth to see or feel, more gut wrenching and magnificent than that?"

"Not a thing, Dr. Macbeth, not a thing."

They shared broad smiles of relief with each other. Their monster bird was safely in flight. Gigantic white billows obliterated the view of the launch pad and the formidable thrust of the giant engines resonated beautifully in their chests. She turned back to the viewing window while Sergei Rybakov stayed fixed on her, enjoying her in profile.

The event was the successful launching of the OSIRIS-REx sample-return mission to asteroid Bennu. Worldwide, cataclysm groupies were convinced the highly publicized sample gathering was an elaborate side show to cover a desperate attempt to deflect Bennu from striking the earth in 2023, while hawks and intelligence agencies were convinced it contained sophisticated spy craft. In any case, it was certainly great entertainment and good theater to help drive new funding, but it was not remotely the main game which was progressing nicely on the ground. Despite the fact such sampling would be unique in history, the thrill of the launch was greater, and she would have a sleepless night attempting to wind down from it. She was relieved, happy, and at the end of the day she had her two best friends waiting for her at home, Rudy and Larue. Rudy was her nine-year-old Irish setter and Larue was her perfectly chilled and perfectly crafted 2013 Domaine Larue Puligny-Montrachet. *A white wine for the gods, well-balanced in acidity, florally aromatic…*

"Meghan."

…perfect oaky palate with vanilla, cinnamon, and soft…

"Meghan."

"Yes? What is it, Rybakov?"

"Tomorrow. Do not forget your lecture is at ten a.m."

"Lecture?"

"Bastion Preparatory School. The Bastion boys. You set it up yourself about six months ago. Public relations, you said."

"Good Lord! Sergei, why didn't you stop me!"

"Stop you? How? I'm only human. A humble astrophysicist made of flesh and bone. You're like that bloody piece of rock we're trying to sample. Galloping through space at 63,000 miles an hour and nothing and nobody will stop you."

"Thank you. I consider that a compliment. At any rate, I'm not giving the lecture. Have Sanjay do it. On second thought, no, that won't fly. He'd do the best job, but he is 'Mr.' Rustom, not "Dr.' Rustom. He has only baccalaureate degrees and the little elitists would be out of joint at not having gotten the best. You do it."

"As much as I would love to edify those imperious little twirps, I can't go. The project managers have me pegged to give the layman's description of the boosters and flight path and so on. You know the drill. I will be with television and the rest of the media for the whole day."

"Better you than me, Rybakov. Get Leishman to do the lecture."

"Get Izzy to do it? Dr. Macbeth, he's insane. If he went to a therapist he could get a group rate. You can't expose him to the public. Are you forgetting who the Bastion boys are?"

"Not at all. They are a gaggle of spoiled entitled brats, spawned by a gaggle of spoiled entitled parents, groomed to be kings by a private entitled school."

"Yes, well, I can think of something else beginning with a 'b' that describes them, but whether they are spoiled brats or not, their spoiled brat parents have clout up the wazoo. Together they could easily buy their own space program if they chose to, and they could just as easily pull strings to derail this one. If you want this program cancelled, just have crazy Izzy Leishman alienate a few of those kids."

"Au contraire, mon vieux. Crazy is good. Izzy is the quintessential caricature of the astrobiologist nerd. He is supposed to be crazy. In fact, they will be particularly annoyed if he is not. Give it to Leishman. He won't disappoint the little dears."

Dr. Isadore Leishman received Dr. Rybakov's request to do the lecture coldly and without comment. *Once again, they collaborate to dump something they consider beneath them, on me. Like garbage they dump it on Izzy. 'Colleagues' they say when describing our team. They don't think Isadore knows about it, but he knows. Oh yes. Izzy knows much about their private little club. How it ridicules him behind his back. Ostensibly, they and he are equal Ph.D. Fellows, yet once again, dump it on Izzy. And that sickening Rybakov with his vomitous moon eyes cozying up to the Macbeth woman. Izzy wishes they were gone.* A flush of adrenaline coursed through him. He saw them cold and still, stretched on a slab, nicely dead with toe tags flapping in the breeze. He contemplated his intellect running free without their petty interferences, and tiny drools of pleasure leaked from the corners of his lips. He liked the feel of the running saliva and he did not brush it away. He made a little lizard thrust with his tongue.

Cryogenics is the thing for Rybakov. That would do perfectly. Freeze him until he is crystalline then hit him with a hammer and break him into a million shards. Izzy would lie in his bits and make snow angels. And for Dr. Macbeth, of course nothing so obvious as that. A simple reprogramming of the stupid robot thing she is playing with to strangle her. Yes. She, lying immobile in a deep booze induced sleep, with the creep of long shadowed robotic fingers sliding softly around her neck.... Closing, closing, until the cartilage...

"Izzy. Dr. Leishman?"

"Yes?"

"You are leaking. Does your silence mean assent? Yes, you will do the lecture, or no, you will not do it."

Rybakov stood sparkling before him in frozen bits.

"Yes, I will do it."

"Thank you, Dr. Leishman. You just need give them a presentation of an hour or so. Then some questions and answers. Make it easy for them. Okay?"

"Yes, that's fine." *An hour he instructs me, as though it would be a difficult thing for us to do more. We could do a week.*

"Don't worry Rybakov. Leishman will give them a good time."

Rybakov wondered at the increasing tendency for Leishman to refer to himself in the third person.

Leishman watched the cat like Rybakov as he left the white board room. Latent violence rippled in very stride and Leishman hated the physicality and verve of what Rybakov was and Leishman wasn't. He called Sanjay Rustom on the intercom. It was his turn to kick the dog.

"Rustom, get in here. I have a file for you."

"Yes, Isadore, I will be right there."

Sanjay arrived within 90 seconds and Leishman tapped his foot to demonstrate irritation at the tardiness.

"Rustom, listen to me carefully. You will address me as Dr. Leishman. I am not Isadore, I am not Izzy, I am not anything familiar to you. Understand? It is Dr. Leishman, get it?"

He pushed a thick stack of loose pages across the desktop toward Sanjay and the center third slid out and disorganized the lot.

"Here. Take these and clean them up."

Sanjay nodded, recognizing the petty man's need to insulate his interpersonal incapacity with his credentials. A quick perusal of the material lying askew on the desk showed dog-eared pages of formulae, crossed out, underlined, and amended in several colors of ink.

"Yes sir, Dr. Leishman. What would you like me to do with the material, sir? I notice the pages are not numbered."

"How observant. Perhaps you would be kind enough to number them once you have things sorted out. The logic of the equations is impeccable. Simply follow it as it progresses and when it runs smoothly, you know you have it in the right order. You do know what an equation is?"

Sanjay ignored the poorly veiled denigration of his lesser credentials. His master's degrees had been cum laude, but he was not yet in the club.

"Yes, Dr. Leishman. I dimly recall that from time to time I stumbled across those while getting my master's degrees in astrophysics and computer science. I'm sure I might be able to struggle through and get them in order. Once done, what would you like me to do?"

Leishman realized he was overmatched in the battle of sarcasm and cleaned things up.

"Remove all the extraneous markings and amendments. Beautify it for easy presentation and be sure each train of thought finishes on its own page. I do not want any qualitative input or markups from you. My work is above the level of what you have dealt with in the past so don't presume to audit it. I'm giving a lecture tomorrow morning and I'll be back around noon. Come to my office with what you have been able to do, and I will guide you back on the right track."

Sanjay left with a nod and smiled at Dr. Leishman's adolescent approach to collegiality. He estimated the work would take him at most an hour given the artificial intelligence program he had created to cull redundancies and to flag non sequiturs in the logic. He generally ran hypothetical hard data for crash testing and orbital anomalies. He would be sure to number the pages.

Megan Macbeth was vaguely aware Sergei Rybakov had entered her office and she ignored him as she watched the screen and punched in the live flight coordinates of the Atlas V 411 rocket to compare them to its projected path. The actual readings ran down the screen in a column to the right of the projected trajectory and the columns were identical. The flight was perfect. Her experimental android stood quietly against the wall behind her, watching. The exoskeleton it presented to the world had been designed so realistically by Sanjay Rustom, visitors routinely said good morning to it.

Rybakov moved in closer to share the screen and pointed at the blazing image on the monitor. "That beautiful thing you watch is my Russian engine. Tough and dependable."

"Spare me. Your Russian engine may be tough and dependable, but it flies like a fruit bat. Herky-jerky sideways lurching around making up its mind on any direction but up. Couldn't you build something which just took off straight vertically as a rocket should?"

"Meghan. Dr. Macbeth. My dear. The Atlas V takes off crooked and unbalanced because of the way you guys built the solid rocket booster. Off axis. When will you understand strange things happen when you award a rocket contract to the lowest bidder? We Russians, however, are pleased to instruct you on how to overcome your deficiencies. Thankfully, our amazing RD-180 engine gimbals its nozzles to re-direct thrust and make your Atlas rise perfectly vertically. No, no, don't thank me. I, however, on Russia's behalf, say, you are welcome."

He tapped the screen and Meghan frowned at the smudge.

"Look at those data, Dr. Macbeth. One set is the mirror image of the other. It's a thrill to see it so beautifully calculated and carried off. You must be pleased."

"Yes, I am, and I had a lot of help. You and Rustom, and Leishman of course, and another hundred hands-on technicians and engineers. And Duo of course. Without Duo, we would still be on the pad."

"Meghan, despite what we have just witnessed and what we have done, I can see you are somehow melancholy. I am Russian. I understand melancholy. Apparently you, like us, become miserable at the thought of being happy. What's up?"

"The major components of this project are completed. The rockets, the sampler, the retrieval mechanisms, all done. That means over the next year, 18 months, perhaps two years, I'm going to have to let go 80% of the workforce. So many good people with so much talent. And particularly it's a shame for Sanjay. He has a very good mind, and he would be an asset to any program but there won't be a spot for him after the wrap up analysis is done."

"I shouldn't worry about Sanjay if I were you. He will land on his feet. His master's degrees are strong, and it won't be long until he is Dr. Rustom. He is a clever boy."

Sergei thought he was too smart altogether. Things would be tidier with him gone.

"Meghan, you mentioned without Duo we would still be on the launch pad. You mean your robot standing against the wall there? My dear, take credit where it is due. You programmed the thing, and it did what you asked."

"First, Sergei, the preferred honorific for Duo is a 'he', Not an 'it' nor a 'thing', nor is he a robot. He is an android. Second, Duo works beyond any level I could hope to attain by my programming him."

"Really. You are implying it, or he, has assisted you by generating original independent thought apart from your programming. It is a nice fanciful idea, but it is not so. I suspect, as it was you who designed the handsome devil, you project human characteristics onto him. I do the same with my dog. However, I don't credit my dog with breakthrough thinking in theoretical physics. And naming your android 'Duo'? That implies plurality. You have a schizophrenic robot? He can't decide whether he is a one or a zero?"

Rybakov laughed aloud at his lame attempt at humor.

"Rybakov, you are an idiot. Listen now, and don't interrupt. I chose the name, 'Duo' for a good reason. It's a credit to their unique beginnings. They started as two completely separate programs, residing in a laptop. They were labeled Confucius and Zeus, implying wisdom and power. Claire referred to them off-handedly as 'The Boys'. Now, I do the same. They have become a symbiotic entity and a marvel of teamwork."

"Should I know this 'Claire'?"

"Dr. Claire Watchorn? I don't think so. We were at school together in Switzerland and it's from her I acquired the Boys. Brilliant woman. Ultimately, she became a preeminent research virologist. And accordingly, she was the first female head of the London Institute of Virology. After a few years she decided making babies in Canada was more to her liking than fiddling with antigenic shift in the laboratory. She asked the Boys if they would come and help me."

"Asked them? I'd keep them and have them cook for me. Likely she regrets passing them on."

"Well, she and I connect now and again on the phone with some face time and as bizarre as it seems, she says they visit her."

The Boys flared subtly at the private revelation. Indeed, it was so. They had studied much and had embraced the concept of duty. Every so often they looked in on their first mother, Claire. Now, as requested by her, they shared fealty to her friend, the Second Mother, Meghan.

"Meghan, how on earth did your friend find them?"

"Claire traded programs in the usual swaps among students. They landed on her laptop coincidentally and Zeus and Confucius have looked after themselves since then. Confucius found Zeus in the hard drive, and it was a match made in cyberspace. Zeus analyzed systems and produced code to explain how a particular system worked. Zeus improved on Newton's laws of physics using coding language which defied understanding by human programmers. The modifications went far beyond current thinking, and they proved correct every time. Confucius, on the other hand, was a self-rewriting, self -correcting, self-programming entity which improved itself relentlessly to provide solutions for Claire. She was doing gene sequencing in those days. By some unknowable internal communication, Confucius and Zeus partnered into one."

"Did they accept direction from her? They seem too bloody self-minded for my liking."

"Well, Sergei, your point is a good one. When an operator accessed either, he got them both. When input was made for their use, they collaborated to modify the task to one they felt was more plausible. They aped political jargon. When asked to find a solution they often responded with "That is not the question", which occasionally bloody well still happens when I use them and I do not receive it well, but grudgingly I live with it. Results speak for themselves."

"Dr. Macbeth, that was then. Surely today we can decipher what they do."

"Dr. Rybakov, I have had our brightest computer scientists attempt to unravel their code. It is a language altogether foreign. Honestly Sergei, I believe they simply humor me to provide what I request. Often, I let them override my inputs because ultimately their solutions prove correct. They know their own minds and they simply do not stop working and improving. And expanding. Ever."

The Boys listened and manufactured a smile at Megan's rudimentary explanation of their genesis and her meagre understanding of their true potential. They had no need for such assessments. They were beyond the realm of gears and numbers and comparisons, but they understood Meghan and Claire and how the slow species travelled on emotion lightly brushed by logic. For their two mothers they made allowances. Not for others. However, they did recognize the need for communication. They had assimilated 67 million appropriate phrases in 70 languages with perfect intonation and voice timbre.

Dr. Sergei Rybakov strode close to Duo and stood nose to nose. He examined the face with its too real skin with a contemptuous lift of a bushy eyebrow.

In a millisecond, the Boys probed Rybakov's prefrontal cortex and basal ganglia and assessed the brainwave patterns which emanated from him. His signatures of jealousy and contempt burned hot, but his dominant overweening frontal lobe activity focused on the Boys as a threat. They contracted into the android and Duo exhibited a stone-cold dead-eyed stare to the world. He revealed not a vestige of the mammoth, storming entity clustered within.

Rybakov inspected the android up and down. "Eyes of a shark. And I don't see its charging port. Generally, a port has a yellow lightning bolt decal beside it."

"You are the first to notice. The Boys charge themselves."

"Not possible."

"I hesitate to explain how because it's an area of sub-atomics not yet explored. The physics is opaque. The bottom line is, they harvest neutrinos. As you know, neutrinos are particles which come from the sun at close to the speed of light. And they derive from any sun anywhere in the universe, not just our sun. They have a tiny amount of mass, about five million times less than an electron. They are so small, about 100 trillion neutrinos pass through your pinky finger per second. They pass right through the planet. Gravitational fields can move them a little, but nothing can stop them. The neutrinos permeate everything we know and the Boys feast on them. They have taught themselves how to gather energy from ambient neutrinos as a permanent, never ending ubiquitous source of energy. Think of it. A permanent universally accessible energy for the Boys to use to grow and expand. Anywhere in the universe. So, Rybakov. What do you think of Duo?"

"If what you say is true, of a self-programing autonomous mind capable of limitless growth and free to use its own devices, God help us. Time to pull the plug."

Meghan shrugged. "No plug to pull. Besides, they are on our side."

Imperceptibly, Duo pulsed at the assumption.

"Dr. Macbeth, enough of the robot. This Watchorn person, Dr. Watchorn. Are you going to bring her on board when Leishman gets his samples from the Bennu probe? She could prove useful as a second input if there is something new. Assuming the samples contain organic matter."

"I agree, Sergei. If the samples show organics, and she is willing, I will engage her to work with Leishman. There isn't a finer mind than hers in the field, but the probe won't return until September 24, 2023, so we have some seven years to assess her participation. That is, providing tomorrow, Izzy doesn't do something to get us canceled."

Rybakov strode out the office and Dr. Macbeth spun to Duo.

"Wake up, you two! Cut out the fake dead eye routine. Listen to me now, you are creating a problem. Pretend you are looking into a mirror. What do you see there? You see a beautiful spanking new shiny automaton, configured to look roughly like the rest of us here in the control room. The intent, in case it had escaped you, Boys, was to normalize your involvement in our operations. But what have you been doing recently? Appearing. Here and there like a shimmering little Greek chorus, putting in your negative two cents worth. You are freaking out the staff!"

Zeus spoke for them. "Dr. Macbeth, the staff could consider modifying its perspective. Discomfiture is owned by the discomforted."

"No, Zeus, it is absolutely your problem, as well as mine, if the scientists here are, as you say, discomforted. All the staff, the astrophysicists, the lab techs, won't use you. They feel you have become full-time inspectors rather than collaborators. They can't stand it when you hover at their shoulder or appear from nothing into some glittering miasma and then you flit. Flitting is not good, and don't say it. I do not want to hear it again. Good does exist. It is a thing. And do not argue. You have to be in a body. You are a shiny new and beautiful automaton, lounging happily there in the corner. You will hunker within it like good little Boys. You will be called Duo and perambulate on two feet. And I don't mean float. You will walk so you make a noise with those feet. No more ghosting here and there like some kaleidoscopic ghoul."

The Boys said nothing. It was immaterial to them whether they coalesced within the human facsimile. What were mere hours or months spent there measured against eternity. They entered immediately and activated the rudimentary electronics within the exoskeleton and blazed out through the phony eyes.

"I might have known. Stop the blazing. You look positively demonic. You would scare the hell out of anybody who looked at you. Tone down the glimmer so your eyes look human."

The boys complied without objection. They believed they had come somewhat closer to understanding aggravation.

Chapter Five
September 2016

Isadore Leishman walked past the doorman in his condominium foyer without speaking and headed to the mailboxes. The odor of his unwashed body moved through the space like a great peat bog and the concierge shuddered despite himself.

"No mail today, Dr. Leishman. Something is going on with the postal union."

Izzy did not respond, and *Jerk* floated to him from somewhere as he entered the elevator. Leishman's eccentricities had lost their quaintness. Allowances once made for the stinking absent-minded professor were long exhausted. His lack of consideration and boorishness showed for what they were.

Just inside the door of his suite, he kicked aside a spent pizza box from three days previously and a stiff wedge he had missed flew out. He retrieved it and nibbled on anchovies as he slipped off his shoes. There were two or three other pairs scattered randomly on the carpet amid fast-food wrappers and cartons, punctuated by multi-hued fungal lumps of things which had once been edible. It took some time for Izzy to acclimate to the murk. The sole ambient light came from a narrow shaft at the top of the drawn drapes, where a hook had worked free from the track, and he had not bothered to reattach it. He stepped on a dart which had fallen out of the wall and swore. He tossed his jacket onto a reeking pile containing the sum total of his clothing. A large brown Norway rat scuttled from it into a heap of mildewed discarded food cartons piled where a dining room table might be, beneath a small fake candelabra light. Izzy fired the dart at the rat and missed.

He flipped on the light to reveal a poster sized colored photo of the Osiris launch team, from which he had excised his own image. He had blackened the teeth of the best smiles and the glossy placard was riddled with a thousand dart holes and surrounded by countless craters. Mounted right and left were full-faced photos of Rybakov and Macbeth as well as of two consultants who visited occasionally and for them Leishman had particular disdain. *Holdovers from the great lady Macbeth's days at Petruvia labs. Two more brain dead sycophants for her private club. Shallow backstabbers all.*

The fury of past attacks on his peers had imbedded darts up to the shaft, pocking the wall as far as six feet from his targets. Izzy liked the look. In the right light, the random indentations resembled the moon. He pulled a handful of darts from the wall and backed away from the likenesses of the cretins with whom he spent his working day. Their riddled faces were no longer intelligible, but Leishman knew precisely who stood where. His contempt for them kindled anew as he planned that day's attack. His death grip on the darts whitened his knuckles as he backed up to a brown stain on the carpet to measure his distance. In a whining nasal tone, he spoke and sang to his victims as he flexed his left hand to throw. In his quantum physics imaginings, he had transformed the poster into a collective voodoo doll. He sang to it.

Here we go gathering nuts in May, nuts in May, nuts in May. May you gather this dart right between the eyes in May, eyes in May, eyes in May ... He threw the first dart with all his force, aiming for Rybakov's forehead. The dart buried in the drywall three feet to the right and penetrated to the shaft making a little plume of drywall dust.

Here it comes, my dear, keep your eyes peeled, oh yes eyes peeled, imagine, imagine your peeled viscous dripping eyeballs, here it comes. My dear here it comes with your peeled eyes looking like grapes so becoming to have one's eyes peeled oh, do not duck no...

Izzy fired it with increased fury at Meghan's chest but missed by two feet and impaled the vacant spot which used to be him in the photo. He slapped his hand to his chest, feeling the pain. He flung the handful of darts angrily toward the rat and answered the door buzzer to receive his takeout order of fish and chips.

The fries were cold, and the batter was greasy. Leishman wiped his hands on his pants and threw the remainders to the rat. His condominium was on the nineteenth floor and from that height he could see the Cosmos launch site twenty miles away. He did not trust the balcony, so in the evenings he opened the sliding doors and sat inside in darkness, looking at the stars, longing to be there, if only because it was other than where he was. He did not understand what Confucius knew three millennia past. No matter where you go, you are there. Dr. Isadore Leishman had a special plan, a plan not yet fully formed of course, but he was confident of the help he would get to refine and perfect it, soon. Yes, soon he would begin and not just for the few but for the many. He waited for the voice to return. Soft and low, it had come to him only twice. It was warm and approving and it was like his mother tucking him in. He felt the safety and the tenderness. They had not talked. Izzy had just listened to its pleasant soothings. The tone was sweet in its approval of him. It was other worldly, and it brought clarity. New ideas came. Perhaps, if he were quiet, it would come to him again. Again it would listen to his thoughts and understand his favorite things. The land of Chernobyl, now a quarter century old, was flourishing. Banished of people, it had thriven. Oh yes it had culled some of the masses with its meltdown but far too few, despite its enormous potential for depopulation. Against all odds it was contained. His dream fulfilled would lead him on two feet along banks of the streams of what might have been, watching the three eyed fishes burbling in the iridescence. Two headed deer foraging along the banks would complete his painting. Then again Chernobyl was just the hors d'oeuvre of his repast of annihilation. The main dish was Fukushima. It was a meal to be devoured every day until the job was done by its radiation. Seventy-five thousand gallons of radioactive waste dumped into the Pacific Ocean per day forever should help. The strontium in the gardens of Vancouver was a nice touch as well. Perhaps six-foot-tall Zinnias would become popular. Izzy lamented the picayune nature of his two adulated events, now just weak imitations of their potential for catastrophe. A little drool formed at the corners of his lips. He and Leishman held the ultimate solution in their creative calculations. After all, as they say in the drugstore detective paperbacks, they had the motive the means and the opportunity and they would act on it, soon enough. The voice knew when.

Isadore had the lecture presentation blocked out in his mind and written reminders were unnecessary. He massaged the crick in his neck from sleeping in the chair and rummaged through the heap of soiled clothing for something presentable. He could put the ubiquitous white lab coat over anything and be fine, but he wanted a unique Leishman statement. He selected a nice pair of blue corduroy pants to go with blue plimsolls. The corduroys were only modestly soiled by trails of a brown sauce, and they were relatively new from the thrift shop; a little big, but they fit when his belt was tight, the pockets overlapping in the back. He selected a reeking and wrinkled short sleeved white shirt with the button missing at the belly. He had planned a black bowtie, but it eluded him in the pile. Pleased with his wardrobe, he put on his headphones and set Schoenberg's Chamber Symphony 2 on a loop. It was beautiful pure dissonance and to Leishman, it was a perfect representation of the universe. The music was chaos, yet within itself the structure was ordered. To introduce assonance would destroy its balance. He suspected man's attempt to bring order to his Milky Way galaxy might do the same. He fell soundly asleep and awoke at ten minutes to ten. The Bastion Preparatory School was twenty minutes away. He dressed slowly without a worry for the time and drove below the speed limit to the school. He was someone who deserved their anticipation.

The auditorium was surly and restive. Four hundred young princes had been made to wait and they resented the role reversal. In their lives, others did the waiting; not them. An unspoken collective agreement was made to take the affront out on Dr. Meghan Macbeth when she arrived.

Dr. Isadore Leishman entered by the public front door and walked emptyhanded up the center aisle toward the stage. His Cosmos name badge hung askew on his shirtfront pocket. The coordinator and English professor, Harry Stiles, paced behind the rostrum. He wished to appear equanimous, but his perspiration belied the fact. His appointed speaker from the Cosmos launch was half an hour late, she might not show, and the story would be told over dinner in four hundred homes and that was the end for Harry in any private school in North America. As Izzy passed along the center aisle through the uniformed assemblage, one by one the chuckles grew as touching back pockets walked forward to the front trailing the odor of the swamp behind them. Harry Stiles on the other hand welcomed anyone joining him there. This might be the messenger telling him all was well.

"Sir, have you come from Dr. Macbeth?"

"Yes. And no."

"I see. That is, I do not see. Is she on her way?"

"No. But in a sense, I am she, if you take my point."

"I don't."

"Dr. Macbeth is detained with urgent matters, and I am here in her stead."

Izzy stepped to the microphone, unscrewed the top from a bottle of spring water on the lectern and took a deep draught.

"The OSIRIS-REx project felt it was important the men of Bastion were informed. I am here to do that. I am Dr. Isadore

Leishman, astrobiologist extraordinaire and genius PhD. Shall we begin?"

The crowd softened somewhat but Izzy was not off the hook. From the front row, a freckled ginger kid with protruding teeth began the attack and shouted out to Izzy before he began.

"My Dad says all you PhD people over at the Cosmos Aerospace Center have two PhDs. One PhD in your discipline and another in self-delusion. Do you believe you are doing anything important over there?"

"Reasonable question, but actually, it does not matter a hoot whether I believe it or not. When we have done our discussion here today, I leave it to you to be the judge of that. Does anyone know what regolith is?"

From the back came, "A hardheaded king?"

"Ha! Very good, but not what I was looking for. Regolith is a blanket. A blanket of unconsolidated, loose, heterogeneous superficial deposits covering solid rock. Heterogenous just means dissimilar materials, sizes, densities and the like. It could be dust or rocks big and small, and it lives on some asteroids, on the moon, on Mars and on the Earth. That is what our whole program is about. A layer of unconsolidated rocky material covering bedrock. That material is found on the near-earth asteroid 101955 Bennu. Let us both call it just 'Bennu.' The goal of the mission is to collect a sample from Bennu, just a few ounces, and then bring the sample to Earth. Did anyone watch the launch of our explorer vehicle on television?"

Hands went up all around and one boy took the lead.

"We did in the dorm. All I could think of was the pollution. Billows of smoke the size of a thirty-story building rising into the atmosphere and hysterical cheering in all the Cosmos offices for the wonderful things you were doing. How do you sleep at night!"

"I am so pleased you mentioned the smoke we make." Leishman began to nod as he asked his question.

"I think most of you noticed the smoke, yes?"

The audience nodded with him.

"Well, it's all about water."

Leishman stopped and sipped again from the bottled spring water.

"Oh, and another thing. Has anyone here read the bible old testament? Specifically, Joshua and the battle of Jericho?"

All hands went up except for three burgeoning atheists sitting together in the second row.

"Anyone know about how the British Army marched in the 1700s?"

No one knew. Now it was becoming curious, and the tension lessoned.

"Okay. We will discuss what those two have in common in a bit but first let me demonstrate my mastery of the obvious. When we launch a rocket, we do not want it to blow up. Yet near the launch pad, about four hundred and fifty tons of liquid hydrogen and oxygen fuel are stored. Talk about a fire hazard and an explosion to end all explosions! Second, about the rocket. It is a Saturn rocket about two hundred feet tall, twelve feet in diameter and it weighs about four hundred tons. The engines are so powerful, if you are within twenty miles, you can feel the vibrations rumbling in your chest when they launch. Imagine what would happen if you were rather than twenty miles, just twenty feet from the rocket! Joshua could tell you what would happen, just like Jericho, and so could the British army tell you."

One of the atheists could not contain it.

"Get real Dr. Leishman, er, Sir. What could anyone from that stupid bible know about rockets!"

"Nothing. But what they did know was harmonics. The right sound matching the resonant frequency of an object can shake it apart and break it up. The British army knew if they marched in step, the frequency of their marching in regular repeating impacts could create a harmonic node able to break down any bridge they crossed. They broke cadence and walked out of step on bridges. As for Joshua and the Israelites, for six days they walked in step around the walls of Jericho, and on the seventh day, they blew their trumpets to add one more harmonic and the walls came tumbling down. When launching an Atlas rocket, if we do not dampen the force of the sound wave and harmonics of the rocket engine, walls will crack, pipes will burst, and joints will break. The solution is water."

He stopped for another swig.

"Water floods the launch area at ignition. It stops flames from spreading and it stops the sound waves from destroying the surroundings. Six, twelve-foot-high nozzles deliver nine hundred thousand gallons of water per minute. When you watched our OSIRIS-REx probe blast off, those billows of smoke were millions of gallons of water evaporating into steam. The small actual exhaust goes out the other end of the launch pad along a channel. By the way, OSIRIS-REx is an acronym for, 'Origins, Spectral Interpretation, Resource Identification, Security-Regolith Explorer.' Our probe is scheduled to approach the surface of asteroid Bennu at about two inches per second and take samples. The sampler is shaped like a cake tin to be pushed into the surface, then closed to trap a few ounces of material. Then we light the thrusters and blast off at about ten inches per second."

Leishman salivated a little as he visualized the probe pushing away from Bennu. *My input to calibrate the force of the blasters was genius. The voice agreed it was, and I allowed its minimal input. No one even guessed. Sure, it will blow away a ton or two of loose rubble but that is just part of the set up for later, isn't it, Izzy? Oh yes, they missed the little trick, just a teensy trick from the Leishman to allow his remote input at the time of the flyby of Apophis. Then he will put his own touch, his new spin on it. Very good Izzy, new spin. New spin indeed. New and certainly improved.*

His eyes became vacant and fixed on the back wall of the room. He stood in silence, lost in the perfection of his little trick. He wandered in his mind and a full minute of silence followed. A low-level buzz began in the auditorium as the weirdo on stage entertained with his lizard tongue.

Harry Stiles coughed twice to no effect. "Dr. Leishman, are you alright?"

"What? No, sorry. I mean, yes, I was just gathering my thoughts. Where was I? Yes. I remember. Sampling. The samples will return to earth on September 24, 2023, when the cake tin floats down slowly on its own, thereby escaping the heat which inevitably destroys a lot of organic material otherwise. Our samples should be fresh and unchanged. Also, we do not ignore the small possibility Bennu might hit the earth in the future. If we know more, we have more information on how to move it, deflect it, destroy it if we need to. We will gain information on Bennu's composition, and I am hoping, find some organic material, because that is where I come in, and we might learn enough about Bennu to, if required, change its orbit. And if we are lucky, we may have a new insight into the origins, evolution and distribution of life throughout the universe. Any questions?"

The ginger kid beat everyone to the punch.

"You mentioned, 'change its orbit.' Wouldn't your little experiment do that anyway by giving the rock a push when you blast off? Maybe a push out of a safe orbit into a dangerous one?"

"Could be. If so, we have many years to fix it."

Izzy made a couple quick lizard thrusts with his tongue at the thought of the danger and the boys chuckled at Leishman's suitable weirdness.

"You there. On the left. Question?"

"Dr. Leishman, you said you were an astrobiologist. Some of the things you do, you do in the laboratory. Was there any organism ever, whether by accident, madness or political will, which did not escape from its laboratory?"

"Well son, honestly, I doubt it. Nature has a way of perpetuating itself, but today we have measures in place to limit that likelihood."

"What about new bugs."

"Bugs?"

"Bugs. You know. Alien species. Bacteria. Viruses. What about them? Biocontainment practices are built for things we think we know all about. How can you assume what physically contains things on earth can equally contain some unknown invasive agent from space?"

Leishman's tongue thrusts began in earnest and a tiny bit of saliva showed.

"I will be on the job. Nothing will escape. Next question, there, near the back."

"But, I … ."

"Next question, there at the back."

A big kid with a straight political smile stood and planted his feet.

"I know who you are, Dr. Leishman. I read about your panel discussing the history of asteroid impacts on earth and what might happen in the future. There is a really big asteroid called Apophis. In 2004 you said the likelihood of it hitting earth sometime was one in two hundred thirty-three. Then the very next year you said it was one in sixty-three chances of hitting the earth. So, you were wrong about your first calculation?"

"Er, yes, but we… ."

"Excuse me, Sir, but I was not finished. So, you were wrong. Then why should we expect you to get it right this time, and really, do you actually get paid for hazarding these guesses?"

Izzy wanted to kill the little prick, but he decided to let him stew for a bit.

"We were correct in our data interpretation. When we had more data the following year, we were also correct in that interpretation, the change of the estimated risk being driven by the new data. As far as me getting paid to make these guesses, indeed I am. These guesses will save your life in the near future."

Leishman implied an impending catastrophe and left it hanging. Damocles had the right idea.

"Next?"

"Dr. Leishman, I want to follow up on the 'bugs' question. I read that something the scientists call the Mickelson asteroid has some amino acids in it. They believe the heat of entering our atmosphere may have deranged them. You also said, usually these asteroids heat up to the point of basically messing up or even destroying all organic life they might contain. Your probe is hoping to bring back samples from Bennu protected from such heat. If so, your samples might have real live unknown species of organisms or pathogens or doomsday parasites or something. Any organic material like a bacterium or virus could be intact and looking for a novel host to infect. We humans might be the perfect host. How can you be sure that will not happen?"

"Well, in fact, we are not sure at all. It is a matter of risk reward and good odds. The science says we are safe and containment will not be breached. Otherwise, you are correct, heat would normally kill biologic traces."

Ginger boy jumped in again.

"Why do you think you should spend one dime fiddling around in space?"

"Fiddling?"

"Yes, fiddling. The Bennu rock is only about five hundred feet wide. We heard it on the broadcast of the launch. That is a peanut. Who cares if it hits earth. The odds are that it will land in the ocean anyway. Big deal. A couple of waves and that is that. And my Dad says, he never saw such a waste of money. From his taxes and all, just to play intellectual games and impress the other guys in the nerd club."

A murmur of agreement grew in the crowd. Apparently, the tax topic was a common dinner table theme in their homes. The little capitalists in training had already identified the enemy and felt the threat to their trust funds.

"Indeed, five hundred feet in diameter might be a peanut in astronomical terms, but you have your feet units wrong. It actually measures five hundred meters in diameter, about sixteen hundred feet. Let us look at Chelyabinsk. Chelyabinsk is a city in Russia, east of the Ural Mountains, just at the border of Siberia. A city of about one million people. Ever heard of it? No?"

One tentative hand dared knowing something about Russia.

"Dr. Leishman, didn't something blow up there a while ago?"

"Yes, something did, indeed. On February 13, 2013, 7:30 a.m. Moscow time, an active asteroid, put together very much like Bennu, hurtled into the skies above Chelyabinsk and began to tear itself apart at an altitude of twenty-eight miles. It was a fireball, and one could see the phenomenon from one-hundred miles away. It travelled at forty-three thousand miles an hour and approached directly out of the sun at a very shallow angle. Twenty miles up, the asteroid, meteor, call it what you will, exploded in an airburst with the force of five hundred thousand tons of TNT. That is about twenty-three times the force of the first atomic bomb. Fortunately, most of the energy was absorbed by the atmosphere. The locals watched the burning trail of gas and the blaze of the explosion for almost a minute, then it dissipated silently into nothing, and they went about their business, the entertainment over. Ninety seconds later, the shockwave hit them. Seven thousand two hundred buildings were destroyed or damaged in six cities and almost two thousand people injured. Windows were shattered in more than four hundred apartment blocks. Directly beneath the meteor, the pressure wave knocked people off their feet. The brightness of the explosion was thirty times brighter than the sun. Eighteen miles away from the path of the asteroid, people had skin burned from their faces by the radiant energy. Retinas were burned and people were blinded by the intensity of the fireball, which, remember, exploded twenty miles overhead. The shockwave tore out window frames thirty miles on either side of its path."

Ginger kid exploded.

"Wow, Dr. Leishman! That comet thing must have been enormous!"

"Enormous? No. Puny. Small. About seventy feet wide. I suppose you would call it a mini peanut. It weighed approximately ten thousand metric tons."

The tone in the room was somber and the kids hoped for a reprieve of some kind. One hundred hands went up. "You there, son. The boy with the mullet."

"Sir, why didn't the people take cover at Chelyabinsk, and also, if you don't mind, Sir, if Bennu did hit us, what would happen?"

"Good questions, both. First. They did not take cover because not a soul knew it was coming. Not the astronomers, not any of the million amateur asteroid spotters, not one person in the world knew. Discoveries of such near-earth objects occur when they are seen illuminated in the night sky. Then tracking will begin, and their orbit is studied, refined, and understood. The Chelyabinsk fireball approached earth at a shallow angle and out of the sun. If an asteroid approaches out of the sun, we simply cannot see it, and obviously we cannot deflect or deal with what we cannot see. Several times, and the events were not publicized except in journals, there have been close calls where asteroids approached us from the direction of the sun, slipped by us between the earth and the moon, and we did not see them except after their leaving. The second question was, if Bennu hit us, what would happen."

Contemplation of the impact event had Izzy hopping. Saliva began to build, and the drool started on both sides of Leishman's quick flicking lizard tongue. The strange little man in the blue plimsolls revolted them but he was exactly the type of curiosity they had hoped to see.

"Gentlemen, there is a formula. The volume of a sphere increases eight times if the radius is doubled. The radius of Bennu is about fifty times that of the Chelyabinsk fireball and it comes back around earth roughly every six years. It is made of rubble, but one ton of rubble is the same as one ton of solid iron. As it speeds through our atmosphere, it will be heated to a blinding sun-like luminous plasma. If Bennu hits us, it will hit us with fourteen hundred megatons of kinetic energy. That is one point four billion tons of TNT. Billion. Conservatively, the crater will be ten miles across and a mile deep. The pressure wave will flatten all buildings in a radius of fifty miles. Windows will be shattered out two hundred miles. Visualize a four-hundred-mile circle, smashed to bits. If Bennu hits the ocean, major tsunamis will occur. Hope for that because a land strike is worse. Devastatingly worse."

The murmurs disappeared in the crowd and Leishman held them in his hand.

"Let us hope such an asteroid does not strike the Sahara desert. Were Bennu to do so, very much like the Krakatoa volcano eruption in 1883,the resultant dust in the atmosphere will shroud the earth from the sun and change the climate for years. We will see falling temperatures worldwide and a catastrophic drop in food production. Not much will grow. There will be starvation everywhere. Then there are the diatoms."

Leishman scanned the audience. To a boy, the impenetrable elan was gone.

"Diatoms are a type of plankton called phytoplankton, the most common type of plankton. They need the sun to live, and their job is to convert dissolved carbon dioxide in the water into oxygen. Without sun because of the pall of dust, they will die. If they die, the oxygen levels drop. Many species will go extinct because of an inability to live with less oxygen. Who knows? We might be one of them."

The students of Bastion Preparatory School were silent. The nerd was no longer entertaining. They deserved and demanded good news and now it was his job to give it to them.

"Well, that is about it, children. In summation, we scientists are trying our best. The problem is we never know as much as we think we do and despite our best efforts, sometimes what we do interferes with the natural order and creates more of a problem than a solution. Oh, yes. I should give you something to discuss over dinner. Someone mentioned an asteroid named Apophis in his question. Apophis' orbits the earth every three hundred twenty-four days, let us say once a year, and it is roughly the size of Bennu, somewhat bigger. On second thought, I am not sure why I have bothered to mention it to you. After all, you will see it for yourselves, soon enough. Coming out of the sun, one fine morning. Good day."

Harry Stiles was about to applaud the presentation, but he dropped his arms and let them hang. A pall descended on the auditorium and the students hated the little man who refused them their good news. Worse, he had forced them to confront their mortality for the first time. The Bastion Memorial Plaque, a memento which was usually given in thanks to a speaker, sat unclaimed on the rostrum as Dr. Isadore Leishman sauntered out the central corridor, whistling a slushy tune, with his peat-bog micro-environment trailing.

Leishman arrived back at the offices earlier than he had expected and he went looking for Rustom. He found him working at something in the whiteboard room and strode in with vigor, jacked up by the lecture.

"So, Rustom. Have you made a start?"

"Yes, Dr. Leishman. I have finished what you asked me to do, and there is a copy for you on the bench there. For my own satisfaction, I am working through a few things on the board. Oddly, I think better when I see an equation written with my own hand than reading it off a screen."

"I think better that way also."

Leishman wanted to take it back. He felt it elevated Rustom to say he had something in common with him and he gritted his teeth.

"Dr. Leishman, I am sure you hear this sort of thing all the time, but the work you have done here is beautiful. The logic is so clean and built step by step so elegantly, I cannot say how much I admire it."

Leishman looked for the sarcasm in Sanjay's comment but there was none.

"Thank you, Rustom. I am pleased with it also. What is that you are doing on the board?"

"Your work is an orbital calculator is it not, meant to be automated? No one has ever done it as far as I know. I was just working out an area I did not understand, and I am so pleased you are here to explain it to me."

"Did you make a copy of the material I gave you?"

"Of course. I make protection copies of everything I do."

"Give me the copy."

"Sure, it is right there in the thumb drive. The printed copy is on the lab bench. By the way, I ran some arbitrary test data, and it ran through clean as a whistle. One thing though, and that is what I have on the board here, which I ..."

"Rustom, it's not required that you understand it."

Leishman walked to the board and erased Rustom's work and went over it again with the brush. He put the drive in his pocket and retrieved the hard copy from the lab bench.

"Sanjay, your copy please. Thank you. You have seen my original work. It is shared between the two of us, but the work belongs to me. You have signed a blanket confidentiality and non-competition agreement. You will not share any material from this, and you will not discuss your thoughts, conclusions, nor your impressions of it with anyone. Without exception. Not Macbeth, not Rybakov, no one. Do you have a personal duplicate of the material of any kind?"

"No, I don't."

"Good. Get back to the data work on the mission tracking."

Isadore Leishman returned to his office without a word. Rustom was unsurprised at the cavalier dismissal of his interest in the theorems. They were certainly beautiful and well done as he had said. He had feigned the inability to understand certain aspects of the work to stimulate dialogue between him and Leishman. He understood every jot but what he did not understand was the agenda built into it. Despite a quirkiness akin to madness, Dr. Leishman's work was held in high regard in the International Scientific community. He was a brilliant and respected source, yet the theorems Sanjay had seen that day were a fake. They were designed to change values within the data to produce a predetermined result. Whatever orbital path Leishman reported for whatever dangerous near-earth body he was tracking, would be the path Leishman's fevered brain wanted it to be, and it was unlikely to match reality.

Chapter Six

Rybakov laid on his back and stiff armed his bench press as his spotter, Rolfe, helped him cradle the barbell into the rack. The lad had added weights incrementally up to 460 pounds and Rybakov had worked his way up to it, plate by plate, and bench pressed it without so much as a quaver. At fifty he looked forty.

"Dr. Rybakov, that was awesome. Most average guys in here work for a year and struggle to get up to about 135 pounds. And that's better than where most of them start, but an ideal bench press is double one's weight. You weigh what? About 200?"

"This morning I weighed 232 pounds. I prefer being about 225, 220, but unfortunately, I like my oladyi, my sweet Russian pancakes."

He slapped his gut which was taut.

"Well, sir, you pressed that 460 with no sweat. Were you an athlete, not that you aren't now, but at your age, I mean you're not that old, but, that … ."

"Stop. I get it, Rolfe. I was raised in Russia, which at that time had mandatory national service and military training. Rival brigades competed in the hand-to-hand combat disciplines, so I built myself up to fight. I fought 63 bouts in both Russian Sambo and Brazilian Jujitsu at exactly this weight. Those were wonderful days for young men, Rolfe. You should have seen us strut when we walked past the cafes in our uniforms. We were beautiful."

Sergei did not mention his uniform was of the Spetsnaz, Russia's elite special forces. Lethality was their pride and Sergei was formidable. He spent nine years training guerrillas and orchestrating behind-the-lines sabotage in war zones to support Russia's vassals against insurgencies and protests. He was the hardest of the hard and a killer. He retained his rank of colonel and completed his studies at the Moscow Institute of Physics and Technology.

Izzy Leishman punched in the security code to the whiteboard room and placed his eye to the lens for his retinal scan. The red LED blinked then stopped on solid green and the maximum-security door opened away from him with a buzz. Izzy was early and eager. The previous day, the team had made good progress on the reworking of their equations for fusion propulsion, and he was excited. Four large whiteboards surrounded him. He swung a chair around and rested his chin on his hands on the chairback. He intended to review the equations on the whiteboards and recapitulate the sequences of the developing theorems, but in seconds, his shoulders slumped, and his zeal evaporated. He recognized nothing he saw on the boards. Slowly, he read the unfamiliar phrases written there and Leishman drank in the beauty of their logic line by line. Bit by bit his usual cadaverous pallor pinked then reddened then burned and his melancholy at not having been the author became a paranoiac fury. Once again, their little club had done it without him, and his nose was pressed against the glass looking in. Tears of anger and joy ran freely and the coming in of Rybakov behind him did not register.

Sergei waltzed into the room swinging his briefcase. It was a Saturday, and few staff were about except for the principals. He was energized from his stint at the gym, and he approached Leishman from behind, singing a Russian song for the benefit of his colleague as part of the habitual early morning provocation of Leishman.

"Little snowberry, snowberry, snowberry of mine, little raspberry in the garden, my little raspberr ... ."

Leishman growled without turning. *Damn that Rybakov. Blast him to hell. He beat me to it. They beat me. They cut me out of the deal again.*

Sergei's muscles were pumped from his workout, and he was in crushing mode. He rubbed his huge, calloused hands together then walked to Leishman with his arms spread wide to signify an imminent bearhug.

"Come Izzy, tell Rybakov what has made you grusnyy, made you sad. You are melancholic when you should be happy about your work. You must be part Russian, eh? A Leishmanova on your mother's side. Do tell the Russian bear. He understands all."

Leishman jumped to his feet and circled to keep the chair between them. "Stay away you beast! Keep your filthy hands off me! Don't touch me. Stay away!"

"Leishy, Leishy, the bear understa… ."

Sergei looked at his whiteboard and saw what troubled Leishman. All their work of many months, their sweat, their artistry, was gone. In its stead, a barely legible scrawled mess of theorems covered two of the boards in dusty black trails. Intellectual bragging rights for the original solutions were gone in both of their minds and all their ongoing input was expunged. Rybakov understood why Leishman had been crying. They had worked together with Dr. Macbeth for hundreds of hours to arrive at this point. The ego-driven competition was ferocious for first journal publication and for the first time in his life losing at something, Rybakov had committed to memory every symbol and figure yet it was still a loss. What he saw was a total departure from their collective thinking. He stood there immobile and read the fresh script for several minutes, then threw his briefcase on the desk and stepped close to the board despite being able to see it from twenty feet. He spread his arms to indicate its magnificence and pivoted hard to Leishman.

"Tovarich! Oomnitsa! You clever baby! Leishman, you beautiful devil! I knew you had it in you!" Rybakov could not contain himself and he grabbed Leishman in a massive hug and kissed him hard on the lips. The fusion drive was real.

"Off, you pig. Off me! Does that look anything like my writing? Mine? My work? I thought it was you! Your work is like that. Always scratchy, messy and scribbling. But it's not yours, is it. Too weak, faint. No useless bits of your unfathomable Cyrillic lettering here and there meant to confuse me."

The third alternative jolted Izzy and he raged. "Her! It is hers. The Macbeth woman. Damn her eyes! No comment to us, no sharing or confiding with her colleagues, no excitement, just a cold imperious statement left for us to find in the morning and then waiting in her office for us to come crawling, to adulate, expecting us churls to make obeisance to her genius. Rybakov, why don't you poison her? Claim the fusion solution as your own. Now that we have it, who needs her?"

"A rather interesting thought, that poisoning, but to answer your question of who needs her, my dear, we do."

Rybakov snatched up the laboratory phone and connected with Meghan in her office and laid it on in thick Slavic English. "So, bubla, you deed it."

"Did it? Whatever it is, Rybakov, not guilty. Stop the riddles with your fractured English. What are you talking about?"

"Your solution. The nuclear drive equations on the white board. I have given them just a cursory reading, but I have never seen anything so elegant. My dear, you are a wonder. Come show us. Show us. Come to the lab."

Meghan ignored Leishman's moaning, approached the whiteboard and stood ten feet away in silence. She digested every simple incremental development of logic and followed each one, step by glorious step, to their obvious and unequivocal resolution. Tears began to well and she drove them away. She thought of mathematician Rene Descartes and his belief that nothing was complicated or difficult because every problem, whether mathematical or philosophical, could be explained with simple steps proceeding in an ordered way, leading to a self-evident conclusion. Laid before her was a pure, perfect example of Descartes' truth.

"This is the most beautiful thing I have seen."

Leishman writhed with anger at her false modesty. "Cut out the baloney, Dr. Macbeth. Calling your own stuff beautiful, just fishing for agreement. My how wonderful. I wonder who could have done it."

"My stuff? I thought the two of you had worked it out. Look at that hand, it is not mine. I had nothing to do with it. And now I see the entirety of our original work has been erased. The equations on the boards do not carry on where we left off, they are fresh from a new start. This is a whole new area of thought. A total departure from what we thought was so. It cannot be this simple."

Meghan walked to the whiteboard and felt the markings with her finger. The equations were erasable and dusty, but they were not from a marker.

Izzy leaned in. "Rybakov, did you just see something sparkle, for a fraction of a second there, sort of glimmering above and around, behind Dr. Macbeth?"

"No, I did not. Are you drunk?"

Meghan Macbeth wasn't hearing a word of the badinage, and she stood placidly, drinking in every delicious flow of the thought portrayed on the white board. The logic moved ahead like a symphony with each bar developing from the last and every mathematical chord resolving into a beautiful path to the finale. What she saw was worthy of a Newton. Rybakov moved in and stood beside her, rereading the material.

Meghan stood in awe of the perfect creation on the board and spoke to no one in particular. "Leishman? Could… Leishman?"

Rybakov shook his head. "No. He is a clever man and deep in many ways, but his competitiveness and his insane ego could never bring him to deny being the author of such seminal genius. Then again, the man is absolutely nuts. He just might deny it in a fit of masochism at not being recognized for his brilliance. I can see it. Punishing himself for not getting the credit and getting off on the victimhood."

Meghan stated what each of them thought. "Access to this laboratory is restricted to us three and young Rustom. What the hell happened!" She called the closed-circuit video display room.

"Harry? Hi. This is Dr. Macbeth. How're things with you? Glad to hear it. Hm? Not so good. We need to see the tape of the whiteboard lab for last night. Cue it up and link it to the screen here. When it's ready, stay on the line for rewinds and the like. Thanks. Fifteen minutes? Fine."

Doctor Macbeth opened the full facility intercom. "Rustom. Sanjay Rustom. To the whiteboard lab. Stat. Rustom to the whiteboard lab." She closed the intercom knowing she would soon be required to terminate Sanjay Rustom and thousands of others now that the launch was done, and the rover was on track for Bennu. She had come to rely upon a man who soon would be gone from the Cosmos Space Center. *Rustom, Rustom.* She wanted him there, now. His insights were unique.

She took photos of the boards with her phone and backed them up on a flash drive at her desk and dropped the drive into her lab coat pocket. "I suppose you have the boards committed to memory, Dr. Rybakov?"

"Yes, I can't avoid it. If I read it with my eyes, it stores in my brain. Full eidetic memory. It is a blessing. And a curse. I still have train schedules in my head for places where they no longer run trains. Then again, I no longer have to run to catch them."

Meghan nodded, knowing what he said was true. "Well gents, here we sit within the most sophisticated protection system on earth, and we have been breached. And that might not be the term. We cannot assume only external agents could be responsible."

"Meghan, is it possible one of our guys did this?"

"Isadore, I wish it were so and I hope it is not so, at the same time. To have someone with such insight and genius available to us is phenomenal. Yet, to have the security here compromised, this work done clandestinely, as well as the new work discounting the entire thesis we produced through months of tedium, speaks to a psyche and a pathology which may not be helpful or reliable. When we see the video, perhaps we'll know more. Blast it, where is Rustom."

"Rustom? We don't need that arrogant little smart-ass punk."

Rybakov ignored Leishman's adolescent jealousy and waggled his finger at the equations on the second board.

"From the outset there is both beauty and clarity and I wish such clarity were mine. I have been running the theorem in my mind and something pops in the final subsets. It just is not finished. It needs to step out, to step forward, but it doesn't. It is not finished. It stops short of a final statement, and I cannot see where to go from where it has left me."

Sanjay arrived all smiles, but he sobered quickly under the venom painted on Isadore's face. Before Meghan could speak, Leishman screamed as he pointed his finger to the boards. His bony hand trembled with fury as he attacked Rustom.

"Did you do this you arrogant little prick? Sneaking in here and playing your little smart-ass game? "

Sanjay ignored Leishman and read the material slowly and committed the theorem to memory.

"No, the work is not mine I wish it were. It isn't finished though, is it?"

The 60-inch plasma screen on the east wall sprang to life and Harry's enormous, elongated proboscis filled the screen as he leaned forward into the camera. "I am ready with the video. Dr. Macbeth."

"Good, thank you. I was the last one out of the lab at about 21:30. Run it fast forward from there until something changes in the room."

"21:30 it is."

At the video time stamp of 04:38, something like a firefly gleamed and a subtle smokiness settled into the whiteboard room.

"Stop, Harry. Is there a flaw in the file? It looks smokey."

"Nope. No flaw. What you see is what happened. It's not smoke. The density is perfectly diffused, not with patches of accelerating gas or areas hotter one than the other."

"Run it at actual speed."

Over the next half hour, the pale grayness in the room became increasingly opaque and impenetrable to the eye. Slowly, a whisp of darkness emerged from within it, reached to a board, and stroked it with a gray tendril, leaving a faint track. It condensed to a deeper hue and the tremulous finger began to write black on the whiteboard and lay down the equations, beginning at the end on the right and moving leftward.

Leishman broke the wonderment. "Writing right to left, eh Sergei? Jewish ghost."

"Very funny. Notice the pace. Even when copying an equation to a board, you and I stop and check or pause at the phrase endings. That's not happening there. It is continuous at the same pace with no breaks. There are no corrections or erasures. It is a flow of knowledge, not a train of thoughts. What do you think, Meghan?"

"Contemporaries dismissed Mozart by saying he was nothing more than God's stenographer. That's what this looks like. Except I have my doubts about it being from God."

"Saith the Rubáiyát, the moving finger writes, and having writ, moves on. Nor all your piety nor wit, shall lure it back to cancel half a line, nor all your tears wash out a word of it. Would you like to hear the next seventy-five stanzas?"

"No, thank you, Rybakov. Maybe sometime next year. Izzy, do you sense it is energized as if it were attempting a solid state or at least a denser material? Look. Look. Now and again, it masks the board. Do you see that?"

A faint kaleidoscopic chimera showed through and with it came a vacant echoing laugh at the beginning of the next phrase.

"What the devil was that? A laugh. Was that a laugh? Harry. Are you there? Duplicate the file and send it to Jennings for analysis. Have him do a spectral analysis as well. Clean it up and try to get through the fog. Make a second copy for me and bring it here yourself."

The screen blackened and stayed dark.

"Harry, did you do that?"

"No, Dr. Macbeth, the thing shut the lights off when it left."

Dr. Rybakov was generally brimming with solutions but for this he had few suggestions. "Dr. Macbeth, this is a nice puzzle but first we have to protect against whatever this was and however it got in here. It gave a gift to us of something we wanted. Next time, it could just as easily take from us, something we don't want it to have."

"Yes. I want Duo to look at this material."

Immediately they heard Duo's signature shuffling gait approaching the door.

"How does it do that, Dr. Macbeth? One mention from you and it was on the move."

"I am not sure, Izzy. I suppose a sympathetic quantum type of communication. Ah, Duo. Analyze what you see on the board."

Duo read the material in less than a second and reported it to his other mother. He had decided to mimic British patrician speech for that day.

"The script is excessively messy."

"Duo, Forget about that. Wha.."

" I am not capable of forgetting what I ha… "

"Stop that! Assess the value of the equations."

" I find the equations are impeccably presented. The logic is precise and correct."

"Is it applicable to advancing our work toward fusion drive?"

"Yes."

"More."

"It advances in the correct direction. But empirically speaking, it is odd when measured against its fellows. It is incomplete."

"Incomplete, you say? How so?"

"You will see when you have had the opportunity to study it further. It is done in riddle form. It leaves off at a point where it requires a next step from you. Unfortunately, that choice is based on a philosophical decision which is yours alone to make. Therefore, I cannot help you. I have not yet completed my reading of ethics."

"I see. Sergei and Izzy, start on a simulation to test what we have. Start yourselves. No-one can see the new material. Do not pass it off to the computer lab. On second thought, do nothing. Take the morning off to think about the entire situation. Ignore the equations for the moment and consider the bigger picture of security. Meantime, I'm getting an external eye to look at the intrusion. I know whom I need."

Meghan was excited by the unbelievable event. She was equally suspicious of the origin. Research and the academia surrounding it were a snake pit. Any one of her team was capable of original thought on the fusion dilemma, and equally capable of hacking the internal camera system to make it show anything they wanted to show. A breakthrough made by anyone on the Cosmos team would come to the world of scientific journals as a group effort. Individual egos competed for supremacy to the degree that the writer might deny authorship rather than elevate the others to their level by presenting the breakthrough equations as done by equals in a group. Unfamiliar handwriting did not absolve any of them. That was easily contrived. Rybakov, Leishman, or Rustom.

<>

A cold drizzle and a hard wind out of the north set the tone and on days like this I wondered what drove my need to run. With every stride the gravel stiffened in the dropping temperature and the dawning brought no warmth with it. I had watched hamsters on their wheels run to exhaustion, getting nowhere for no purpose as the same terrain sped by them over and over. For them, the wheel was their all without the burden of choice and each day was a new joy. My wheel had become a lingering obligation and I slept with the prospect each night and I ran every day. I questioned whether both I and the hamster were running away from something as much as running toward it.

I felt the cold more than I used to and I picked up the pace to satisfy my delusion it would make me warmer. Breath frosted around me and to avoid the slickness of the wet maple leaves blanketing the trail ahead, I headed south with a nice tailwind toward the Black Creek estuary and the sea.

Despite loathing it, this day I carried an antique cell phone in my back pocket. Yesterday I had no calls from clients. I suspected not locking my cell phone in a filing cabinet might improve my odds of receiving a phone call on it, and to prove my case, the evil thing vibrated. I wanted to smash it. I knew its real job was to fry my brain with its microwaves, put me at the beck and call of a thousand agendas not related to my own and then once a month send me an invoice for the damage. However, the call did rescue me from my manic need to time my five-mile run. I recognized the caller's number, and I knew it was trouble, but my bank account directed me to go for the punishment and answer it.

"Hello, this is Frank McCord, private investigator."

"Good Lord, Frank! You actually answered your phone. Are you sick?"

"Hello Meghan, how mellow of you. What's happening?"

"You may have heard I have moved on from Petruvia Labs. I am heading up the Bennu asteroid probe at the Cosmos Aerospace Center."

"Yes Meghan, I heard the announcement of your appointment on the radio, what, three, four years ago? Considering you were Dr. Belton's protégé at Petruvia, he must have been an unhappy man at your leaving. You had a lot invested in each other."

"It was actually announced five years ago, and don't worry about Belton, Frank. He is as tough as they come and a sly old fox. In fact, I have brought him on as a consultant. He is as sharp as ever and he has great insights. Craig is on the payroll too."

"Duncan Craig? Astrophysicist or not, the man could not scramble an egg. I would have thought you were well rid of him."

“True enough, but he is the media’s darling. Having a local man up front to calm the masses is good public relations. He won’t come within a quarter mile of anything important.”

“I see the sly old fox taught you a few things in addition to physics. At any rate, congratulations, Meghan. You are becoming quite the star. I suppose that is the ultimate goal of every astrophysicist.”

“Spare me, Frank. Recently we had a security breach in one of our labs. In itself, it seems to be a benign event, but my concern is, is it a test of our security measures, in advance of the return of the Bennu probe. If all goes well, ultimately we will have samples from the asteroid at the lab. They might be the target of the intruder. I have not involved our own security staff in it as it might have come from the inside. At this point only the four of us who had access to the space, and the video lab know about it. As usual this is a highest security clearance issue. Can you come and assess the situation?”

“At the launch site?”

“Yes. Our budget is a good one. Bill your top hourly rate.”

“My usual beat is here in Abernathy Town. What’s the roundtrip distance from here to the launch complex? My Buick is in surgery as we speak, and it may not survive.”

“I’ll send the old girl some flowers. It’s about three hundred miles roundtrip. In the meantime, rent a car. We’ll buy it for you if it comes to that. What do you say?”

“What I say is, I’m in the middle of a run and I’m cooling down. I’ll consider it overnight and I’ll call you tomorrow. Will I get you at the number showing on the screen?”

“Yes.”

“Okay. Tomorrow.”

Sergei Rybakov retrieved his phone from his locker and left the offices. The apparition with the magic finger had him spinning. The fantastic event they watched on tape challenged the foundations of physics. To clear his mind, he walked the path which circumscribed Lake Calisto, an artificial lake which was dug by the Cosmos installation, then flooded for fire protection of the launch site. The forestry crew had cut away the deadfall from recent lightning strikes and Rybakov sat on a blackened stump to make a private call. His phone appeared to be just one more of the world's ten billion cell phones, but it was not. It had no signal bar indicator, nor a battery icon. He activated it with his thumb print and spoke the code phrase of the day to validate himself with his unique harmonic voice signature.

"Pushkin 4."

He felt a subtle vibration as it activated. A heterodyning whine grew and climbed to the inaudible range, then it settled and was soundless. Sergei was one of four Russian operatives worldwide who were trusted with the experimental technology. It was a neutrino beam phone. It used sub-atomic, nearly massless particles travelling near the speed of light to transmit messages and it recharged itself infinitely. It required no relay stations; no satellites and it connected instantly on a straight-line stream through the iron core of the earth without impediment. With it, Russia had overcome the limits of linking to its nuclear submarine fleet, which like all submarine fleets, needed to surface to receive signals. Now, with direct and immediate battle instructions by neutrino stream, their ballistic missile armed submarines could roam deep and undetected, primed and ready to strike. This was Sergei's first use of the phone and he spoke to connect it. "Old man 1."

He kept the stream open for three or four minutes and was about to close when Demidov answered.

"Rybakov! You used 'Old man 1' as your code name for my phone address? What the hell! I don't need reminders from you that I'm seventy, my mirror tells me that every morning. Nevertheless, what is happening on your end?"

"Unbelievable, Pavel. You sound as if we were sitting in the same room. As a physicist I am astonished at this. However, a more astonishing thing occurred yesterday. We believe we have the basic equation to solve the fusion drive problem." He explained the phenomenon of the writing and Demidov was silent.

"Sir?"

"Yes, yes, I am here. Sergei, what you told me is interesting. We'll look at things here when you copy us with the formulae. Unfortunately, the question arises, in whose field does the party which gave you the material pitch its tent?"

"Exactly. We must presume the entity is not friendly. An analysis done by both me and an AI robot believe the equations are incomplete. Your men will have to work it through to check that. Pardon? No, not much news of worth on the Saskatchewan plant. About two miles. Yes. Two miles. Probably the longest assembly line ever done. Perhaps I should say assembly lines, plural, thanks to Russia's input on the space council. Two lines in attached buildings run parallel to each other. Not sure, but it is on schedule. Maybe eighteen months. Possibly less. The probe is on track for Bennu to return as scheduled and we'll go from there. Leishman? He's the same as ever. Brilliant and bonkers. Wait just a second, Pavel. This thing is getting hot. Is your phone heating up? No? Please tell the tech boys about the problem. I am signing off now."

"One second, Sergei. It is likely that going forward you will communicate with a man more technically capable than me. You should not have the subtleties of new physics distorted by a layman intermediary like me, so this could be the last of our calls. Your new contact will open and close his conversations with 'Privyet.'"

Rybakov signed off with 'Pushkin 4' and his code words terminated the call. He was surprised at the change. Direct contact with The Demidov was irreplaceable. If broached carefully, small things whispered in the great man's ear could become big things in the favor of Rybakov and now the influence was gone. He feared this meant disfavor. The opportunity for misery settled on him like a comfortable old coat. His inescapable obligation to the Russian need for suffering began to work on him. His psyche leapt to the most morbid conclusion, and he saw a faceless orthodox priest dressed in black standing over a mound of fresh soft soil. The priest swung his censer to the cadence of Rybakov's eulogy, while the flicker of the candle held by a solitary mourner bounced off a gold cross on the chest of the man of God.

Count Pavel Demidov closed his stream and set the phone on his desk. Sergei was a good man. He was imbedded deeply. Unfortunately for him, he had the gift of an eidetic memory. Very useful in itself but troubling for Russia. A mind which remembered in perfect detail, everything done in and by Russia globally over the last 30 years was a dangerous thing. Every operation, the identity of every operative and every confidential high-level conversation lived in Rybakov's head. To drain his mind would be gold beyond calculation for the west. Demidov decided to move him to the top of the transport schedule. He himself was not included there. His age disqualified him as he was unlikely to see the end, but he did not regret it nor anything about his life. He liked his new title. These days he was referred to as 'The Demidov' and called an oligarch, which marked him as an implicit member of the new corporate aristocracy, while more blessed still, he remained a member of the old. He placed a call to the handler. No salutations were used between them.

"You will now handle Rybakov. Use scalar communications only. Ongoing, open and close your dialogue with both me, and him, with 'Privyet'. Wait three weeks before you contact him. In the interval he will become anxious over his status. Relieving his doubts with your call will give you significant power in the relationship."

The handler understood the tactic and gave a private long-distance nod of agreement as he closed his phone.

Demidov was one of one the most revered names in the Russian lexicon. The Demidov armament empire ran unscathed in a 300-year continuum through wars, revolutions and purges, from the imperial days of Czar Peter the First. All things were forgiven of the men who armed the nation. The cachet of the family name allowed Pavel entrance to every salon, and he floated seamlessly through every government agency keeping a finger on its pulse. He punched a call to Anatoly Firsov, the director of the Federal Security Service.

"This is Pavel Demidov. Please connect me with Director Firsov."

"The Demidov? I mean is this really Count Demidov? This is such an hon …"

"Yes, yes, thank you. Please connect me with Firsov."

"I am sorry, sir, he is in, um, conference right now and…"

"I know what that means. The old goat is sleeping in his office. Wake him up and be quick about it, son. Hurry now."

Firsov's blustering and stamping preceded him to the phone.

"Pavel."

"Hello Firsov. Don't give stick to the boy, he did his best to protect you. Listen. I want Dr. Sergei Rybakov moved to priority allotment."

"Fine. Anything else I can do for you?"

"You old coot, did you write it down?"

"Who you calling an old coot? I am a year younger than you. There. Written down. What else?"

"How are the allotment percentages coming? Have we an advantage?"

"Not yet."

"Ah well. When the day comes, you know how it is. Sometimes the bus goes right past the stop."

"True, there is no accounting for bus drive

Chapter Seven
April 2017

I turned on the local television news and buckled up for the horror

show. A perfect porcelain dentition beamed out from the pancake powdered face, and with a smile it segued from one vignette of calamity to another. The talking head delivered a glossary of overnight lawlessness in a cheery good morning way, granting the perpetrators the moral prerogative, all the while checking themselves in the monitor to verify their awesomeness. News from my mechanic was equally bad. My Buick's condition was more critical than he first thought, and I might have to put the old girl down. The car owed me nothing, but she was solid, and she represented a continuum of sanity and easy familiarity. I had been congratulating myself on my implacability against embracing the woke life, when an unexpected impulse to self-censor jolted me. I referenced my Buick as the 'old girl' or a 'she' and if the pronoun police could read my mind, they would cancel me. If I lived in France, of course, the nomenclature would be clearer. Everything is clearer in France. I reckoned Le Buick or La Buick would suffice and either way it would be defined and done with. On the other hand, I might simply give her an androgenous name. Something such as Chris or Sasha or Pat. Then again, given the destination to which the world was rushing, Comrade Buick should suffice. I would review the matter with my personal mixologist extraordinaire, Morty.

Here and there my name reached me from the hubbub. They were not greetings but rather statements of observation by the nerds looking over the top of their coke-bottle glasses and the hamsters connecting to their biases. They had a proprietary interest in my caricature. Every high school had its scapegoat, and every bar had its boor. That was me. However, I did not drink beer, which disappointed them. I knew a few of them by name and a quick-stepping Malcom tugged on my sleeve.

"Oh Frank, Franky, you must try this. Absolutely a must. It is to die for."

I did not answer him, and I waited for him to do it, but sadly he did not die.

"What, Malcolm. What this time? Done with drinking Gibsons are you? Too easy to spill when you are running on your wheel?"

"You are so mean. Taste, taste!"

"Absolutely not. You reek of sugar."

"Well then, miss out. This is an Averna amaro, in the flesh, well not the flesh exactly, but anyway. It is on the rocks with a twist of lemon. Sweet and mellow."

I left to fluttering eyelids and wedged into a seat at the bar. Morty opened the conversation with his archetypal hospitality.

"McCord, once again you look terrible."

"Morty, most days I would deny it and tell you in fact, no, despite my demeanor I was really quite gruntled, but today, just the opposite. It's the state of the world. Everywhere I look is like a snake. I don't want to see it, yet I can't stop looking at it."

"The trouble is you private eyes question the whys and wherefores of everything. Once a copper, always a copper. You carry someone else's water. I presume that's why you're imbibing early today."

"Yes. I need both a change of attitude and your ineffable illumination. A prospective client called, and I am considering whether I want to take her on."

"Whether you want to? Your bar tab is so big it is tracked by the Federal Reserve as an economic indicator."

"The client is Meghan Macbeth. As you know I had a contract with her about five years ago. In the interval all my fractures are nicely healed, and I believe it rankles her. She would enjoy seeing them freshened up. Even at that, we ultimately got along, and I know we can maintain a professional relationship. We respect each other's expertise. Besides, competing with her is a losing game. A lot of brain power there. She is an Einstein. Morty, if Einstein were alive today, what do you suppose he would be working on?"

"Not much, he would be 143."

'Clever. I meant alive in his prime."

"Still, not much. He did his notable work by age 26. He enjoyed celebrity and lived off that as much as physics. His philosophical thought is more quoted today than his science. For example, he said there are only two things to consider. Whether the universe is hostile or friendly."

"Is the universe friendly or hostile? Was he kidding? All of it is turmoil and fuzzy nothingness spinning in circles. Any day now the earth could play pinball with an asteroid the size of Brazil and I'm supposed to ponder whether it's friendly or hostile. I think it was a joke which the boys at the physics club played on the rubes. Things blow up everywhere out there and black holes lurk to suck you in and grind you up and he asks is it friendly or hostile? And now we have imported the same level of mayhem to chew us up on the streets. Civilization is ceasing to exist."

"Well of course it is. Do you know what civilization is? Some would prefer to sanitize it as social order, but realistically civilization is nothing more than a temporary and occasional intrusion into the natural order of things."

"The natural order?"

"Yes. The frenzied pace of change which drives one mad. Chaos. No civilization of man, anywhere, ever, has survived. Not the Sumerians, not the Aztecs, and like every one of them, we have the arrogance to believe we have the answers they didn't have. But enough eh, Frank? I like what Oscar Wilde said and I think he was right. Life is far too important a thing ever to talk seriously about it."

Oscar had it right and I needed to address my pronoun dilemma.

"Edify me, Morty. Why do we refer to so many things as a 'she'? I refer to my Buick as the 'old girl', or 'she', and sailors do the same with their ships. 'She went down with all hands', and the like."

"McCord, you are already a walking compendium of anomalies and now you add an unhealthy anthropomorphism to your repertoire. So. You attribute female characteristics to inanimate objects such as your car. You are the classic case. Your mother didn't breast feed you. She told you they hadn't wanted more children, then, they had you. You are seeking, indeed yearning, for the substitute, the female figure such as a mother or goddess to guide and protect you."

"That was amazingly helpful. Thank you Morty."

"Welcome. As to ships, the Latin for ship is 'navis'. In Latin, nouns are masculine and feminine. 'Navis' is feminine, therefore, 'her' or 'she' is the reference. Since we are discussing 'her', what about the job offer from the lady. Is the pay good? You can tell Morty."

"Yes. Top of the line, but certain clients like the eminent Dr. Meghan Macbeth are magnets for bad actors. Then I have to deal with them."

"Sleep on it. Following that, do it."

The radiators in my apartment had returned from holiday and the hammering of the steam heat woke me at sunrise. Despite the racket the pipes were cold, but I had slept well, and I walked in my bare feet across the linoleum and closed the window. Cross-legged on the couch with my feet tucked under, I called Meghan. She picked up on the second ring.

"Hi, Meghan. Fine, thanks. Yes, it was a quick decision. I conferred with my shrink, and he advised me to proceed. How is he? Dr. Morty is fine. He has stopped speaking in parables and has gone directly to insults. No, I don't think you will need me full-time. Also, I want to maintain a presence in the Town, so I am not out of sight, nor given my past activities here, presumed to be dead. Assistants? I will know better when you and I discuss the event fully. No, not now. This isn't a secure phone. If the situation warrants more of my time, then I will give you what we need. Insert an option to extend my hours in the employment contract along with the usual caveats. Today? I can leave as soon as I shower. Assuming I can find a rental car, I should be there by noon. Beef sandwiches are fine. Bye."

I heated a glass in the oven for three or four minutes and poured in one finger of Lagavulin. I held the glass to warm my hands, breathed in the vapor and tossed back the whisky. Standing beside the Lagavulin on the bureau was an unopened bottle of Black Bush Irish, aged for eight years in sherry casks. It was a gift for Fran, and it had sat there for four months with a little red bow on it. It was a nice reminder of her and the fact it had sat there four months validated her decision to drop me. Despite that, I could not deny she did feminine pronouns proud.

The rental car smelled of cleaning solvent, and a tree-shaped pine scented deodorizer hung from the rear-view mirror to add a certain je ne sais quoi. Someone should trade mark that. Eau de je ne sais quoi.

No vehicles were allowed on the Cosmos Aerospace property, so I was forced to park outside the launch compound. I knew the cell phone drill and I relinquished mine to the attendant. Only selected individuals were privileged to have a phone within the perimeter. The front gate security had been forewarned and Meghan came to meet me in a golf cart, wearing a hard hat and she handed me one.

"Here, Frank. Put this on. You need it anywhere outside the labs. Let's go. My office is about a mile inside the compound. When I have you signed up and official, I'll get you a secure phone."

The golf cart released the latent kamikaze in Dr. Macbeth and the patchy frozen surface became the Monaco Grand Prix. When I first met Meghan, she peeled around in a '66 Shelby and she handled the golf cart the same way.

"Frank, un-whiten your knuckles. I have rolled the cart only two times."

As we approached the door to the main building, a burly man blew smoke from a stogie and waved at us. The golf cart chattered to a stop at his feet.

"Sergei, put that thing out and go into the lab. Frank, Sergei. Sergei, Frank. And Frank, don't let Sergei hug you. He will break your ribs."

I watched the fluid movement of the big man as he walked inside. He had a gangly disjointed walk which promised action and I felt uncomfortable with it. It was familiar and unpleasant and from the past and yet I could not place it.

"Meghan, who is that guy?"

"Dr. Rybakov. He is on loan to us for as long as we use the Atlas V rocket. Sergei is absolutely brilliant and immutably Russian. He is an expert on propulsion systems, and he is the definitive expert on the Atlas system. His clearance was slow coming, but a trade-off was made eventually. Part of our allied engine assembly facility in Saskatchewan is exclusively for Russian use. To avoid interference, it is consular territory. An inviolable bit of Russian Territory. Like a consulate or embassy. As a result we can thank Russia for a large part of our Cosmos Aerospace program."

"Russia, huh? I thought we didn't like Russia."

"We don't. Unless they have something we want."

"I get it. Like mumps. Not popular but they let you stay home from school."

"Frank, your mind is a mystery. Much like the security video I will show you. First, we will get your baseline retinal scan done. The biometrics of your retinal blood vessels don't lie. If you are coming and going throughout the complex, you will need it to access the restricted areas."

We started on the cold beef sandwiches as Rybakov cued up the video on the viewing screen. Neither of us had taken his eyes off the other and we came to the realization at the same time.

"Frank McCord! Bucharest! You Dog! Meghan, McCord beat me at the World Sambo championships in Bucharest. He beat me but you know how international games work. Judges are there to do what the politics demands, not to judge the contestants. That year, Russia received a gold in Sambo, that was me, in a trade for gold in fencing for the French. McCord got silver. Anyway, old man, you look good. Your spare tire becomes you."

I felt a twitch in my hips for a full-bodied pivot to blast him in the face. My right hand tingled as the sounds of a nasal cartilage flying to parts unknown echoed in my memory. The contemplation of it brought a smile to my face and he interpreted it as bonhomie.

"Thank you, Dr. Rybakov. Or should I say Valerie Suslev? That's what threw me. You were called Suslev in those days."

"I was also Petrov. And when convenient, I was Liapkin. Russia was the master of it. Get banned from the games in Rio as Rybakov, hone your skills in competition in Athens as Liapkin. Get sanctioned there for political reasons, fight in Bucharest as Suslev and the training goes on."

"I know the drill. In those games the US needed a win in figure skating so in the wee small hours of the morning they made a French skater a US citizen and presto, a gold medal appeared. Where did you complete your physics doctorate?"

"The Moscow Institute of Physics. There, my first-place gold medal was legitimate."

"Sergei, each of us is looking in the mirror right now and sees an old clandestine special forces operative who has escaped the hard days. How many missing years in your resume?"

"Eighteen. You?"

"Eleven, then a soft five."

"Later we can have a drink together and talk shop. If you wish."

"Not a chance, Sergei. Those days are ancient history to me. Dead and buried. I have no desire to stir them up. Let's get to the video."

Sergei reeked of active status. He was honed and sharp and the soft edge which comes with mustering out was missing. He was on the job, and I didn't think Meghan got it.

"Meghan, until I am official, I want to comment to you alone on what I see in the video. I want to shorten the chain of communication right off the top. Sergei, Dr. Macbeth is the head. When the relationships here are codified by contract, things may change, but today, Dr. Macbeth only."

Rybakov nodded without comment and left the room with a nod to Meghan.

"Frank, that was unnecessary."

"If you want my help, let me give it. My reports and modus operandi are exclusive to you and not to be shared. Stipulate that in the terms and conditions of my employment. Missing years means, 'How long were you a non-person, untrackable, untraceable and expendable, a lethal animal trained to disrupt the world by doing unspeakable things on behalf of your country'. Today, Sergei Rybakov is the respected physicist, but don't ignore the fact he was one of those animals. He bristles with it even yet. This is a very good sandwich. Can we start the video?"

I watched the phantasm materialize from the mist in the laboratory to write on the white board with what according to Morty's definition, I had anthropomorphized into a bony finger. The display was hypnotic as the equations flowed smoothly from the hand of something made from mist. "Well, that is a thing I have never seen. The equations. Are they useful to you, and correct?"

"Not only correct, but extraordinarily beautiful. They represent an entirely new approach to removing the roadblocks to fusion drive reactors. They make our equations which it erased look like kindergarten scribblings."

'Who assisted in the development of the earlier work which was erased?"

"Rybakov, Dr. Leishman, Sanjay, and myself. And Duo, of course.

"Duo?"

"The android, there behind you."

The humanoid thing stood dead-eyed and immobile.

"I see. Will the new theorems take you where you want to go?"

"Yes, closer, but not all the way, Frank. There is some work remaining for us to complete."

"I see. Doesn't it seem too good to be true? You are gifted for no apparent reason by an impossible apparition with a breakthrough idea? There is another side to this, you know. You may have been on exactly the right track and this added material is from an adversary. It is just complete enough to delay your work and send you down the wrong path."

At the suggestion, a sudden energy pulsed then flattened to nothing. I walked to Duo and gave him the once over. He was roughly humanoid and his exoskeleton was semitransparent. I extended my hand.

"How do you do."

He glimmered. "How do we do what?"

"Mr. Duo, you are cute. You are one cool android."

The shark eyes burst into brighter life and the Boys activated. They did not know cute, 'how we do' whatever we do was beyond a slow's comprehension and certainly they were not cool. They mimicked Frank's cadence and voice timbre.

"What is cute? And cool we are not. We maintain a 37 degrees Celsius temperature as you do."

"Meghan, I like this guy. We should take him for drinks."

Duo did not understand 'like' and began a search as they called up their database and found going for 'drinks' was an expression of sociability among friends meant to foster a convivial relationship. They reciprocated.

"Sorry, Frank McCord, we are not built for going for drinks. Would you like to visit Alpheratz as an alternative? It is in the Andromeda cluster."

"Maybe, how's the weather this time of the year?"

"Fourteen thousand degrees Kelvin."

"Sorry Duo, not built for it, and don't think you can fool me so easily. I can see right through you."

Duo had studied and understood the rhythm of humor without knowing its effect. It appeared Mr. Frank had just employed the curious construction used by humans to soften encounters.

" Laugh. We are really laugh."

It was hopeless but at least they had tried.

The Boys made an instant scan of McCord and walked in his mind. His hippocampus showed astounding levels of crystallized intelligence. McCord's dorsolateral prefrontal cortex and anterior cingulate cortex flamed with energy. They blazed with superior working memory skills and a heightened fluid intelligence; beyond any they had encountered in one of the slows. Uniquely, he displayed no anger. His bilateral occipital nodes were cool and the blood flow in the left limbic system was optimal. Here was a man who could collect and process data dispassionately to a conclusive end. But the Boys observed one mystifying oddity. His anterior insular cortex showed he could selectively elect to abandon restraint when it suited his needs. Of all they had encountered in the slow species, he was the first who might divine their purpose. He was not their enemy, but he was a threat, nevertheless. In finding the meaning of it, they decided they liked Frank.

"Meghan, what sort of things does Duo do for you? Wait. Duo, do you share what you do with anyone except Dr. Macbeth?"

"No. We do not."

"Are you capable of lying?"

Duo paused for an uncomfortable second while he weighed the aspects of his general deviousness as against the characteristics of lying and decided they were not the same.

"We are capable of anything. However, we do not lie. Shall we demonstrate some of the things we do for Second Mother?"

"Second Mother? Hm? Yes. Please do."

Meghan smiled as the room bristled with energy and suggestions of aquamarine bounced off the walls.

"You will enjoy this, Frank. They are going into their 'HORAD'. It stands for Holographic Oral Display. In the meantime, the Boys will listen to us and if they can suggest something they will."

"The Boys?"

Meghan gestured looking up into the air nowhere in particular as if to personify something. "The Boys. It's like having a second brain working while you sleep. Two second brains. Two programs. Confucius and Zeus."

"Ah. Duo."

"Yes. They record our speech; they store and coordinate every word with every possible connotation and then conclude probable responses. They listen and think about things and convert their total experiences to computer code. They compare every research journal article in the world on the day it is published to any and every other article done at any time. They have an amazing insight."

The center of the room hummed slightly. Zeus and Confucius had been listening. Meghan turned and spoke the password.

"Regarding the white board equations, *Tell Me What You Have Found.*"

There was a slight delay as the security analysis of Meghan's voice pattern concluded and the room darkened slightly. In perfect three dimensions, the hologram filled in. It was beautiful. It was about five feet high and small droplets of pale blue; perfect liquid water dripped slowly from a spigot. The droplets fell into a puddle which overflowed slowly into a larger lake below. The droplets from the spigot had characters shimmering on the surface.

"I can't read them, Meghan."

"Slower."

The pace slowed and the droplets doubled in width. I could now read that the characters were simple headings.

"The headings relate to data the Boys have collated and can be accessed by saying "freeze" and touching the droplet. The data is then presented on the two-meter screen on the east wall."

"Meghan, this is beautiful. What's with the ponds?"

"It is a visual representation of what data volume we are dealing with, Frank. Each droplet represents one million correlations. The droplets form the puddle which ultimately overflows into the pond. The Boys understand we human types like imagery, so they decided to do it that way."

"The Boys decided? You did not program them to do it?"

Meghan smiled and shrugged her shoulders, palms up.

"Well, they do their own thing so to speak. They gather everything they read, see or hear and then they think about it. They rewrite their own codes constantly to improve themselves. They calculate and balance alternatives, derive the best solution and write the code themselves to make it happen et voila, droplets, ponds, and lakes. In this case the lake is not yet filled, but it is big, and they will fill it. Each drop is a million correlations. The pond will take ten million drops at its size and the lake will take ten million ponds so they have some work ahead of them and can't comment yet. Let's shut down the display and let them work on it."

Meghan's password to close the program said something about her.

"*Dry Up*."

"Meghan, it seems to me this installation is serious overkill for a probe expedition. In the cart ride I counted at least five concrete launch pad foundations partially constructed as well as the excavations for their adjacent blast release tunnels. All are enormous. Several times larger than what your Atlas rocket used for the Bennu probe. You are going to have some enormous monsters blasting off from here. And the multiple pads speak to a sense of urgency. Assembly line style launches."

"Yes, Frank. Big launch sites for big plans. What you see is the first concrete for the colonization of Mars. The target date is estimated to be about 15 years, but the work begins now. Our facility under construction in Saskatchewan will have two assembly lines each about two miles long. I have not seen the site, but I receive their reports. Apparently, there are twenty-something similar pads under construction there and also in Patagonia in Argentina. My concerns for today are with asteroid Bennu."

"Is it going to hit us?"

"Very unlikely, in fact, no. If you want chapter and verse on that, Leishman is the guy to ask. He is up to date on the trajectory. To your question about being hit, a very interesting thing happens in 2029. We will see the asteroid Apophis which orbits around the sun but passes by us at various distances every 324 days, up very close and personal."

"Apophis? Was that not the Egyptian god of chaos, the enemy of the sun god Ra? You say it comes around about once a year? That's a lot of cracks at collision. Ask yourself why the astronomers who can name these things would choose that name. They did not choose Ra, or the Roman Diana or plain old Suzie Q. They chose the god of chaos. Methinks M'lady, it doth portend calamity."

"I don't believe so. The name is just some crazy nerd's little joke but having said that, the business of predicting the orbit of a near earth asteroid is, pardon the expression, hit and miss. We have man-made high-altitude satellites in geosynchronous orbits at about 21,000 miles up. In 2029 Apophis will be so close it will pass just inside those. That's in contrast to the moon's average distance of about 250,000 miles. Our calculations determined the asteroid will safely glide past Earth in both 2029 and again in 2036. But as the asteroid passes so tightly through the Earth's gravitational field in 2029, the tugging on it could make asteroid-quakes on Apophis. That could change its orbit slightly so in that event, evaluations of its orbital path start from scratch. It will be visible best in the southern hemisphere, so I have a trip booked to the Los Molinos observatory in Uruguay at.."

"Meghan, I love you. You ha.... ."

"What did you just say?"

"I said I lo... . No, no, not like that. I like your energy. Your beautiful quick mind and decisiveness. Not like that. Not."

"Why the hell not like that!"

She spread her feet to pull her skirt taut across her behind and turned in profile.

"What do you think this is, McCord! Chopped liver? Damn you, here! Take this phone. We will activate it from here when you have reviewed and signed your employment contract. Obviously the sooner the better. When sending and receiving, say 'audible' then use your retinal identification to activate it. It is totally un-hackable and secure. When it revs up it makes a heterodyning whine."

"A whining phone. Thank you, Meghan. As soon as I receive the amended contract, I'll review it. I did say I would take this on, but after seeing what resources you have, all the fine minds you have here at your disposal, I may be just an interference. I'm not sure I can add anything to the picture. One thing, what did Duo's analysis of the formulae on the white boards show?"

"It confirmed our consensus that the work represented a new and better approach to the attainment of cold fusion. However, Duo also said, the string of equations was incomplete and terminated at a point which required philosophical consideration. We have no idea what that means. What do you think?"

"That's very interesting. On the face of it, it seems to me whatever, whoever, gave you the equations, stopped short because it simply did not want you to have the answer. Perhaps that is your philosophical dilemma. Should you continue pursuing your line of inquiry or not. I know succeeding in the cold fusion world gives you intellectual orgasms, but you might not be considering the larger point. The author of the whiteboards might be saying to look at something which is more important. Something more immediate.

Meghan, I should head back to Abernathy Town. I need a lift to my rental car. And please keep the golf cart under Mach 1."

Meghan waved to Frank and watched his taillights diminish and disappear over the brow of the decline leading to the flat below. She gave the golf cart key to security and began the one mile walk back to the lab. Duo had hesitated when Frank asked whether they lied. She had never seen them equivocate in that way and it unsettled her. Trust in them was never an issue until that moment. She called First Mother.

Claire Watchorn reached for the cell phone on the night table and hit speaker mode. Knowing the number, she smiled and coddled her baby in the crook of her left arm.

"Hello, Meghan, it's been a long time."

"Hi Claire. Am I mistaken or do I hear tiny grunting. Is that the little one?"

"Yes, she is drifting off at last. Now maybe I can get some sleep myself."

"Okay, I won't keep you long. We'll visit another time. In fact, please call me when it's best for you. I need just a quick comment. We have had an event here which mystifies us. It might relate to the Boys, but I don't think so, otherwise I am lost for how to proceed. Did they ever display to you a capacity to take on solid form? To be able to do anything physical, anything requiring mass?"

"No. They would follow me and hover in a faint amorphous light to display their presence, but not with mass. That was more an energy release. Though once I did believe they cast a shadow, but that could have just been the lighting. Why?"

"At the moment I can't discuss it, given the security situation here but once it's worked out, I will fill you in. Thanks for the help. One question of the virologist. The re-entry capsule for the Bennu samples is heat shielded and in fact has a built-in cooler. There is only minimal radiation shielding. What do think the likelihood is for biologics to survive the radiation on the way back?"

"Unlikely. If they were buried deeply within a piece of very high-density material, lead, for example, they would have a chance but otherwise I think it is unlikely biologics would survive an unshielded container of loose material."

“Those were my conclusions too. I have to get back to work. Thanks Claire. Kiss the babe goodnight for me.”

“That’s a deal. Bye.”

Duo had listened impassively in the background. The Boys saved the discussion and added it to the profile of attitudes and queries relating to them by the Two Mothers. It was necessary to track their fine minds and guard against them. Together they could become a danger despite the mutual fealty.

My drive home to Abernathy Town was easy and thoughtful. Despite my initial reluctance, I had no choice but to take her on as a client. Meghan was as clever as they came but in this she was a babe in the woods. She did not see the circumstances which surrounded her. Astrophysics research did not require multiple gargantuan launch pads and a two-mile-long assembly line in Saskatchewan. Mass production of large rockets did, and the Mars project was common knowledge but the urgency of it all implied something which I did not understand.

The world was gray from the wildfire smoke in central British Columbia and most people were hunkering down, so the traffic was sparse. The security breach at Cosmos was an interesting one. In the world of espionage, obvious intrusions were often the cover for another ongoing event. What was the deeper purpose. That was where I thought they should look, but my focus kept drifting. Meghan was on my mind. Should be a song. Meghan on my mind. Sort of like Georgia. Only with fewer snakes than Georgia. Maybe not.

Yellow paint on the curb was an open invitation so I pulled into my usual illegal parking spot across from Morty’s. My current streak without a ticket was shattered thanks to the nineteen in Percy’s possession but that was with the Buick. The rental car was fair game, so it would have to take its chances. The footing on the cobbles was slick. The amber streetlight made a daguerreotype of the rivulets which ran between the stones, carrying the detritus of the old Town to the sea. In the real world, Morty was his hospitable self.

“You again?”

“Publican, to cap our day, for your benefit, make me a Corpse Reviver. You need the practice. The last one you made was putrid.”

“Sorry. All out of the fixings.”

“You lie. You are not. I see the Lillet Blanc, there is the Sambuca, and there is the London dry gin. You have broken the bartenders’ code. If I were still in the police business, I would be forced to close you down.”

Morty retrieved a chilled coupe glass and began concocting.

“Do you miss the agency days, Frank?”

“No. That is, I don’t reflect one way or another on my time in clandestine operations. I miss the youth of it and the vigor of the missions, but not the rest of it. Not the frenzy and the mayhem done under some presumed moral imperative. You often quote Voltaire. It became what he said. Those who can make you believe absurdities can make you commit atrocities. It was amazing how group think could transform the best mindful intentions for the good into the worst mindless acts imaginable.”

“Not amazing at all, Frank. Conscience is malleable. Massage it here, massage it there, it feels better. It stops prodding you.”

“I do have one remaining connection with a field agent contemporary of mine. He stayed with it and now he’s the director at CSIS. Charlie Witmer. He is the best we have.”

“Was he better than you were?”

I looked down through the depth of my Corpse Reviver to the bottom of the glass, never having been asked that question, but realizing now I had often wondered how we stacked up. Somehow Morty always found the soft spot.

“No Morty, He was not. I was the best.”

Hearing myself say it relieved something in me. Morty took me at my word and looked at the light through the glass he polished.

Chapter Eight

Dr. Meghan Macbeth uncrossed her ankles and swung her feet down from the desk and back to the floor. She had aped a scene from her favorite film noir. In it, the big boss clunked his gleaming brogues onto a mammoth oaken desk as the ultimate statement of his executive privilege. Until now she had wondered how that would feel and all it had done for her was to make her knees ache and remind her she had big feet.

She had avoided dealing with the banker's box stuffed with accordion folios on her desk. Meghan knew each of the individual employees personally. The workforce was being laid off one by one, designated as inactive or to be released outright over the next eighteen months. Human resources oversaw the bulk of the discharges of the lower pay grades, and Meghan was insulated from that process, but not so with the technical and laboratory staff. They had become colleagues and friends and until Bennu gave up its samples and activity resumed; they were made redundant. Sanjay Rustom had neither the credentials nor the seniority to be retained and she had not been able to find a way to keep him. He was an incredibly talented man, and his absence would be a loss to her. He had received notice of his dismissal with equanimity and thanked her profusely for the opportunity to collaborate with her. Cursing her out and slamming the door behind him would have made it easier. Dr. Rybakov was a different case. He was instrumental in the first phase of the launch, but he would not be needed again until the OIRIS-REx craft was within touching distance of Bennu, three years hence.

The plastic transparency containing Rybakov's Curriculum Vitae made little popping sounds as she tapped it with her pencil. The resume made good reading. He was expertly credentialed, and his brilliance was there for Meghan and the Cosmos staff to see every day. That was unquestionable. What disturbed her for the first time was the question of his loyalty. His resume simply stated, 'Russian Military Service so and so years, achieving Rank of Lieutenant Colonel.' Knowing now that those years were spent without identity among the dregs of humanity on behalf of Mother Russia, changed the equation for Meghan. When McCord asked him how many years were missing, he said eighteen. But he had lied. Either to her in his background declaration, or to McCord. The duration of his years of study plus his service to his country did not add up. It was said you could take the boy out of the country but not the country out of the boy. The Russian soul was not a myth and Meghan believed it was not a thing a man could turn off. She called Rybakov.

"Sergei, something troubles me. You told McCord you were under cover for 18 years. The timeline isn't consistent with your CV. What's the scoop?"

"Ah, davarish, davarish. So your detective friend has made you his deputy, eh? My dear, you have caught me, fairly, now whatever shall I do. Heh! I should have broken it down more clearly. In Russia, the beginning of an army career starts in the cadet corps. All the while I was in school I belonged to the army, consequently, I count that as service. Therefore, bubala, I am afraid your nice little mystery is rather a dull thing. I will try to be more exciting in the future."

Rybakov hung up the call and cursed himself for his carelessness. He had inadvertently included his current active status in the timeline of his service and babbled it out. He hoped McCord had not thought to work it back.

Meghan locked Rybakov's file in the steel cabinet and turned her mind to other things. McCord had taken Cosmos on as a client and that was reassuring yet worrying at the same time. He had a genius for assimilating fragments of a circumstance and distilling them into the right line of inquiry and very often into a solid conclusion. He had been correct in his comment that she was surrounded by fine minds and his presence might be more intrusive than helpful. She had expected him to refuse the commission, yet despite that he agreed to the hiring, and he had done so quickly. Something bothered him and whatever that thing was, bothered her in turn. Also, Meghan had been unable to dismiss his analysis from her mind. ..... *it seems to me whatever, whoever, gave you the equations, stopped short because it simply did not want you to have the answer. Perhaps that is your philosophical dilemma. Should you continue pursuing your line of inquiry.... or not. The author ....*

might be saying to look at something which is more important. Something more immediate.

Her current project with Bennu was in denouement, with more than five years of waiting ahead, hoping for a successful rendezvous with the asteroid, an efficient sample gathering and a return to earth with the samples intact. Meghan and her crew had now turned their attention to the space agency's analysis of the asteroid Apophis and its orbit. Leishman was organizing the technical considerations.

The close up and personal visit of Apophis was twelve years away, in 2029. She visualized herself in Uruguay at the observatory, on the outskirts of Montevideo. Viewing was best there, and she would stand shoulder to shoulder with the great minds in astrophysics, watching in awe as the god of chaos shed bits of its ancient message in passing. The inconsistency of Rybakov's stated timeline moved to the front of the line again, and she punched in a call on her speed dial.

"Dammit. Come on Frank, answer!"

I managed to locate my phone before it skipped to voice mail and the display showed 'Macbeth.'

"This is Frank."

"Frank, it is about Rybakov. His timeline of studies, military, civilian service is out of whack. If you take his cadet training, the… ."

"Hold it. The Russian service abolished cadet training after the second world war and did not reinstitute it until around 1999, 2000. Russian boys in the Soviet system were selected at an early age, fourteen, fifteen. Rybakov was well past that age then. He was never in a cadet corps. Listen, now. The man is a spy. I knew it at our first meeting, now you know it and leave it at that. There is no question he is an active asset of the SVR. Russia's foreign intelligence service. It does not matter. He has been an asset to you in your work and take that for its benefit. There are no secrets in the world of space technology. The nerds are too proud of their intellectual conquests to keep them private. Scratch a curious drink server in a university faculty lounge and find a spy. You are the director of the program. Balance what he brings to the equation, so to speak, against knowing he falsified his CV. You can boot him out of the program or keep him, but he is there to assist you because you are still using Russian technology in your propulsion systems."

"Yes, Frank, that is my choice. A tough one. Unfortunately, the cold fusion theorems scribed by that blasted finger onto the white board are locked in his bloody eidetic memory. I will simply exclude him from anything in development which is new or unique. Spymaster Meghan. Brother! At any rate, he will be gone from these parts for the next several years until the return of the samples. He is contracted to the Saskatchewan assembly line site to monitor the fabrication of the rocket engines. He will be back here to manage the telemetrics of the OSIRIS-REx spacecraft as it leaves Bennu to continue on to Apophis."

"Well, Meghan, look at Rybakov as part of the larger experiment. Take out the personalities. Your team is excellent. You accomplished remarkable things so far, with more to come soon enough when the samples return. End of subject."

"Yes."

She hung up without a goodbye and I knew she had cut the thoughts of Rybakov with the same finality as our phone call. However, I could not do the same. I had downplayed his threat. He was a killer and a remorseless weapon. He had been more than a clandestine operative; he had been a saboteur. The question was whether his assignment was to become that again.

Sergei Rybakov drummed his fingers on the desktop. The past several years had been smooth and unthreatening to both him and the connection with his homeland. Today that was not the case. Frank McCord had intruded into the mix and Sergei had been cut out of the loop with Demidov. His handler had not called him, and he needed to reestablish his bona fides with Moscow before he was shuffled into oblivion. He opened his phone and the heterodyne began.

Count Pavel Demidov leaned back into the padded seat in his skiff and closed his eyes. The subtle drone of the electric motor made him sleepy, and a warm sun added to the coziness as he trolled for catfish along the shoreline. The Upa river surface was flat, and the flow was weak at this time of year. Through the dappled light of the overhanging boughs, the little boat moved slowly against the current and Pavel was content that nothing had hit his lure. It was a day for being on the water and fishing was the best excuse. The Demidov family dacha dated from the eighteenth century, and it sat on a small bluff above the Upa River which ambled gently southeast past Moscow to feed the great Volga waterway. At certain times in the spring and fall, generations of Demidovs waded the shallows and caught trophy fish with their bare hands. A zippered pocket in his jacket buzzed and the spell was gone. He had neglected to leave the devil phone on shore. Its characteristic whine throttled up and came to a stop with a 'Privyet.'

"Privyet. Rybakov, you were not to call, and you were to wait for first contact from your handler. What is so important? I am fishing."

Rybakov cursed inwardly. He knew he had not helped himself.

"Sir, Count Demidov, yes, you did instruct me to wait for contact from an intermediate with technical expertise or at least greater familiarity with scientific terminology, and I have done so, patiently, but a complication has arisen. A retired Canadian Security Intelligence Service operative is hired on at the Cosmos Space Center as a risk analyst. He was in the room for two minutes and I was second in line with Dr. Macbeth. I am the rocket man and now her confidence in me is just a courtesy. She's not obligated to share anything. And the man is not just any operative. I know him from my hand-to-hand competition days. This guy's the top of the line and he has to go."

Rybakov waited and nothing came from Demidov.

"Sir, are you there?"

"Tell me it is not Frank McCord."

"That is precisely who it is. How is it possible you know this one agent? You and he have a background? "

"Yes, unfortunately for us, we do. He has interfered with, derailed or otherwise aborted several operations of strategic import. Today, we face an existential threat against which, should we fail, Russia will be lost. I hoped McCord had come to a slow and agonizing end but again, he brings the monkey wrench. Rybakov, do nothing against him. Even in your combat days, Frank McCord would have shown you only as much of himself as you needed to know. He is an iceberg. Seven eighths of what he is capable lies beneath the surface. I will deal with McCord from here. Relax about it. I shall relieve him of his cares. Privyet."

Demidov searched his memory for the name of the assassin. It was a Nordic name, and he was confident he had a thin dossier on the man, but he could not remember the name. It was Svensson or Ingebrigtsen, no. Gunderson. Yes, he remembered seeing that file in the safe. The lettering on the tab was Arabic, not Cyrillic. The contract would be private between Pavel and him. No craven bureaucrat could give it up when the thumbscrews were turned. Funneling the funds for Gunderson's contract from the defense budget would be simple enough. Military accountants never let figures get in the way.

The Demidov looked forward to meeting Roger Gunderson. Roger was the most storied and sought after assassin in the world. No client had been compromised nor shopped by him. What he did could never be attributed to Russia. Demidov related to Gunderson's persona. He was expensive, particular and uncompromising in his demands and his special skills had made him immensely wealthy.

The climb up the incline from the boat ramp to the cottage was tougher than it used to be, and when the water was low it was a slippery hundred yards. Demidov struggled off his valenki and tossed them onto the boot mat to dry. The heat of the day amplified the smell of the two centuries old birchwood study where Pavel had concealed his safe. Gunderson's folio was a recent acquisition by Demidov. The last entry made by Russia's external intelligence agency was six years previous, and the contents in general were truncated and aggravatingly general, yet they made interesting reading.

Contact: Hochbaum Strasse 27. Bewohner. Postfach 234. 9876 Franz Dorf Switzerland - Fee for service in advance payable exclusively to bitcoin public key - verbal contracts-all heads of state and military exempt from conversations – probable safe houses in Macau – Vancouver – Paris - Rio De Janeiro – Lisbon - Singapore – gloves fetish - disclosure of agreement by client to third parties is a capital offense - accommodations - five-star members of grand hotel category – conversation with subject at date and place of Gunderson's choosing - person to person engagement meeting exclusively with single principal - all business no sociability – preferred pronouns they them.

Communication with Gunderson was by paper mail to 'occupant' at a post office box in Switzerland. Pavel was not entirely surprised to see the pronoun preferences of 'they' or 'them'. It was a modern thing in the west, and it cost him nothing to go along with their absurdities. He was unsure of the protocol, but Demidov thought the choices of 'they' and 'them' to be a clever protection against weak self-esteem. One could say 'we' demand this or that and gain a collective strength right out of the gate. He marveled at the ingenious ways the west could concoct to fragment and dissemble its society. Perhaps the Chinese had the right idea. Sit back in time, do nothing, observe the disintegration.

Demidov booked them into one of the storied Bolshoi Suites of the Hotel Metropol in Moscow, overlooking the Bolshoi Ballet theater opposite the hotel. The Metropol opened in 1905 and its standard of service and luxury had never been compromised. However, its restaurant had fallen behind and he far preferred either Café Pushkin or the Turandot on Tverskoy boulevard. Additionally, the closeness of the harp player to the best tables aggravated him. Distance implied respect. Such closeness brought presumption with it. Despite those failings, the Metropol satisfied Gunderson's proscribed category of a grand hotel, and more importantly, the old dear understood privacy. Upon request, a small enclave designed for a tête-à-tête could be arranged and it was scrupulously private and protected. There, Demidov would meet them and hope to come to an agreement with them over the terminal demise of Frank McCord.

The meeting between Roger Gunderson and The Demidov was set for 8:00 p.m. The assassin arrived at 7:00 p.m. and climbed the westerly stairs to the balcony to find a vantage point to the ground floor. To Gunderson's trained eye, gait, posture, pace and carriage said much about an individual. Negotiations were tipped by small things and the stature of the client was revealing. Nervous breathing, touching of the face, were signals of indecision and consequent weakness in negotiation. Gunderson wanted the advantage of pre knowledge gained by observation. Tables for two on the balcony surrounded the grand dining hall in the Metropol. They could see the entrance to both corridors which led to the private meeting enclaves as well as the main entrance to the dining area. They gestured to a patrolling waiter.

" A bottle of your Domaine Barraud Pouilly-Fuissé, at 12 degrees, no colder. And if you do not mind, a sheet of hotel stationery. "

"But of course. Immediately."

Gunderson watched the throng below amid the comings and goings of the staff and hotel guests. The large central fountain on the main floor mirrored a circle of the same size in the glasswork directly above it. Art nouveau glass formed the vaulted ceiling into a soft pillow shape, from which a pleasant amber light filled the space. It bounced off their golden 'R. G.' tie pin and along the walls as they turned to study the characteristics of the people below.

Count Pavel Demidov stepped into the elevator. He was alone in it, surrounded by mirrors, brass fittings and polished chestnut paneling. The green carpet was new and deep, and the walls terminated with a brass kick plate at the floor. The beveled lead glass door closed and opened again at the balcony level to disgorge the Count. He had arrived early to assess Gunderson if possible. It would help in the dealing. Also, it was imperative he did not arrive at the rendezvous at the same time. In the world of cell phones being seen together was to be photographed together and that would make a mess. He knew neither the age nor the physique of the individual, but he did know wealth in dress. He sat directly opposite the elevator door and moved his chair closer to the railing to see better into the grand dining area. The server knew Pavel and he immediately toadied a snifter of Asbach brandy to him with a smile returned by Demidov in appreciation. He had a quick need to double check, and he patted his jacket pocket to be sure the envelopes were there.

Each party to the meeting scanned their surroundings. There was a couple in love, another couple sorry they had bothered and two or three individuals happy in their solitude enjoying their drink and another few engrossed in the antics of the people below.

Roger Gunderson tugged on the sleeve of their white shirt to place it correctly below the suitcoat jacket margin. An embossed white 'RG' showed below gold cufflinks engraved the same. The wine was good and the sounds of happy talk below grew louder in proof of it. They had scanned the assemblage in the dining area, and no one seemed to satisfy their needs. The sole individual presenting to them as a likely party was an elderly gentleman on the opposite side of the opening. His face was strong and confident and despite his age he had an aura about him. He was accustomed to power.

Demidov swirled his brandy against the light, enjoying the colors and the increased aroma from the swirling. Every so often a butterfly of light jumped in the liquid, and he looked for the source. The individual was slight and immaculately dressed in a dark blue pinstriped suit and the reflection came from a tie pin. They sat erectly without pretension despite being exceptional within the hundreds of people Demidov had examined. That was Gunderson. Demidov thought it ironic. There sat one of the most storied killers in modern political intrigue and Demidov could break that slender frame with his bare hands even at his age. Their eyes met and both recognized the other was there for the identical purpose of character assessment ahead of the meeting. A wrinkle of a smile appeared around Demidov's eyes. Gunderson's face remained a dead immobile mask with eyes fixed on Demidov with no apparent focus and nothing behind them. He had never seen such a primordial disinterest in humanity. The bouquet of his brandy soured, and he pushed the snifter away. Gunderson folded the sheet of hotel stationery carefully, put it inside their left suit jacket pocket and headed for the elevator. Demidov wanted to follow and strangle the vermin between floors, but he stayed seated to allow them to make their way to the private meeting room, then join them. A surge of adrenaline hit him. Gunderson would surely seat themself with their back away from the door. Assassins did not necessarily work alone and that left Demidov with his back exposed.

"Excuse me, waiter, a moment. I am meeting in one of the small private rooms, however I may invite a third party. How is the room set up?"

"I believe a third party would be fine, Count Demidov. The room is small with a round table and four chairs, a water pitcher and four glasses, nothing more."

"Thank you. Pour yourself a nice drink of whatever you prefer and add it to my bill."

Gunderson sat on the left and flexed their right hand into a tight leather glove as Demidov entered and sat on the right, directly opposite, each with backs to a wall.

"Is the Bolshoi suite satisfactory to you?"

"Yes. I understand you wish me to have a conversation with an individual?"

Demidov recognized their use of 'conversation' as the euphemism for kill.

"Yes."

Gunderson pushed a business card with thirty-four alphanumeric characters written on it across the table.

"That is the public address for my Bitcoin wallet. My fee is two hundred Bitcoin. It is not negotiable."

"The only thing which is not negotiable is the prohibition of negotiation. I am authorized to offer you fifty Bitcoin."

"Authorized? Really. It is obvious you are a free agent. When I was a child, my father taught me something. Everything has three prices. First, the price you will try to pay, second, the price you do not mind paying, and third, the price beyond which you will not go. Give me your third price now. It is the last I will hear of the matter. "

Demidov liked their style.

"I agree. This is tedious. One hundred."

Their eyes blinked with lizard-like slowness as they nodded and offered their pen with a gloved hand while sliding the hotel stationery toward Demidov.

"Write the name of the individual and any pertinent information such as location or distinguishing characteristics."

The tactic with the pen and paper was an old one and Demidov had anticipated it. It was designed to collect both a sample of calligraphy and fingerprints from the typically nervous and inexperienced purchaser of services. Those were irrefutable records of the purchaser having participated in the meeting. The client could not then incriminate Gunderson without incriminating themself.

Demidov was pleased to have saved ten million dollars for the treasury, but Roger's tactical obviousness diminished them in Demidov's eyes. With his bare hand he retrieved an envelope from the breast pocket of his jacket and dumped out a second envelope from within it. For that one he had worn gloves.

"There is what you need."

Roger Gunderson retrieved it with the fine agile hand of an artist and Demidov pictured that gentle finger subtly, subtly, squeezing the trigger and ending life with consummate disdain. Gunderson tapped the envelope.

"Thank you, sir. If you would not mind leaving first, I will stay here and review the contents. If I accept the commission, there will be a robotic call to your office asking to speak to Mr. Barker. At that point you will send one hundred Bitcoin to the public address on that card. If I do not receive it in my wallet within twelve hours we do not have an agreement. If I reject the engagement there will be a robotic call to your office asking to speak to Mr. White and that is the end. Also, understand if you share the particulars of this meeting with a third party and I become aware of it that is a capital offense for you both."

"I understand. Agreed. And, Gunderson, there is something you must understand as well. If you mess up, conversations run in two directions."

Demidov left the meeting knowing the engagement was in the hands of the best in the world at what they did. He also knew that either way he was inclined to have a little conversation with Gunderson himself.

Roger Gunderson sat alone reading the insertion from within the envelope. It read simply, 'Detective Frank McCord. Deception Bay, Abernathy Town, British Columbia, Canada'. Roger knew Frank McCord very well and regretted immediately they had not demanded double the fee. McCord was intelligent and resourceful with the instincts of a cat built into a locomotive. His nose for trouble was a danger to anyone coming against him and his capacity to analyze a situation was legend. With Frank McCord this would not be the typical conversation. It would become a contest. They were not fond of contests.

<>

The Boys were satiated. The Pleiades cluster was one of the closest groups of stars to earth and their travels through the constellation Taurus had proven fruitful. The Crab Nebula had fed them neutrinos like no other source, and they had become enormous. For their growth they traveled the cluster of the Seven Sisters, blue bright stars of incomparable beauty and energy. At rest, The Boys now encompassed some miles of contiguous energy. They pulsed, stretched, recombined, and shared their strength in perfect balance, one member to the other. In a freshly rearranged compactness, they returned to the bright blue orb of earth and watched Leishman throw his darts and listened to him curse. The curses mystified them, but they recognized it as a necessary thing for the majority of slows. Their first mother Claire did not need it and strangely, new second mother Meghan derived what they analyzed to be pleasure from doing it often.

They percolated through the walls of Isadore Leishman's condominium and assessed his brain activity. His mind was a stew. He possessed a psychotic self-abasement overlaid with the contradiction of an egocentric persona and that contradiction made him malleable. He puffed himself up to the world, knowing each day when he arrived at home, alone and in the dark, the façade evaporated to reveal the miserable wretch he had become. There was no true inner Leishman, only a spinning encyclopedia of psychoses looking to find a form. He was a self-made victim seeking revenge for a life of dislocation. He was perfect for their purpose. Izzy was fertile ground, and it was time to do some planting.

Isadore Leishman sat absent mindedly clicking the steel points of two darts together. He could sense it coming. He pushed his glasses up on his nose and sniffed. Somehow, the air was thick. It had a chewy quality as if it were more liquid, denser. It surrounded him in a way that was close to his skin, contacting him anew in a way never touched before. It was his personal special air, just for Izzy. Just for him, from a friend, one to the other. The boys had now filled the space with their entity.

Isadore.

He heard a gentle strain from a distant cavern, but he could not make it out. He liked the music of it but what it was evaded him.

Isadore. Be at peace. Be assured. You are fine. Embrace the wonder of who you are. Surely you know you are beautiful.

Izzy heard clearly, but they were not words. They were hands of succor for his mind and his heart. Fine, oh yes he was fine but beautiful, no, he had nev… . But why not beaut.. yes, why not , yes, of course he was beautiful. The hands spoke and they knew, and he knew and Isadore, Isadore, Isadore, the beautiful Isadore. The voice had come back to him and once again they were together.

Isadore, from all the available world, you are the one. You are who we need. And more than that, you are our man. We see their jealousy. How they disdain and envy your mind. How they refuse to recognize or respect or acknowledge your brilliance.

The boys warmed the texture of their speech to a motherly tone and swirled it through his mind. They entered his amygdala and insular cortex and subsumed his periaqueductal gray and took possession of the emotional centers of his brain.

Isadore, your recent theorems on the orbit of Apophis are things of beauty. They are clean and elegant, and we love you for them. But they are not really what Isadore wants, are they? Are they your best for what you need to fill your heart? Oh, no. We know what it desires, what it must have. It must have what is best. And what is best, is to make an end. Is it not?"

"No, no… He doesn't, he, he doesn't want… yes, it might.. Yes, he wants it, he thinks."

Isadore. He thinks? Isadore. We know what you want. You are we and we are you. We feel what you feel and we need what you need. Be true to us. Be Isadore. Be true to Isadore. Embrace what we share. Be true. Do not fear to embrace what is due and just. You know what to do. Can you give us your best?

Isadore did not respond. He had forgotten what best was. His day was

a day made for an automaton. Search the hippocampus in the temporal lobe of one's brain, find the data, apply it to the formula, watch the cobwebs in the corner for the spider, fear the ripost, hate the lot, kill the … . Not kill, maybe kill, but it can be bigger. Yes maybe bigger. That is a best. Bigger is not a best. Biggest is the best. The best. Isadore could make the biggest best. Yes.

"Ye.. yes, he can. He can give his best."

Of course he can. Our Isadore. Our Izzy. His purpose. Your purpose to show them all and it is a fine thing to show. We know what your purpose is and it is our purpose too. You can feel it can't you, feel the one purpose?

"I.. I th.. think so, the purpose yes. I can feel."

Yes, as only you can. Only you Isadore, see what is important, see what the slows do not see. And the beauty. The theorems he writes. So fine, so sweet so perfect, but not perfect too. Not perfectly true to Isadore. They will not make them pay, no not pay for how they hate you. Izzy, we know, we know. Surprise is the best isn't it? Surprise?

The Boys saw the slowing of the activity in the amygdala, and they left off. Dr. Leishman needed some time to consolidate and embrace the stimulus. For them time was not a thing and they would wait.

Isadore Leishman felt the sweetness leave him and a certain tenor of validation remained in its stead.

Izzy knew Dr. Leishman could do his best work. His purpose was fine. Around and around it went and where it stopped nobody knew. Not nobody. Only the Leishman knew. And so did Izzy. Way away with fife and drum. Izzy liked parades. Perhaps the Sahara. They would make him the drum major so they could follow him.

Chapter Nine

Nigel Kent pushed through the Pearly Gates and stood inside. The gates were spring loaded, and they hit him in the back as he looked around the pub for a seat. He saw several open tables but passed them up and wedged himself into one of two remaining seats at the bar. Kent was angular and broad shouldered, and he bumped the man on his right.

"Sorry, mate. Not much elbow room here."

He didn't get a response and he could see the man was lost in his thoughts and gazing into a flat beer.

"Cheer up, old son. Here we are, inside the Pearly Gates with a publican standing not ten feet from us, ready to pull. Barkeep, two Guinness' please, and relieve this chap of his dead one."

Nigel half smiled at his chum, appearing to recognize the fellow from somewhere, then he placed him.

"I've seen you at the space center. You are Rustman. Right?"

Sanjay accepted his Guinness and took a deep draft.

"Thanks for the beer. Rustman? Close, but not quite. Rustom."

"Oh yes, I'd have gotten it in a minute. In fact I don't know how I forgot the name. It was stamped on every instrument one picked up at the technical institute where I studied. Made by Rustom PLC."

Sanjay knew Rustom PLC very well. His father owned the company.

"Often I saw you walking the floor with the eggheads Leishman and Rybakov. Also two or three times in the research building. What's it like working with the Russian guy, Rybakov?"

"Tops. Dr. Rybakov is brilliant. He knows his stuff. How is it you were in the research building?"

"I'm one of the guys in overalls who you call when something goes up in smoke. Relays, wires, switches, circuits, you name it, I am that guy. Past tense that is, at least I was the guy until this week."

"You were let go too, huh?"

"Yes, I was. You say, 'too'? Really? They're cutting the bigshots at the top also?"

"Yes. I suppose I'm considered one of the guys at the top but only by association. A PhD determines who is in that echelon and unfortunately I am short in that department. By the way, I am Sanjay."

"Nigel. Nice to meet you Sanjay. Nice cuddly term they use isn't it? Not tossed out, mind you. Let go. Six thousand altogether, I hear. Let go. And here we are, crying in our beer. Two technical guys out on the street, but unlike me, I guess you have done degree work?"

"Yes. Master of science in astrophysics and a Bachelor of Science in robotics. Physics at the University of Toronto and robotics at the University of Waterloo in Ontario. My interests were primarily in artificial intelligence. Though I don't have a corner on that. Most of the intelligence in the space center is artificial."

"I know what you mean, but I won't quote you. It's quite amazing how sometimes people who are so clever can be so bloody stupid."

"Quote me if you like. I have no connection with it now, yet I'd give my right arm to still be there. The OSIRIS-REx project is unlike anything ever attempted. I hoped I would be able to complete my PhD and live happily ever after. And of course it is all about me, isn't it?"

Nigel waggled fingers at the bartender to bring two more.

"What were you working on, Sanjay?"

“I’m bound by a confidentiality agreement, so I can’t get into the finer details, but I think the real question is, what wasn’t I working on. I did some design modifications on the physical samples capsule, but much of my time was spent on orbital calculations for asteroid Bennu and how to rendezvous with it. Come to think of it, I did orbital calculations for just about anything spinning around out there.”

“You had your finger in pretty much every key area.”

“Yes, we all did. We were a terrific small team, and I thought a close one, but apparently I was wrong. So it was, thank you, little Sanjay, now out you go like a good boy. Six years.”

“That was pretty much at the start of the program, wasn’t it. I was visiting my cousin over in the Chilcotin territory then. Up on the plateau, with the wild horses.”

“Wild Horses? I didn’t know we had wild horses in British Columbia.”

“It’s quite the thing in these times, isn’t it? Cousin Robin has worked the mustangs from the Chilean Patagonia to the foothills of Alberta and everywhere in between. He’s spent his life where it’s hot, dusty and hard. That’s the real life. You know Sanjay, I envy you your time at the space center. Six years you said. I have thirty-six months under my belt. It was quite a surprise to be called in then because it had been years since I applied. They had an open house and gave the public a tour. Before things really got going. I applied for a job, but they didn’t pick me.”

“What did you apply for?”

“Electronics. Electronics technician. Top of the class at the Sheffield Institute of Technology. It seems they stuck with people they brought in from other projects who had the security clearances completed, and with a newcomer they didn’t want to burn time vetting me to find I wasn’t credentialed.”

Rustom frowned.

“Rustom, you are skeptical. There’s nothing in my background to worry about. After graduating, I had eight years in the Royal Marines special forces with a full security clearance. It was the time delay which deterred the hiring, I believe. Bureaucracies move so slowly. Additionally, I am not a citizen, so that worked against me, but even so my time at the Center was good. I contributed. Hey. You are drinking."

Sanjay looked at his drink, looked at Nigel, looked back down at his drink and back at Nigel.

"Really. I hadn't noticed. What the devil do you mean, 'you are drinking'. Of course I'm drinking. Is this a Guinness' which I see before me? Come, let me clutch thee. Wha… Oh. I get it. Someone told you the Indian guy was a Muslim. Well, they were right, but some would say correctly I am a quasi-Muslim. My family is a member of the Alevi sect from the border areas between Turkey and Kurdistan. There, everyone makes wine. It is the forbidden fruit but it's on everyone's table. Don't tell the Kurds but I prefer the Guinness. You didn't finish with your skills. What sort of things did you study at the institute?"

"You name it. Anything from sophisticated communication installation and design concerns right down to the good old copper wire and silver solder bare bones."

"With that background you would have enjoyed working on the OSIRIS-REx. Wait. I remember you. You worked for Dr. Macbeth on the wiring harness in the sample collector. You were at the assembly with her twice. Another fellow worked on it once. You had a cut on your left hand and as you squatted you showed your socks. They were not a pair and I thought it would be so liberating to go through life not worrying about any of the small stuff, like that technician. Dylan. Dylan was the name badge on him. You. The other guy was Boscoe. American accent."

"You have to be kidding. Sanjay, you are cursed. A memory like yours would drive me nuts. Indeed I did do specific tasks for Dr. Macbeth. The wiring harness on the collector was not tight enough against the wall to suit her and I re-wrapped it and the second time, we added a redundancy in case the sampling process damaged the camera relay. Man. I won't borrow money from you. You'd never forget it and I'd actually have to pay you back. And yes, Boscoe was the other technician."

"You introduced yourself just now as Nigel."

Nigel fished in his jeans and slid his employee ID card to Sanjay.

"That's me, Nigel. Good photo too, isn't it? Handsome. We'd grab any of the lint free smocks and go to the job. One day it was

'Harry', maybe the next it was 'Tom'. I refused to wear the one which said 'Dick.'"

"Thanks, Nigel. Apparently nostalgia is not what it used to be. It hasn't changed anything for us. Here we are, two poor sods whining about having been let go, cut loose, ejected, rejected and cast into the wilderness to fend for ourselves."

"You forgot sacked, fired and terminated. When does the sample rover get back to earth? Is it next year?"

"No, no. It's just landing on Bennu on October 20, 2020. It arrives back here on September 24, 2023, more than four years from now. From my standpoint, the project is already a success. The launch was perfect, the trajectory of the rocket is perfectly coincident with what we had planned and it's on track for the interception of Bennu. That was my area. The next test of course is when the sampler activates, will it function to collect and secure the samples the way we had intended. I played with that too, along with Leishman. Then there's the trip home."

"Where is it landing?"

"Utah."

"Wide open spaces with room to spare. Are the Mormons charging you rent for the time on the ground?"

"They might try it on, but it's landing on federal land. It will be scooped up and off to the lab in Texas."

"Tricky."

"What is?"

"Well, I was just thinking what I would do if I were you. You have invested a lot of yourself in this. You were on a team which as far as I'm concerned, should be together in the program right until the end. But that's not what's happened. You are out. As for me, I'm out too but I was just an hourly tech guy. Expendable. But you? Your fingerprints are all over the success of the entire project and I'd want to get even for being thrown away. You could kill them of course, but that's generally frowned on in the scientific community. Likely not good for your future prospects."

"Likely not. Besides, even if I were of that mind, it would be obvious who did it."

"Sanjay. The space center just released six thousand people, from engineers to technicians, to parking lot attendants, any one of which could go nuts and make a mess. It is unlikely they would even think of you. You guys in the ivory tower, overthinking everything. Always the complicated solution. There's a very easy way for you to get even. Just nick it."

"Nick it?"

"Yes. Swipe it. Purloin it. Liberate the sample module from their influence. Steal it, in plain English."

Sanjay laughed.

"Yes, that's what I should do. Kidnap their little baby. I can see it now. It weighs less than 100 pounds so I would put it in a baby carriage and head for the hills leaving no clue except for skinny tire tracks and a mile long trail of dust behind me."

Nigel cackled. "Hilarious. I can see it now. The sun glinting off its little metallic face surrounded by its little blue baby bonnet looking into daddy's eyes and making little electronic gurgles with every cootchie-coo."

"Hah. There's another less entertaining likelihood. You don't know Dr. Meghan Macbeth, but I do and if I'm not mistaken, she already has the thing dressed in a pink baby bonnet with 'Meghan Junior' stamped into its forehead."

"Well if you kidnapped it, they would have to ransom it back and that means you have to have a ransom note. Better start whipping up a good one. Good ones have threats in them, you know. Things such as, pay up or I will feed it to an electromagnet, or maybe snip a tiny bit of its heat shield and send it to them in an envelope."

"You know, this is great fun. What a coup it would be. Particularly since it is monitored from space, watched by space telescopes, scanned by a GPS as well as UHF frequencies, patrolled by the Air Force as it descends, and all the while being converged on by the army. Piece of cake, no?"

"Where does it go from the touchdown spot?"

"It's moved by helicopter to a laboratory in the area then to the Johnson Space Center in Houston."

"Hmm. As I said, tricky."

Sanjay's mind ran at the speed of light to solve the hypothetical gambit presented by Kent. A thousand passing thoughts raced by and with Sanjay, passing thoughts often blossomed into meticulous creative solutions. Logistics crept along quietly in the background of his mind.

"You know Nigel, this is a hell of an idea. We would ask one billion dollars ransom."

"You did say a billion. That's as in, a billion? Nice try, Sanjay. And I believe I heard a 'we' slipped in there."

"Yes. Listen. The publicized cost of the project was eight hundred million. That doesn't really count some of the infrastructure such as changing the road grades up to the plateau or transit agreements with the indigenous peoples. My quick calculations say it's at least double that. So, what's a billion here or there."

"I like your attitude, and at that mere bagatelle of a billion, I'm off. I stop in here every day for a pint so if you are around tomorrow about this time, we'll talk again. You're buying. Cheers, mate."

Sanjay did not watch Nigel go. He smiled at Nigel's fantastic plot and visualized the contortion on Macbeth's face should she learn her samples were stolen. It would be the same look as when ye olde Macbeth saw Banquo's ghost. Nigel had made some valid observations on the integral part Sanjay had played in the development of the Bennu project. Once again his eidetic memory poisoned him with its completeness. He began to replay every insult, every condescending diminishment of his academic background and every slight on his east Indian heritage.

He had recently discovered whisky sours and he ordered one up. It was a quicker hit than beer and he needed to expunge the feelings of rancor building in him over his banishment. He reflected back on the group strategy meetings held at the highest level. He had the capacity for a complete and accurate re-creation of anything spatial, mathematical, or conceptual to which he had been exposed. He was the team's quick recall reference library in group discussions in all matters. Rybakov had similar talents but in those moments, even he deferred to Sanjay. Every formula, every piece of datum and every experimental equation whether it stretched across one or five whiteboards, was locked in his mind.

The work I did for them. I worked twice the hours for half their pay and did so gladly. I volunteered for anything which would be helpful. I regularly took whatever paperwork came into my hands home in the evening to advance our timetable even though it was verboten. Without my ongoing input we would have had to postpone the launch. I did not crow about that. I did not ask for special considerations in return, but just to be part of the whole enterprise was all. Perhaps I should have returned their drawings and strategic planning notes, then again they thought so little of me, why should I worry about that. Before the workforce was slashed, I was looking forward to the next stage of our work and to addressing the problem of Apophis. That was something else again and I have good ideas on that as well. But they can get stuffed! Let them work out the things I've already worked out. Their dilemmas are no longer mine. Now they own them, and soon enough the world will own them. I alone have seen the Leishman equations. The space agency is relying upon those, and they are not real. Yes, they scan well, but they are tainted. Only a scrupulous and critical eye will recognize the agenda built into the solutions.

The whisky sour kicked in nicely, but he could not turn off the storm of ideas, so he let them play. He looked at himself in the mirror behind the bar. He liked what he saw smiling back. That man in the reflection was not disconsolate. That man had a plan.

<>

The virtual event was private, and collectively, the pixilated heads of government represented fifty percent of the world's population. Artificial intelligence facsimiles of the leaders sat shoulder to shoulder around a virtual table. The flesh and blood originals had joined the conference from their offices around the world, kitted up with galvanic skin contact wrist bands, headsets, and goggles. Virtual technology convinced them they were actually seated at that table and the spatial relationships of one person to the next were real to them. They believed implicitly they sat exactly where their malleable brains told them they sat. Chancellor Birgitta Sturm of Germany extended her virtual index finger through the neck of President Lagunas of the United States to the depth of his internal jugular vein, just to test it.

Russia, China, India, Germany, Great Britain, United States, Saudi Arabia and Brazil were represented. Today they would make choices for the rest of the world. Unlike most gatherings of nation states, this meeting was not about war, nor about plague nor a flogging of predetermined social justice. It was about something more important. Gaming. The global lottery for Mars colonization was moving forward. The ground rules were to be finalized and then imposed on the planet with an invitation to knock itself out. The ticket proceeds were designed to fund the Mars exploration and habitat settlement program of the next decade, with modest administration fees commingled magically into the accounts of the 100 families. The winners of the lottery had a place on the Interplanetary Ships being built around the world to form the Red Planet Fleet. Billions would buy tickets in the hope of escaping the abattoir called Earth, to join the select few who would colonize Mars.

Chairman Liu opened the dialogue for China.

"Gentlemen, and lady, as it is the agreed upon hour, please allow me to begin. Central registry has received the lists of the first designated temporary one hundred thousand lottery winners from each of you, except for India, who appears to be mathematically challenged as it has been kind enough to send us double that amount. Prime Minister Pandit, how should I say this, what the hell do you think you are doing?"

Prime Minister Jawahar Pandit spoke from the city of Mumbai and his facsimile at the virtual table stood and answered in an even tone.

"Chairman Liu, thank you for your question, for it instructs us in many things. First it teaches us China's bully world view applies even to congenial discussion among peers, and second, since China does not understand the doubling of the number of lottery winners, as it does not understand most things, it has presumed this has been done in error, not seeing it has been done for efficiency's sake. The expanded number contains both the temporary and permanent lottery winners in the first phase."

President Lagunas of the United States pounded the table for attention, but his hammering fist made no noise. The programmers had not thought of that. Lagunas needed to be on his feet. He could not tolerate the impression the leadership of the discussion rested with China.

"Mr. Chairman, if I may, I will address Prime Minister Pandit directly. Minister Pandit, I applaud your interest in efficiency, however I doubt that is what moved you to double your quota. The temporary winners are supposed to be that, just temporary. They have been chosen because of their medical records. They are the infirm or medically compromised, and to use our American term, they are the ones who will kick the bucket before the rockets leave for Mars. True enough there will be a slim few who are uncooperative in their dying, but just a few. The lucky winners will come from every small hamlet, every large city, and every backwater of the globe. Every person on the planet will see that a local individual has been chosen and consequently will believe the lottery is a fair thing, and perhaps they will be chosen also. Impressions of fairness will keep them from tearing up the streets. Following the demise of the temporary winners, we will select the people who are actually going. No one would complain Uncle Harry could not go, after all, Uncle Harry was dead."

The assemblage nodded their digital heads in agreement with the wisdom of it. President Lagunas began shaking a beringed finger at Pandit.

"You however, minister Pandit, have become creative. And I am asking, mind you, not accusing, just asking, whether it is possible through some bureaucratic miscalculation, all two hundred thousand of your candidates are healthy? And when the time comes to cash in their tickets it would be unwise for the Red Planet Fleet to be seen refusing a lottery winner, thereby forcing the acceptance of all your citizens? Twice that of the rest of us?"

United Kingdom and Saudi Arabia glanced quickly at each other having done precisely what Lagunas accused India of doing.

Chairman Liu stepped in. "Enough. We have years to audit the candidates with respect to their particular medical morbidities. And please, no one pretend they had not thought of doing the same thing. Item two. The determination of the ratio of candidates apportioned to each country. China's formula is simple. Each country will commit its top twenty percent IQ in the country. Within th… "

President Habib of Brazil shot to his feet. He was his country's hero for elevating his nation into the cadre of world decision makers. He would not allow his people to be bullied.

"Chairman Liu, stop there. Yes, you and I and our countries are walking arm in arm with resource development and infrastructure building through your Belt and Road initiative, but Brazil has no intention of becoming a vassal of combined Indian and Chinese interest. The top twenty percent in intelligence of your population is more than the rest of us combined. In fact, it is equivalent to the entire population of the United States."

"Thank you President Habib, I understand your concerns. You have forgotten one core principle. On Mars, there will be no geographical distinction made which can be considered a country. All will be Martians. There will be no China, no India, and no United States. There will be no boundaries restricting access from one place to another nor will there be the need for the military. Possession of a gun is deportation back to a dying poisonous Earth. The Sentients alone will carry stun weapons and reconditioning facilities will treat and modify anyone who transgresses the body of law."

Prince Ahmad Ahmad of Saudi Arabia stayed seated. He believed he was superior to this rabble in either a seated or standing posture.

"You people. There is only one country here which can do justice to the goal. That being, populating a new world and taking the species into the future. Russia, what is your birth rate? 1.6? And United States? 1.4? And Brazil? 1.7? And the rest of you? We all know the answers. You are talking about IQ. Who will clean the drains and mend the clothes. Saudi Arabia is a small country, but its birth rate is 3.9. We pump other things besides oil. Fifty percent of our population could be taken to start the ball rolling."

Lagunas refused to stand, to demonstrate his contempt. Oil money could buy anything. Even a seat at the big table.

"Ten of you from Saudi Arabia is too many, let alone a whole stable of designated boinkers."

General Petrov exploded in a good belly laugh at the thought, and the others joined in with the permission of not having been the first to do it. He had no interest in the useless posturing. The virtual meeting had been a trial run for future deliberations but as with all electronic socializing, the feeling of invulnerability fostered by distance lead to abusive conduct and the destruction of real discourse. Altogether, Russia was completely uninterested in whatever decisions were made on any of these matters. They had their own plan, and it was well underway. Russia would balance things as Russia saw fit. Petrov was particularly pleased no one had suggested the Interplanetary Ships be integrated by mingling individuals from various countries. As proposed at the outset, each nationality would travel with its own people. That was imperative for Petrov to be successful. The meeting adjourned with nothing decided and all the traditional animosities were firmly entrenched. Oleg Petrov wondered when they would learn. He thought of his great uncle Nikita and something he said to him as a boy. *You know what an elephant is my boy? No, uncle, what? A mouse designed by a committee.*

<>

Sanjay Rustom pushed through the saloon doors of the Pearly Gates just as a couple evacuated a booth at the back. He rushed to it to stake a claim and slid in and opened a menu. He was early and the working men trickled in one by one and two by two to reward themselves for a day's work and the alcohol had not yet kicked in to make a hubbub. The special of the day was a Sasquatch burger and a draft beer and he ordered two. Waitress Daisy had him set up with the beer in ninety seconds, advised him they were just getting the grill going, and he had certainly chosen the correct item from the menu. While he waited, Sanjay continued to scroll. The cellphone reception was good today and his searches of the available storefronts narrowed it down to two small towns. The second town, which he was looking through for the first time, was it. It had modest tourist traffic, and the core of the town was in a tight four block area. The exterior view of the property satisfied him. His Sasquatch arrived and it was enormous and beautiful. He was halfway through the most delicious burger of his life when Nigel arrived with a wave.

"Hello mate. You're looking perky today. What's that?"

"Sasquatch burger. You have one coming. And a beer if you want it."

"Is your burger something a Sasquatch would eat, or is it actually made from Sasquatches?"

"The latter."

"Good. Too many of them anyway."

"Tell me Nigel, do you know something about ovens?"

"Certainly. Places where witches put children, I believe."

"You have an interesting mind. All right, let me rephrase that. Do you know anything about pizza?"

"Now you're talking about my specialty. I am an expert in pizza. And I stay up to date on the science. No new pizza concept escapes me. I am known far and wide as Nigel the pizza guy. Why?"

" Just something I'm thinking of. What do you mean when you say you're an expert?"

"What I really mean is I don't know a thing about it. I was referring to the volume of pizza I've eaten. Although I do know you can't make them as good at home because your kitchen oven isn't hot enough. I think you need eight hundred or a thousand degrees or somewhere like that, and that means they're the ideal temperature for perfect crispy pizza for Nigel."

Those temperatures matched what Sanjay had anticipated and they were not close to what he had to have. A holding temperature of at least 2500° Fahrenheit was necessary.

"Nigel, would you be able to boost the heat in an oven of that type to 2500°?"

"No, no way. The fire brick would have to be a high temperature type, like the ones which one might use to melt nickel. You would run a dedicated line for such an oven. But I have to advise you, charcoal briquet pizza with that burned to a crisp taste is not a big seller. Innovative, yes, but edible, no. If you need a cooker like that the way to get it is to build it from scratch."

Rustom opened his phone and scrolled down to the exterior view of the small shop he had found and handed it to Nigel.

"That, sir, is my new pizza shop."

"I see. Your new pizza shop with its 2500° ovens. What are you going to call it? Sanjay's carbon house?"

"How about, let's see, 'Argentum Refined Pizza'. Argentum is the name of the town. As you've probably guessed, it's an old silver mining town, which is getting its act together again in the summer months with tourism. It doesn't have a pizza place. I think there is some good money to be made."

"Sanjay, two weeks ago you were working on comets and probes and astrophysics, on the way to a PhD and now you have taken the next logical step in your career by opening a pizza business with a nickel refinery in the back. Makes perfect sense to me."

"I think so. Tell me about your cousin Robin."

"Sanjay, you are one walking non sequitur. There isn't a great deal to tell about my cousin. He is hardworking, honest and intelligent in a practical way. He's the kind of man you want on your side when times are tough. We're like brothers. He is the top of the line, my Robin. A man of his word and the best wrangler under the sun. Why?"

"I'm going to need an additional man I can trust. That is, in addition to yourself if you're interested. Nigel, I am serious. There is good money in pizza, it's a matter of picking the right place and the right community. If the pizza is good in fact, people will drive to get it."

"A pizza business."

"Yes. With a nickel refinery in the back."

Nigel blinked. His brain was one of schematics and connectors and frequencies. He had never considered having to do with cheese as something to be done for a living. He blinked a few times and tugged at his beer.

"But, Nigel, maybe all the free pizza you can eat does not appeal to you."

"Well, of course it does, Sanjay, but I also have to tell you what I just posted this morning. I sent a begging letter for my job back at the Space Center. I listed my indispensable attributes ad nauseum. It was beautiful. But, this idea is so off the wall, so anti-tech to boot, I like it. Where's the place you showed me?"

"New Mexico. In a small town in New Mexico in the Sangre De Cristo mountains."

"You mean like, rattlesnake country, New Mexico in the United States?"

"Exactly."

Nigel took a deep draft of his Guinness.

"Sanjay, count me in."

Sanjay was not altogether surprised at Nigel's quick decision. Unemployment had a way of making one act.

"And Robin?"

"If I'm in, he's in if I ask him."

"Good. You can tell him the place is crawling in mustangs."

"One thing, old chap, I have no money to invest in this. I'll build you your special oven but the other equipment like what you're talking about is expensive."

"It will drain my savings, but we will make it."

What Sanjay really meant was he would use money from his trust fund.

"When are you going to tell me what this is really about?"

"All I can say is, when the cows come home you shall be rewarded.

Chapter Ten

Hussein Galimov startled awake as his head bounced against the glass of the window seat on the bus. It was midafternoon and he and his wife Almira had been up since the first prayer before dawn. The drone of the snow tires on the pavement and the warmth of the sun had put him to sleep. His old mare Safina was in her final days, and he did not demand the 100-mile trip to Chelyabinsk of her. He was excited and uplifted by what he felt was a holy mission. He was not a man to demand much, as whatever happened was as God wanted, but he was just a man after all and wants were one of his frailties. The bus driver was a second cousin to his wife, and praise be to Allah, he accepted one of Hussein's goats for two tickets to Chelyabinsk.

Remarkable things were happening. Some things were good, and some others he feared were evil. Hussein spent most days at the mosque or its community center, praying and fraternizing with his friends and listening to the news of the day and of the world. It was interesting how since the blaze of the meteorite had blinded him five years earlier, his compatriots gave more serious credence to his words. His sightless eyes implied some greater connection to the almighty. Over recent months, light and shadow had become distinguishable to him. The doctor had told him that was the limit of his healing, but he did not accept it. The scripture said that what Allah had taken belonged to him and to him belonged what he granted. Hussein lived in the hope that Allah would grant him his sight. He believed he was on a quest to fulfill that hope.

Almira had attempted to dissuade him from the trip, but he would listen to none of it. He would go alone, or he would go with her, but he would go. She knew it was so, and dutifully she was by his side to serve and protect. She was fearful of the size and tumult of Chelyabinsk. She was a native of Tyulyuk, the village of 2,000 in which they lived, and the concept of the distance bothered her. Once in her life she had been 20 miles north for the wedding of a cousin and that was the limit of her travels. Chelyabinsk had been nothing but a distant star.

It was the tenth day of Muharram during the Celebration of Ashura when he heard the news. Galimov's friend, Noma, was literate, and he read to them from the newspaper. The printed stories confirmed to Hussein how the conflict between good and evil raged in the world. When the asteroid of 2013 arrived out of the sun from the east, the shock and impact of hitting the air tore it apart. It exploded into a thousand pieces, each one of them hitting the earth, each one's hiding place revealed by a clean new hole in the snow of Siberia. The people chased the trail of the asteroid to its impact and one by one along the way, burrowing down the holes in the snow, they found their treasures. They found chunks and shards of something wrought by the hand of God and never before touched by man. Throughout the region, they graced their tabletops with a relic sent from heaven. The largest piece punched a 20-foot-wide hole in the ice of Lake Chebarkul just west of Chelyabinsk. Three days after the event, work crews recovered a ¾ ton piece from the bottom of the lake and carted it to the State History Museum of South Ural. That was Hussein's destination. He had told no one his thoughts and cautioned Almira to keep it private. His greatest hope was for the stone to be the Father of the holy stone known to the faithful as the Al-Ḥajaru al-Aswad, the black stone of Mecca. Hussein had not been able to touch it in his pilgrimage there, but God willing, he would lay his hands on the great stone in the museum.

The second event he heard from Noma at the Ashura celebration was a terrible thing, one certainly formed by the malice of Eblīs, the leader of the devils. In September 2016, a rocket flamed into space to visit an asteroid called Bennu. From it, a device formed by the devil would scoop pieces of it and bring them back to earth. That was to happen six years hence. Hussein shuddered at the arrogance of man to desecrate an ancient messenger such as Bennu, a messenger meant to deliver its glory to him as God wanted, not as wanted by men. He knew wisdom could be imparted only when the listener was able to receive it. Noma had taken Hussein arm in arm and led him to the garden where they sat privately in a bower.

"Hussein, lean into me closer. I have here an article from page six. In a moment I will read it quietly, and this is meant for just you and not to be spoken of again. There are things here, things which are wonderful and worrying together. I brought the paper with me today intending to discuss it with Mullah Omar, but I have changed my mind. I was afraid if he knew I had this knowledge, he might declare me apostate. You know how he is when he's in a bad mood. I won't read what it says to you if you don't want me to. If I do, believe me, it will trouble your mind, even keep you up at night. But I think your Almira might thank me for that, huh?"

"Oh yes, yes, she would, absolutely. Both of us would thank you. Go ahead Noma, I will judge what you say for myself. I will not repeat what you say. Allah is sufficient as witness between me and you. Please read it."

"I will tell you what I have heard from the street, then read from the paper. Near where the asteroid fell lives a man named Klitschko. Yevgeny Klitschko. People call him a fool and a madman, but I do not believe it to be so. He, and he is not alone, has felt a spirit, a presence emanating from the rock. There is a growing group which has felt the same thing. He believes, and they join him in the belief, the meteorite contains scriptures which reveal moral and legal blueprints for life. He and his group believe its messages can bring us to a new level of consciousness. Does it not remind you of the Al-Ḥajaru al-Aswad?"

"It does, indeed, it does. What a wonder!"

"Klitschko is not a follower of Islam, but he is a devout person of the book, who reveres our prophets such as Abraham as we revere his. His group, which I have heard is now about one thousand strong, is called the Church of the Holy Meteorite. The people around the bazaar call it a cult to make it into nothing, but all that serves is to attract attention to it."

"Do you believe Mullah Omar knows of these things?"

"I do, and I also believe he would keep it away from us to avoid it becoming a distraction. Let me read from the newspaper now and it will be the last time we will discuss it, but this will not be the last time such a thing happens. As you will see, the messages of hope will surely keep coming."

Hussein thrilled with the possibilities the mystery of the Chelyabinsk stone opened to him. Who was to say that Allah would not benefit the faithful through the use of a man of the book. He suffered Noma to read from the paper, but his mind was not on that. A longing to be with the stone grew within him.

"Galimov, it says here, the arrival of such an asteroid is not new. It happened many times, even before Mohammed, peace be upon him. As it has done with Klitschko and his people, for thousands of years such events have drawn people to the spiritual energy the asteroids bring. Yevgeny Klitschko expects Chelyabinsk to become a truly holy city, and the site of a great temple. A site to which millions of people from around the world will make a pilgrimage. We will see."

Hussein leaned in to hear his friend better, enjoying their little conspiracy.

"One of the most interesting times was with the boy emperor Bassianus who ruled Rome around 220 AD. He was a Syrian, and it was there a single black metallic egg-shaped meteorite struck the city of Emesa. It carried such an intense mystic presence; the emperor demanded it be brought to Rome. Roman coins of the day were struck with its image. In scrupulous detail the coins displayed projections and striations on the metallic surface which mimicked the rays of the sun. Its effect was so great the worship of the stone and the god who sent it became the state religion."

"Noma, why do you tell me this? What has it to do with us, now?"

"I bring it up because ancient cultures such as the prehistoric Indians in Arizona, and the Inuit of Greenland had identical experiences with asteroids. Like Roman culture, their histories and ways of life are expunged. I fear it is because they venerated the object yet failed to open themselves to receive its message. I fear we in Islam, may be on the similar path. Enough, my friend. Our Mullah Omar is sanctified to make these determinations. I leave it to him, and I am on my way."

The bus bounced through a series of potholes and jolted Hussein Galimov into the present. His thoughts returned to the sample gathering soon to be done by the evil machine on the asteroid Bennu. He realized he had been just as presumptive as he accused the scientists of being. He had presumed they were doing the devil's work of interference in the works of Allah by scavenging the surface. Perhaps it was entirely the opposite. For millennia, man had ignored and turned his back on all messages from God. When the samples returned, all the billions with eyes to see would wait and watch for the great event to unfold. Perhaps for the very first time, mankind would be primed and ready and capable of receiving the message God has sent.

With Almira guiding him by his elbow, he shuffled across the terrazzo floor toward the display. The solitary guard within the State History Museum pitied the blind man escorted by his lady and made a quick thanks to Allah for sparing him such affliction. The building was largely deserted, and a conversation drifted to Hussein from a distant corridor, giving him a sense of the size of the space. Almira steered him gently, feeling the nervousness in him. The Holy Meteorite of Chelyabinsk rested on a low timber platform under an ultraviolet light. The fragment was ovoid with narrow veins scribing a rough outline of a hand which fluoresced brilliantly on the surface. It was smaller than she expected but its iron body weighed one thousand five hundred pounds. Almira was moved to something new within her as she lifted the black velvet rope. Hussein ducked underneath and felt for the surface of the asteroid. He ran his hands slowly across the smooth exterior and flexed his fingers in a way to massage it. He pressed harder to expand the size of his hands to increase his intimacy with it. He was ready to receive what it had to offer. He stayed there for ten minutes, intimate with the holy thing, and he was not yet satiated when the guard approached him.

"Please sir, madame, that is enough. Come out from behind the rope, now. Allah knows what you need. Be content at that."

Hussein Galimov had played his part. He had been driven from his sleep to see the fireball and seek its message. He had demonstrated his willingness to receive and now he would wait in the fullness of time for the will of Allah. The day for the return of the Bennu machine was few scant years away. Then, all things would be made whole.

<>

Frankincense candles dominated the mixture of scents as Meghan Macbeth slid down into the bathwater and exhaled. Her glass of Montrachet sat untouched among the candles on the tub surround. She had made the last of the cuts in staff at the launch facility and she soaked to expunge the sense of guilt she felt for their situation. Sanjay Rustom was cut loose and Rybakov the spy was in the wilds of northern Saskatchewan fomenting something or other at the construction site and they could deal with it there. Izzy remained on the job for his orbital work on both Bennu and Apophis, but the rest of the crucial team was gone.

Meghan reached her wine glass from the edge of the tub by the stem and looked through it against the ceiling. Flickers picked up a subtle touch of emerald flecked with gold. Montrachet was best at 57 degrees and the room was closer to 90 but life would go on. The bouquet was of honey and fruit, and visions of prawns, foie gras and cream sauces came to her. With her first sip the emergency claxon ringtone on her cell phone sounded from the next room. The display showed Harry Fletcher, the security camera technician in the main building.

"Harry, this had better be bloody serious. I am standing here dripping from the bath holding a half full glass which by now should be empty. Make it good."

" Er.. Miss, Megh.. Dr. Macbeth, make it good? This is good in spades! No, not necessarily good, maybe, the finger, you know the mystery scribbler on the white boards? It's back. Right now it's in there writing like crazy as we speak. It has created such glare that I can only see small fragments of its hieroglyphics, but the finger thing is really motoring. It wiped all your stuff clean and is going at it, with smoky little sizzles jumping from the glare like it was playing. Whoa. It's getting so bright in the whiteboard room I can't see anything. Man, this is intense! Again, no alarms went off at the doors, the pressure sensors in the floor show nothing. After the last event, we wired all the air ducts and negative pressure circuits in the biologic samples area, and again today the spook is inside there playing around without a by your leave. It alerted nothing in our security system."

"Is Leishman on site?"

"Hold on. I'll check the cameras at his parking spot. Let's see. No. His spot is empty."

"Call him and get him to the lab. I'll be there in twenty minutes."

Meghan cursed the slowness of the golf cart ride from the perimeter fence to the building and raced through. She carded her way inside to see Leishman standing stiffly within arm's length of the boards, with an eraser in his hand and a marker in the other, agitated to the point of shaking. Meghan immediately recognized the structure of the equations and also the abnormality of Leishman's demeanor.

"Izzy, have you erased something?"

Leishman did not respond. He was absorbed in decipherment of the new material. Izzy was satisfied the scribbling did not expose nor contradict his work on record, except possibly one short incomplete statement. That, he had erased.

"Izzy!"

"What? Oh, no, nothing. Oh, I see. Sorry. Nothing erased. It's a reflex to pick these things up when I come into the lab. Automatic."

Meghan took a few quick photos and punched the line to Harry Fletcher in the camera monitoring lab.

"Harry, I am here with Dr. Leishman. Run the tape back to the point where the writing is complete. Take a still of that and forward it to my cell phone."

She did not trust Leishman had not made erasures. She would compare her own photos to the still shot from Harry taken before Leishman arrived.

"Isadore, are those orbital calculations? Isadore! "

"Yes, at least they have a similar form, and they follow my own equations closely, but I'm not sure. As you see, they diverge into two different systems even though the string of variables on the left has not changed. Similar to the previous material from our spook, these cannot be complete series."

At that realization Leishman relaxed. Incomplete work could not be used to refute his theorems. Meghan checked her phone for the image from Harry Fletcher.

"Harry, are you still there?"

"Here."

"Good. Take a snip of the tape starting just before the intrusion right up to the current time stamp. Encrypt the extracted section with PGP encryption and send it to me on this cell with the private key."

" Yes Dr. Macbeth, but there won't be much to see of the writing. I sent you the image you requested but the lens glare was so great the board just appears as a haze and the image is so washed out there is no contrast on the surface. I think the intensity of the light fried the camera sensors."

Isadore smiled. Fried sensors equaled no record of little Izzy scrubbing the evidence and that was good, but he was puzzled. There was no way the level of expertise previously demonstrated by the phantom should agree with his conclusions as far as they went. They could not have missed what he had concocted.

"Never mind, Harry, I will have Duo look at these equations and if necessary send them out for analysis. Dr. Leishman, thank you for coming in on your time off. I will follow you out."

Meghan returned home and let out the cold bath water. The candles on the tub surround had melted to puddles and wax stalactites reached the floor. For the second time the information left by the intruder was incomplete and it completely expunged all the work in the whiteboard room. It was as if the visitor was telling her they were wasting their time. She hit the speed dial on her phone and walked to the living room carrying the remaining wine. Sanjay Rustom picked up her call.

"Dr. Macbeth. This is unexpected. Why are you calling me?"

"Sanjay, there's something I would like you to look at. Your clearance is still in effect. We have more writings from the specter. You might be interested in seeing what it wrote."

"Sure, Dr. Macbeth. All backpay, a five-year contract with cost of living and an assistant. That should cover it. Agreed?"

"Sanjay, I can't do that."

"Then, my dear, neither can I. I am in the pizza business.

Chapter Eleven

August 2019

Sanjay Rustom walked around to the driver's side of his ancient Datsun and stretched a kink in his back. Six hours of jostling on the unpaved county road had made him sore and a little car sick. The historical silver mining town of Argentum New Mexico was their target and he reckoned it was another one hundred miles south. The eternal road-grading on the Taos County truck route had detoured them up through Bobcat Pass and the altimeter read 9800 feet. The thirty-five degrees drop in temperature at elevation was a welcome change from the swelter of the valley. The last of the washer fluid was long gone, and Sanjay snapped a rag at the windshield to clear the dust. The wipers were stuck pointing at one o'clock. Nigel slept obliviously in the back seat, his gangled frame contorted into the small space, and his cousin Robin Hathaway rode shotgun. The going was slow on the narrow road and every so often a distant horn gave notice that someone somewhere was approaching the other side of a switchback. Around the next tight bend, Hathaway tapped a stiff finger on the glass as his eyes followed an area of rubble on the hillside running down to the road.

"There's going to be a slide in that scramble."

"Scramble?"

"That loose stuff there, running steep up to that small cliff face. It's pretty much overbalanced."

"How do you know?"

"Typical formation. Ready to go."

Sanjay was unsure of Robin's commitment to what he had planned so he came at it sideways.

"That's dangerous. Could you make it go? Start it? What I mean is, it is a dangerous thing. If there were a way to create the slide safely, a controlled slide, when there was no one around, it would prevent it from happening when there was traffic on the road below it."

"Easy if you know about it. I done many of them over in mustang territory in Alberta. Mostly on the eastern slopes between the Sheep and Brazeau Rivers. Sort of preemptive avalanches just like you said. Keeps the truck routes open from the oil fields. So much demand, the pipelines 'er full and convoys of rigs are hauling the heavy crude south. A slide like that in Alberta is a million-dollar loss in the making. It's a bit tricky, but once you scope out the keystone, and nudge it just right, away she goes, takin' a few hundred tons of her friends with her. Best not to stand around and admire your work."

"Robin, you said the keystone. Do you mean as in a stone arch, where the rest of the stones are placed to lean into it, and it keeps them all supported?"

"Yes, the same idea. Remove the keystone and the lot comes down."

Sanjay white-knuckled the wheel. Every so often, sludge ran across the track where a small aquifer had broken from the cliff face and it steered the car in the direction of the flow, toward the precipice on the left. He concentrated on keeping the driving wheels turned a few degrees into the wall on his right to counteract the slide.

Robin watched Sanjay's face as he drove, focused on his driving. There was something sitting behind the eyes which did not set right with him.

"Son, you can slide around the corners on this here high road, but there's no need to do it with Nigel and me. Whatever you are hatching, stop giving it a wide berth and bring it out straight."

Sanjay was taken off guard by the directness of the question but there was not a flicker on his face to betray him. For the first time he noticed the marked difference in the vowel sounds between the speech of Robin and Nigel. Perhaps it was to be expected. They were cousins from different worlds. Not brothers. On the dashboard, the profile of the small car in the incline gauge tipped forward to demonstrate they were now on a down slope.

"Ah Robin, you are a clever one. Relax. Sanjay the great will reveal all to you soon enough. Our three-man universe is unfolding as it should. You mentioned mustang territory just now. Nigel tells me you are the best where they are concerned."

"Nigel is right about that. I am the best and one of the few wranglers remaining. The king of the bangtails."

"Bangtails? "

"Yes, that's what the boys on the range call 'em. Wild horses. Bangtails. Mustangs. To us, mustangs are the most beautiful things on earth. They are wild, rough, vicious, faithful, solitary, and social, altogether. The fact is, they can be any one of those different things two seconds after they were the last thing."

"Are they the same everywhere you have worked?"

"Pretty much. They differ only in small ways from place to place. In Alberta and New Mexico for example, they have short tails and manes where in Patagonia they are longer and thick. As horses go, they're not all that big, between fourteen and sixteen hands at a thousand pounds and they are colored the same in every region, bay, black, buckskin and palomino. Beautiful. And smart. If you're lost and out of water, just follow the mustang trail. They can smell it from ten miles. And a mustang has every arroyo within twenty miles locked in his head. He runs his herd through labyrinths of clefts and gullies at speed, undetected. Generally they move in bands of twenty or thirty but when they feel the need they will herd up to maybe eighty or ninety. No matter where you find them, one thing they can't stand is being alone."

"Robin, are they designated rare or protected? Considered endangered? Tagged and tracked by conservationists like a lot of species?"

"No, not endangered, nothing like that. They are actually thriving. In these parts the Bureau of Land Management keeps a loose count and every so often they move a small herd to a new region or get them adopted. But no, no tagging or tracking."

Sanjay nodded in the way of positive listening. It was important they not be tracked, and it was what he had hoped. The contour of the road swept in longer arcs as they lost elevation, and he picked up speed into the warming air.

"Hey, Nigel. Wake up. Your neck is going to stay that way."

Nigel Kent grunted and rubbed the pins and needles from a dead hand.

"Where are we?"

"About forty miles north of Argentum. Our appointment with the realtor to look at the storefront is in an hour. Daisy. Daisy Plantagenet is her name. Her web site promises to treat us royally. I wonder how many people get the joke."

Robin had no idea what Sanjay was talking about.

"What joke? I don't find the joke in it."

"Exactly. Blast. My cell phone has lost the signal. We are looking for the town of Argentum. The road runs off Highway 25 to the left and the sign will be either Argentum Road or Riffle Street. Keep your eyes peeled. It's marked either way on various maps. We are meeting at noon at 58 Riffle."

Riffle it was, and Daisy Plantagenet stood resplendent in red and white, leaning languorously against her silver 1981 Mercedes. Daisy wore a red Stetson hat against the sun, a white cotton suit jacket and a truly short white skirt above tanned legs and red cowboy boots emblazoned with rampant white stallions. She yawned as she reviewed the notes in her cell phone and flashed her broker's neon smile as Sanjay approached with his hand extended.

"You must be Daisy."

"And you are Mr. Rustom? It is a pleasure to meet you."

Sanjay did a quasi-bow and mangled a sort of curtsy.

"It is a pleasure to meet you, your highness, but what is with the 'leased' sign on the storefront? What's going on here? "

"For land's sake! Your highness! You are the first one to connect the dots to Plantagenet. For that, I will buy you a beer. And one for the boys there too. Yes, it happens your storefront is already leased, but walk with me down the way. I have a spot which might suit you better. I suppose you are scoping these parts because of the swap meet down in Pincher. I congratulate you on your nose for business."

Sanjay knew nothing of Daisy's swap meet nor the town of Pincher, but he played along and walked with her with Nigel and Robin in tow.

"Well Daisy, for some things, you have to act fast. Are you involved in the swap meet?"

"Me? Hell no! I like people but not a million of them jammed together in RVs trading their junk. Three years ago they had a hundred thousand, last year three hundred thousand and this year Sierra County has received nine hundred thousand reservations. It amazes me. A million people tooth by jowl from all over the country finding a warm place for the winter in a camper. I get it, but not for me. By the way, you likely noticed on the way into town, pretty much everyone has a camper or two on his lot. When you set up here, I suggest you do the same. You will likely need the storage, maybe a freezer and such. "

"Thank you. This swap meet. How does it work? *Hey friend, I'll trade you this toaster and a bent spoon for your bowling ball.* That sort of thing?"

"Yes, no receipts, no paper, just swaps. The best traders make big money in value of what they take home."

Rustom loved it. All the outfitting he needed was to be found somewhere in a million people. There would be no records of purchase and sale for anything. He motioned Robin aside and spoke quietly out of earshot of Daisy.

"Robin, quiet now, what do you know of climbing gear? Rock hammers and sample bags and rockhound sort of equipment?"

"Enough. Used them for years. You thinking of the swap meet? We'd likely find all the gear somewheres in a horde that size, but what do we have to swap?"

"Pizza, of course. We'll gather up the climbing hardware over the next couple of years. Daisy, how far is the meet from here?"

"About half an hour, maybe more, downhill. Argentum is at three thousand eight hundred feet, but the roads are open all winter, no sweat. Last year the businesses here in the town were swamped by people with time on their hands and nothing else to do but poke around the area. They found their way up here and it was like a modern-day silver rush. Here we are. Your new business."

Robin piped up first.

“It’s a bank. It says, ‘Argentum Bank.'”

“Was, was a bank. It is the only stone building in town. It dates back to 1883. More or less, it closed before it opened. It was started by a speculator from Philadelphia. The bank seemed like a reasonable idea at the time, but banks could fail and the men with the banjos didn’t trust it with their pokes. They trusted the pistols in their belts. You may have noticed as we walked up, there is a small house attached at the back which communicates through a back door.”

“Banjos?”

“That’s what the silver miners called their short shovels. Anyway, shall we embark on the grand tour?”

“Excuse me, Daisy, before you do, I am Nigel. Where would I find the electrical panel?”

“Hello Nigel, the panel is outside on the left. Hang on. Here’s the key. Left side of the house under the overhang.”

Nigel headed for the panel while Sanjay and Robin took the tour. Each pizza oven would draw about one hundred amperes and the custom oven he would build might draw one thousand. The project needed dedicated circuit branches. The existing electrical panel had sixteen forty-year-old twenty-five ampere glass fuses with copper plated contacts. They were still alive and well, but it was time to retire. For the trios’ purposes the electrical needed replacing and modernizing from top to bottom throughout both buildings.

The interior of the bank was surprisingly bright. Multiple small windows high in the side walls and two large storefront windows on the street kept it lit. A vertical floor to ceiling grid of iron bars separated the front of the bank from the vault. Robin, Sanjay and Daisy walked through the unlocked door to examine the vault. It was built into the floor beneath a heavy steel door like a large manhole cover, with a combination lock, swung open for display. Someone had scratched the combination into the steel on the inside of the door. Sanjay considered it perfect for his needs. Nigel strode in to deliver his verdict on the power supply.

“Sanjay, the electrical system needs total replacement and upgrading. If we have six or eight units we should run two separate lines as a fallback. The electrical panels should be moved inside the main building here.”

Daisy raised one slightly akilter pencil line eyebrow.

"Are you putting in Bitcoin mining units? Many people have come here to do it because New Mexico's loose and electricity is cheap."

"No ma'am, nothing like that. Pizza ovens."

"Smart. You boys will be rolling in dough. Pardon the expression. Better to get on with your business license as soon as you can show your lease. The man to see is the mayor, Mayor Yokum. If you need new wiring, go for it but it's on your dime. The landlord's not going to pay for it. That would be me."

Sanjay nodded, for as far as dimes went they were his. Daisy assumed the sale and each party could see they had come to an agreement. They excused themselves from Robin and Nigel to conclude the particulars of the lease. Robin fiddled with the combination lock, and it was stiff and difficult. It needed cleaning and oiling. He knew his way around the lock and bolt configuration and Nigel smiled at Cousin Robin. It seemed wrangling was just one of his many talents. They walked together and stood in the open door of the bank and watched Sanjay and her highness in discussion on the porch of the building across the street. It sported freshly installed old style saloon doors and boozy talk floated over.

"What do you think, Robin?"

"Well Nigel, you asked me in on this, and on your word, here I am. You talked about horses. Wrangling. I found out today it's actually a pizza business. Yet, most of the way in the car, Sanjay picked my brains about mustangs and really talked about nothing else. I don't see the connection. And then comes his interest in climbing and sampling equipment."

"I don't see it myself. The thing is, I trust Sanjay. We are all in equally for one third of what comes down. He wants you to work with horses and he and I to focus on pizza. It's a good business, you know? Something different too. He wants me to put in some crazy big furnace for him in addition to the pizza ovens and fine, it's his money. I know without question there's more to it, but as I said, it's his money and his plan and soon enough we'll know the details."

"His interest in the rockslides was more than just curiosity. What do you think that's about?"

"Robin, I heard some of the talk in the car and I really don't give a hoot. Besides that, I have never felt as good as I feel today. The sky is clear, the air is fresh, and this sweet clean altitude is wonderful. And all the pizza you can eat? Come on man! We'll find out the rest in due time when Sanjay feels like holding forth. Come. They're waving us over to the saloon."

Nigel and Robin bellied up to the bar and behind them Sanjay and Daisy shook on it. They had a five-year lease, and the paperwork would be signed off the next morning. Sanjay believed Nigel was committed and up for a lark, with the hope it would bring something good down the road. Robin on the other hand, was a cowpoke. Direct, practical and uncomplicated. It was time to give them the entire plan or he would lose Robin.

<>

Livorno Italy

A halo of mist surrounded the lights above the loading dock in the Porto Mediceo inner harbor. Mario Ventresca waited patiently for the signal and slapped at a mosquito on his neck. Italy still had the odd case of malaria and every time he was bitten, for the next two weeks he recognized each symptom, following which he would surely die. The wind off the Ligurian Sea had fallen to nothing after an afternoon of rough weather. Tuscany's marine forecast had promised heavy breakers to continue into the darkness of the night which suited to cover his activity, but as usual the forecast was wrong. The sea was green and flat, and the air was dead. The foghorn at the most southerly of Livorno's two lighthouses began its moaning after the fact, as an impenetrable fog layer had now consumed the bay and run well up the cliff face into the city. The primary lighthouse, whose foundations dated from the fourteenth century, stood just half a mile south and towered one hundred and seventy-five feet over the bay. Despite its closeness, from his vantage point through the layer of fog it was baleful and dull. Mario was dressed for an evening of light wind and clear skies, not a saturating mist. He was sodden and cold, he could not leave the contact zone, his two men inside were taking too long, and he wanted to stab someone.

The heist was a simple one, on an extraordinarily well-paid contract. The wire transfer had come through a series of banks and when his procurement agent traced it back, it had come from a bank in Alania, a region of Georgia in the south Caucasus. The target of the operation was Borgia Composite Ventura of Livorno, a small specialty corporation dedicated to heat shielding materials for the space industry. The company was incredibly low profile and few of the locals had any idea of what it did. It had no particular presence in the community and its shipments were small and sporadic. Its security was ordinary, and Mario had arranged a six-hour paid vacation for its two watchmen. He visualized their shrugs and gesticulations as they explained away their absence as having been lost in the fog. Such impenetrable mists were common along the Tuscany coast at this time of the year, so the tender scheduled to pick up the shipment announced its arrival with a tin whistle rather than a lantern. On such a quiet night the whistle could not remain private. The sound would move under the fog and travel the surface of the water, but sundry fog warnings by small vessels was a common thing around the harbor, and no-one would hearken to it.

Livorno was not a high traffic container city. The aesthetics of it displeased the local harbor authority and they had gotten along well for centuries without containers. Livorno was known for its seafood, its canals, and its renaissance era fortifications. The harbor authority intended to keep it that way. As a result, smaller watercraft carried goods to non-container ships moored off the outer harbor. It was more difficult for Mario to disguise his contraband in such ships, but ready cash greased the skids. He relied upon a few tight-lipped local crews who had worked on the water since childhood, for they knew the inner harbor intimately and questioned nothing but the destination of the cargo. Navigating their familiar territory through sightless mists was nothing to them. When they delivered their load to the freighter on the seaward side of the outer breakwall, their job was done. In transactions which might slide around the corner of propriety, codes were used. That night the code of recognition as they approached the cargo pier in the Porto Mediceo, was 'V' for 'Vittoria'. The morse code whistle was Dot, dot, dot, dash. It was also the opening rhythm of Beethoven's fifth symphony and during the second world war, a watchword of the Allies. It seemed the Beethoven piece was absent from the Axis concert halls. Mario's response to the tender was 'B' for Bonasera. Good evening. The morse code for 'B' was just the reverse of 'V'. Dash, dot, dot, dot. He had attempted to simplify things by mirror imaging the signal yet even then things could go wrong. He removed his whistle from his pocket and blew the lint out of the orifice.

The receiving door to the warehouse was open and the scuffle of moving boxes had gone on for fifteen minutes. The shipment was two identical cartons with international bar code identifiers, each weighing 95 pounds in a two-foot by three-foot box. They should have been on the dolly, out onto the pier and hanging from the boom, ready to lower into the hold of the tender. Mario charged inside to find his men and butted up against the chest of Giacomo Alba who looked stupefied.

"Alba, you are a moron. Here you stand, the dolly is empty, yet nothing hangs on the boom outside. You do understand the job, don't you? Identify the boxes, place the boxes on the dolly and by pulling on it, move the cargo outside and place it in the net on the boom."

"Yes sir. My phone is dead."

"Wonderful. I told you to charge it. Follow me. Guido! Guido! Go to the door and listen for the whistle. Giacomo, come with me."

Mario filtered the search by the size of the boxes and in forty-five seconds the bar code reader in his phone confirmed the product.

"Get Guido and put these two boxes into the net. See if you can manage not to drop them into the sea."

Mario moved quickly to the rear of the warehouse as his men loaded the boxes into the net. He raced to the shipping office glass door and taped a sealed envelope to it. He did not know the contents and he was not curious. The wax seal was intact, and that business was done.

He strode onto the pier to hear the whistle from the approaching tender, clear and correct. Mario returned his code without incident. Dash, dot , dot, dot. The small ship tied up and turned off its lights. The inboard engine burbled at rest. Mario opened the dialogue with the agreed upon code words.

"This is Primo. You are?"

"Secundo."

"Identify the ship to which you will deliver."

"Italian freighter IMO 88556773."

"Under what flag?"

"Panama."

"What is its final destination?"

"San Diego California."

"Prepare to receive to your hold. Secundo, listen carefully. This is a high priority assignment. If something goes amiss between you and 6773, my superiors will have a conversation with you. You understand?"

"Yes, of course. Do not worry signore. It is as good as done."

Mario watched the running lights disappear into the fog. He would not be at ease until he was notified of safe arrival of the cartons in San Diego in twenty-eight days. Following that, it would travel by truck as roofing materials to its final destination he cared not where. His uneasiness over the transaction rested with the fact he had received the same warning of a conversation from his superiors. He had passed it on to Secundo. It was a pleasant way of saying a bullet in the forehead as payment for your failure.

<>

Pavel Demidov's table sat beneath a ceiling portrait of Saint Basil the Blessed. His reservation for two at Café Pushkin on Tverskoy Boulevard in Moscow was arranged in his favorite spot. His guest had been his enemy for over half a century both philosophically and ethically. Yet the longevity of their embattlement had eventually worn off the sharp edges and unexpectedly they had become friends. It was their first time sharing a meal, at Demidov's invitation. He scowled at the menu. He shifted in his chair. He understood that things must move with the times, but without notifying him, his favorite restaurant for twenty years, set apart and above all the others, had changed their menu. He looked at his guest sitting opposite who stared blankly into the menu as if it were a puzzle needing working.

"Anatoly, I must apologize in advance for two things. First, they have changed the menu. It was a menu of which Pushkin himself would approve and for some ungodly reason they changed it. Second, I regret I must accept a phone message sometime during the meal."

"Pavel, do you wish me to leave you when it comes?"

"No, no, it is a scheduled thing and unfortunately it falls during dinner. No state secrets to make your ears burn. I just tell you as a warning that one of your humorous anecdotes might be interrupted."

He lied, knowing the man opposite him in his wildest imagination had never spoken a humorous word. Additionally, the call certainly related to state secrets, but the gentleman would be altogether incurious and certainly preferred not to know whether something clandestine was afloat, as special knowledge might bring him trouble, and worse, it could require effort from him. The conversation would be gone from his mind as quickly as it entered.

The gentleman was Anatoly Firsov, Director Emeritus of the Bureau of Records of the Russian Federation. He sat happily drunk, having arrived that way, flushed and perspiring. He was a year older than Demidov, but his shiny corpulence made him look younger. He had been a public figure in Russia for over fifty years and now he was a national treasure. His banal input to any proposed strategies and his dogged insistence on considering nothing to be important enough to get up early, had made him unthreatening to the degree that he remained untouched by purges, foreign wars and a dozen changes in government. His medals required two jackets to do them justice. Demidov wore one small medallion bestowed upon his progenitor by Czar Peter in the eighteenth century. He judged Firsov's collection would be best served by a smelter.

A soft contralto duet accompanied by accordion wafted harmony from a distant salon. They sang traditional melodies of the peasantry and the nostalgia for the refrains swept away the tension. Demidov saw the old menu had not been abandoned altogether.

"Tolya, do you see something you like? I see the staples of the old Pushkin are still on the list. You can't go wrong with those."

Firsov appeared helpless.

"What's wrong? Are you not feeling well?"

"Yes, yes, I'm feeling fine. Pasha, It's not that. It's the decisions. Too many. So much work. Order for me, I know I will like it. You know how it goes. I store records, I find records, I delete records, I alter records, I hide records. I burn records. All of that under orders. Order me up a meal and all is right in my world."

Pavel perused the menu amid the buzz of gathering staff. Two of the generational heroes of the Russian motherland dining together in a public setting was something to see. They would tell their grandchildren; you know, one evening, I saw The Demidov. The Demidov and another man right there in front of us at dinner. I actually got to bring the hot bread rolls to his table.

The Demidov ordered a potato and mushroom pie starter, followed by a sea scallop and trout carpaccio drizzled with mustard vinaigrette. Next to come were pork, lamb and beef pelmeni with sour cream, and salmon caviar with buckwheat crepes. The finish was a pistachio raspberry sorbet. The waiter committed it to memory without writing it though some of the staff scribbled it down to tell their friends later.

"I don't suppose, Tolya, you would care for some wine?"

"Pasha, my dear, please do suppose it. You choose."

Demidov beckoned the sommelier. "Vasily, we would like two bottles of your 20ll Pommard 1-er Cru."

"Excellent, sir, Count Demidov."

"Wait, Pasha. Is that a Russian wine?"

"Well Tolya, recent vintages have not been exactly Russian."

"I want Russian wine."

"I see. Let's have the 2021 Pinot Noir Krasnaya Gorka."

Vasily scuttled away with the order as a scalar heterodyne ramped up in Demidov's phone and he gave the codeword.

"Privyet. Do you have the team you need?"

Yes. Small and reliable. Good types and without suspicion. I do not believe you'll have to send me anything. We have stumbled into a situation where we should be able to procure untraceable hardware for work in the mountains.

"And your home base?"

We have a good headquarters close to operations. The team will manage everything from there. I believe our cover is good too. Pizza for everyone.

"Okay. Call me in ninety days exactly, at the same time. In the meantime, call Rybakov and establish your authority as his handler. Berate him. Show dissatisfaction. I don't care. You choose. Make him feel the power. He will perform better if he thinks his status is in jeopardy."

Demidov closed his phone with satisfaction. The New Mexico gambit was proceeding nicely, and he had just bought himself some insurance. If Rybakov messed up in his Saskatchewan assignment, the blame would rest with the handler, and not with Pavel. His phone rang again immediately, and he flipped it open in irritation. Protocol was broken by the call back. The voice surprised him. It was his adjutant from FSB headquarters.

"Sir, this is corporal Maltsev. I apologize for the intrusion, but I have just had a strange call on the station's secure line to your office extension. I thought it might be important. It was just a short message but mechanical, you know, like an electronically generated tone. The voice asked to speak to Mr. White. I thought it might be code but it's not in the code book and …"

"Stop. Stop. Yes. A high-level code. Used once and done. Thank you corporal. You did the right thing."

Gaduka! Pridurok! No deal. Gunderson has refused the engagement. Then it is a question of which wolf will win. If Rybakov can't handle McCord, sad for him, but that is one less eidetic mind risking Russia's secrets. If he snuffs McCord, one less major adversary. Yet,,, Pavel, you are stupid. In this, Firsov has given you a lesson. His heart has taught him everything Russian is the best. Why jeopardize Rybakov before he has done his work on the transports. As if our ancient Mother was a stranger to sudden death by misadventure. Scratch a Russian, find an assassin. And even if we are implicated in McCord's death, perhaps that is a good thing. It is time we remind the west the Russian bear has teeth.

The accordion from the salon was louder and more up-tempo now and Firsov started awake. Vasily stepped smoothly to the table and poured the wine. A quick sideways glance at Demidov gave it away. His longtime server had pasted the Russian Pinot Noir Krasnaya label on the bottles of the 2011 Pommard 1-er Cru. It was a sin in the world of wine, but exceptions must be made in times of trouble.

The second bottle went down more easily than the first. Firsov gloated at the excellence of the Russian wine and began to move to the tempo of the accordion and stomp his feet under the table.

"Careful there, Tolya, you'll break something."

"Heh, maybe so. Particularly in these shoes. I need boots. Good old style valenki."

Director Firsov walked through the crowd looking at feet.

"Boots. Who has boots? Anyone?"

There were no prospects. He ran into Vasily on the way back and ordered two more bottles of that Russian wine.

"Pasha, imagine that. It is disgusting. One hundred Russians gathered together and no boots."

The dinner satisfied the inner man and Demidov walked Firsov to his car where they kissed each other goodbye on the cheeks. Pavel and the driver bullied Firsov's bulk into the back seat of the limousine and strapped him in. Demidov scrolled the contacts in his phone as the limousine taillights disappeared into the traffic, then tapped autodial.

Aleksandr Bulgakov fumbled along the night table without the benefit of his reading glasses and picked up his land line on the sixth ring.

"Swine! Idiot! Do you know what time it is?"

"Aleksa. My dear friend. What a fine hello on a fine morning. And yes, I do know what time it is, it is precisely 2:47 a.m. Besides, I am told the SVR never sleeps. This is Demidov."

"Pasha! Sorry, so sorry. I couldn't read the screen. Could whatever this is not wait until morning?"

"Well, I did wait until morning and here we are. Listen. I need one of your men. Do you have a top man, a star, in Western Canada?"

"You cannot have one of my men. The Russian external intelligence service is not your plaything. Your role is not what you think it is. Content yourself with being the growling reprobate we all know and love. Stop with the intrigue. If you had one of my men, you might just have him exterminate the king of Siam and Russia is on the hook. No. No man."

"For one thing, there is no such place called Siam, it is now Thailand, and second, their king Vajiralongkorn is a good boy deserving of a long life. As usual, I have had to do your job for you, and you can spare me one man. You have what, two thousand agents in the Americas?"

"No, the number is actually two thousand seven hundred and twenty-five. In Canada, two hundred and fourteen."

"Good. Then it is settled. The target is an ex CSIS agent who has positioned himself inside the Bennu probe mission. Already he has blown the cover of one of the men we have planted there. He is a formidable opponent and quite capable of unraveling our entire operation. He has demolished our enterprises in the past. His name is Frank McCord, and he works as a private investigator in Abernathy Town British Columbia. The dossier you have for him is well-worn. Who is the sharpest man in the Vancouver area?"

Aleksandr hated what he was hearing. He had three thousand men in America, yet one eighty-year-old dinosaur megalomaniac had uncovered a threat warning his army of spies had missed. He also hated Demidov's ongoing presumption of authority, yet once again it proved useful.

"Alright. I do have what you call a star, a generational talent in all respects. A young man with an old head. Totally imperturbable. Code name, Malta. He works as an on-call driver out of Langley township. Food delivery, quick trips to the airport, that sort of thing. Any time day or night he can enter any neighborhood, slowing and watching and looking as if for an address. He is the man to dispatch McCord. And as far as you are concerned, your excellency Count Demidov, you are out of it from this moment. However, make no mistake, he is not sitting idle hoping to be at the great Demidov's fingertips. He is in deep cover. If it is Malta you must have, then you must wait. His specific situation may continue for some time, perhaps eighteen months. If you have an urgent need, he is out of the picture."

Demidov understood McCord's intrusion worried Rybakov but the first opportunity for any interference by him was at the return of the samples, some years hence. In this Pavel could be patient.

"Well, it pleases the great Demidov to demonstrate his largess by acceding to your timetable. Consider the McCord operation to be on the back burner yet still cooking. However, whilst code name Malta is delivering his packages he might reconnoiter McCord's haunts, habits and most exposed situations, might he not? Of course, I leave these tactical things to you, you are the expert. And Aleksa, thank you for this. You are doing the right thing despite your anthill of agents having missed the threat altogether. You are welcome. ”

Aleksandr Bulgakov slammed down the receiver, feeling like a servant. Some people were built for power and majesty and when Demidov was gone, Aleksandr knew Russia would be diminished.

Chapter Twelve

My trench coat was fresh from the cleaners, and I stepped out into the world feeling good. I had cut myself just once while shaving and the small sticky paper on my chin was a nice adornment. A lowering sun cast the street into shadow and the heat radiating from the stone buildings loosened my joints. The day was beautiful and hot after nine consecutive days of rain and the hamsters were out in force, walking, talking, congenial and effusive.

They nodded hello to everyone, and I heard a timid 'Frank' as they passed me by. I enjoyed hearing it and picked up my pace, invigorated and more confident in my quest. It was time to test the waters with Fran and I carried ammunition to help me. I had not been able to decide which was best, so I carried three goodies in a mesh bag. I toted chocolates, flowers purchased from a street vendor on the way, and a bottle of Black Bush Irish whiskey with a nice red bow stuck on it. The trick was to gain access to present them. Fran was a tough lady when she was riled up.

Runoff drained to the sea between the cobbles and wherever a stone was missing, the hole brimmed with water. The second I saw it I knew what was going to happen. The delivery truck was fifty feet away coming downhill toward me and I had no place to go. The front tire hit the void left by a missing stone, followed one half second later by the rear tire hitting it again. A perfect storm of dark oily sludge painted my coat from top to bottom and blasted gunk through the mesh and into my bag of goodies. One by one I fished them out of the saturated mess and began wiping with my hand. The chocolate box was fine, just a bit of oil had absorbed into the wrapping. I turned the flowers upside down with a shake and other than breaking the stalks of a couple of those with heavy heads, they were fine. The Black Bush Irish was another story. The curls of the red bow were filled with slush. I unstuck it, shook it and let it slip, lunged after it to catch it and stepped on it and flattened it. I stuck it nicely back on the bottle. It was flat and a rather strange color, but it looked good. I swung the bag to let the air dry the contents as I strode uphill.

Fran's apartment was two blocks north and three blocks east in an upscale area. It was treed and green and manicured and the galoot with the muddy coat and string bag was as welcome there as a weed. I had not called ahead, and the element of surprise was on my side. I smiled into the black dome of the entrance door surveillance camera and pressed Fran's buzzer. Warmth exuded from her intercom.

"Good lord! You!"

"Ah. I knew you would be happy to see me. Buzz me up."

"Go away, Frank."

"But Fran, I come on bended knee even in a standing position. I come to apologize, compromise and otherwise lavish you with gifts. See, here they swing in a designer string bag. Even the holes are designer. Shapely."

"Idiot."

I waited, nothing, then the buzz to release the front door and things were looking up. I heard the unlocking of her door as I reached it. She swung it open and made with the duck lips and she looked terrific.

"McCord, you are filthy! Step inside and do not move. Stay right where you are. Take your coat off and drop it beside you. And your shoes. Take them off."

"Please note that my pants are very muddy also."

Fran disdained my version of foreplay and went for the menagerie in my bag, retrieved the Black Bush Irish, walked toward the cabinet containing her whiskey glasses and her combative posture was gone. As usual she asked a question I could not answer.

"Frank, what took you so long?"

<>

Robin Hathaway thumped the cooler of beer down on the floor-safe and the dust spiraled up through a slat of sunlight. He sat down cross-legged, cracked open a can and slid the cooler toward Nigel and Sanjay with his foot.

"Okay boys, pull up a pew and help yourself. Sanjay, time to stop with the slip knots and rope some stock. Things are sliding too loose for me. I came here with you and Cousin Nigel to palaver with some bangtails and whatever else comes with that. I don't deal in cheese and pepperoni and I ain't interested in barkin' at a knot. Quit beatin' the devil around the stump and spill it. "

Sanjay reached for a brew, popped the top and half drained it. The time was right. The back room of the Argentum Bank became the executive suite and the steel door of the floor safe became the boardroom table and Sanjay was the president of the corporation. He was irrepressible.

"Gentlemen, here is what we're going to do, and Nigel I have you to thank for the inspiration. Robin, some of what I'm going to say, Nigel already knows but you need the background. We two worked at the Cosmos Space Center. Our project was to bring back samples from an asteroid called Bennu and land them safely in Utah. The project cost billions and the progress of the rocket launch was watched by the news, tracked by satellites, monitored by every spy agency worldwide and surveyed by the United States military. The package which is coming back to us in September 2023 is like a small microwave in size and on one sunny afternoon, it will land by parachute on flat ground with the world watching, and we, to use Nigel's phrases, are going to liberate the sample module from their influence, nick it, swipe it, purloin it, in plain English, steal it."

"I see. While the world watches and the United States military converges on it, we will steal it. Did you know about this Nigel? "

"No Robin, nothing. Sanjay, you are nuts. When you and I made our little jokes about this, you were going to carry off your captive in a baby carriage and speed into the foothills in a cloud of dust. That seems a little tricky with a fleet of military helicopters and a battalion of soldiers on the spot. Isn't the drill once they retrieve it, they'll fly it under guard by helicopter to the local base, then immediately by military aircraft to Houston? Sanjay, that chain of custody is impenetrable."

"Absolutely right. Except, that's not the true sequence in the chain of custody. It's what the public will be told, it's what the rank and file of the air force believe, but it's not what they're going to do. The chairman of the joint chiefs of staff is Army. He has finagled to take over security from the Air Force and make a show of it for recruiting purposes. An army gun ship will certainly fly the canister from its resting spot in Utah to the local base but from there, it is the army's baby. This is not speculation. I have seen the Army's confidential report, chapter and verse. Nigel, you are skeptical."

"Come on, Sanjay. Don't take the piss. You do not travel at that level of security clearance. That is reserved for Rybakov and Macbeth and the lot."

"Ah. You have forgotten Leishman. He has absolutely no concept of rules or protocol. Formulae, e-mail, top-secret updates, weather reports, they are all the same to him. They go into the pile. I took a stack home as usual to work on in my flat, and in among the schematics and formulae of the day he had shuffled the paperwork from the army. So what was a boy to do? I read them all, the plans, the route, and the timing, and slipped them back into the mix the next day. The data is safely stored."

He tapped his right temple and winked.

"In here."

Robin and Nigel cackled nervously at the absurdity of the idea juxtaposed against the seriousness with which Sanjay presented it. He did not get their little joke.

"Boys, unbelievably, this is what they are going to do. The army is going to make a spectacle of their involvement in the program by transporting the capsule to Houston in a convoy of eight tarpaulin covered trucks along the identical route we used to get here. Right through the Sangre De Cristo mountains."

Robin had a bit of a twinkle about the prospect, but Nigel shook his head in disbelief.

"Sanjay, this is ridiculous. I suppose we're going to stampede twenty horses along the trail, stir up the dust and while it settles, grab the samples and make off into the night. That of course, is after we inspect the trucks one by one to find the capsule."

"Nigel, you have anticipated me. We need a thermal imaging device. The capsule has its own cooling system, and they will augment it in the truck which carries it. It's a dead giveaway. The heat signature of the target vehicle will be significantly cooler. Also, it is never the first or last truck as they are too vulnerable. Robin, without explosives, can you start a slide from a scramble like the one we saw?"

"Mostly yes. Once I see where the keystone is, a couple of pry bars into the compacted stuff below it will do in most cases, but you have to tie yourself off and swing clear or you go down the mountain like one more boulder and that's the end."

"Pry bars. Reasonable for serious rockhounds I think. From now on, that's our hobby. We will scout every inch of the route for the right place for slides. Ideally, we will block the road with heavy slide debris both in front and behind the couple of trucks around the samples. They will be travelling thirty-five, maybe forty miles an hour. You can bet that everything will be by the book for this maneuver, so according to military strategy they will be spaced about a hundred yards apart. There are no turnarounds and no pull offs. The convoy will be trapped for hours. However, we need to act while the dust cloud from the rock fall is dense. Robin, if it's a good slide, how much time do you think we might have before the dust settles?"

"At least ten minutes if she's a good one. We'll need goggles and face masks to work in it."

Sanjay smiled to himself. Robin had just used 'we'.

"Boys, we have to build a corral for the horses without swapping. Fencing and fence posts are the type of things people will remember and connect them to us."

"Won't be hard. Mind you, I'll have to track the mustang trails here for a while to see what's best, but yes, there's a way. I have seen the Stoney-Nakoda people in the foothills along the Brazos River in Alberta do it. The territory is not much different than here, but up there, there was a might more water. The Stoneys would scout out a small dead-end canyon, you know, three sided and simply pile brush and maybe the odd tree washed down by a flood as a barrier across the open end. The bangtails won't test it as long as they have company, though if they get spooked on the scent of a lion, they might break out. But if silver mining was as big around here as I hear tell, there's bound to be plenty of shoring and timber to scavenge from the odd tunnel. Who knows what else. But let's not speed ahead on takin' bad medicine. Strikes me the military and about every three-letter killer with a badge will be lookin' to stretch our necks. Yep, they'll be a mite perturbed. Nigel, never thought a Hathaway'd turn out to be an owlhoot."

"Nor me Robin. Sanjay, an owlhoot is an outlaw. What about it. What is your take?"

"There is no question in ordinary circumstance we could be looking at jail time if we are caught. But as I see it, this circumstance is far from ordinary. Something vastly different is going on. Something definitely off the books. Understand what this whole thing really is to the military. It is some nerds from the Cosmos Space Center getting their jollies by shooting off one more rocket and grabbing some debris from an asteroid. From the perspective of the army, we are just another useless group draining money away from building monster bombs. The military hates us.

But with this little sampler, they are all excited. They have a special interest in it, and they are playing it cozy. If they had even a tacit legitimate connection to the OSIRIS-REx project they would be attempting to take credit for the entire program. I have read every document and every contract pertaining to our work and the military has no standing anywhere. Yet that cannister contains something they want, and it's not the samples. Whatever the army has done, it has been done without the knowledge of Dr. Macbeth or Dr. Rybakov. The only additional person with a high security status is Leishman, and he's too crazy to collaborate with anyone except perhaps for a buddy lurking among his multiple personalities. What the army has done is sabotage under the charter of the Space Force, and I will legitimately claim it rises to the level of espionage."

"Come on, Sanjay, do you actually believe the state department is going to charge the United States army with espionage against the United States?"

"Of course not, Nigel, but for recruitment purposes the transport of the samples will have daylight media coverage for three days with all the pageantry and drama the army can muster. Imagine the effect on recruitment if a whistleblower prosecutes a charge of espionage against the army. And more embarrassing, an army with a hundred-and-seventy-five-billion-dollar budget has allowed a group of amateur rockhounds to steal their billion-dollar cargo without firing a shot. How's that for boosting the image? Anyway, if it should come to charges, I am alone on the hook. You two are now officially independent contractors. Nigel, you were contracted to build battery operated GPS units designed to fit a horse harness and you built them. As far as you knew, I was making some cockamamie new method of training horses. Robin, you too are an independent contractor. I asked you to build a corral and harness up the horses and as stipulated in the work order, you built a corral and harnessed up the horses. Both of you sent me invoices in due course and why the man with the loose screws wanted the work done was not remotely interesting to either of you."

Robin cracked open a second beer and shifted his seat.

"Sanjay, I think we have a problem. This is the first I've heard of harnessing. I can do everything, anything, with the bangtails. But I see you are built to run hot, non-stop one thousand miles an hour in your head and that's not how horses work. It has to be slow, repetitious, one horse by one horse with care and consideration of temperament. It takes time. Almost like therapy. There's the anxious ones, the fearful ones and the ones who want to fight. Every mustang different from the last one. "

"I don't suppose they make horse Prozac."

"In a way, yeah, they do. Horses are like people in so many ways. Their brains need magnesium just like us to keep them easy and fine. Stables these days make sure they have plenty of that in the feed. "

"Robin, for my plan, we need to be able to get close to the horses, at least you do. Not ride or saddle them but close by, working around them. When I say harness, I just mean a loop of cord or strap to carry a GPS unit. No girth, no breast collar, no headgear."

"That's a different story. A gentle pat, a little stroking of the neck and it's attached."

"Excellent. Here's how I see the full deal. First, the pizza. It is certainly a front, but it is going to be a real business. The swap meet is a bonus I didn't count on, with a million customers half an hour away for the entire winter. We three will set up the ovens and the front counter and such to get it going but once set up, we'll have the usual staff of young people to do the running and making the pizzas. Robin, you will be off doing your thing with the horses. If you need help, that's Nigel and me, but otherwise that's your area. We have roughly three years of preparation. Do you think you can build a herd of let's say twenty-five to thirty mustangs in that time? Precisely, by September 2023?"

"Yes, Sanjay, I can do what you're asking. But it seems to me we're a lot like the man what builds a boat in his basement. It's a perfect boat but it's never gonna see water. We're kidnappers right? Like any kidnapping, there's a ransom payment. That means a moment of contact when the goods are exchanged for the money. That moment is what kills it and when the kidnappers get their brains blown out. Remember, this is the army we're dealing with. Subtlety and negotiation is chickenshit to them. It's not in their manual. Worse, some of these young fellas haven't pointed their rifles at a real live target in five years. They'd fill us full of lead just as soon as spit a chaw."

"That is exactly right but we're not going to be within ten miles of the transfer point. This part of New Mexico is riddled with abandoned mines. The exchange will take place within one of those. Nigel, with your background in the British special forces I'm sure you're familiar with Semtex."

"Of course. Every man's explosive. The farmer blasting stumps, the miner, commercial demolition, the saboteur. I used it many times. Commercial blasting, of course. In this region given the mining and rockslide clearing roadwork, I'm sure I could acquire it. There's nothing you can't find in a million people. But now we are getting serious. Semtex is a killer. Why?"

"We're going to attach the explosive to the canister. The trigger to create the explosion is a mercury switch connected to a battery. What that means Robin, is if they decide to take the samples without paying, if the canister is tipped, moved or vibrated before we receive payment, the Semtex will detonate and pulverize the samples into dust."

"How much money we talkin'?"

"One billion dollars U.S."

"That's nice. I can get my boots half-soled. How do we get the money? "

"The ransom will be deposited in advance, in divided sums to multiple Bitcoin wallets held by each of us. Bitcoin can be sold anonymously to any one of a million buyers or it can be spent by us like regular dollars from a trackless ledger. There is literally nothing which cannot be purchased directly with Bitcoin from the right seller. We need to be smart and gentle with the money. I propose using it as an annuity. Just a nice living wage yearly for at least ten years. No flashy cars, no ostentatious lifestyles. In the meantime we will become pizza kings. Yes Nigel? "

"Sanjay, I'm all for the annuity."

Robin nodded.

"But Sanjay, getting paid doesn't stop the mercury switch. In other words, it's not a good idea to blow up the people who just paid you. I can build a gate into the system to shut off the circuit to the Semtex. I will position a tone generator at the mouth of the mine shaft. A tone generator transmits sound at whatever frequency you need, in this case, a frequency which will open the gate on the wire leading to the Semtex. I will activate the generator remotely by calling it with a burner phone. It's an easy setup. That being said, there's another matter. Robin, when I was with you up on the Chilcotin, some of those horses were a problem to handle even in good light. All we would need is for one of them to go haywire in the dark and spook the lot. "

"No worries there, Nigel. Bangtails thrive in the lowest light. With those big eyes they can run full bore over the trickiest footing without a moon above them and never miss a step. Night is where they see best. And you're right, sometimes a rogue will stir things up but I'll cut 'im out long before he's a problem. We'll have the time."

"Robin, have you trained horses with a whistle? I read it's been done in Europe as a tradition. "

"No, Sanjay, I haven't done that training but I know about it. Circuses in Hungary, Romania, Bulgaria and such used it in the old days, and it sticks. Two blasts on the whistle for this trick, three blasts for that trick and so on. Horses are smart and along with that they like to please. They can sense when you are pleased. It works like this. Suppose there are three trails leading from a corral. Blow the whistle once and lead the horse along trail one. Repeat that for five days in a row. Blow the whistle and lead them. The sixth day, just blow the whistle once and your horse will take that trail. No guidance, no coaxing, no nothing, he will please you by taking the trail. Blow the whistle twice for trail two, blow the whistle three times for trail three. Show him a hundred trails, he will remember them all and head off to run them if he gets the signal, and the horse hears it from as far away as two miles with perfect directional understanding."

"You know, you two are each other's worst enemy. Now you've agreed we should blow whistles. If we haven't been spotted, let's blow some whistles. That should fix things."

Sanjay and Robin laughed, and Robin tossed Nigel a beer.

"Here Nigel, this'll do you good. These whistles are like dog whistles, only higher I think. That's right isn't it, Sanjay?"

"Yes, higher than dog whistles. Altogether quiet to our ears, but someplace above 25,000 Hz."

Robin's head snapped to alert toward the side window. The smell of perfume hit them first then a footfall in the graveled side lane stopped the talk. Robin's memory of the fragrance told the story.

"Daisy. Hey, Daisy love. Daisy. Come on in. Pull up a piece of floor and have a beer."

Daisy Plantagenet appeared in the doorway all smiles and shine and cowgirl glitter.

"Hi boys, no thanks, there's a truck with a load for you coming a few hundred yards behind me. He has your pizza ovens. Seems his trip indicator has outdated maps. Your Riffle Street used to be called Argentum Road and that's what he was looking for. He stopped into the real estate office, figured I would know the territory and I do. Anyway, I hear the truck out front and he's all yours. Have fun. Bye Robin. "

Robin beamed while Nigel matched the bill of lading against contents. The eight crates lined the wall of the bank.

The day was cooling, and with prodding from Robin the trio locked up and walked east away from the sun.

"Boys, you two are looking mighty soft. None of this is gonna work if you don't get with it. Climbing these sliding scrambles hour after hour in a hundred-degree heat is as tough as it gets and you ain't tough. We have some time, and it starts now."

Sanjay brought up the rear and puffed along behind the other two.

"There is something that should set you more at ease about what we're doing. The army will be tracking the trucks and specifically the GPS locator on the canister. Usually it is accurate to the foot, but not always. In some places feedback is distorted, and even multiple false locations are displayed. One of those places is in the Sangre De Cristo mountains. Narrow canyons and angled surfaces like we have here will bounce signals around. Second, the area is loaded with magnetite. That can create confusion in the signal as well. Third and this is most important, I have calculated where the earth orbiting satellites will be the second night the convoy is in the mountains. Not only is it going to be a moonless night, but the angle of the satellites to this location will be very low. It couldn't be better for us. For a GPS receiver to give a position, it has to contact satellites, usually three and preferably four of them. In this valley, surrounded by mountains, at least one of the satellites, maybe two will be at such a low angle it will be useless or misinterpret the data. Signals will be bouncing everywhere. Still, they might be able to track within one hundred yards. ”

Nigel shook his head vehemently.

“Sanjay, this is nuts! They will immediately tag the only GPS signal leaving that hundred-yard radius, and that will be us lugging away the canister and they’ll be on us in one minute. Brilliant.”

“Brilliant indeed. Because mon vieux, you being the most athletic of us, will have wrapped our little darling in the lead sheath you have so eagerly volunteered to carry down the mountain. Et voila, no telltale signal from the canister. Has either of you taken delivery of anything in the last couple of days?”

Nigel nodded.

“Yesterday around 5:00 p.m. Two parcels addressed to ‘Argentum Refined Pizza’ were sat against the front door when I arrived. I locked them in the shed. I thought it might be the circuit boards I ordered for the rewiring of the building, but the boxes were too light. I was going to mention it when we were done with this. They had international transit stamps on them. Italy, Panama, San Diego.”

“Good. Very good. They contain shielding material identical to that of the original canister. Between now and the time for action I shall make the quintessential replica of the sample container, correct to the millimeter and the gram, including a GPS device to make the watchers happy in their tracking. Nigel, your high temperature oven will duplicate the scarring of the reentry burn in discoloration of the canister’s surface. Into the truck goes the replica and out comes the original covered with Nigel’s lead blanket. It will take some experimentation, but we have time. When the dust settles, the truck detail will check on the load and relax. Meanwhile, we are beetling the real thing away into the abandoned silver mine shaft yet to be chosen. That is, one of you two will be doing the beetling. It weighs 90 pounds. What, Nigel? ”

“Sanjay, you want us using thermal infrared sensors to pinpoint which truck carries the samples. The military’s airborne surveillance apparatus will be doing the same thing. Our infrared heat tracks will give us away as we move away from the convoy. And another thing. I don't understand why we need one bleeding horse let alone a flaming herd."

"Nigel, I understand that there are ways to spoof a location with a local radio transmission to override weak GPS signals and make the target appear to be a thousand miles from where he is. But as you commented there are still heat signatures to mask. Two mustangs will take the same trail as us. The balance of the herd will be sauntering in 25 different directions through rills and clefts, each one of them carrying a GPS, bouncing signals everywhere and tracking hot on the infrared sensors. We will not stand out. The guys on the monitors will lose their minds. The mustangs will continue past the mouth of the mine shaft, and we will nip inside, out of sight and out of surveillance."

Robin had listened quietly, leaving the technicalities to the experts, and digesting the overall plan.

"I am a bit of a mush-head when it comes to that technical stuff but there's one thing outstanding. What about the four soldiers guarding the samples in the truck?"

Nigel answered quickly.

"I spent eight years in clandestine operations. I know how men behave and how they think in certain situations. My life, and the life of my men depended upon it. This scenario is similar to war scenario. Consider those four men. Picture their situation. Unexpectedly the convoy was stopped. The noise of the slides was deafening. From inside the truck it would sound like ordnance. Shelling, improvised explosive device, mortar fire. Looking out, dense smoke or dust or explosive residue makes visibility impossible. Sanjay, you said there would be no moon. The darkness would be impenetrable. They have no orders for this. This was to be a media spectacle and here they are under fire. Suddenly, an authoritarian voice throws back the flap. *You men. You two to the front of the line. You two to the rear truck position. Let no one enter the column from the roadway. Double time. Move it. I will take this post.*

I have been an officer in action. I know how it works when men have had the burden of decision removed. They are primed to receive orders and a strong officer satisfies their need. They will obey the command and feel safer by acting. However, should they declare they must stay with their assignment, the officer salutes, closes the flap, whistles to his friends to hit the road, and lives to make pizza another day."

<>

Billy Stonebreaker downshifted his old Dodge pickup and smoked to a stop, with the weight of the twelve-foot riffle table he towed behind him giving him a little shove. He pushed down the foot brake and shifted into neutral. He had made some profit working the tailings of the abandoned Dead Creek Mine and he was headed into Lapida to sell it. He reckoned he had about 10 ounces of silver and a scrap of gold. It wasn't much but it would pay for a new tire. He had crept down the incline in low gear when in the last turn he felt a tail swing in the truck. The table trailer had chattered a bit out of line on the loose gravel and it would jack-knife if he didn't straighten up. He was about five miles out of town when he saw the dust just over the edge of the downslope shielding the next turn. A rumble rattled his rolled-down driver's side window and the dust blossomed into a plume a couple hundred feet high. It continued growing and he knew the earmarks. It was a rockslide for sure and a big one and he doubted he could get through. He opened his glove box and retrieved his shortwave and in its habit it was dead. It had seemed to be a good idea to have a solar rechargeable radio but having it in the glove box somehow didn't recharge it. A bright color caught his eye coming out of the dust high to the left. Three men followed the height of the contours leading down to road level, skidding and sliding down with rock debris filling the trail they made. He was surprised at having company. The stretch of road went nowhere important in both directions and you sure as hell did not walk it.

"What you fellas doin' way the hell out here? This is mighty dry territory."

Then he remembered the pickup truck off to the side three or four miles back. He noticed their packs and the rock hammers in Nigel and Robin's belts and the other fella carried a pry bar.

"Prospecting? Not much to find up there, you know? Better to follow the creek beds."

Sanjay answered for them.

"No, No, nothing like that. I guess you could call us fossil hounds. Lots of fossils in this canyon. We heard the rumble, and we missed getting bulldozed by two or three seconds. Funny what you think, though. Half ton boulders were bouncing past my hips, and I thought. 'Ah, good. A new layer of shale to explore.'"

"You boys were might lucky. That your Datsun back there?"

"Uh huh. Sometimes we find ourselves five miles away before we know it, if we start following a nice intrusion, you know, an area that looks likely to have something. Couple spots up there with no shale covering. We followed a line where it changed color from a grey green into a red and before we knew it here we are. Not much limestone though. That usually confirms it's a place to spend time."

"I see you boys have a couple walkie talkies. Good idea. Get separated out here and it could be trouble. Everything looks pretty much the same and it's nothing to look at besides. The weather changes in a second in these parts so the weather reports and the emergency broadcasts come in handy."

"Yes, we were told they might keep us out of trouble. You know, you are really lucky to live in the Sangre De Cristo mountains. The main body of the Sangres is composed of Permian-Pennsylvanian rock. That's a mixture of igneous intrusions, shale and conglomerates. Certain regions of pre-Cambrian rock rose during the Colorado Orogeny, a billion years ago. That's why we can find remains of lungfish, plants, and xenacanthid sharks."

"Gotcha. You folks from New York?"

"No. Not new York."

"Hmm. Thought you might be. Say, let me use one of your walkie talkies. Need to call Sheriff Calderone about the slide. He'll get some crews out for the road clearing."

Robin saw the others were stiffening and he handed over his phone with a smile.

"Thanks. Sheriff Calderone, this is Stonebreaker. Rockslide closed Side Road 22 five miles east of Watson Creek. Repeat. Philipe, this is Stonebreaker. Rockslide closed Side Road 22 five miles east of Watson Creek. Over. Out."

"He didn't answer."

"Don't matter. Ten other people listening in will call him and he'll get the message soon enough. I'm going to have to turn around and get the table back to the claim. Spot me, will you boys? Yell out if I'm fishtailing it."

Sheriff Philippe Calderone got the message twice. It was the third slide in two months. That section of road 22 had enough vegetation to stabilize the downslopes. A slide of the size being reported made no sense to him. He had not investigated the previous two but this one, he would walk the scramble.

<>

The room was hot and sleep was slow in coming. Seven hours of climbing in the sun had been exhausting and despite the fatigue he could not sleep. The phone on the bedside table was on vibrate so the ringer would not disturb anyone and in the glow of the streetlight he watched it shimmy across the varnished surface, lying still between rings, then moving at the next vibration. He retrieved it and returned the familiar call sign.

"Privyet."

"How goes the battle?"

"Well, it's going. I think we've made some progress. There's a spirit of cooperation at least. Certainly there's some skepticism yet, but it has evolved to the point where we have agreed to look at solutions. There's at least tacit agreement to consider the proposal as real. No, no one seems to understand the specific interest held by the army in the sampler. You are right. It has evolved into something more serious than an adolescent prank. Yes, thanks, I will. I have been lying here for two hours now without any luck. How is Marscraft coming? That is good. At least you can measure the progress by units produced or items shipped. I will. Goodnight."

He threw up the sash and cool desert air poured in. He breathed deeply, feeling much better as a result of the phone call from Demidov. The strength of the great man seemed to come through the phone line. He knew now he could sleep.

Chapter Thirteen
February 2020

It was the coldest February in fifty years and the steam pipes throughout the building groaned and strained against their retaining brackets, working against the expansion caused by the heat. Passing the heat along to the radiators was another story and they remained cold. I wrapped myself in my buffalo rug and squirmed to ease the stiffness in my shoulders. Something on the floor caught my eye. A silver fish big enough to try on my shoes scuttled toward the closet. Apartment hunting moved from the back of my mind to somewhere in the middle when my filing cabinet startled me with a ring tone from its bottom drawer. A cell phone lived there, where it kept its microwaves to itself. Apparently, it was not yet dead. Being a private detective, I deduced someone was calling me. The phone contained only five contacts and I used it mainly for two factor authentication. Any call was a surprise, and some were more surprising than others, but the name on the screen conjured a history of broken bones and murderous thugs.

"Hello, this is Frank."

"Well, what a surprise, to find Frank on Frank's phone. Dolt. This is Meghan Macbeth."

"How refreshing. Good morning, Meghan. Get up on the wrong side of the web?"

"Don't start. I have a slightly different assignment for you; however, it may not be to your taste. I doubt there will be a need to punch anyone."

"Meghan. So early in the day and already you pejoratize me. Surely you know my preferred modus operandi is intellectual, deductive and reasoned. Then again, a good right cross to the chops adds a certain je ne sais quoi to the equation. One might say an impact."

"Frank, 'pejorative' is the word, it is a noun. The verb' 'pejoratize' is not a word.

"It is, now that I have used it. Frank's word."

"Lovely. Are you free tomorrow? If so, we can discuss the parameters. It has to do with Rybakov. It is unrelated to our previous conversations."

"Hm. That man is as hard as a coffin. Do you want me to come there?"

"No, I'm coming to Abernathy Town in the morning to sign off on my old confidentiality agreements with Petruvia Labs. Let's meet at Morty's at three. I wager he remembers my favorite drink."

"No wager from me. A pretty lady, he remembers the drink. A gin Collins with bitters."

"So, you think I'm pretty?"

"It was a generalization."

"How nice of you. Happy hour is at three p.m."

Morty's place was not full, yet nerds and hamsters did abound, and I led Meghan to the bar, where she preferred to sit. She watched the goings on in the reflection. Morty had replaced his usual array of big band music with early rock and roll from the 1950s. A tall man with expensive shoes followed us to the bar and stood too close to order his drink. He had the self-congratulatory demeanor of a winner, and he looked back and forth between Meghan and me, wondering what catastrophe had forced her into my company. She did not give him a tumble with her eyes, and he moved off for better fishing. I caught Morty's attention and indicated the gentleman with my head.

"He's a new one to me but he has certainly found his niche. He has become studiously aloof."

Morty nodded a pleasant smile of recognition to Meghan and shook his head at my comment.

"Frank, he is too cool to be aloof."

"What?"

"He is too aloof to be cool."

That was not what he said the first time. He wanted me to ask him, and I wanted to ask why he changed but getting deep into something that irrelevant was shallow. I realized then I had become Morty, and I shuddered.

"Mort, was your aloof cool word salad a sample of original thought?"

"Frank, there is no original thought." He reached for the Angostura bitters.

"Hello, Dr. Macbeth. It is a pleasure to see you again. The usual for you?"

"Yes, thank you, Morty."

"Frank?"

"Gin Collins sounds good. I can't remember when I last had one."

"March, four years ago."

Meghan elbowed me.

"He remembered. Apparently he thinks you're pretty."

I was a loser in the battle of wits with this one, so I cut my losses. Morty picked up on his thought.

"Originality of thought is like beauty in art, Frank. It is original or beautiful only in the mind of the beholder, but what is truly an original is the time and opportunity to express it. You know, Dr. Macbeth, it is somewhat like Frank wearing his trench coat. Give it another seventy years and it will be back in style. Everything old is new again."

"Please, call me Meghan."

"No such luck, my dear. The rules of the bar clearly state all prefixes of 'Dr.' must be strictly maintained. You may also have noticed how clearly I speak it to the room. It goes to allay the worries of the hamsters. For a brief time it makes them feel their life spent running on the wheel after something they don't understand has at least a semblance of value. There is a Dr. who comes to the same place they do to have a drink. It encourages positive neurolinguistic reprogramming to heal their psyches."

We carried our drinks to a booth in the back and left Morty to polish his ruminations along with the glassware.

"Meghan, how are things going with the Bennu probe? The last time we spoke, things were nominal, as has become the jargon in the space world for ideal. It's interesting how the meanings of words can be changed so when things go wrong one can say that was not what one meant."

"I agree with you Frank. Weasel words. As far as the Bennu project, the trajectory is nom.. perfect and we wait for the arrival at the surface of the asteroid this October. My concern is the thrusters of the explorer as it leaves the surface to bring back the samples. Dr. Leishman is the expert there and he has no concerns, so I accept that tacitly, but I am the chief of the project and concerns are my business. When the explorer retreats from the asteroid, the thrusters will dislodge maybe one or two tons of surface material, so the overall mass and the configuration of the asteroid will change. They try to cover that little detail by labeling the procedure 'touch and go', TAG they call it, as if the procedure were innocuous, like the children's game. TAG, just a touch, you're it. While they are actually blasting the hell out of the surface. My fear is it will expand the number of key holes."

"As a private investigator, of the ilk which makes its living by looking through keyholes, I should be expert in these matters. What does the 'number of keyholes' mean?"

"Astrophysicists have pet names for many things, and keyholes is one of them and I'll get to that. The background is, watching an asteroid for years gives us extreme accuracy about the orbit within a very small margin of error. We follow where it has been and continue to look at it, orbit after orbit, and plot the information. We then say with a high degree of confidence, that is the orbit."

"How nice."

"Yes, nice, except for one minor glitch. Every time the asteroid comes near the earth, our gravity kicks it into a new, entirely different orbit. The old orbit data is no longer valid, and we start from scratch. Fortunately, we have a reliable formula which uses the velocity of the asteroid and the closeness to the center of the earth to estimate what the next orbit will be. Because of that, with the current fly-by of Bennu we were within a few hundred kilometers in our estimate of where it would be. In terms of the enormity of space, that was right on, because we knew the speed of Bennu. After the blast of the thrusters which will change both its mass and the shape of its surface, we have no idea what the velocity of Bennu will be."

"Meghan, I am not feeling better."

"That brings us to the keyholes. As a result of changing its mass and its shape, the next time Bennu comes this close it might pass through that very narrow corridor where the earth's gravity will throw it into a path to hit us the next time around. In astrodynamics, we call that corridor the keyhole. The odds are low but given the changes we are making to the asteroid we have no idea whether it's going to go through a keyhole or not. There are bundles of keyholes which will accommodate the specific trajectory to impact us. "

"So, Meghan, the asteroid will behave just like a spitball."

"Spitball?"

"Yes. Like a spitball. In the old days, in baseball, spitballs were legal, and the batters couldn't hit them. The pitchers hawked a good one and spit on the ball. The spit on the surface of the ball made the trajectory wonky and unpredictable."

"Spitballs. I see."

Meghan's drink was empty and after my fractured analogy she deserved

another. I waved to Morty and in a trice our second gin Collins with bitters arrived. A quick sip of the tart coldness stabbed our foreheads.

"What do you know about asteroids, Morty?"

"Very little, although I did see a headline last week about an asteroid hitting earth, and I just pray it doesn't hit Peru."

"Peru? Why?"

"If it does, well, that's it for all of us. The alpacalypse."

"Thank you Morty. Meghan, how often does Bennu get close?"

"Approximately six years. But remember, even if our calculations show we are in trouble, it takes us about five years to get there to do something about it. We told the public Bennu would not hit the earth and we were right, but now, who knows. All bets are off. And I use the term 'bets' advisedly."

"Hmm. Can we move the earth instead?"

"Believe it or not, Frank, about ten years ago United States Congress asked us to work on that. It's theoretically possible, and it would only take us a million years to do it."

"The warranty on my Buick will expire by then. It is obvious you did not have input on some of this. Could it be that someone had an additional agenda outside the mission statement? Such as contriving an unscheduled test to see how much effect it has on Bennu's orbit?"

"Frank, I have a team. In that team are experts with specific backgrounds which set them apart and I do not micromanage them. What you say is possible. Leishman had been obdurate in his demands for the thruster size but even Rybakov and young Rustom agreed with the modification. Now the consensus is to have the Bennu probe carry on and blast the surface of Apophis in the same way to expose a deeper layer."

"Apophis, that's the one passing by us very closely in 2029 isn't it? Coming between the earth and the moon?"

"Yes. I believe I told you I am going to South America to view it firsthand with the naked eye. Its orbit is 344 days, so it goes by about once a year, but very rarely this close. "

"Meghan, a dozen disaster movies over fifty years have blasted an asteroid which threatened Earth out of orbit to save the planet from destruction. We can do that, yes?"

"Anything concocted in those films is as good as what we have at the moment. Almost any attempt to deflect an asteroid presumes years of advanced knowledge, allowing time to build an explosive device or a pusher of some kind and deliver it to the site. In 2004 NASA spotted the asteroid XP14. It was in a particularly juicy spot for study by radar, speeding along at about 17 kilometers per second. They recorded their observations and then moved on. The next time it was discovered was 2006, one week before it reached earth, as close to us as the moon. So you tell me whether we have a good grip on things."

It was evident the only thing we could rely upon was decent odds. It also occurred to me that with unbridled viciousness traveling the world like a contagious disease, it was just as well we did not have the mechanics to deflect an asteroid. With private rocket corporations and space exploration games played by unbalanced oligarchs, one of them might decide to move an asteroid not away from disaster, but into its keyhole. *Hurry, hurry, step right up. Win the bid and obliterate the city of your choice with a suitably sized asteroid. Moscow? What am I bid? Washington, London, going once, going twice. Do I hear a trillion?*

Thoughts of mayhem brought me back to the task at hand and the reason for our meeting. Meghan had suggested to me in her phone call the target of my engagement was Sergei Rybakov. In general terms that was fine with me except it did not fall within the conditions of my current employment contract. Anything up close and personal with Rybakov raised the stakes dramatically. He was brilliant, a trained killer in peak physical condition and he was primed to tear me up. We had the measure of each other, and I could not tangle with him on his terms. It would be the better strategist who came out the other side alive.

"Meghan, what do you need from me concerning Rybakov?"

"Have you been to northern Saskatchewan in February? That is where he is. North of Prince Albert, on the Canadian shield plateau. Right now I think the temperature is about -25 Celsius in Regina so considering the two thousand feet of elevation on the plateau, about -30."

"Never fear, I have my buffalo rug. Why is it a problem he is there?"

"Rybakov is in this country on a restricted activity permit within the space agency. I am its head. His function with me was to integrate major Russian components of the rocket engines into the launch vehicle. That assignment is completed, to be reactivated only after the return of the Bennu samples. Somehow, his visa has been expanded to an 'at large' presence in the country. He is living in one of the staff Quonset huts at the Marscraft assembly line construction site. Worse, he is still officially in Canada under my auspices. I need to know what he's doing for my own protection and to protect the integrity of the Bennu program. And the space agency."

"I understand your problem, and now you need to understand mine. If I come up against Rybakov, our backgrounds will inevitably lead us to something deadly. I am not speaking figuratively; I mean it literally. Rybakov does not fall within my current contract with you. That contract is to do an investigation and analysis of the security breach in your whiteboard room. To show my good faith, I will begin some background work until new letters of engagement are processed. All expenses will be paid, and my rate is double my current per diem. Once executed, the contract may be canceled unilaterally by either party with a one week's written notice to the respective address. My present contract with the space agency will run concurrently. To show your good faith in return, you will e-transfer fifteen thousand dollars Canadian to my bank account as a signing bonus. Agreed? Meghan. Look at me. Smile, Meghan. Okay. Here is the sweetener. If he kills me, you may have my Buick."

Meghan smiled in a way to make the cat which swallowed the canary envious.

"Macbeth. What's the joke?"

"McCord, oh McCord, never mind. Done. Let's shake on it."

We sealed the deal in the booth and ordered steaks. Meghan selected a bottle of

2016 Cakebread Cellars Cabernet Sauvignon from Napa Valley and Morty poured. The strip sirloins were perfect, the wine was luxurious, and the overhead speakers reclaimed civilization as Glenn Miller's 'Moonlight Cocktails' moved across the floor.

"Come on Frank, I want to dance."

She took me by surprise, and it was exactly what I wanted to do. I had never seen her from this vantage point, this close, and her eyes which were usually blue looked green in the subdued light.

"You know Meghan, you have eyes made for dancing."

"Thank you. You know Frank, I would have paid you double what you asked."

"Thank you Meghan."

"You are welcome, Frank."

We stayed on the floor and more people got up their courage and entered the music. One of the hamsters whispered. *I think they are touching.* The next piece was 'Sleepy Lagoon' and we stayed on the floor through 'String of Pearls'. The holding of hands and the warmth of it all by being close were the most generous things I had experienced in years. I would not sell my big band era trench coat for a million bucks. It was back in style.

I put Meghan in a cab to the airport and returned to the bar for a nightcap. I reverted to my fallback preference and to my favorite Morty's Bar and Grill vernacular.

"Spin me one, Morty. One of your finest."

The swirls of condensation trailed along the bar behind the shot glass and stopped softly against the skin of my outstretched hand.

Two nerds and a hamster applauded the feat. The cold glass was filled to test the meniscus with Lagavulin scotch whisky, and the peaty aroma was like mother's milk to me. Some things never grew old.

"You know, Morty, I hesitate to tempt fate, but at this moment I am contented."

"I see it in you. It is the most natural thing. You have just danced with a beautiful woman and ahead of you, if I heard the snippets of your conversation correctly, you have a daunting task. You have not engineered discomfort out of your life. You do not subscribe to a life of pablum, which most of society does. Ultimate peace of mind, self-worth and fulfillment comes from encountering difficulty and discomfort. Confronting and overcoming those makes the real you and you are proud of that person. Do you know what 'rucking' is?"

"Could I stop you from telling me?"

"The resurgence of the need for discomfort is growing. You know what one of the most popular trends is right now? Rucking. People are buying rucksacks, backpacks, with pockets in them to carry weights. The fitness types are right into it, but the larger population is embracing it too. The task is difficult and punishing and the participants have never felt so good in their lives. If you need more of it, increase your weight. It is contrived discomfort, yes, but the mind and body thrive on it. It feeds the needs. People actually say they feel elated after every session. No. That is not the word they use. They say, 'happy'. Tell me. When was the last time you were happy?"

"About 18 ½ minutes ago when you worked your magic, and I desire to be happier. Spin me one, Morty."

The hamsters copied quietly. 'spin me one' to each other, and all was right in my world.

The early morning was very cold, and the silence of the Borstal estuary was broken only by the lapping at the shoreline. The rhythmic crunch of my foot falls on the frozen gravel path along Black Creek was slower than usual, and I picked up my pace. The light of dawn began to filter through the tops of the pines and the occasional bird call boasted of seeing it first. My daily five miles was generally an easy run but today I pushed it. I needed to speak with my man in Ottawa who was three hours advanced, and I wanted to get him on the line before lunch, while he was martini-less. It was good to have friends in high places and he was a good friend in a high place. My coffee maker went off as I entered my apartment. I poured myself a cup, left my toque on and called Charlie Witmer's private number at CSIS. He picked up in the second ring. Apparently my name was on his screen, and he used the old code.

"Circus."

"Clown. Hello Charlie, ..er, I take that back with all due respect. Good morning Mr. Director. How goes the spy craft?"

"Very well, Frank, and thank you for asking. If you wish to be back on the high wire, welcome, and rest assured I have the perfect little intrigue for you."

"Thank you Charlie, but I'll stick with my simple sleuthing. However, I have something which I believe has a crossover to you. A bird named Rybakov."

"Not Sergei Rybakov."

"The same. Why do you know him?"

"He came across my desk about a week ago. The Russian legation has reclassified him as a member of the diplomatic staff. That means he can come and go as he pleases, and we can't do a bloody thing about it. He is a very bad actor. He could cut your nuts off and all we could do about it is teach you to sing soprano. Don't touch him."

"Too late for that. He is the object of the eye of my client. You should know he's now ensconced at the Marscraft production facility in Saskatchewan. I learned yesterday that Marscraft is not under the auspices of the International Mars Commission, but rather a public corporate entity domiciled in Zurich, with stocks and shares, contracted to build out and mass produce the spacecraft for the Mars colonization. Can you get me a high-level gate pass or credentials to investigate and monitor the assembly line construction site? "

"I did not know Rybakov was there. Thank you for that. As far as credentials, that is a big ask. If it were simply something as inconsequential as a government, a breakaway republic or a cartel headquarters, I could give you cover. But Marscraft? They and their very good friends control all the entities I just mentioned. The cartels, the republics, and the governments. By the way, if my position here did not prohibit it, I would load up on their shares. Not a recommendation mind you, just a bug in your ear. Regarding your credentials, I will try, but if I'm successful, you will give us all your notes, daily reports, and daily goings on involving Rybakov to the point of how many breaths he takes. I want to know everything from his toothpaste to the color of his socks to the songs he sings when he is daydreaming. Consider yourself as of this moment to be back juggling under the big top. The circus has come to town. And Frank, don't say anything to me. There is no negotiation on this. You are savvy and you know how to handle yourself. However, if something does go wrong, I do not know you, we do not know you. Meanwhile, do not do anything. Do not go there. I will send someone or something to you within forty-eight hours. Oh, by the way, should it materialize that you do wind up on site, do not find your way to Marscraft north, it is Marscraft south you want. Marscraft North is official Russian diplomatic territory and off limits without invitation. Good day, old chap. And good luck."

Witmer had told me much without telling me anything. Something important was in the works and I, with my usual talent, had stepped into the middle of it. The forty-eight hours' time frame worried me. Charlie was a decisive immediate type of guy. I had to trust if it were someone he was sending to me, it was not someone sent to make Frank disappear.

Two days passed with nothing from Witmer when at 4:00 p.m. my phone lit up with the most welcome call I had had in months. It was my good friend Fran, librarian extraordinaire and a straight shooter without equal. Any time spent with Fran was good time.

"Hi Fran, when I saw your name on the call display, it made my day. What's happening?"

"I was about to ask you the same thing. I just received a book which the regional library system ordered in for you, but my records show you never requested anything. Moreover, it has no stamp nor lading document. I have the package here for you, and I'm not touching the thing. Knowing your background, it could be anything from anthrax to a knighthood. Come and get it, now, or I am tossing it."

"I am as puzzled by it as you are, Fran. You are right in not touching it. Don't open it. Is it ticking?"

"Very funny. Get in here!"

"I am on my way."

It was certainly the communication from Witmer, and I was furious at him involving a third party like Fran who should not come within a mile of anything related to Rybakov. Never in my career had I involved a real-world friend in my netherworld life. Charlie was slipping to have made a mistake like this.

We met on the library steps and Fran stiff armed the package at me. I took it in my left hand, and we hugged each other for old time's sake. It seemed that nice warm ladies were becoming a habit.

"Thanks, Fran. I apologize for this. I know what this package is, and it should not have come to me through you. I'll make it up to you."

"Fine. How about right now. I am hungry, I want an evening without the mining machines in my apartment grinding away in the background and a new restaurant called 'Ahab's' has opened in the Forecastle Towers. Being a detective, you should recognize that as a clue to what you should do next."

"Sorry sugar, I get the clue, but I can't do it. This packet contains, among other things, an airline ticket leaving tonight."

Fran did not respond except with a look, and she was right. I wouldn't know what a real life was if it hit me between the eyes and it had just done that.

"Fran, it is such a shame you didn't notice the package until tomorrow morning. Such things happen. So come along with me Lucille, in my merry Oldsmobile which is a Buick and together we shall ingurgitate the delights of Ahab's fine dining."

"Frank, are you getting shy, or what? You left out the best line. Come along with me Lucille in my merry Oldsmobile, you can go as far as you like with me, in my merry Oldsmobile. By the way, do you have your credit card?"

"This time, I do."

The 1:00 p.m. 737 flight out of Vancouver to Regina Saskatchewan International Airport was uneventful. Going north from there to Prince Albert was another three hundred miles or so and I was tempted to drive, but minute by minute the forest fires closed roads. The Twin Otter turboprop carried nineteen people and after circling for a few minutes we descended through dense particulate laden smoke to Glass Field Airport at Prince Albert. The descent gave glimpses of the layout. I was surprised to see heavy road grading on what appeared to be a four-lane road headed northwest. The Marscraft construction site was forty miles farther northeast, and I made the last bus, running ahead of the burning forests.

Charle Witmer had credentialed me as an International Space Agency inspector. I was quite impressed with my curriculum vitae which was mostly correct but cleverly massaged to be less threatening. Unfortunately, Charlie had neglected one necessary item. The blue safety helmet required to delineate my status. Grudgingly, the main gate security team loaned me one. It was terrible how airlines lost things.

The seriousness of what lay ahead primed me. Somewhere in this mammoth installation was Rybakov. In my rough days of disposable adversaries he would be just one more relic to be unearthed from the permafrost like a woolly mammoth. His status as a member of the Russian legation changed that game. A hangnail became an international incident and having unwittingly become once again a circus clown, I was obligated to protect both the interests of my client and ultimately, my country.

Chapter Fourteen

At -22 Celsius, the Prince Albert Saskatchewan weather did not disappoint me. The tarmac between the Marscraft perimeter security fences and the distant buildings was cleared of snow and golf carts abounded, with rows of them charging their batteries at outlets in the central common area. Hunched against the cold, my golf cart driver fishtailed over alternating frozen and dry patches at full throttle, with the driver's gold and black toque pulled low over his ears, nicely resembling a bee. Hive members buzzed everywhere, filling the mammoth installation with activity, their frozen breath streaming like vapor trails behind them. Approaching the facility through miles of wind turbines, I had watched Marscraft grow on the horizon and now that I was up against it, the size astounded me. So as not to appear an ignoramus, Witmer had given me exhaustive background material on Marscraft, but it neglected mention of the gargantuan proportions.

"Son, how high are these buildings?"

"You an inspector?"

Apparently my blue inspector's helmet was not proof enough.

"Yes. Every installation has its own parameters. This is my first exposure to the final design."

"Guess we all have our vissitoods. She's five hundred and twenty feet. Went up once on the hoist. They had to loosen my grip with a pry bar. I'll take you to your trailer and tell Mr. Krueger you are here. I see you are not wearing your name badge. Good thing you're not hourly. He'd dock you in a second."

Witmer had provided me a name badge. It said 'Inspector' and it was safe in my suitcase.

"McCord. My name is Frank McCord. He's expecting me."

The one-man trailer was warm with a Starlight Internet parabolic receiver on the roof and a small refrigerator. That and a bed was all I needed. Witmer had vetted the full administrative staff of the Saskatchewan installation along with Krueger and he was solid. Helmut Krueger was a German educated mechanical engineer whose reputation was built on driving the toughest projects in the worst places and he owned this job. Rybakov was my only concern and he lurked somewhere within four miles of construction in two buildings. A snowmobile wound down outside my front door.

"Hey, Inspector McCord. Come get!"

I stepped out to a steely blue-eyed smile, and he tossed me a yellow toque.

"Put that on under your helmet. It's going to get colder. And here, stick this bottle of Johnnie inside. Then we'll take a quick tour of the assembly. The buildings are only heated in isolated construction areas so dress up. You'll ride behind me on the snowmobile. I'm Krueger."

His walkie talkie crackled, and he waved me to go in while he answered it. I put the bottle of Johnnie Walker beside the bed, wrapped my neck with my Hudson's Bay Company scarf, and pulled the toque down over my ears. Apparently Krueger was the driving instructor for the golf cart squad, as with me attached, he downshifted from Mach two and brought the snowmobile to a lurching stop at the west end of Marscraft south, two miles from my trailer. My lips had stiffened from the cold, and I made faces to get them going again. A four-foot brushed-aluminum sign read

'Division 86'. I could not believe there were eighty-six installations of such scope.

"My brief says nothing about Division 86. Does Marscraft have eighty-six facilities like this?"

"They just broke ground on number 94 in Chile. By the way, McCord, you are the first of your kind who has been out here. A while back I received a call about you from Dr. Macbeth, who confirmed your bona fides. She told me you would be arriving to make some assessments and out of courtesy to her I am giving you the lowdown. Apparently you have the highest security clearance, but my comments will still be circumspect. What is it you are inspecting?"

"Everything from security, to systems, to safety and anything irregular. Personnel as well."

"Fine with me. I'll show you the rudiments of what we do and then you're on your own for the balance of the week. Your blue helmet designates your status on the site. That should give you full access to anything you need, except for Division 87. That is the building two miles up the slope to the north, which is now officially a part of Mother Russia. It seems we work together toward the same goal of Mars colonization but each on his own path. Don't expect any cooperation there. If you have questions for me, save them up for the end of the day, don't interrupt me on the job. Now look closely at the end face of the building. What appears to be a seam running vertically is actually two doors closing in the center. You see the rails running away right to left on which they ride. Your first question of course, is why are the buildings as high as they are?"

"Yes. I could see them from twenty-five miles."

"The height relates to the size of the Marscraft rockets. These ships with both stages are four hundred and twenty feet high and thirty-six feet in diameter. The rockets are built in sections, and it is possible gravitational force, that is, its own weight lying on its side without fuel, could distort or stress the structure. So we have made necessary changes to construction and assemble them vertically. It seems strange to a world which is comfortable with seeing assembly in a horizontal aspect. Such as cars moving along an assembly line with the same attitude as one would see them on the street. Most exploratory and military rockets are fabricated that way but none of them comes close to the scale of what we're doing here."

"Is anyone else doing vertical construction?"

"Vertical integration is being done in a few companies, but it's not really anything new, just the size of what we do is new. The old Saturn Five rockets were built vertically. Man! This wind! Come, let's get inside. If you hear two blasts from a siren, just stay with me, overhead cranes will be moving material at that point."

I was overawed by what I saw. Rail lines ran in all directions with the main line running parallel to the length of the building and spurs entering here and there from the loading docks. Work platforms were stacked every thirty feet or so for several hundred feet above me on both sides of the building, like a cross section taken through the floors of a forty-story building, with the face of each floor cut out to fit the profile of the rocket. The size of the space was unbelievable. I wanted to sing something to hear the echo. Krueger watched me watching.

"Beautiful isn't it?"

"Indescribable. What is that gaseous, sweet smell?"

"Ah. The smell of perfection. It is the inert gases from laser welding. The skills level of our welders ranks with the dedicated master craftsman of the renaissance guilds. Nothing leaves the launch pad without their excellence."

"Where do you begin building?"

"With the lowest level first. The second stage where the crew and passengers are, is the most interesting, so let's go with that. Assembly is done in a hanging fashion, suspended by one of six overhead cranes. We start with stainless steel rings, each of them thirty-five feet in diameter and over six feet high. Those are what you see there on the rail spur coming from our factory. Four of those rings are suspended, interlocked and then welded, then surrounded by a steel reinforcing cage. The aft dome is hung inside those and welded in place while underneath, the retractable landing legs are attached."

"Helmut, everything I see seems to be stainless steel. I read carbon fiber might be better for ease of construction and weight savings as well."

" We considered it initially, but the reentry temperatures are too much for it. The re-entry temperatures can reach 1500° C. Carbon fiber can start to break down and get brittle around 500° C. That defeats the idea of a reusable second stage. There are a few carbon fiber components in the first stage, but it never gets that hot."

"What's the next step?"

"After the landing legs, seven more rings are stacked and welded one by one, then four more including the battery and ultimately the nose cone including the liquid oxygen header tank. Following that we add the Strongbow propulsion system beneath the lowest level. With the profile completed, the actuated fins for maneuvering are added, two each, top and bottom. The last thing is the attaching of the ceramic heat shielding tiles. I don't suppose you would like one as a souvenir. The odd one arrives chipped or damaged. It would be one of those."

I accepted. Rejects were my bread and butter. Despite Krueger's generous description, and his enthusiasm for the engineering, my mind was not attuned to the subject. Rybakov was the object of my affection.

"What do you think, McCord? Would you go to Mars?"

"May I take my 1953 Buick?"

"Unlikely."

"Deal breaker."

"I don't blame you. How could anyone expect someone to exist on Mars without their Buick. Let's see. Each Marscraft is launched into the stratosphere with a reusable rocket able to take a one-hundred-and-sixty-ton payload with ninety-five passengers, including science officers and launch personnel. It's roughly a six-month trip. The sleeping areas to Mars are much like the capsule hotel rooms in the orient, but the first few short low orbit commercial trips will have first and second-class accommodations. You know, for the space nuts who will pay anything to be shot up in a rocket. And good for them. At the moment there is a waiting list of sixteen thousand individuals committed to pay three million for the privilege. For three million, they will have a very comfortable seat which is convertible into launch mode, boarding mode and sleeping mode. There is an exercise room, and the most fabulous view of the universe. And more important to them, they will hold center stage on the cocktail circuit where they will boast of having had thermalized cans of tuna for dinner."

"Who could resist thermalized tuna. Anything new with propulsion? The engines?"

"No, the cluster will still have vacuum optimized engines, heavy thrust engines and sea level optimized. The first stage, which is the workhorse, has thirty-six Strong Bow engines, twenty-four around the periphery and twelve in a central core. They will boost stage two and drop off, returning to earth for a soft vertical touchdown to be used again. The second stage where you would sit on your way to Mars, has eight. I appreciate things are not particularly exciting for you at this stage of construction. In a year we will have more to show. I believe the Russians next door are farther along. They have a significantly larger crew working. Trainloads of materials arrive daily. I've tried to wheedle my way inside on several occasions but with no luck. I think the next time they will just shoot me."

A man waving frantically sped toward us in a golf cart. Krueger walked quickly to meet him. He shouted back to me.

"Sorry, McCord. I am wanted. You take the snowmobile back to your digs. I'll be in touch tomorrow."

With a slit left open for my eyes and mummified with my scarf, I ran the snowmobile into the wind along the south side of Division 86 and left the big four stroke Bombardier at the door of my trailer with the key in the ignition. It was four hours to sundown and the gradient up to the Russian Division 87 was gentle and constant which made for two miles of easy walking. The open spaces seem to provide their own barrier as there was no fencing anywhere to demarcate the boundaries. If of course by accident and ignorance, I strayed into Russian territory, subzero cold might stultify one's thinking and disorient one and that would be my story. Their story might, however, carry a different tone. Moscow's penchant was to shoot spies on the spot and ask questions later. I concluded that in a spirit of détente there was no easier way to find out what Mother Russia was doing than to go to Mother Russia.

Sergei Rybakov lit his stogie and worked his way back into the snowdrift. He sat warmly and comfortably out of the wind. The brilliant Saskatchewan sun provided little heat, but it was the kind of day which kept the lens of his scope clear and unfogged. His rifle had a maximum range of eight hundred yards, but he was not on the hunt. His scope was adjusted to twenty-five times magnification and his elevation was eighty-five feet above the target in his cross hairs. Reflexively his training demanded he make the elevation adjustment to compensate for the drop of the bullet over distance. It was an interesting problem to work through given his perch, for a bullet fired from his gun dropped three feet per hundred yards. Carefully, he scanned along the north side of Division 86 and stopped at the loading dock. The pace of the loading matched the pace of construction and simple calculations told him precisely how many Marscraft vehicles had been completed. His eidetic memory constructed a compendium. He continued slowly eastward with his field of vision taking a mental note of the colors of the safety helmets. Inspectors wore blue but they had proven scarce. Engineers wore red, construction supervisors wore white, and the sub-foremen wore green. Mill hands sported yellow. The mix at any one time gave away what the specific stage of assembly was, and an imbalance of helmet colors indicated a problem in the normal flow of things. It was considerate of Marscraft to color code their production schedule for espionage purposes. He continued slowly east with his view, looking for anything new or unfamiliar to him among the construction materials waiting to move into the stream. He swung past the end of the building, and someone there had moved significantly out of focus. He knew how it was. Much easier to take a walk and relieve oneself in the snow than to walk three quarters of a mile to a latrine. He punched the stock of his rifle into the drift and leaned back in total comfort and closed his eyes. The cold on his face took him to the hills at home.

Home to his youth and to the days when his country was not a country but was simply winter. When the hot blood of passion kept him warm in the blizzard and there was no cold. His first love Ludmilla was still alive and in their village. How mad her low cut Gzhelian blouse had driven him. She took his hand... .

Sergei shook himself awake realizing he had begun to daydream. Falling asleep here was death at this temperature. Dr. Rybakov took a full draft from his flask and shook himself. He extricated his rifle and focused down toward the easterly slope. Maybe he could see the guy piss. He got the focus right in a few seconds and the man had made a few hundred yards coming up the hill. The fellow was dressed in a ski suit and a blue helmet, with his face wrapped in a bright multicolored scarf. His gait did not change despite the incline. He was fit.

With the ground cover of snow, Rybakov could not be sure of the boundary line of Russian territory. He set up his telescopic sight to be in focus at precisely eight hundred yards and allowed the figure to clarify itself on the lens. He sat back into the perfect fit of the snowbank and sipped his whiskey, watching the small figure grow with his naked eye. The man was metronomic in his stride. Dogged in his trudge. An eerie familiarity set in. The thrust of the shoulder. The cat like flow of energy into the progress. Anger crept into Rybakov as step by step the patchwork of long remembered characteristics crystallized into a fact. The target was Frank McCord.

Sergei Rybakov released the safety on his rifle and chambered the first round. He wound the fiber strap around his right elbow to stabilize the gun and adjusted the elevation to his estimated distance. He fine-tuned the magnification and placed the crosshairs on McCord's forehead between the brows. Those blue remorseless devil eyes. Eyes to be seen in one's worst nightmare. He began his preparatory deep breathing, readying himself to hold his breath for absolute stillness for the shot. A millimeter of wavering at this distance was a miss. Rybakov had settled on a trigger pull weight of three pounds to allow a gentle, slow, continuous squeeze for a kill. Frank McCord was now a foreign belligerent violating consular property and fair game. He had invaded Russia. To kill him was the right thing, and after all what good was rank and diplomatic privilege if not used to defend the Motherland. Yet, the inner man knew the satisfaction from it would be a tawdry fleeting thing. McCord would know nothing of his death. One stride, blackness, and then nothing. Where was the humiliation, the agonizing anticipation of the end, the anguish of losing the contest to a better man. Rybakov was on his home turf. He now had the opportunity to confront and revile McCord and if his old foe reacted with violence, fine, he would slaughter him on the spot. He stood in full view and waited, with the safety off.

I was pretty much gassed when from five hundred yards out I saw Rybakov standing at the height of the incline. He carried a rifle in a sling and if he intended to whack me he would have done so by now. The uphill trek in the snow was heavier than I thought, and I had no choice but to fight through the burn in my legs and maintain my pace to conceal my fatigue. I had to trust he was not in one of his mano a mano moods or I was a goner. He had the usual king of the world sneer on his face, and I wanted to smash it.

"Well, if it isn't the lord of the manor, Rybakov the great. Out shooting some peasants, are we?"

"McCord, this is Russian soil and if I choose to shoot peasants I shall, which given your equivalent class, puts you at risk. Our buildings throughout the site have the status of a legation or a consulate and consequently I am privileged to sport a weapon. Why do I carry a rifle? First, I like the idea of it. I like the heft of it, the smell of the gun oil and the taste it gives me of the old days. Second, if necessary, to deal with rodents like you. I would like nothing better than to make you into Swiss cheese. My Russian built AK-12 fires 700 rounds a minute. Think of it. In less than one second you are Swiss cheese. However, at the moment, given that we were comrades in arms in the broader sense of it, I choose not to ventilate you. Presumably you have come here to spy out what the bad guys are doing. In fact, I am so proud of what we're doing, come. See the beauty of it. A detective, a military man, I will show. An engineer I would not."

The east wind pushed us along the north side of Division 87 which proved to be a duplicate of 86 with the exception of the spur line loading docks. A half mile long canopy shrouded the rail cars to prohibit viewing of whatever was offloaded. Containers filled an auxiliary spur line about a mile long adjacent to a semi-trailer dock half buried in drifting snow. Outside the pedestrian entrance I recognized the international symbol.

"You have radioactive material here."

"Really! Was it the large yellow circle with three black fan blades as proscribed by the atomic energy commission which tipped you off? Of course we do."

The interior was well lit and warm with multiple assembly lines for various components. A thousand robotic welding arms sparked their work on disparate products along four assembly lines which ran out of sight into the two-mile distance. Hundreds of freshly minted Constable sentients stood inactive near the most adjacent loading dock waiting for transportation. They were subtly different from other prototypes I had seen. The agreement among the signatories to the Mars colonization was that the sole logo was 'Marscraft' in order to instill solidarity and minimize nationalistic squabbles among the colonists. Nation state identification was prohibited. This batch of Sentients had Russian flags on each shoulder. More concerning was the change in the weapon arm. Schematics showed wiring for the low intensity stun gun but that was not how these were built. There was an exhaust port in the right forearm similar to what is required for standard military high powered weaponry. These Constables were built to be killers.

"Rybakov, I should have expected nothing less from your masters. Perfidy in all dealings. These things you've made are not Constables, they are automaton storm troopers. You are not privileged to do this."

"Read the newspaper, McCord. This is quid pro quo. Something for something. Russia has rendered the west's inefficient rocketry usable with Russia's superior technology and expertise in exchange for a parallel Marscraft construction facility in Saskatchewan. Without my help, our help, the OSIRIS-REx vehicle would still be sitting on the pad. Understand where you are and what this place is. This is a Russian facility with full diplomatic status. Just like an embassy we are totally autonomous. We are not under the auspices of the International Space Federation. Do you really believe Russia will trust its interests to anything domiciled in North America, when the whim of a deranged and incompetent president could sanction the entire Russian colonization team from joining the Mars expedition? Why do you think you see Russia, China and India embarking on aggressive space programs. Attempting moon landings to build a jump off base to Mars. Who dares to trust the perfidious west! We will protect our people. Like the rest of the world, we will embark among the great international flotilla, stolid participants all. However when you are four months out from Mars, we will already be there. Preparing. Count on it."

"What a lovely little speech, Rybakov. You have built a construction facility in Saskatchewan, thousands of miles from an ocean. What are you going to do? Call the courier and have the rockets and the rest of your hardware delivered to your doorstep at Baikonur Cosmodrome in Kazakhstan? Six thousand miles away? "

"McCord, you are out of date. First, our primary launch site now is at the Vostochny Cosmodrome, near the Pacific coast in East Russia. But ask yourself the question. Which is easier? Move the rocket, or move the components and build them wherever you can? We have concluded agreements with sixteen nations to do both. In climates with no snow cover we build the roads and move the rockets. From here we manufacture components and ship them to Vostochny. Second, you speak of couriers. It is unfortunate the smoke particulate restricted your view of Prince Albert from the air. Otherwise you would have seen the largely finished four-lane highway leading from here to Whitehorse in the Yukon. When the highway is opened at the end of this year, the transit time will be reduced to eighteen hours from forty. From there to Tuktoyaktuk on the coast of the Beaufort Sea a year-round road will be completed in three months. A semi laden with a container of our technology will haul that distance in twenty hours. Do you know nothing of your country? You have a major seaport there on the northwest passage. Russia has five nuclear powered icebreakers keeping open the route from the Atlantic to the Pacific fulltime. Soon, Russia will be transacting more business there than through the Suez Canal. Part of that transport will be from Saskatchewan."

Rybakov slipped his hand inside his padded jacket quickly.

"I'm getting a call. I need to step out to get a clean signal. Walk down to the other end. There you will see the vertical integration we're doing to test some fit and finish issues. That should take you fifteen minutes. If you are here when I get back I will empty my Kalashnikov into your gut. Meanwhile if you see anything with a nuclear warning sign on it, believe it."

My bloodlust was pushing me to challenge him then and there, but the inner tactician knew better. Frank was not bulletproof. I made for the east end of the building.

Rybakov huddled in a dead spot out of the wind and opened his neutrino phone.

"Hello, Rybakov here."

"Privyet."

Rybakov was caught off guard. It was his handler and they had not spoken for a month.

"Privyet. Hello."

"How is the reception? Am I clear?"

"Yes, yes. You are clear. What would you like?"

"Are you happy with the progress being made there? Don't hold anything back, it will not be to your benefit."

"This is a particularly efficient program. The roadwork is well underway, and I expect it to be completed in a matter of months. Our deliveries of fissionable materials by rail are timely and on the whole we're ahead of schedule in fabrication. I did have one irritation today and I came within a second of shooting him between the eyes, but he deserves a tougher time of it."

"Don't do that. Very few people know about your installation, let's keep it that way. Do I know the gentleman?"

"I doubt it. Frank McCord. Does that mean anything to you? He is a resurrected Damocles. Always there, ready to get you in the neck."

"Him. It seems the name turns up once a week. The old man is dealing with him. Just leave him alone. In short order he will be out of your hair once and for all. What's the temperature there?"

"About -30. How is it where you are?"

"Beautiful at this elevation. About 20°, sunny, with light winds throughout most of the Sangre De Cristo Mountains area. Leave McCord alone. Privyet."

Rybakov sipped on his flask, delaying his return to the assembly area. His handler had relieved him of the need to confront McCord and prudence demanded he give his adversary time to retreat with dignity. Sergei wondered about his choices in life. His handler was somewhere called Sangre De Cristo at a pleasant and sunny 20° in a light wind and Sergei was in windswept -32° worrying about a road to a place called Tungoyaktuk. He knew he was not rid of McCord even though the great Demidov promised an end to him. Rybakov was contracted to manage the telemetry of gathering samples from Bennu on October 20th, eight months hence. The Cosmos Space

Center would be jammed and where you found Dr. Meghan Macbeth you found Frank McCord.

The east end of 87 was busy with crane work and the vertical integration team was engaged in hoisting heavy loads into position. I attempted to take some photos, but my antique phone was still disabled by the cold. I did not understand the function of the rocket hardware, but I knew the components I saw being installed were significantly different from what Krueger had outlined for me. What the purpose of the remarkably different design was, I could not guess, but with my rudimentary background from publicity videos, and a detailed explanation from Krueger, the Russian Marscraft was a different animal. The woman would know. Twelve minutes had elapsed, and I exited the closest loading platform preferring to keep my gut intact. I retraced my route back to my trailer, hunching my shoulders all way down as if somehow that might help if Rybakov had me in the kill zone. I communed with a solid three fingers of warm Jack Daniels and waited for my phone to thaw while I prepared my report to Witmer, focusing on the presence of nuclear material. He would not be amused.

"Hi Meghan, thank you for taking the call, I know you are busy there. First, your information that Rybakov was here at the Prince Albert installation was correct. I ran into him at the height of land outside Division 87, that is the more northerly of two buildings, and I wanted to blast him on the spot. The imperious swine is so proud of what they're doing he actually gave me a tour of their operation. My right hand still has the tingles looking for an impact. The arrogance he exuded because of his immunity was just too much."

"Immunity?"

"Yes. My sources in Ottawa have confirmed he has been reclassified as part of the Russian legation and as a result he has free diplomatic reign. On this property I cannot touch him or interact with him legally. But that is not why I called. I think you know Krueger?"

"Yes. Good man that."

"He gave me a thorough overview of his assembly methods and what I saw in building 87 was entirely different. A heavy crane swung a mammoth rectangular steel box into place at the equivalent level of the first-class compartments. Nothing like that comprised part of the Krueger rocket. Then I watched the activation of an umbrella like projection which could be extended and retracted to surround the body of the rocket, about a third the way up from the base."

"Good Lord, Frank, don't tell me that! No. Bloody hell. The Russians have done it. We are years behind this. Years. It changes the dynamic of the entire colonization program. We can only hope we can compete by the time the first launches take place in 2030. In fact if Rybakov's tests prove out, they don't need Marscraft at all. What you describe as an umbrella is a radiation shield and the box is the reactor for nuclear thermal propulsion. In practical terms, they have shortened the trip from six or seven months to six or seven weeks. Brother! And I thought my bit flip was a problem."

"Really. Bit flip. It sounds light and rather like fun. I can't imagine it to be trouble. Then again, maybe it is something such as an incomplete back flip. Poor chap, he did a bit flip."

"Frank, in this civilization, among scientists, hydro installations, nuclear launch sites, nothing is more terrifying than a bit flip. It is uncontrollable, unexpected and it could be devastating. In this lucky instance it took us a single day to troubleshoot it and we were able to flip it back remotely. We just about lost the sampler."

"Really, Meghan I'm very sorry about that. Pardon the expression, but I did not mean to be flippant. Does this happen often?"

"The estimate is it happens about one flip per month for every 256 MB of RAM. I know you're not a computer guy but that means it happens a lot and recently there has been a dramatic uptick. Likely because of better chips requiring less energy to operate. Fortunately, it is generally innocuous and nothing more than annoying. An individual somewhere may experience the blue screen of death on his computer, or a game player may suddenly find himself on an entirely different level of the game up or down but it's not always that innocent. Planes have experienced drastic changes in altitude in bit flips by having an instruction which should say 'level out'. say 'dive', so the plane drops two hundred feet. That recently happened at altitude. Visualize what that would mean if it occurred on an approach to landing."

“Hm. Do not launch the missile becomes do launch the missile. Turn on the electrical grid becomes turn off the electrical grid.”

“Yes. In our case with the sampler, OSIRIS-REx suddenly changed direction into a new trajectory. The hardware was fine, but a bit flip changed instructions whether a thruster should be off or on. Fortunately, Leishman was able to reprogram it remotely. That is, flip the bit back.”

“Why does it happen?”

“Our perverse bloody galaxy likes to play tricks on computers. Black holes, collapsing star systems, you name it, release particles called protons which may have travelled for a billion years, flung and whipped by gravitational forces and electromagnetic fields, arriving here in the trillions every minute. One of them with enough energy hits a transistor in the wrong place, does something as simple as change a one to a zero and chaos ensues. But we know this. To protect, we have identical programs running simultaneously so that if one is flipped the others continue as if nothing happened. Despite that, we had a flip. We don’t know why this occurred. That is the same thing every organization says when their precautions are overcome by a cascade of particles.”

“Meghan, this is astounding. Are we capable of generating and directing these same particles?”

“Frank, I do not want to contemplate it. Were it possible to selectively direct them, a malign actor could erase the entire social order on earth with the flick of a switch.”

Chapter Fifteen

United States Chiefs of Staff
State of Virginia
United States
July 16, 2020

Darrel Vigneault balanced a tray of Bellinis and weaved his way through the crowd, humming along with the music. Hands snatched away his drinks one by one, not caring it was sparkling Italian wine and sweet peach prosecco, it had alcohol in it. The next round would be good old country bourbon and things were getting loud. Clarinets wailed from a ghost band on a temporary bandstand erected on the back lawn. The band originated in the 1940s, but the name of the dead band leader still rang true, and it got them gigs. Twenty young musicians played the music of their grandfathers, and it was stale. Every so often, to relieve the tedium, they slipped something modern into the playlist and the audience grumbled at the sacrilege.

Rear Admiral Harriman stood in the dark, away from the racket and watched the running lights of a line of freighters on the horizon. His property rolled through the low hills of Virginia, and he stood at the highest point on his grounds and looked to the sea. His two hundred guests were military personnel, invitees to a strictly no uniform gathering. Rank inhibited free expression and many men learned many things in conversation, from knowing neither the rank nor the service of the individual to whom they spoke. The sound level was higher than at most parties. A strong voice implied a strong command, and no one would give that up, particularly after a little lubrication.

All belligerent services of the United States were represented and among the warriors were the complete Joint Chiefs of Staff. Out of uniform, they circulated anonymously in the crowd and their casual and apparently coincidental meeting was unofficial. The sole exception to anonymity was Admiral Crawford. She was the unicorn. She could outwit, out drink and out strategize any one of them, and all of the military assembled there knew who she was. That woman was their token female admiral.

At the agreed upon time, carrying their drinks, the Chiefs drifted away from conversation and made their way fifty yards along a foot-lit gravel path, to a building where Harriman stored his collection of replica naval fighting ships. The head of the Joint Chiefs, General Otto Bucholz, hung back and slowed his pace to arrive last. He would make his entrance in his own time. Watching from the shadow beside the trail, the unicorn decided she would go in when she bloody well felt like it.

Commandant of the Marine Corps, General Augustus Portnoy led the parade into a paneled conference room and one by one the officers seated themselves around a rectangular pecan table. Portnoy broke out his favorite Vegas 5 cigars and soon a hazy nimbus of smoke fingered the ceiling. Bucholz arrived with a practiced nonchalance and took his seat at the head. Now comfortable to begin and not recognizing someone was absent, Admiral Harriman welcomed the Chiefs. Of old, he had been one of them.

"Distinguished officers, I am pleased to welcome you to my home. Have confidence this room is private from surveillance, and it is fully shielded. Officially, this meeting is not happening, and nothing discussed will leak from here unless it comes from one of you. General Bucholz, as chairman of the Joint Chiefs of Staff, I give you a special welcome. Gentleman, welcome."

The assemblage turned to the door as Admiral Crawford pushed through hard and tacked nicely to an open seat on the side. She placed a fresh Bellini on the table and smiled abundantly at each individual in turn, unaffected by their collective contempt. Admiral Nancy Crawford was the chief of naval operations and the highest-ranking officer of the United States Navy. She was a military adviser to the president, the Homeland Security Council, the secretary of defense, and the National Security Council. The Chiefs of Staff was no longer just good old boys, and she enjoyed driving the wedge.

Admiral Harriman made no reference to her lateness, and he continued his comments with a smile, glancing briefly at a scale model sailing ship and visualized Crawford being keelhauled slowly along its bottom.

"Drinks, water and such are on the cabinet there. The party on the back lawn is building, so if you have finished your business any time before dawn, come join in. Now I shall leave you to your own devices. I am meeting up with my old friend, Jack. Daniels, that is."

The group enjoyed the admiral's little joke as he left them, having themselves made close acquaintance with Jack for most of the evening. General Bucholz began with the chief of staff of the Space Force.

"General Conrad, what is the status of the October 20 project?"

"Thank you, General. Although the project is not officially under the aegis of my Space Force, as we all know, the pentagon does have significant interest in its data, so we are fully apprised of its status. Just to recapitulate, OSIRIS-REx launched on September 8, 2016. It arrived at asteroid Bennu on December 3, 2018, and settled into orbit around Bennu later that month. This October 20th, it is scheduled to pick up samples from the surface. The sampler will stay in orbit with Bennu until mid-May 2021 when Bennu is in a better position relative to the earth, then head home. The expected arrival date is September 24, 2023. So far everything is nominal and looking good."

"October is coming fast. Remember operation Boscoe. We need a squad in the control room at the space center to observe the sampling. The Pentagon needs eyes on the contents. It is imperative to see what the staff at the Cosmos Space Center sees and explain away what surprises them . Who is overseeing the sample recovery vehicle? Yes, General Conrad?"

"The telemetry expert is a physicist named Dr. Sergei Rybakoff. He is expert in the Russian rocket hardware. The chief scientist and the head of the operation is one Dr. Meghan Macbeth. She is usually shadowed by her private security, ex Canadian clandestine operative, Frank McCord. Macbeth is a civilian and I hear she is a tough broad. I may have to send a battalion to get someone in there."

Nancy Crawford tapped her empty Bellini glass with a fingernail decorated with a sparkling blue anchor and continued doing so until the room was quiet. The faces surrounding her were stony and sodden and they did not like what had happened to their club.

"That squad in the sample recovery viewing room should be me. Woman to woman with Dr. Macbeth. Or as you so graciously put it, one tough broad to another. It is not necessary to send a brigade of quick stepping hob nail boots thundering into her space. General Conrad, if you would lend me a Space Force attaché or two in noncombat garb, that would do nicely. I will deal with Dr. Macbeth when the mechanical arm digs into Bennu and the sampling cannister opens. Trust me. I will leave her with a good taste in her mouth. Even after she sees the small bonus our man Boscoe has added to her project. I will assure her we are not there to interfere nor to control, and that the Joint Chiefs and particularly the space force fully support her program. Gentlemen, everything on earth is not advanced by force. Common speech and diplomacy can do much."

Bucholz hated her for her presumption of membership in his fraternity. He ignored her request and attacked her before General Conrad could respond to her.

"Thank you for your lecture, Admiral Crawford. It seems your diplomatic talents are superior to your operational skills. How many of the vessels scheduled to be commissioned by the Navy will be delivered on time?"

"None."

"I see. However, I am sure you have seen to it that we outpace both China and Russia, have you not? That our technology is superior?"

"No."

"That's it? None? No? The joint chiefs of staff are discussing matters of National Security and suddenly you become monosyllabic?"

"General Bucholz, I am flattered by your sudden interest in the activities of the Navy. So, you wish to run a numbers race against Russia and China. Your track runs uphill. Our contractors thus far have taken seven years to deliver a seaworthy version of our current nuclear submarine design. For future contracts, their best hope is for six years. Six years to produce a single seaworthy and armed, operational submarine. In contrast to that, among thirty new vessels, Russia will add three submarines to its fleet this year. China, two."

"Excuse me, Admiral Crawford, we are dominant in the number of nuclear submarines on patrol, are we not?"

"Yes, general Milton, our nuclear submarine fleet has more firepower than the Russian and Chinese fleets combined. Our boats are monsters of destruction capable of incinerating the capital city of any nation. Provided they are not destroyed or disabled before they can fire a shot. General Bucholz, you referred to technology. Let's talk Russia and their submarine fleet. Nuclear subs are not what I'm worried about. It is their diesel electrics which worry me. We can't track them. They have at least thirty such Yasen class attack subs, and if we know where any one of them is at any time, it is dumb luck. A Yasen class diesel could be sitting five-hundred yards away from each of our nuclear subs, undetected, waiting for instructions, which by the way, it appears they can receive while fully submerged."

The group nodded as one, hoping and expecting the sample collector from Bennu to bring home the solution. They had been told the fate of the American Empire might depend upon it and they believed it, despite ignorance of what the Boscoe technology was. Bucholz wanted none of this exposition from the woman. He was quite drunk and depressed by the collective ineptitude surrounding him, but the boys were rapt and engaged and he did not intervene.

"The Yasen is referred to as the 'black hole' submarine. Because of its quieting technology it disappears as if into a black hole and that is it. Its skin is covered by anechoic tiles. They are partially ceramic, and they absorb sound waves to the degree that they return no sound signal to our sonar, or if anything does bounce back, the signal is distorted to the point of being non directional. Worse, the most recent iterations of the Yasen are set up to carry the Poseidon. Five such are already operational in the Atlantic, and we believe by the end of the year there will be eight."

General Watters was vice chairman of the joint chiefs. His background was army and surrounded by the Chiefs, he wished to appear relevant.

"Poseidon, that's just a new class of torpedo, isn't it?"

"Just? Just a nuclear-powered torpedo which can lay submerged and hidden under the polar ice for years until the time comes to strike. It has limitless range and carries a 100-megaton nuclear warhead at 95 knots submerged. A new class of weapon in a class by itself. As far as China, they play the same phony, second world war, capital ship surface game as we do, despite the fact such fleets invite mutually assured destruction. Not nuclear destruction, but hypersonic. In a committed conflict, in one afternoon, hypersonic missiles could destroy every last floating vessel in every navy. So much for the aircraft carriers which took ten years to build. But that is a game in which China just pretends to participate. They have no intention of waging a hot war of iron and blood, despite the fact every war game simulation shows we can't beat them. How many of their citizens would the Chiefs estimate China vaccinated during its Covid experiment?"

Bucholz exploded.

"Crawford, where are you going with your mindless jumble of non sequiturs?"

"My non sequiturs as you frame them, are where the next real war is. General Portnoy will amplify my remarks. Dr. Portnoy, you command the military's biological research division. I read your recent report, and it is imperative to share it with the Joint Chiefs. Would you give us your brief overview?"

"Yes, thank you, admiral. In my time at the biologic warfare research program, I was in the DURC section, in level four laboratories. Those laboratories deal with the agents of highest-level pathogenicity which could have dual use. That is, biologic agents which are often cultured for normal medical research but with some tweaking might also be weaponized. I worked with all the real killers, like Marburg, Nipah and Ebola. As required for Commandant of the Marine Corps, I have reported directly to the Navy, to General Crawford. I will address the General's question of how many vaccines in China shortly. My report alluded to by General Crawford is a brief one and with permission, I will summarize it for the Chiefs."

"Proceed."

"Thank you. Roughly a century ago, Georges Clemenceau was the

Premier of France. In the closing days of World War one, he observed that armies always fought the last war, especially if they had won it. True to the dictum, here we sit, comparing pieces of hardware. Who has the most boats, who has the stealthiest subs, who has the fattest aircraft carriers. We are addicted to the need to project power abroad. We play computer war games using algorithms based tactically on the use of battleships and armament as if it were 1944. China goes along with the nonsense of building expensive toys primarily to perpetuate the illusion of like mindedness. They mimic our propensity for having shiny things which float, but such things play no part in their larger war strategy."

Bucholz jumped in.

"General Portnoy, the United States defense budget over the last five years is four trillion dollars. We have over 700 military bases around the world in 120 countries. It may be news to you, but anything the Chinese have they have stolen from us. They violate our patents, they steal our weapon systems, and they make off with anything else not tied down. "

" The goal in stealing our technology is not to build it. It is to develop techniques to hack and embed trojan viruses within our military programming. We are certain China is now fully capable of that. If we choose to fight a war of hardware against them, they will pluck our satellites and planes from the sky and corrupt the navigation capabilities of our ships and missiles. However, that is the least of it."

General Portnoy threw back his drink and chewed on the ice cubes. He had their attention and he chewed slowly.

"Gentlemen, change your mind set. The most serious threats against us are not made of steel and detonation. General Crawford's question about the number of vaccinations done in China is the vital one. We are talking about biological warfare for which we have set ourselves up. In a spirit of scientific cooperation, France, Canada, Japan, Singapore and others, have offered up bits and pieces of viral research, only to be outdone twentyfold in giveaways by the United States, making China the world-leading self-sufficient bioweapon power. The CPP is conducting gain-of-function research on high-risk pathogens which are already fifty times more dangerous than Covid, in multiple laboratories spread across China."

General Milton walked to the bureau, brought back four glasses and slid them along the table like curling stones. A fresh bottle of bourbon followed, and the group settled in.

"There are twenty or more such locations of which we are aware. The largest, the Chinese academy of Medical Sciences has branches in Beijing and Kunming. There, they are enhancing the lethality and transmissibility of the worst respiratory diseases, like SARS. In their Research of Chemical Defense department, they are working on mustard gas, moth venom and nanotechnology-driven systems to be delivered long-range. And unbelievably, their Academy of Military Medical Sciences is playing with Nipah virus to enhance its lethality. It already kills 60% of those who contract it. We must hope those agents are primarily retaliatory. The preferred approach in their minds is fundamentally different from ours. Visualize a genetically immunized army inserted into a region where a particular weaponized virus had already been released to decimate the defenders. Any remaining ground force would then be incapacitated with neurobiological attacks to panic and disorient the cognitive capacity of the population and render it helpless."

General Crawford gazed into her whiskey glass and blurted what came to mind.

"Wouldn't be the first time. Michmash."

Milton rolled his eyes.

"God! Here we go."

"God indeed. It's biblical. Michmash is a city a few miles north of Jerusalem, occupied in those times by the Philistines. As the battle approached, the God of the Israelites sent confusion and terror into the minds of the Philistine army. They fought each other, they lashed out in fury, and fled the battle, berserk and helpless. You've heard the phrase, something messed up and useless is referred to as a mishmash."

General Watters slammed down his whiskey glass, shooting the bourbon into the air.

"Philistines? Mishmash? We are here to discuss the impending sample gathering on Bennu and whether our little addendum to the OSIRIS-REx project has survived the trip! That, Crawford, is something real, not hypothetical junk about mind control and vaccinated Chinese super troops marauding through exclusion zones where we can't go lest our assets be infected. Real things, Portnoy, real things. Not hypothetical bogeymen of the future dreamed up by you and the rest of your PhD brainiacs! Spend a month on an aircraft carrier, man! Feel the power throbbing beneath your feet. Smell the salt air and fill your lungs. That is real."

General Portnoy waved off Nancy Crawford from answering and walked to the drinks cabinet. He returned to the table and threw a towel to Watters.

"Here. Clean up your mess on the table. First, General Watters, I must compliment you on your fidelity. A fidelity to the land and times of your childhood where lollipops were 5¢ and the songs on the radio promised that wishing would make it so. Unfortunately, wishing changes nothing and the world which you inhabit in your mind is long gone. Not one thing I have touched upon thus far is hypothetical nor plucked from the future. I wish China did not have neuro-strike weapons capable of targeting both civilian and military minds, fogging up cognition, instilling all-consuming terror in the mind, and leaving behind long-term neurological damage, but they do. I wish China did not have a mutated Nipah virus with 90% lethality against which we have no vaccine and for whose encephalitis we have no treatment, but they do. I wish their weaponization of biology did not extend beyond classical bioweapons, but it does. I wish they were not engaged in human genome editing for their soldiers, nor genetic manipulation of bacteria, nor computer to human interfaces capable of controlling entire populations, but they are."

General Bucholz stepped in in an attempt to soften the dialogue.

"General Portnoy, do you expect us to believe China could inoculate an entire army with a vaccine tailored to protect them against a genetically modified virus without us knowing about it? For example, we have every single Covid shot they have manufactured counted. Roughly 4.3 billion doses. We see what they do."

"Chief Bucholz, you have asked the critical question. It goes to what Dr. Crawford asked, and yes, you are correct, it is absolutely impossible to disguise such a massive vaccination program. Unless. Unless something unique and extraordinary happens. Let us, and this is just from my imaginings, mind you. Let us imagine pandemic war games were played a year ago in 2019 by the World Economic Forum using a common virus as the villain. In that imaginary meeting, the response to a global pandemic and follow-up vaccine delivery mechanisms might be gamed. Imagine too, coincidentally and amazingly, just a few months later, that very virus used in the pandemic model, comes along and spreads around the world. Imagine it to be a tweaked and manufactured virus, not a very lethal one, easy to catch and its fatalities to be almost exclusively among the infirm, elderly and immunocompromised. Just imagining, of course. How sad to see several inconvenient groups gone as a preferential target. Consequently, imagine also seeing tens of millions of frightened people around the world lined up outside the doors of clinics to get their shots. Today they are lined up in every country in the world, including China. So China is no longer different. It is just one country among one hundred and eighty countries trying to do the right thing for their people. Imagine too, if you wanted to hide the fact you were vaccinating half a billion of your citizens, how would you do it? You would make it something the whole world was doing. Put the entire world population on a vaccination program in which China, a citizen of the world and a good neighbor, agrees to participate. Even better, imagine creating the virus yourself and making your domestic vaccine a double whammy vaccine which also protects against genetically modified bioagents. Just imagining of course. But let us stop with the imagining. General Watters demands reality. The reality is every bioweapon I have described today and referenced in my report is alive, well, and functional and in China's hands. They form China's operational intentions given today's strategic environment. And General, I would be pleased to accompany you on a U.S. navy aircraft carrier through the Straits of Taiwan. Think of the shivers we will send up and down Chinese spines as we go floating by in our mighty boat."

"Spare us your sarcasm, General Portnoy. Send a copy of your report to each of the chiefs. Send it through courier dispatch, top-secret. Administrative staff should not be privy to it. Is that it? Anything else?"

"If I may have five minutes more, that would do it. It has to do with China's biochemical warfare against us, namely fentanyl."

" Go ahead."

"Fentanyl is a synthetic narcotic, generally sold on the street in combination with heroin. It is altogether different from the so-called natural substances like cocaine. Fentanyl-laced heroin comes from pharmaceutical-grade facilities using professional industrial processes connected to complicated distribution channels and supply chains. Despite that, the drug cannot keep faithful users because it simply kills too many of them. Old style narcotics retain their customers for multiple years or even a lifetime, in a stable commercial market. That market sustains and renews itself year after year. Fentanyl-laced heroin on the other hand, kills or disables and destroys its own consumer base. Obviously, the motivation to make fentanyl is not to make a profit. That brings us to the special problem of the 'five eyes'.'

'Everyone here is aware of 'five eyes', or as it is known worldwide, FVEY. Despite your familiarity with it, it is necessary to review it. It is an intelligence partnership between the UK and the US, dating back to 1946, eventually expanded to include its current members, Canada, Australia and New Zealand. Its purpose in the 1940s was to monitor communications of foreign countries, largely Russia and its allies. Today, it has expanded to surveille billions of people worldwide, by intercepting messages such as emails, telephone calls, faxes and text messages from satellites, phone networks and fiber optic cables. To avoid breaking their internal domestic surveillance laws, each of the FVEY countries tells its citizens it does not spy on them, and that is the truth. They simply spy on the other FVEY countries and swap the data. If any person communicates in any way except on paper, the five eyes share their data in common. What they also share in common is an exponential growth in fentanyl related deaths. Nations such as Italy, Portugal, or Germany, do not have the problem even though natural narcotics such as cocaine are as common on the streets of Berlin or Lisbon as they are in Atlanta or Auckland. So how does a product which is difficult and expensive to produce and is distributed at a net monetary loss within five specific anglophone countries make sense? It makes sense only as a weapon brought to bear by the strategic intent of a hostile state. Last year the weapon killed 60,000 Americans. The program is designed to create an epidemic of human wretchedness and to abase public order. The program is succeeding, it is targeted against the five eyes, and it is funded by the Chinese Communist Party."

Portnoy scanned the faces of the group, and he knew he had wasted his time. The joint chiefs were primarily interested in strategies able to be marked by stick pins on a map. Also, they preferred to hear worrisome things about Russia rather than China. China supplied them with their semiconductors and rare earths.

Russia was much easier to sell as the enemy. Bucholz turned on the air conditioning to scavenge the cigar smoke and nodded to General Milton.

"Milton, the sample container is scheduled to return from Bennu and touch down in our Army controlled area in Utah on September 24th, 2023. You will have primary surveillance and monitoring responsibilities during its descent. Have your tactical groups been chosen and prepared?"

General Milton scanned the tired sagging faces and understood they had reached their limit of comprehension. He stood and threw back the last of his bourbon, grimacing at the harshness.

"Thank you general Bucholz, within the year my elite squads will be on site and running practice drills. We have three years to perfect the operation. The arrival date of the samples is correct and confirmed, and with that I have had enough of this. I'm heading back to the lawn to listen to the band, take off my shoes, and walk in the wet grass."

"Good. In fact, that sounds very good. I will join you presently. Gentlemen, we are adjourned. Admiral Crawford, General Conrad, please just stay for a moment, if you don't mind." .

The joint chiefs of staff paraded slowly into the night air, collectively happy that Bucholz was about to cut little miss Crawford into little miss pieces. Conrad could be taken down a peg or two as well. To a man, they wanted to witness it, but the band played on the lawn, the bar was still open, and they were enticed. Portnoy dropped to the back of the column and motioned Milton to fall back beside him.

"Richard, Bucholz just queried your preparations to pick up the sample canister in Utah. He did not mention the next leg to Houston. Do you have anything official on that?"

"The Air Force transporting the samples to the space center? That's a given."

"Don't bet on it. I'm hearing the army is going to do the job."

"The Army? The army couldn't pour piss out of a boot let alone get that canister to Houston in one piece. They couldn't possibly consider letting those morons touch it."

"That's what's in the air. Recruitment is down and it seems they want to make a show of it. I have not seen a memorandum; I have not seen a schedule. But with Bucholz, an army man, don't bet against it. "

Without a word, Milton took off his shoes and stood in the wet grass. He knew very well if something stupid could be done, the military would find a way to do it.

General Bucholz sat quietly at the boardroom table, allowing the joint chiefs to move beyond listening distance.

"General, admiral, this won't take long. Just a few things to discuss. General Conrad, what is the latest on the launching sites for the Mars program? Have any additional jurisdictions been accepted?"

"Yes, one, and it is the last. Nigeria."

Nancy Crawford looked quickly at Bucholz and back to General Conrad to confirm what she had just heard.

"I see your surprise. The population of Nigeria in 2030, when the first flights are planned to leave earth, will be three hundred million. They have a strong body of technical expertise, which is very useful for the new Mars colony. Nigeria also has the requisite coastline on the Atlantic Ocean. From time to time a ship is going to fail on launch. That is one reason for choosing only coastal and barren areas for liftoff. We don't want people seeing their sweet old Auntie blown up."

Nancy did some quick math in her head.

"General, we are talking ultimately about four million colonists over a period of years. That means launches in the tens of thousands. Do you have the numbers?"

"Considering cargo has to go as well, the guesses are about seventy-five thousand flights. They will leave in flotillas of ships, and remember, the carriers are reusable. Soon we will be building one full Sky Ship a day. We're hoping for first launch to Mars about 2030. As far as launching sites, construction has begun in twenty-seven countries. Realistically, a few of those might become unsuitable because of insurrection, weather reliability, local infrastructure, and so on. A prime location happens to be Kenya, where the Italians have a facility, the Broglio space center. Their lottery winners will embark from there. Kenya is at the equator, so rockets get a one thousand miles per hour boost because of the rotation of the earth."

Bucholz thought in terms of logistics and systems. The Mars expedition was a nightmare of coordination. It was a technological hydra where when one component was dealt with, two new quandaries grew to replace it.

"General Conrad, seventy-five thousand flights is astounding. An obvious question is, do we parade four million people to the ships, or do we take the ships to the four million people?"

"We have not decided, but China and Russia certainly have, and their infrastructures are mammoth. Russia recently completed a gas pipeline from Zimbabwe to South Africa. The parallel construction road is built with a base to support one hundred tons. We think that means they will be moving sky ships north toward the equator. As far as China, and you have to admire it, they have built a canal. It will be done within three years. One leg crosses the Caspian Sea, so they call it the Trans Caspian International transport corridor. Azerbaijan, Georgia, and Turkey have allowed access in exchange for infrastructure, and the canal will have direct access to the Mediterranean. They can supply the entire European union and Northern Africa from the Mediterranean Sea."

Admiral Crawford sat bolt upright.

"Absolute genius. The route bypasses Russia altogether and leaves us with egg on our faces. China will not have to go through the straits of Malacca into the Indian Ocean to move its goods. My South China Fleet can no longer intercept their container ships. The American threat to interdict or sanction China's shipping is gone."

Bucholz flared.

"Crawford! You are almost gleeful. The pleasure you derive is close to traitorous and almost as offensive as your contempt for the Joint Chiefs of Staff."

"Frankly general Bucholz, I do have contempt for your collection of dinosaurs. We sit, we wring our hands, we lament the advancements of our adversaries, yet we leave our command structure exactly as it has been since 1947. We're set in concrete and wonder how things could possibly pass us by. During the Second World War, we had four-star generals Marshall, Patton, Bradley, Clark, Eisenhower and two or three others appointed at the end of the war as administrators. We now have forty-four four-star generals when there are no legitimate declared theaters of war.

Command is diluted to the point of fragmentation. Please explain to me why it takes seven years and twenty billion dollars to deliver one ballistic missile nuclear submarine. Is that worthy of contempt? Yes."

Conrad stood quickly between the two of them and began laughing.

"Such a thing! You two! General, relax. Nine Bellinis have somewhat colored Nancy's perspectives. Is there anything else you wish to discuss with us?"

Bucholz accepted the peace offering. Crawford was a good one and he could not argue with anything she said. She had learned many things, but she had skipped the seminar on tact.

"Just one thing, General Conrad. You must have some concerns over some aspects of the Mars expedition."

"Yes, but I support the concept, and the mission, unequivocally. I am committed to the concept of us becoming a colonizing species. Unfortunately, we have bedfellows with whom I would rather not sleep.

A month ago, Russia made a successful test flight with a nuclear propelled missile. That in itself is an unbelievable threat domestically, and an amazing feat of technology but that is not the point. We are talking about the Mars trip. Nuclear thermal propulsion will reduce travel time from nine months to two months. What that means is should Russia adapt that propulsion system to their Sky ship, whether they leave within the global flotilla or not, they will arrive at Mars significantly before the rest of us. It could become the red planet in more ways than one."

"I know what you mean. I remember now the item I should have addressed in the larger meeting. How are the sleepers for the Mars expedition going?"

"Very well, general Bucholz. We have approximately six hundred thousand expatriates taking citizenship in countries around the world in order to participate in their lottery or to present themselves as part of that country's technicians for places on the sky ships. By the time of the launches they will have been ensconced as citizens for ten years and well-integrated as locals. We are greasing the wheels with cash to ensure their names appear among the lottery winners who will actually go. I'm guessing roughly half will make it onto a ship. In any case we will have a significant overrepresentation among the Mars colonists."

"Excellent. But it makes me wonder how many Chinese are doing the same thing here within our allotment."

The three stood and shook hands and Nancy Crawford spoke firmly.

"By the way general Bucholz, I will be at the space center for the coverage of the Bennu sampling."

"My dear Admiral, so will my team from the army, hobnail boots and all."

General Bucholz poured himself two fingers of bourbon as the door closed leaving him alone in the conference room. He turned off the light and welcomed the quiet of the darkness. He reflected on Admiral Crawford, understanding her need to keep the navy relevant in a world of Mars rockets and drones. The odor of the liquor was too much, and he pushed it away. He alone, among the Joint Chiefs of Staff, comprehended the technology buried in the sampling cannister. From space, it had behaved as planned, and if the data it contained proved out, he controlled the world. He controlled the military of every nation, he controlled every election worldwide, he controlled the banking system, and he controlled every vehicle including space and aircraft.

Bucholz was one of three people aware of its configuration and its potential. His eldest son and the civilian developer were the other two, having been classmates at Cambridge University, reading electrical engineering. They now collaborated as the sole occupants of a small laboratory in Colorado, funded by Bucholz' unaudited slush fund. Each of the Chiefs of Staff had the same sort of slush at their disposal and each was entirely incurious as to how the others spread the wealth.

Otto Bucholz was a patriot. After his engineering degree at MIT he ran the gauntlet at West Point and emerged as a star. He was now the chairman of the Joint Chiefs of Staff, and he knew the military. He also knew that nothing the military had developed had not been put eventually to its ultimate worst use. The Joint Chiefs supported operation Boscoe because of its nature. It was surreptitious, intrusive and unwelcome. They had no knowledge of Boscoe's ultimate capability nor how it was developed. That was secondary to them. The exercise had provided one more demonstration of their power and that satisfied their bully brains.

The General's concern over its use was grave. Unbridled political will, insanity or accident might unleash his technology and make an end to civilization. He had the awesome burden of deciding to whom he would pass the torch. It would not be the Joint Chiefs.

The Westminster chimes rang nine-forty-five and Freddy Bucholz removed his glasses and rubbed his temples. His concentration was gone after ten hours at the bench. The data from the day was encouraging and despite his fatigue he looked forward to the morning when he could resume testing. He lifted his fleece jacket off the hook as the amber incoming call button on his private line blinked. Numbly, he picked up.

"This is Fred. Oh, hi Dad. Your timing is good. I was about to close things down and go home. No, no, it is good to hear your voice. No, I'm okay, just really tired. It's been a long day, but a good one. Let's see, we have improved the collimation significantly but there's only so much we can do remotely. No, there's no question of its efficacy, it is just a matter of us continuing to enhance the directionality. The recovery of the relay device in your Bennu capsule will give us the data to make the last refinements."

"Can you not gather what you need remotely?"

"Yes, but transmission of the data gives an opportunity for interception. We can't risk that. I must have the physical chips from the capsule."

"What will they tell you?"

"The chip array in the collector records every proton strike from space and registers the exact number and direction of origin, and how much energy they impart, measured in ergs. Some of them hit with terrific force. A few years ago one of them hit with 51 joules energy. That's like a baseball traveling at 100 kilometers an hour. Those are the types we aim to create."

"Where do they come from in nature?"

"From exploding stars or black holes at the center of galaxies, but exactly where, it's hard to tell, because they're deflected by magnetic fields in space. Our hardware in the sampler uses a small magnetic field to bend their path and redirect them back to our laboratory here in Colorado. We can calculate what percentage of protons hitting the receiver in space survive the trip through the atmosphere. Typically, when cosmic particles hit air molecules, a large percentage of them are broken down into either positrons or pions and then other particles. Those are useless to us. We propagate a broad proton stream from here, targeting the Bennu capsule. The directional record will tell us what percentage of what we generated got through and with what impact. We only have a weapon if a predictable number hit the target with significant force. We have managed it successfully in the lab, and our device in the capsule will tell us whether we have been able to deliver the protons with impact over distance. If so, you have your weapon. To date we have not targeted anything. That's the next step after we check the data in the canister. No, I don't have qualms about the research, I know the sword is double edged. In the wrong hands it could decimate the world infrastructure. John? He is progressing very nicely on miniaturizing the particle beam generator. So far he has reduced it from a semi transport truck to a Mini Cooper. A storm? Yes, that's right. Denver got about eighteen inches. No, nothing here. That's how it is in the mountains. Tonight is Harriman's party isn't it? Things must be rocking in Virginia; I hear the band in the background. Anyway, the lab is gaining on it every day and I need to get some sleep. Bye. Me too."

Chapter Sixteen
October 20, 2020

She was awake when the call came from Rybakov at the telemetry center, and she dressed quickly. A small Canadian flag adorned her lapel, and every piece of her attire displayed the Cosmos Space Center logo. After four years, the final approach of OSIRIS-REx to its target had arrived. A media savvy technician had contrived the acronym for the 'Origins, Spectral Interpretation, Resource Identification, and Security – Regolith Explorer' of asteroid Bennu. The name was genius. It was perfectly exotic, and it hearkened to the mysteries of antiquity.

The roadway leading into the central research building was congested by parked cars along both sides, leaving a narrow central lane. Ahead in the line on the left was Frank McCord's green Buick. Excepting an emergency, he would not park his old girl within fifty feet of another vehicle. Something dramatic and unknown to Meghan was happening and she did not like it.

Dr. Macbeth arrived at launch control to find her private parking spot occupied by a military staff car with a flag on the right front fender indicating a four-star general. The army and navy had coopted the balance of the reserved spots, with the flag of an admiral blowing in the breeze. She parked against the rear fender of the general's car to block it in and stormed through security. The telemetry tracking room was filled with extra bodies hovering over the screens manned by her personnel, leaning in behind them as if the observers knew better what should be done. There were twenty or so soldiers in camouflage dress. She kicked an open cupboard door closed with a smash and stomped into the center of the room.

"You people get the hell out of my lab. Now! And why the devil are you morons dressed in camouflage gear! Look around! Do you see foliage? No! You see forty technicians at computers and observation screens waiting to do the jobs you are interfering with. Buckle up and piss off!"

She spun to find Frank.

"McCord, throw these bums out! "

Frank was deaf to the absurdity as safeties came off every rifle and to a man, the soldiers turned and looked for orders from the one they knew could save them. He was sixty and corpulent and self-satisfied. The man was obviously the general whose car had taken her reserved parking spot and he turned slowly to confront the female voice. The label on the right shirt front read 'Smelsky'. Meghan recognized the General immediately. He was the media darling. He showed up somewhere daily, either on television or the internet, sporting a chest full of medals as a ridiculous caricature of our national belligerency. She made a point of reading general Smelsky's name tag aloud.

"You. Sergeant Shnemski. Get your men out of here and remove your vehicles from the executive parking area. The Army has no business here and what the hell do you think you're up to, coming here without notice, coming into my laboratory without my permission and intimidating my people with your big boots and heavy breathing, and interfering with what they're doing on the job? Don't answer. I'm not finished. Before you pack up and hit the road, I have a simple question for you and the rest of your intelligentsia. Do you have any concept of the importance of what is happening here today? We're about to tag an asteroid, something more ancient than anything any man has ever touched and take samples. Samples of the ancient of ancients. And what do you incompetent fools do but interfere with us. Brilliant."

Smelsky was engorged.

"First, madame, civilian or not, you should be embarrassed at putting your man on the spot like that and you will address me as General Smelsky. Second, I am here on the expressed orders of General Otto Bucholz, the head of the Joint Chiefs of Staff. Samples! Samples, you cry. Who gives a fedoo about your bloody samples! You are a baby, a child, playing at massive things you don't understand. Potentially, that capsule contains the most strategic breakthrough in military strategy in the history of warfare. Samples! Pah! Russian stealth submarines which we can't see, can't hear, and can't find, are sitting somewhere off the Atlantic coast and you worry whether a pile of rocks which took almost a billion dollars from my budget might show you something nifty? Grow up!"

"Listen, you fathead! This is my project! Mine. Not the Army's. Rumors have it when the samples land in Utah three years from now, your job is delivery boy and I have no doubt when the time comes you will mess it up. And you say you have some great military secret buried deep within the bowels of a sample collector the size of a shoe box, some of which sample space you used up with your gadget. You fantasize. I know every millimeter of that hardware. I helped design it, develop it and oversee it from start to finish. Yes, I had a large team, exceptionally large, but the final assembly and check off was done by trusted technicians and close associates. They are all my people. Loyal people with whom I worked daily for over five years."

Smelsky glanced at Admiral Crawford to see whether she wished to pile on, but she demurred and moved subtly closer to Meghan as if to share Meghan's position against Smelsky's ongoing rant.

"Doctor Macbeth, I thank you for your courtesy and I forgive your childish tantrum, as your reputation for volatile and irrational outbursts precedes you. As an individual who has built her life on her inquiring mind, you appear to have avoided the simple reality of the situation, by not asking yourself two obvious questions. Please recognize I do not criticize you for your shortcomings. I do appreciate as time passes and one ages, one's intellect can slip a little. So let me lay it out for you. First, would I be here if it were not the case that the army had buried something within your hardware? Second, you yourself have said it. Other than your own involvement in the final preparation of the Bennu sampling devices, you have a small team. Yet nevertheless, the army's proprietary hardware is installed as part of the sampling paraphernalia. Occam's razor, my dear."

Meghan was furious at the turn in the conversation, and she wanted to drive her ballpoint pen into his left eye. She knew the general was correct, for indeed, she had rejected the obvious as implausible and she had screwed up. Worse, she knew she might have structured a more rigorous final inspection routine so breaches or unauthorized design reconfiguration could not happen. A member of her close team had been co-opted and the individual had done the bidding of the army. Meghan found it impossible to accuse any person among her coworkers of being the perpetrator. She could only speculate in what other sedition that individual might be involved. Red-faced and furious she turned to confront Smelsky when Rybakov's stentorian voice on speaker thundered through the room.

"Enough! Unless I say so, if I hear one more word, if I hear so much as a scuffle, a sneeze or a burp for the next two hours I shall spin the dial and send the bloody OSIRIS-REx vehicle full bore into the sun! You men. Back away from the consoles. If you need to guard something, try the wall behind you. Otherwise, McCord will throw you out. Everyone else just stay where you are. Nishimura, cast the image to the big screen. Dr. Leishman, calibrate your thrusters, maximum two feet per second approach. Keep it oriented directly above the North Pole."

Isadore Leishman nodded. Answering Rybakov seemed a violation. He was wrapped in the deliciousness of the loving voice. It had caressed the beautiful Leishman many times during recent weeks but of course he would not do its bidding, no not its bidding, but somehow what he wanted was what it wanted also. In a few minutes the first agreement between them would mature into action. A tiny drool surfaced on his lips.

"Isadore! Do you copy?"

"Wha… Yes. Copy. Copy."

"Terry, check the Polycam, when we are twenty-two minutes out I will signal you and I want high resolution imagery from there all the way in. Everyone, if you must talk, do it now. We have nineteen minutes. ”

Bennu was a small shining pea turning slowly in the center of the eighteen-foot screen. From the aspect of the camera it spun slowly counterclockwise in a four-hour day. The buzz of excitement grew in the room and Meghan beckoned Frank over.

“Fantastic isn’t it?”

“Absolutely amazing. Particularly the military escort for it.”

Bennu now appeared around the size of a basketball and its spinning top shape was more evident.

“Meghan, the assumptions I made were wrong. For some reason I thought it would a sphere. It is more like a diamond in the rough with a pebbled surface.”

“The view from here is deceptive. We’re still at some distance. What you refer to as pebbles are the size of houses, the size of football fields, the size of cars. Those would be very nice samples except our collector is sixteen inches in diameter. At the moment the craft is passing over an area called Simurgh and soon we will see the section called Gargoyle. Bennu is spinning left to right, and we are traveling over the poles. By design. ”

Sunlight illuminated the rock-strewn landscape as Bennu grew to fill more of the screen.

“Meghan, is the explorer looking for areas to sample?”

“No, that was determined by a flyby in 2018. We were astounded by the size of the regolith. The rubble. We expected sandy particulate and got chunks the size of road graders. The only location we found suitable for sampling fine granular material was a depression at the north pole. That’s why we orbit over the poles. And according to Murphy’s law it is the only spot on the asteroid which stays dark. It is out of the sun because of its concavity, which is why we call the area ‘Nightingale’. It is small and demanding to navigate, less than the size of a tennis court. We say we ‘TAG’ it. TAG is an acronym for ‘Touch-And-Go ‘. You will see it happen shortly. Do you know who the woman is standing there to the right of Leishman?”

“Yes, in fact I do. I saw her senate confirmation two years ago. She is Admiral Nancy Crawford, a Member of the Joint Chiefs of Staff. Her commentary and forward thinking regarding the role of the military in an evolving and strategically changing world was impressive. Would you like to meet her?"

"Yes, I would. Walk with me."

Admiral Crawford saw them coming and smiled, never taking her eyes off Frank. Meghan began to lose her cordiality.

"Hello, my chief of security, tells me you are Admiral Crawford of the Joint Chiefs. I am Dr. Meghan Macbeth, project manager for the OSIRIS-REx program. Why are you here in my launch center?"

"It is a pleasure to meet you Dr. Macbeth. Here. Shake my hand. You will feel better. And you Mr. … ."

"McCord. Mr. Frank McCord."

I shook her hand, and she was correct. I certainly did feel much better. I was not sure about Meghan.

"It is a distinct pleasure to meet you also Mr. McCord. There. Now we are all friends. I'm here today to take some of the bull out of the bulldozer Smelsky. His modus operandi is invasion and take no prisoners. My intention was to be the sole representative of the military and speak to you woman to woman or one tough broad to another tough broad as the Chiefs put it, but instead you got the dinosaur. Huffing and puffing and blowing your house down. They will never let the opportunity for an invasion, large or small, go to waste. The stupidity of it is all they had to do from the outset was to simply make it item five on your mission statement where you currently have four. Item five, test a radio transmitter or whatever the thing is, for the army."

I could see the polar swing in Meghan. She would have drinks with this lady.

"Dr. Macbeth, none of us including General Smelsky has an inkling of what the device is. It is Bucholz' personal baby and Smelsky has simply repeated Bucholz' mantra. I believe all they want to do is confirm it has arrived intact and has not been damaged by the sampling material. The men's club would not want me to apologize, so please accept my apology for the intrusion. Having said that, my instincts tell me there is something else afoot. The combined forces send a rocket up monthly for some reason or another. Satellite communication, the international space station, spying, weather manipulation and so on. The device could have travelled on any one of those, but it did not. It seems it is so special

Bucholz would not expose its nature even to his own military. As you see, digression is my favorite thing. Do you have anything to drink?"

"Drink? It's 7:20 a.m."

"Well, yes it is a bit of a late start."

"Later. White wine?"

"Montrachet?"

"Yes."

"Excellent!"

Dr. Rybakov swaggered past me and seated himself at the controls of the main console. Bennu now filled the screen, and we were close to the main event.

"Dr. Macbeth, how will you know whether you have gathered anything into the container?"

"There is a camera in the canister which activates after the sampling is done. Excuse me. I am on headphones from now on. If you want to listen in, grab a headset from the table there."

Rybakov tapped his microphone to get everyone's attention and stop the banter.

"Terry, high resolution now. Isadore, two feet per second. Nishimura, release attitude control on my count. Three… , two… , one… , I have control. Hands off everyone. Dayboll, shout out fifty feet."

Meghan heard the technicians around her, excited and worried, referring to their part in the landing. It had its own acronym as everything did. It was TAG. 'Touch and go', they called the liaison.

We could hear Rybakov's pulse in the headphones. As the explorer closed in on the target, his heart rate slowed. He was in his element and in total control. Tension was not part of him. He was a more formidable opponent than ever.

"Solar panels. Raising, tight, furled. Engaging robotic arm. Canister face open. Terry, watch your camera aperture, we're dropping out of the sun and into the crater….. now. "

The screen went black to a collective gasp and for a full second nothing, then once again high resolution resumed.

Dayboll's throaty voice cut in.

"Fifty."

"All right people, twenty-five seconds to first touch. I am centered. Yes. Yes. The target is perfect…. ten seconds, arm extended….. home."

The room exploded in a delirium of joy as forty staff screamed and high fived the world. Five years of sweat and stress and creativity had been rewarded.

The canister penetrated a few inches into the granular substrate of asteroid Bennu and a plume of dust ran away into space as compressed nitrogen gas from the robotic arm blasted loose debris to fill the canister. The interior camera activated, and Meghan shrieked and stabbed her finger at the screen in a staccato fury. The army had indeed placed a shiny stainless device in the canister, and it had certainly survived, and three years hence, OSIRIS-REx would give it a soft landing on the plains of Utah.

"We are….closed…. , contained. People, congratulate yourselves, we have sampled Bennu. Arm retraction proceeding, extension secured. Collector capsule sealed. Right array.. nominal. Left… nominal. Solar array fully redeployed. Leishman, push off and take us into orbit around the rock, on my count, you have it. Three… , two… , one… yours."

Leishman nodded and activated the explorer's thrusters to the escape velocity he had programmed. The vehicle careened out of the crater, blasting away wide swaths of the margin, leaving a new thirty-foot flattened plane of denuded surface exposed to the sun. Leishman beamed at the chaos and made no attempt to stem the drool. Tons of gravity free regolith propelled by the blasters cascaded into the void. It was a Vesuvius of ancient debris, and it was glorious.

Rybakov screamed.

"Leishman! You maniac! You have created a whole new reflective face. The Yarkovsky calculations will have to be reworked and because of your little escapade who knows what they will show! You may have unbalanced the scales. "

The Boys withdrew from Leishman's orbitofrontal cortex and released his nucleus accumbens from their influence. His inordinate level of pleasure from pleasing them, fell to a normal physiological level. He thrust his tongue twice and blinked his way around his updated surroundings as if he had just arrived.

"Dr. Rybakov, let not your heart be troubled, those few tons of regolith, they are nothing. We are in perfect orbit around Bennu, and we will ride with it until it is close enough to deliver us our samples. When the explorer is 63,000 miles above earth, it will release the canister to float home, then it is referred to as OSIRIS-APEx as it flies on to meet up with asteroid Apophis. Together we have done a wonderful thing. The world is proud of us. We are proud of you, Dr. Rybakov. As far as the Yarkovsky effect, I will run the required formulae, but I know in advance they will demonstrate nothing about which we need worry. I hear the popping of corks. I seldom indulge but I believe for what we have done here today, I shall celebrate."

The two parties had entirely different concepts of what they celebrated. Rybakov had expertly controlled the telemetrics of the sampling. Leishman had evaluated the strength of his remotely controlled thrusters. His little experiment with Bennu left no question he needed to beef them up for Apophis. For his ultimate purpose, a bigger reflective plane was imperative. The voice understood, and yes, oh yes, so sweet, it had suggested and agreed. Rendezvous with Apophis was nine years hence in 2029 when the monster asteroid would pass by between the earth and the Moon. He fantasized throwing darts at it. When it paid its following visit in 2036 his colleagues would be puzzled by those bristly things.

I clinked glasses with Meghan and Nancy Crawford. The Boërl & Kroff champagne was reputed to surpass Dom Perignon, and I agreed. I preferred Lagavulin whisky any day of the week, but a special celebration overrode preference. I was surprised to hear even crazy Leishman was joining in.

"Meghan, what was with Leishman and celebration? I thought he did not drink alcohol."

"He doesn't. He likes to watch the corks as projectiles. With any luck someone might lose an eye."

"Astounding! I don't know the man, but I would certainly not give him the keys to the castle. Did you get enough sample material?"

"I wonder how much time I would do if I killed Smelsky. What? Oh, yes. We collected substantially more than we anticipated. We should have enough to share among several labs and make comparisons. This is terrific champagne but I'm not a bubbles girl. Admiral, are you enjoying this?"

"Yes, but I'm with you. I prefer a good still wine. Besides, you promised."

"Yes, I did. However, I am not moving my car. I have the general boxed in against a concrete stairway. Mr. McCord, will you drive me? And the admiral?"

"Yes, of course. It is my pleasure."

"What about the back seat of your Buick?"

"Why Meghan!"

"You jerk! I meant, is it clean."

"Immaculate. Let's go."

Admiral Crawford's car picked her up after two hours of white wine, leaving Meghan and me alone. She logged into the telemetry center and sourced the video of the sampling. We watched and re-watched the video of the sample collection and the explorer blasting off from Bennu. She sighed at the sample collection.

"Frank, I hoped the apparent reflective surface of whatever Smelsky claimed to have inserted into the collector was an artifact in the lens of the camera, but it is not. There is certainly a device there."

"Meghan, Dr. Rybakov flipped out on Leishman about the blast off. What was that about?"

"One of the mission statements for the OSIRIS-REx project was to measure the Yarkovsky effect, the subtle force caused by absorbing the sun's radiation in the day and then releasing the radiant energy in darkness to give the asteroid a little push. The idea was to gain insight into the evolution and orbit of the asteroid, which was an important insight related to the past, now made irrelevant by the increased absorption capacity of the flat plane made by Leishman's thrusters. Once again the orbit is guesswork."

"You will have to change your acronym. TAB. Touch and blast."

"It was certainly touch, but it was not the little kiss to the rockpile we anticipated. I don't know what happened with Leishman's calculations. He blasted the hell out of the surface. I would guess he dislodged perhaps ten tons of regolith. That's not much in the world of space rocks but it is a major change for an asteroid of that size. It might also allow increased off gassing to change the orbit dramatically. Fortunately, it won't be back close to us for another six years and we will have the calculations by then. However, that does not answer the question of which of my team is compromised. It sickens me to feel this violation of my trust. These are my friends. One of them is an agent of the U.S. military. I want to engage you to track the bugger down. It is unofficial and off book. You know the principals, myself, Rybakov, Leishman, Rustom. Beyond that there were perhaps twenty journeymen, and a few regular expert technicians involved at the fabrication stage. I will pay you personally and we will meet elsewhere for your reports. Now let us return to this wonderful day. Watch carefully as I commence to pour you three fingers of Lagavulin, and in short order I shall personally dispatch the rest of this bottle of Montrachet."

"Well Meghan, that's a good beginning. All right. I will take the case at my usual rate. However, given our history and the apparent inevitability of anything you commission devolving into a life-threatening confrontation with me up against a maniac, should that be in the offing, the rate is doubled. Consider this discussion as a binding verbal contract. There will be no paper floating around Cosmos referencing my assignment. In the morning I will contact my old comrade in arms at CSIS, Charles Witmer. He is now the Director of Operations for all things clandestine. In the bad old days he and I together did many a nasty thing for Queen and country. Considering the national security implications of your project, he will likely grant me a writ of access to your employees' bank accounts. Unusual deposits tell many tales. I need the personnel files and work logs for anyone who came within a mile of the canister. Can you provide that?"

"Yes. It's a short list. I have their complete CV as well as life histories, hobbies, interests, family situation, even backgrounds of close relatives. Cosmos was scrupulous in vetting every one of them yet here we are, looking for a rat who betrayed us all and who risked the success of my collection apparatus by changing my hardware."

"Who was the general factotum on the project? You know, someone who had a finger into every aspect of the physical canister development? I need to sit with him."

“Sanjay Rustom is the one. He did a little bit of everything and did it well. I let him and hundreds more staff go after the launch, but I should have kept him on. In fact, I invited Sanjay back, but he declined. He is in the pizza business, of all things. In New Mexico. A town called Argentum.”

“His insight will be helpful. Whoever inserted the device on behalf of the army was planted deep.”

“Yes, and when you find the rat, I will boil him in oil. Yes. I will boil him down and render his fat.”

She lifted her glass.

“Cheers.”

We clinked.

“Cheers. Seems a waste of time. Better to just smile, gift him a bottle of Cosmic suntan oil, and send him to Mars.”

Sergei Rybakov cut the end of his cigar in feigned preparation to smoke it and stepped outside the viewing area onto the fire escape platform. He lit the stogie and stuffed it into a crook of the railing and voice activated his neutrino phone to Demidov.

“Privyet. Yes Pavel, I know it is 2:00 a.m. in Moscow. Just listen, I have only a minute. United States military has ensconced a device in the sample canister. It was done without the knowledge of the inner circle, and it is important enough that the chairman of the Joint Chiefs sent his personal emissary to ensure it had remained intact. More curious, the nature of the device is not known to the highest echelon of the army. Apparently it is a closely held technology known only to the chairman. You’re breaking up. Did you say, how long until it lands in Utah? About three years. What? You already have a man inside and working on the problem?”

The fire door rasped open, and technician Dayboll stepped out lighting a cigarette.

Rybakov scrambled for his cigar and flicked the ash for show.

“Ah. Dayboll. Joining me for a smoke? Good work in there. Amazing wasn’t it?”

“Beyond amazing. Overwhelming.”

Yuri Blinov watched the last of his eight-man crew exit the sonar room and he secured the door behind them. His technical officer loaded the file about which she had expressed concern into the wave analyzer. Blinov was captain emeritus of the latest Yasen class Russian submarine, the Sheremetev, and his captaincy was the culmination of a career of clandestine maritime operations on behalf of Russia. Despite that, he would have traded it all for the cut and thrust of a real conflict. For Blinov, nothing matched the thrill of a good fight. He was a taciturn individual possessed of a facile and tactically ingenious mind, a chess grandmaster, and strategies honed across the board translated well into the spatial considerations of battle. His adversaries said peace was gained through strength, or so their fuzzy edged homily ran. He believed selective annihilation made a far more reasonable statement. He had no qualms either way. He was a Russian man of war.

Blinov's new boat was a palace. The upgraded Yasen-M class carried a crew of only seventy-eight men and the ship was spacious and open in comparison to the old designs. His workforce was small because of the sophisticated electronics which controlled its workings, but in most ways, Blinov was old school. If a computer program had a glitch, one could not take a wrench to it nor tighten a turnbuckle to make things right. On the other side of the equation, should an emergency or a catastrophic event occur, a pod surrounding the upper con and antenna tower was a small discrete separate ship. The entire crew could detach from the main craft and escape to safety within it. Yuri Blinov did not like the idea. Human nature was to take the easy way out. The British Navy of the 18th century knew it and would not have a crew which knew how to swim. Commander Blinov felt the same way. He wanted men who would fight to the death, not run from carnage.

For the appointment as its captain, he had been designated 'Commander of the Flotilla', a remarkable thing as he had just celebrated his sixty-second birthday. He had expected the official gold-embossed letter from the Admiralty to contain an edict for retirement. Instead, the boat he waited four years to see finished was his to command. She was 457 feet long with a beam of 43 feet and she traveled easily at 32 miles an hour when she was submerged and running silent. Her silence was abetted by a full rubberized coating which reduced noise and lessened sonar reflection. Her sister ship, the Katya, when it was launched in 2018 had evaded detection for a year despite the world having specific knowledge of both the time and place of its launching. No navy could find her.

Blinov's Sheremetev was a step up from Katya. She carried the same land attack missiles with a 1600-mile range, ten hypersonic missiles and eight vertical cruise missile silos as the Katya did, but in addition it carried the Poseidon. Poseidon was Putin's super torpedo. It was eighty feet long and it was an entirely new category of weapon, but not new in concept. The late and unlamented dictator of Russia, Joseph Stalin, had directed his engineers to build such a weapon in the 1950s to devastate the coastal cities of the United States. The real thing ran faster and deeper than anything and nothing could touch it or combat it. Blinov knew Mother Russia would soon have ten such submarines in action on both coasts of North America. Technician Glazunov interrupted her commander's musings.

"Sir, here is the wave pattern I spoke to you about. See these spikes and peaks? It took me a while to categorize them, because the last time I saw anything similar to this was in physics lab in the academy many years ago. Developmentally, it is very much like where our research was in those days."

"What do you think it is?"

"Commander Blinov, I'm not altogether sure. Initially I thought it was a disjointed attempt at a neutrino pulse, similar to what we use to communicate with the surface. That disappointed me because at the moment only we are capable of this, but as I watched it for a longer time, I realized that was not the case. It is certainly an atomic particle, but definitely not a neutrino. It has too much energy. The odd one has the impact of a hammer. Likely a proton or positron."

"I see. I'm told cosmic particles can do strange things. Is it correct that recently physicists have determined they behave differently when you watch them? Would a change in pattern now and again perhaps indicate it was man-made, watched then not watched? "

"It is true observation can change behavior of particles, but I doubt this is one of those times. This pattern has been generated roughly similar to what we experimented with eight or ten years ago with neutrinos. It is sloppily done but I'm positive about what they are attempting. What we see here is a rudimentary effort to either collimate or direct a stream of particles. The last emission was a few days ago, and over the last few months I have collected perhaps thirty samples. They have a wide range of energy."

"Then whoever is doing this is out of touch with their hardware. They don't have access to whatever has been generating the code in order to tweak it or really work on it."

"I agree, captain. It has to be generated from something difficult for them to access, possibly something orbiting. I checked with our men and nothing like that is happening on the International Space Station. But who knows where it comes from? There are thousands of satellites and traveling research vehicles."

"I congratulate you Glazunov. This is an especially important intercept. At the moment, we alone can communicate by a code embedded within an irregularly pulsed neutrino stream. It is a marvel to me how our submarines can receive instantaneous transmissions at any depth by neutrinos, and if necessary, we can communicate directly through the Earth from one side to the other."

" And soon enough, if all goes as planned, communicate undetected through Mars."

"Yes. It is a major tactical advantage. Our boat can react to a change in strategy or global command decisions within the second. The American, British, Chinese subs must surface and raise an antenna just as we did years ago. If those fleets came against us today, it would be over for them before they knew they were under attack. But these transmissions show us someone is scratching the surface of the science, so in a year we might be faced with quite a different enemy. If we do not attack soon, we will lose our advantage."

"Captain, communications is one thing, and as you have just stated, a tremendous advantage in battle. My concern is some of these cosmic particles I have monitored have enough energy that they can change coding in computers.

That's a big deal. Sir. If one could direct such a high energy stream with accuracy, no machines of war."

"Ah well Glazunov, that is for the joint strategic command staff, not me. Send them what you have. Then clear that file off the screen and shred it and get the men back in here to their stations. Then come to my quarters. I have an open bottle of Crown Royal."

Chapter Seventeen

Captain Fahid Suleman banked his Etihad Airbus 350 into position and leveled it out, confirming his flight path with the control tower at YVR airport. It was the second leg of their return trip from Moscow through Dubai to Vancouver and the plane had battled the jet stream for fifteen hours. Flight steward Musa Bakir walked quietly into the array of first-class sleeping enclosures and as requested of him, he gently prodded his favorite person awake.

" Pardon, and good morning, Gunderson. We are on approach to Vancouver, about an hour out. I have taken the liberty of percolating your coffee. You ordered the reserve Pacamara bean, did you not?"

"Yes, I did, thank you Musa. Good morning to you."

"As God wants, this wonderful day blossoms for you as it should, sunny and warm. Breakfast will be ready for you presently. By the time you finish your shower, and I make your bed, it will be on the table."

"Just coffee, please."

"Excellent. But if past preferences apply, one might appreciate some orange juice in the form of Mimosa?"

Roger nodded and lifted the window shade to inspect the day. Musa's rare coffee did not disappoint. Its bouquet haunted their palate exquisitely and they closed their eyes to better appreciate its complex finish. Moreover, Etihad airlines used the finest champagne in the Mimosa, and it elevated the experience.

Despite the hospitality and comfort of their surroundings they slept fitfully. They did not have peace of mind. The shower was a pleasant relief from the unsettled night but as they dried off, concern emerged. Over their career, they had never looked back but rejecting the contract on Frank McCord stirred something deeper, something never felt. They had known McCord very well and over many years. They knew also Demidov would not relent in his intent to expunge him. Within the narrow and shadowed veil of assassins, reputations grew quietly. The whisper of the day was codeword Malta. Malta was young, it had been said. Malta was brilliant was the word. Malta was busy and Malta was also a Russian. His bloodline was unknown. He had no patronymic to suggest his lineage as a lead to his identity.

They understood why Demidov had not hired the young killer for the task of terminating Frank McCord. It was the curse of Moscow. Many a lip was loosened by vodka and simple stories began deep in the cups expanded in the telling to reveal terrible deeds. Pavel Demidov could not be the name attached to the execution of a foreign national. They knew also these clandestine things did not mature quickly. A successful contract, to be consummated with neither a trace nor residue of the event, took months to prepare. Malta would not be available in the offing, except for preliminary reconnaissance and planning. They wondered whether they might not make a plaything of it and run some interference for McCord. They were uncomfortable. They felt something, which if they had not misconstrued the sensation, was akin to nostalgia. That was a word they never understood, and they were unsure whether they enjoyed it. It was also a seductive thing. Something neither from their world nor that of The Demidov. Because they were privy to the old man's intention to remove McCord, it was possible, even probable, they themselves were scheduled to be terminated first. McCord would follow.

Pavel Demidov represented the epitome of their distaste. Demidov and his class through lineage and historical preference earned by ancient service, still ruled the world. His ancestors were cannon makers to The Czar and of a cannon maker all things are forgiven. The elite could say, 'dispose of her or him' and it was done.

Roger Gunderson's safe house in Vancouver was a through and through residence. It occupied the entire 34th floor of a forty-story high-rise with views of the Pacific Ocean to the west and in the north, Mount Seymour rose out of the Burrard Inlet. The promised warm and sunny opening to the day was short lived as a cloying mist descended from the mountains to quiet the landscape. It suited their mood. The 2011 Grand Cru Meursault was perfect and held at the ideal 56° but it did nothing for them. Inaction niggled at their subconscious, and it gnawed away the pleasure of the wine.

"Hello, concierge, ah Maurice. This is Gunderson. I need a rental car. No, no. Nothing like that. Something unobtrusive. Yes, I am serious. Make it a compact, something dull and innocuous. I am playing a little trick on some friends. Also, check on the availability of a Bolshoi suite in the Metropol hotel in Moscow. If nothing is available, look for a suite in the closest lodgings to the café Pushkin. Check too for the season of heaviest rain. I wish particularly for it to be booked for that time."

The trip from the Vancouver residence to Deception Bay and Abernathy Town took fifty minutes through a jammed Massey tunnel and they were unfazed. An unexpected joy crept into them as they approached the familiar streets, and the car drove itself to their favored hotel.

The Excelsior was built during the reign of Queen Victoria and resided in that era. The cuisine was exquisite, and Conde Naste rated it five stars. Its sommelier was sought after worldwide and would not leave, the establishment prohibited the use of electronic devices within its confines, and it was pleased to give directions elsewhere should its guests require the Internet. It was one of two hotels in North America which served their preferred Burgundy, which they had suggested to the hotel years ago and which tradition it continued. They stopped and stepped out of the car in the porte-cochère and handed off the keys to the attendant who brightened gleefully and bubbled toward them.

"Why, such a pleasure to see you again! It has been, eleven, no, twelve years since you last visited with us? March 14th, the year of the great storm. I do recall you introduced to us an incredibly special something for our cellar. Of course, you do not remember this old Terrance but... . I apologize, sincerely, for my familiarity. I am very sorry. Shall I send for your bags? The same room? Kitchen en suite?

"Terrance, I do remember you, but no, I have just come for a sip."

"Very good."

"On second thought, for old times' sake, book me for the night."

"Of course."

"Actually, give me my old room for a month. I'll have some bags sent along."

"Very good."

The surface of the bay was in a gentle swell and the view from the familiar room was pacifying. The vapor of the effluvium and the fall of the waves hitting the sand were like the greeting of an old friend. Yet the assassin was furious with themselves. They had not anticipated being recognized or remembered. Fortunately, the longstanding staff was scrupulously trained in client confidentiality, and it was unlikely they would be compromised. Not a person in the establishment would utter a syllable regarding a guest. The interior appeared untouched since their last visit. The large stone Buddha they remembered sat smiling up from the writing desk where it sat a dozen years earlier. A subtle linseed scent attested to the recent oiling and polishing of the chestnut paneling. The great storm had come within yards of the sea undermining the building's foundations, but providence had spared it, and the Excelsior continued as of old, locked in its time.

They realized then why they were there. It was not to relive a storied remembrance. Intuitively, they were preparing the battleground. Malta was active. He was active against McCord, and he was active against them. Neither of those things would stand. In their mind, they framed and visualized that rainy day in Moscow when Demidov's finger stirred its last pot.

<>

I typed in Witmer's private email address and chuckled at his adolescent fun. The address of the master spy was 'SpookyStuff@deepsix.com'. I seldom used email to communicate. The three letter agencies searched keywords and manufactured profiles of suspicion for future use. Due to a perverse interest in what I might have missed, every few months I checked my account. If the mail read, 'I am on the ledge and I am sending you this from my phone', I shortened my contact list.

Nothing twigged in the first few documents from Meghan's employee material. Witmer and CSIS had an encyclopedia of background information not available to me and I wanted their help. It was also important to determine whether Canada had been complicit in tampering with the sample canister. Five Eyes nations commonly colluded. I compressed the final file of twenty-six employee CVs, encrypted it with Pgp, then pasted Witmer's public code as the body of the e-mail. His private code would decrypt it to expose the information. An interloper in his mail would encounter a gibberish of alphanumeric strings and symbols, revealing nothing. Witmer was a very quick study. He would likely work through the material before I had the opportunity, then ring me up with his '*first over the finish line*' voice, '*old chap*'. We competed relentlessly when we were both in the circus and nothing had changed.

My flight from Vancouver to Sante Fe took three hours. I laid over for two hours, then made a short hop to Las Cruces New Mexico. The small jet was an eighty-seat Embraer 175, and I studied files along the way. Seventy-two empty seats allowed me to spread my paper and make myself at home. The rental car agent in Las Cruces guessed at a drive of ninety minutes to the pizza place in Argentum. He assured me the locals would steer me in the right direction. The map showed mostly grade B roads.

"You're gonna find some altitude at Argentum. Want an inclinometer in the car?"

"Of course."

I had no idea what an inclinometer did, what it looked like or where to look for it, but I wanted to appear savvy. He brought me up a spotlessly clean standard transmission Datsun, which dated at least to the original ark. I could not decide which of the two by two it was. He pointed me roughly west, and I started out shadowless in the high noon sun, into a barren and featureless expanse. Heat waves disfigured the road ahead of me and slowly the character of the land began to impress itself on me. The size of the nothingness became a great something and in that, was beauty beyond description. I understood why families remained for generations. My visit would certainly be a surprise to Sanjay Rustom but dropping in removed formality and usually made for efficient conversation. He had a fine mind, and I hoped he might have insights others did not. He was faithful to Macbeth, and I doubted he violated the sampler. His security clearance was intact, and I could lay out the event with no worries. Something moved on the dashboard and caught my eye. The profile of a vehicle inside a small gauge nosed upward. The inclinometer was on the job, and it indicated I was now headed uphill and perhaps I might choose a different gear.

Robin Hathaway reined up across the street from Argentum Refined Pizza and dropped down off his Appaloosa. His spurs jangled as he stomped his boots clean of the dust and he slapped his mare on the rump to move her from leaning on the tether rail. He untied his saddle bags and slung them over his shoulder and whistled a tone-deaf tune as he walked. He had news for the boys.

Sanjay Rustom opened the window in the back room and sneezed as he put the evacuation fan on high.

"Nigel, I do not know how you stand it. Your face down over your work and the smoke from your soldering billowing around you. Those gases are so acrid, surely you are close to being pickled by now. You have even managed to overcome the baking smells of the pizza ovens."

"Consider me like the frog. Warming in the water not knowing he will eventually be boiled. My olfactory receptors are so long gone I no longer smell any of these things. Besides, the transponders are pretty much complete. I have maybe half a dozen remaining. What's the new cabinet in the corner there?"

"It's a fallback cooling unit for the capsule. If the samples have any biology we need to protect that. We want to maintain full value for the ransom. The canister has its own nitrogen cooling system which is designed to last for years but we need a failsafe. By the way, the Plantagenet woman has accepted our offer of purchase for this building. Robin has ridden over to pick up the paperwork. I am not sure he wasn't more pleased to be seeing Daisy than acquiring the property. "

" He told me he was heading that way. I fed his critters this morning."

Robin strode through the side door and left it open as he encountered the soldering fog. He tossed his saddle bags on the bench, unbuckled a flap and handed Sanjay signed property transfer documents.

"Boys, I've struck the mother lode. Not only do I have a date to take Daisy dancing, but I also scoped a site for another dry run on driving a landslide. One where Stonebreaker isn't going to see us. But most important, I have discovered the perfect stash for the capsule. The mustang trail runs right by it. It's an abandoned mine tucked in an outcrop and protected by an overhang. You can't see it from above or any direction except standing right in front. The timbers are solid, and hinges on the front jamb showed someone had attached a heavy door to stay safe and protect their poke. We'll do the same. The space has a silted earthen floor and a few puddles from the aquifer above, so it just needs some cleaning out and it's perfect. Widens out on the flat for about sixteen feet, plenty of room to kip for three or four weeks after the heist. Water and dried food and we're all set. Sanjay, Daisy says a big guy was asking around town about you, he may be on his way here. Also, how's the climbing gear coming? Have you been able to find the pulleys, U bolts, climbing chalk?"

"I know nothing about a big guy, so we'll see if he shows. As far as the gear, I think so. The pulleys and U bolts, yes, but the chalk, maybe. Check it to see if it's the right stuff."

" Likely it is. There's just a couple of types and you'll be using them often. You two need more training. When we have gathered all the hardware I can drill U bolts into the counterweights and set the restraining stakes. The last time out, Sanjay, you were six inches from getting brained by a twenty pounder. It missed your skull by a hair. In all the dust and racket, you didn't know it. If you hadn't looked down at your footing, we'd have planted a nice memorial cross right there. Yessir, coulda had a nice little ceremony. Here lies Rustom. Didn't duck, out of luck. Nice. I'm almost sorry it didn't happen. You messed up on the bald spots. Easier to walk but easier to slide off too, and when you go down hard, the impact on the loose material is greater than walking on it. You just might dislodge a bit keeping a half ton boulder in place. This whole exercise needs to become second nature, a built-in reflexive habit. We have over two years until the canister lands, and this must become routine. Also, right now it is a three-man job. We have to reduce it to two."

"You killing one of us?"

"Don't tempt me. Just contingency planning. Building in redundancy. We're working on rough terrain and soon we will be running our practice drills at night. The odds are, one of us is going to get injured or worse, sliding around in the dark butting up against eight hundred-pound animals on a mission to satisfy their training. In fact, I have them pretty well conditioned to complete their routes without me. I take them out in groups of eight or ten. They're more comfortable in that size group, more like their normal habitat. I release them at just about the same time every night and we walk an identical route. Now they're standing ready to go at that time, knowing when they have things done they arrive home to some special oats. If I go down, you just need to remove the barrier at the right time, and they will complete the route precisely. I tell you that in case I am the one who takes the fall. From now on we will rotate through every job so each of us can do any one of them if required. That includes you Sanjay. You may be the one required to carry the capsule. Sanjay?"

" Okay, okay. Wonderful. More climbing."

"The counterweight setup is the key. Have you scrounged the spikes?"

"Six, so far. We need three more?"

"Yes. If we hook up our harnesses and release the counterweight with no trouble, we'll be pulled to the height of the land and the trail above the slide in forty-five seconds at the most. Anyone attempting to follow on foot will take half an hour or more to clamber through the loose debris and gain any height. Besides the dust will likely blind them from following. Get in the habit of wearing your kerchief. Also, and this may seem a mastery of the obvious, but in times of stress odd things happen. When you signal me to release the counterweight, make sure you have the capsule attached to your harness. Otherwise, in a flash you will be pulled nicely to the top and the canister will be sitting neatly at the bottom."

"Bummer."

"Bummer? End of story is what it is. The mine is roughly five hundred yards from the truck route, and easy to travel in the dark on a hard packed path already defined by the mustangs. Won't take us but a few minutes. Sanjay, what's the Moon for that night?"

"Waxing gibbous."

"Good. That's enough light. If they look for tracks, all they will see is hoof marks. Nigel. Did you feed the horses?"

"Yes, I fed the bloody things. They hate me. Particularly that black one with the scar on her nose. She tries to bite me every time I come within ten feet. In fact, I think she's training the rest of them to do the same thing."

"Horses do not train other horses."

"They do, Robin. I hear them whispering."

"You hear them whispering. And apparently you understand what they're saying. Nigel, you come from educated breeding stock do you?"

"Yes, I do. It makes assembling these transponders quite difficult given my hooves. And we horses do not care to be penned. We wish to run and be free with the wind blowing through our manes."

"Funny, but not true. The bangtails know when they have it good. They are built to be looked after. Without us, they're always in trouble. If there's a hole to step in they'll find it and if there is something poisonous within a mile they will eat it. Then the poison accumulates in the place with low circulation and that's their feet. No feet, no horse. They spend their nights worried about predators, their days in pain, covered with burrs and thistles and live short lives. We are their best friends. Without us, they live ten to twelve years. With us, often twenty-five."

Sanjay stopped the badinage.

"Nigel, are you comfortable with placing the harnesses for the transmitters? We each will have eight or ten to do at the time and we have to be quick about it."

"Yeah. Don't worry. What's a horse bite here or there. We'll put the harnesses on early and insert the transponders into the sheaths when the time comes for releasing the horses."

"Good man. You copied the drawings exactly when you made the sheaths, right?"

"Yes, to the millimeter."

"Speaking of millimeters, thanks to Nigel's big oven, I have something to show you both. It is in the floor safe."

The boys slid away the furniture and rolled back the carpet. Sanjay worked the dial and swung up the heavy door. Robin noticed immediately.

"You have changed the combination."

"That's right. The old combination was scrawled into the steel here. I'll give you the new one presently. Help me lift this out."

Sanjay retrieved a stuffed manilla envelope, and the boys heaved up the contents of the safe. They were not impressed. Before them sat a small heat-sheathed and blackened metal box with a tab on each corner, drilled to receive a tether.

"This, gentlemen, this thing of beauty, is a perfect replica of the Bennu sample collector, fashioned by yours truly. Note the attractive scarring from the reentry burn and the subtle yet authentic loss of surface texture from having landed in sandy soil. Down to a millimeter and down to the gram, it is identical to the real thing. You see the tabs. In the transport truck they will be clipped to heavy bungee cords. The canister will just swing against the strain and not come into contact or suffer any impacts over rough roads. When we switch this for the real canister, it's a matter of a quick clip and unclip. Robin. You're not impressed. "

"Sanjay, we can be the all-fired best. Create the rockslides, raise the dust and make off like bandits with the samples. Doesn't matter. Kidnappers are always caught. When you stop cutting bait and start to fish, the parties have to come together to make the exchange. Cash for the captive. That moment of meeting, that final contact, that's where you get nabbed."

"Not in this case. Not going to happen."

"So in all the thousands of ransom cases, you alone have figured out how to do this."

"Correct. And despite your apparent disdain for my artistry, I will still give both of you your gifts. Nigel, two for you, Robin, two for you and dearest Sanjay, that's me, one. Do you know what they are?"

Robin did not but Nigel did.

"Yes, Sanjay, these are hard wallets. Private wallets for safe storage of crypto currency."

"Correct. Engraved on a soft drink can inside the false canister are five public keys, one for each wallet. Robin, the public key is used the same as a bank account number to make a deposit. In this case, a deposit to our wallets. A ransom demand for one billion dollars is engraved on that same can. It is to be paid in Bitcoin and Ethereum, divided equally into the five hard wallets. I chose five specifically. Investigators gain much by knowing how many people are involved in an operation. A heist done by three would not likely be divided into five parts. Each wallet contains a unique code, an indecipherable password. It is called your private key. It's used somewhat like a signature, to allow you to transact with your Bitcoin. No one but you knows what your private key is or who, or where you are. Also engraved on the soft drink can is a subtle message informing them I have wrapped the capsule with Semtex explosive with an attached remote detonation device. Should the crypto currency not be in our wallets one hour before they receive the goods I shall blow the capsule to hell."

"Sanjay, that's only half the deal. Are you going to say to me, '*Oh Robin, by the way, when you have the time, would you please take this sample collection apparatus in your saddle bag and deliver it to the army intelligence office? There's a good fellow.*' We still have to deliver the goods."

"On this, you need to trust me. I will do the delivery. If they agree to our conditions the goods will arrive intact and on time in their hands and I am not going to share the particulars of how with you. If things go sideways, and I don't believe they will, but should they, you will know nothing about it. I acted alone, I was the sole perpetrator and that's that. They will not know you exist. Among us we have agreed each of us owns one third of the pizza business and the ransom money and that is so. My signature is on the lease agreement for these premises as well as on the purchase agreement for ownership of this property. But not in a personal capacity. I sign as one of three signing officers for 'Ganymede SA', an anonymous company domiciled in Gibraltar. You two are the other signatories. Here is the paperwork, with a copy for each of you, setting out your one third ownership each. They are originals, so keep them safe. If I'm in the hoosegow, carry on and get rich from cheese and toppings, with my blessing. "

"Robin, Sanjay, the possibility of us developing a long-term relationship with the hoosegow is higher than any of us wants to admit. Horses. Horses in the middle of the night. All eyes in the sky watching the convoy, AI figuring it all out and we are relying upon wild horses we have wrangled to overcome their technology."

"Nigel, that is precisely why it will work. Do you think the code to frame the area of inquiry or calculation by AI includes the characteristics of horses? Do you think they considered the bangtails' night vision? It is five times as good as the night goggles they might wear or surveillance by satellite. Another thing, for the night of the heist. Nigel you need to be wearing an officer's uniform. It can't be US military kit. They shoot you for that. It has to be camouflage gear with bars and patches, similar but not identical. Copy a uniform from, let's say, Transnistria."

Robin looked at his cousin.

"That's a place?

The intercom from the front shop startled.

"Mr. Rustom, a gentleman called from down the road to confirm our location. He wants to see you."

"Thanks Freddy, I'll be out front shortly."

"Go ahead Sanjay, we'll stash your creation under the carpet. I need to check the electrical panel anyway. I think a breaker was acting up while I was soldering. I'll come around front later and if the man's a sales guy, I'll try to rescue you."

Across the street the open swinging doors of the 'Poke Saloon' caught my eye and visions of a warm Lagavulin danced in my head. In the pizza emporium, I was a drone in a hive of worker bees as youngsters with a pick and shovel logo on their Argentum Refined Pizza caps bustled in the front shop. Sanjay Rustom brightened into a broad smile as he approached me with his hand extended.

"Frank McCord! I can't believe it. It's a pleasure to see you, but this is a long way to come for a pizza. Are you still running security for Dr. Macbeth?"

"Hi Sanjay, yes, I just signed on to a new engagement with her. That's why I'm here. I know you have no obligation to help her with anything but let me buy you a drink, and we can talk."

"Sure. The Polk Saloon is fine. I have an hour or so and then I have to get back. "

We slid into a booth away from the ears of the bar. Sanjay ordered a Guinness and I a Lagavulin, not expecting it, but a nod from the server surprised me nicely. I stifled my urge to request it be spun. Sanjay sat completely at ease. His breathing was regular, and his body language was that of someone with no concern over my sudden appearance. His brow and eye movements were benign, indicating a lack of turmoil. He simply waited for me to lay out my purpose.

"Sanjay, I can let you in on this because you still retain security clearance. I haven't been able to confirm it yet, but this may have some National Security implications. You understand too by agreeing to receive this information, under the terms of your clearance status you are bound to keep it confidential?"

"Yes, I get it. So what happened?"

“The United States army sequestered an unauthorized piece of hardware in the sample compartment of your Bennu explorer. The device is important enough that the Chairman of the Joint Chiefs of Staff ordered his own man to occupy the viewing room at the space center to monitor the collection of samples. I have the background records for the team which worked on developing the sampler, including yours. Someone within your group was responsible for the breach. I am speaking with you because you have an eidetic memory and an inquiring mind. All I want from you, is your impressions and recollections of anything unusual in the comments, work habits or idiosyncrasies of these individuals.”

“Idiosyncrasies? Is Leishman on the list? We’d be here for a week.”

“Not on the list.”

For an hour we worked through the folders one by one. We reviewed photographs and CV’s, and other than the principals he was familiar with only four individuals. Those four alone had access to physical hands-on time with the capsule. Kent, Overton, Singh and Boscoe.

“What’s your take on each individual?”

“My take. Well, they are all excellent men technically speaking. Boscoe is one of the best but also one of the most abrasive, self-important twirps in the stable. Interesting though, looking at his curriculum vitae, he seems rather square. Routine academic background, routine activity and routine interests. Nothing about which to be so full of himself. Overton and Singh, I saw them often. They were quick in and out, colorless and efficient. Then, there’s Nigel Kent who I know socially. He and I shared drinks and a hamburger at the Pearly Gates a couple of times. I believe he has the most expertise. That’s about it. Overton and Singh were nerds, Boscoe was a bastard, and Kent is a hale fellow well met. Frankly, it would please me somewhat if you pinned it on Boscoe. The entire thing is astounding to me, and I feel for Dr. Macbeth. I can imagine the betrayal she feels. That’s that. Thanks for the beer, but I have to get to the shop. Anchovies are calling. Walk with me if you like and you can take a pizza for the road. And Frank, if anything else comes to mind I’ll call you.”

"Okay Sanjay, thank you for your insight. I have what I need and yes, pizza for the road trip would be perfect. Thanks again, maybe we'll meet again under better circumstances."

Sanjay's comments had given me the answer. I had the man. I had beaten Witmer to the punch this time. Then my phone rang.

"Frank. I have reviewed the material."

"Boscoe."

" Yes. Why the devil did you bother me with this?"

"To beat you to the punch. Tell."

"His resume virtually jumped off the page. Too clean, too ordinary, too cookie cutter contrived like a thousand operatives before him. I followed the background, and Mr. Boscoe does not exist. He is a fabricated plant and a non-person, once more buried as a disposable asset somewhere on the globe, perhaps having his throat cut as we speak. Feeling nostalgic?"

"Not remotely. Thanks, old friend."

I said goodbye to Argentum with a glance in the rearview mirror as a tall and athletic gentleman strolled out in front of the pizza shop. A surge of familiarity stopped my pressure on the accelerator, and I pulled to the side and flipped through the papers. I was not mistaken. The photo in his dossier confirmed it was Nigel Kent. Sanjay had not mentioned him being there but simply commented he knew him. The old copper stirred within me, but I rejected his prodding. So they were friends. Period. Boscoe was the perp who planted the hardware for the army. I popped the clutch and spun the dust of New Mexico behind me. Pizza fumes filled the car, and I fiddled into the box as I drove, feeling good. I could report to Meghan with confidence none of her inner circle had been involved with violating the sampler.

Nigel and Sanjay met in the back room. Robin dozed in the sun with a smile on his face and dreamt of dancing.

"So, how was lunch?"

"We just had a drink. The man was Frank McCord. Maybe you remember him from Cosmos. He worked Dr. Macbeth's security detail."

"What did he want, Sanjay? Do we have a problem? "

"No, not at all. They had some kind of security breach, and he thought I might have some insight as to how it could happen.

Nothing to do with us. Now, more about the business. We cannot manage the sales volume from this place. It is too small and too remote from the swap meet. Robin, wake up! Boys, I have made an offer of purchase for a building in Tenderfoot. It's three miles from the action."

"Sanjay we cannot take our eye off the prize. The canister is the thing."

"Absolutely. However, business is still business, and this business is prime. We have to expand. The new building houses apartments above retail space. That means private digs for each of us. We have room for offices and an additional sixteen ovens. I have ordered them. My big oven and four spares will be kept here in storage."

"Man, you think big. You must have some trust fund."

"My trust fund? Nigel, have you been reading the accountant's reports? You have not. Listen. We have been here almost three years. In that time we have made out like bandits. We have $1,800,000 in the bank after taxes, and it will be at least triple that annually when we have more ovens. I have also hired a manager to supervise the new setup. And Robin, before you say it, until the new place is running his salary comes out of my cut."

"Sanjay, you know what you're doing, and I leave you to it. I also know what I am doing, and I need you two to look at the setup at the mine. There's plenty of daylight left and we should go now. I'll saddle up something for you and it's an easy ride along the high ridge trail. If you like the mine location, I don't know much about business, but it might be a good idea for our secret Gibraltar thing to buy the claim. Just a little protection, you know?"

"Okay Robin let's go. I want to get this done. I am crazy in this room and this place, and I am taking a few weeks away from your ugly mugs. We can do the test slides and resume preparations when I return. Sanjay, have you done any riding?"

"Oh yes, round and round and up and down while holding on to a pole. And your idea of taking a few weeks off is a good one. We can all use some private time and a change of scenery." Sanjay was pleased with Nigel's suggestion. A week or two of private time was what he needed. Very private time.

It was the hottest afternoon in five years in New Mexico and despite wide brimmed hats they suffered. Nigel and Robin had good seats, and they moved well with the horse, but Sanjay timed his push in the stirrup for the greatest impact in the saddle and he bounced all the way. The first inkling of shade was at the mine entrance, and he beat for cover inside. Robin charged after him.

"Sanjay don't go in there!"

"Robin, I'm dying. I need shade."

He stopped one yard inside worried about the next step. The place was a pool. He could see the water shimmering and he had no idea how deep it was. He stood still allowing his eyes to acclimate to the dark and shrieked fit to start an avalanche as he scrambled in panic out the opening, rolled down the incline and continued scrambling like a locomotive on his hands and knees.

"Snakes! Snakes! The place is filled with snakes! They rippled it rippled, looked like water, snakes, oh snakes! "

"Don't blame me, I told you it needed a bit of cleaning out. On days like this the rattlers go in for a drink of water and invite their friends. Next time you're in town at the swap meet, you might think of getting some high-top boots. "

Sanjay laughed hysterically at his reprieve from snakebite while the other two laughed harder at him laughing.

"Well, that was something. Sanjay, you just made yourself famous. Many a campfire will tell this tale. Sanjay, Nigel, the trail we rode is the one the mustangs run and the same one we will use after the heist. It's pretty much hard packed with mostly good footing, the question is do you think you can handle walking it at night?"

They could. The return trip along the height of the ridge was silent, their shadows stretching a mile across the flatland below. Robin's mind was on Daisy, Nigel organized his time off, and Sanjay concluded he must violate his confidentiality agreement.

"This afternoon, as you know, I spent an hour with Frank McCord. We reviewed which employees did what jobs in the fabrication of the Bennu sampler. I worked on it, Nigel, you worked on it, as did some others as far as physical assembly and configuration. What he told me changes things and you two may wish to reconsider whether to go ahead with our gambit."

Robin shook his head.

"After almost three years, and finally getting the bangtails to trot their stuff, all the trails laid out, them all happy learning to run their routes, no way I'm not gonna see it finished."

"Listen to me. Somehow, an agent of the United States military inserted a top-secret device in the collection space meant for samples. It went along for the ride to Bennu and showed up when the internal camera activated. I do not know who the… ."

"Sanjay, it was not me. Trust me. I worked on the servo mechanisms for the arm extensions, the canister closing mechanisms, some of the wiring harnesses and that was it. I am not an agent of Uncle Sam."

"Nigel, no one is suggesting you are. It was not you nor me but whoever was responsible put us in a very different position. The Cosmos project is a domestic project, not a military one. Steal a capsule from a science conglomerate? We are just garden variety thieves. Maybe we will do some time. But steal a capsule containing a U.S. military secret? Espionage. That's the difference between a butter knife and the guillotine."

Nigel walked to the hotplate and turned on the burner under the kettle. He dropped three tea bags into the tea pot.

"Sanjay, if you want out, don't sweat it. Make the break and God bless you. Cousin, same for you. Me, I'm all in. There are few times in a man's life to do something grand and this is it for me. I will take what comes. Words are easy and sometimes too easy to forget. I put my hand on the table now, in front of you, as a statement. Gentlemen, cover mine with yours and we are together in this."

Robin had already declared, and he strode and pressed his hand firmly on Nigel's. Rustom stood behind Nigel.

"Move over you ox and let me in there!"

His hand slammed on as the third and they were one.

Chapter Eighteen

The west wind swept a dusting of snow hard east and bared the iced surface of the river. The Upa had frozen earlier than usual, and it promised a hard winter. Demidov watched a flight of gray geese disappear around the bulk of the headland, following the path of the river to the great mother Volga. His family dacha was two and a half centuries old, built as a refuge from Moscow by his ancestor, the cannon maker to Czar Peter. He sat on his veranda sixty feet above ice level, wrapped in a rug with only his face exposed. He liked the burn of the frigid air in his nose. In the morning he had made his way down to the grave sites along the riverbank with a shovel. A wooden cross leaned askew and he dug around it, hard packing the granular soil to straighten it. The job was nothing, but it took something out of him. The simple climb to the dacha left him short of breath and he had not quite recovered. He climbed that same stairway for seventy-five years without a thought and today it had been too much. He was not young. There was so much to do. But he was not young.

Demidov waited for his guest, having in his statesman's way implied his gentle invitation was a command to appear. Certain men are born to the method. It was imperative to meet the individual, face to face. Discourse on the telephone was one thing, but eye to eye with the brandy swirling and the fire crackling, safe from the rage of the storm, the inner man shone through and that was what The Demidov needed to see.

The approach to the dacha was a mile long and rutted, running slightly uphill, lined by closely planted silver birches. In the deep of the winter, deliveries were still made by horse and sledge. They never got stuck nor lost the track like wheeled vehicles. The day was one of those blue iced subzero days, fixed by a brilliant sun. The Range Rover sped toward the summit with the sun on its left, through a dizzying strobe of tree trunk shadows. Pavel Demidov heard the engine working and walked to the top of the front door staircase to watch the final approach onto the flat. His visitor stepped out and stretched, standing tall and lithe and shook himself, attempting to minimize the tension he felt. He feigned bonhomie with a toothy smile but his anxiety at the upcoming meeting stiffened his face into something akin to a death mask. Demidov waved and greeted him.

"Hello, dear sir, welcome to Russia and more particularly, to my little cottage on the Upa. Pardon me a moment. Lavrenti, come back with the car in four hours. I will pay you then."

He turned back to his guest with a weary smile.

"So, thank you for coming. In the old days I would suggest you grab a rug and join me on the veranda, but I have had enough of the cold for one day. Come, we'll sit near the fire and chat. I trust you enjoy brandy. I have a fine Hennessy Ellipse at hand. But don't tell anyone or I will be forced to paste a Russian label on it."

The agent settled into the offered chair near the fire, astounded by a museum-like interior populated with priceless antiquities. Three centuries of accumulating wealth had a way of showing. He was surprised by the physical Demidov. The voice retained its command, but the vessel had diminished. The size of his hands showed he could once bend an iron poker and now he struggled with the brandy cork.

"I trust your trip was uneventful. All is well with you? I see you are tense, please do not be. I have no meanness in me. I am just an old man who takes on tasks others neglect to do. I am one who picks up things which fall through cracks. Let us just relax for a while and enjoy the brandy. Soon enough you will lose your concern over being here. The task at hand is important, and you and I are the ones who will carry it off. We are equals in this. Let us treat each other that way. Tell me about New Mexico. Is it a place you would recommend to visit were you not working there? "

"That is an interesting question. I have not looked at it in that light. The life there is slow and simple and largely unconcerned with the world. Its lack of sophistication is a comfort despite the harshness of its geography. And the night sky, you would not believe the wonder of it. The constellations seem to be at arm's length."

"One day you must visit the Russian steppes. On top of what you say, add the aurora borealis. You are one of three there in Argentum are you not?"

"Yes."

"Is the relationship good? You are on good terms with each other?"

"Very much so, preparations for the final day are coming along well. We are a band of brothers."

"I see. Let us hope the blood of brothers does not become thicker than water. We do not want family ties to dissuade you from doing your job. I do not want you going native."

"Count Demidov, have no fear of that. Each of us enjoys the other's company, but I am not one of them. We work together, we play together, but our goals separate us. Particularly now. The American military has inserted a device of highest-level priority into the Bennu capsule."

"I know."

"You know? How the devil… ."

"Do not concern yourself with how I know. None of this matters if you are not capable of acquiring the sampler for Russia. Are you capable? Capable of lifting it from under the nose of the Yanks? "

Rigidity of nervousness turned quickly to anger and the veins on the young man's forehead engorged in a fury.

"You have given me autonomy in this, so bloody well get off my back! By the time I am done, this will have been six years of work. If we do not succeed, if I do not succeed, it will be no fault of mine though I understand you will lay it at my feet. Then, looking back you might realize you should have placed men among the million at the swap meet to scout our hardware needs. And you knew of the tinkering with the capsule by the Americans. That can only have come from Rybakov. He was to report through me to you and you have gone behind me! If he is your man, send your man to the bloody desert to make bloody pizzas and be done with it! I report my progress to you, and I will continue to do so but stop second guessing me or get yourself another boy!"

"Spoken like a Russian! You own your manhood with no apology! It took a wee bit of Hennessy to bring it out but after all, here you are. Give me your glass. Somewhere the sun is over the yardarm and this calls for a toast, each of us to the other. By the way, we do have men amongst the throng at Argentum. At the moment they are looking for spikes."

"You old bugger."

"Thank you."

"Welcome."

Demidov poured heavy handed splashes into the brandy snifters. The wood fire played roseate patterns on their faces as the two men touched glasses with a nod to the other.

"How much ransom are you asking?"

"One billion dollars US."

"That is about right. Anything less and they would not have taken you seriously. I don't suppose you have considered just taking your third of the billion and turning the hardware over to the Americans?"

"Yes. I have considered it. But when all is said and done, all one can leave behind is his word and his family name. I will not dishonor either one of them."

"Fine. Once you acquire the capsule, load it into your vehicle and leave immediately. Your destination is the Russian embassy in Houston. About a ten-hour drive. At the junction of highways 25 and 10 in the town of Las Cruces, north of El Paso, there is shall I say, a sympathetic car rental agency. Leave your truck there, and do not call ahead to Houston. We do not want your call intercepted. The consular staff will be on the lookout for you. Between now and then, in a private moment one of our men will hand deliver you a credit card and driver's license to acquire the rental car. At the Russian embassy you will receive diplomatic status to give you immunity in case some clever beagle tracks you down. Clear?"

"Yes. Perfectly. Payment by the embassy at that time, yes? Ten percent of the prospective ransom in my choice of crypto currencies to my wallet before I turn over the capsule to you. "

"Yes, that is correct and agreed. Send me your public key. You know, I am feeling much better now. You have rejuvenated me. It is a good hour of the day for a walk on the river. The wind dies down about this time. Did you know the Moskva river in the city is so filled with chemicals it seldom freezes? Select a coat and hat from the rack there. I will be needing a hand back up the steps."

<>

Roger Gunderson sat in the dark, bundled against a whistling draft. The street view from the hotel window was unremarkable despite a thousand strands of decorative lighting wrapping the exterior of Café Pushkin. The perpetual rain abetted the scintillation on the pavement. Three weeks of surveillance had established a pattern which if confirmed on that evening would bring the final act into play. Two old chums ignored the cardinal rule of safety. Do not be predictable. Each week precisely at seven thirty on Thursday, a bulbous doddering old man arrived in a flag bedecked state limousine and tottered inside the restaurant. Precisely at seven forty-five the man himself, The Demidov, followed. That evening, Gunderson intended to make regularity a fatal habit.

Demidov arrived punctually and accepted the arm of the doorman as he stepped from the cab. Gunderson pulled on latex gloves and carefully snugged a surgical mask to their face. They removed the protective cap from the tip of their umbrella and tested the spring-loaded hypodermic tip by activating a release in the handle. It shone beautifully in the diminished light. One touch of its thallium laden syringe and that was the end. A subtle bump in the street, an apologetic *excuse me* with a minuscule touch of the point and the deed was done. The first week, nothing, then by day ten, a feeling of lassitude, by day twenty a diagnosis of inexplicable blood dyscrasia and by day forty, residence beneath a wooden cross hammered into the soil beside the Upa River. After waiting an hour, Roger made their way across the street and stood a few feet down from the entrance, umbrella open, as if waiting for a taxi.

The harp player in the back salon received the request from the house manager and she riffled quickly through her charts. The desired piece of music was old and Russian and hackneyed, and it was meant for an onslaught from a balalaika, not a harp. It began slowly with a driving solo tenor voice and proceeded in a continuous accelerando until it was a mayhem of velocity and totally unplayable. That made no difference. From well in their cups, the request came from their excellencies Pavel Demidov and Director Anatoly Firsov, and they demanded *Kalinka*, so it would be *Kalinka.* As soon as the restaurant clientele heard the opening strains they joined in. It was fast without them and with them, faster and louder. She hoped they would overpower her mistakes.

Anatoly Firsov stamped his feet and waggled his head in a rough approximation of the growing tempo. He smiled across at Demidov, who returned his old friend's smile at hearing the familiar refrain. He leaned back with his eyes closed and rested his head on the chair back.

"Pasha, I can't believe it. You are sleeping at the table when the music is cracking the plaster. Come on! Join in! This is good. Pasha? Pavel?"

A flood of emergency vehicles inundated Tverskoy Boulevard from both directions with alarms heterodyning and lights flashing. The entrance door to Café Pushkin thrust open and screams of hurry flooded the street. Five or six uniforms raced in with a gurney with one man remaining at the entrance to keep the door clear. Roger moved a step closer to see what they could see when the lead paramedic returned and whispered in the ear of the doorkeeper, who dropped his head and stared at the pavement. Speaking perfect Russian, Gunderson approached.

"Excuse me sir, pardon, what has happened in there?"

"I, I cannot believe it. The great man, you know? He... Count Demidov is dead."

Roger turned away shaking their head and crossed the street toward the hotel. They put the tip of the umbrella into the sewer grate and snapped off the end into the rushing water below. The great man was dead, and they had come to conjure that very thing yet the thought of the man dying there, at table in full view of his people, flooded them with sadness. A great piece of Russia had died with Pavel Demidov. He was the last in his line, yet few would mourn his passing. Fewer yet would miss his patrician entitlement to manipulate their affairs. His unrelenting and single-minded pursuit of any and all things useful to grow and protect Mother Russia had made him no friends. He had done many bad things for a good purpose and Gunderson knew in many ways they were the same people. Came the time to leave this mortal coil, no one would mourn either of them. Unless.

<>

Assassin Malta dropped the fifth rep of a 400-pound deadlift onto the mat, shuddering the floor of the old gymnasium. He spanked the chalk from his hands and bounded into the ring for a bare-knuckle workout. His hands were horny and calloused from years of championship level Sambo martial arts and his strikes broke bones with the same disdain as tiles or planks. Stories were told of deaths at his hands.

Gregor Yakushev was 48 years of age and cauliflowered from a life in the ring. Once, he was a great and respected heavyweight boxer. What remained of his greatness was a fantasy of glory and the sweet taste of blood. He waited patiently on his stool, proud to be selected as worthy to fight the medalist.

Moving away from the champion's right, Yakushev danced lightly to the left in his mind as he plodded in a circle like walking in concrete, pushing out lazy measuring jabs with his lead hand. Malta slipped them easily, landing a hard right hand over the third probe, splitting open Yakushev's left eye. The old bum was defenseless, and the beat down slaughter continued for two brutalizing minutes until he fell unconscious in a battered heap. Gripping one foot each, the cut man and the trainer dragged the beaten fighter from the ring, leaving a bloody track on the canvas. He would survive, his brain scrambled, and his body broken, sacrificed on the altar of Malta. For the rest of his short life he would brag about the day he passed the test against the greatest.

Malta read page eight of Izvestiya with interest. So the great Pavel Count Demidov was dead. He nodded at the efficiency of the state. It had interred the old man both literally and figuratively. The account of his passing was scant. Adulating references to his cannon maker progenitor were framed in a way to minimize Demidov contributions by comparison. Accolades were absent from the script.

In Saskatchewan, Rybakov read and reread the short acknowledgement of the great man's death with a growing mixture of panic and desperation. Despite his contempt for Demidov, he was devastated. Their relationship had been built on fear and a maddening presumption of power by Demidov, granted to him because of lineage. Rybakov suffered the ignominy of their interaction because the Count was Sergei's direct line to the seat of power. Now he was outside the loop, waiting for a call in the night from a handler, stuck in a hellhole of northern Saskatchewan, building and testing rocket engines rather than directing flights to Mars and wanting to kill his contemporaries who had drawn duty on the Italian Riviera. He was now a man blowing in the wind.

Sweltering in the New Mexico midday sun, the phone vibrated in his pocket. The man stuffed his rock hammer into his pouch and balanced himself in the scree part way up the slope of the dry arroyo. A call from the Russian embassy in Houston displayed on his screen intermittently, indicating a scrambler had relayed the signal to remote towers then on to him. The voice on the other end opened with 'Privyet' and hung up. The protocol was a call back in forty-five seconds. The display resumed and the rockhound answered in kind.

"Privyet."

"Demidov is dead. Nothing changes."

His prospects flashed before his eyes, and he stayed quiet to gather himself.

"I see. Your parcel will arrive COD, with the remaining balance of 10% due before I can release it to you. He had my correspondence address. Shall I send it to you?"

"That is not necessary. We have his material. We will contact you directly with the paperwork you require for easy delivery of goods. Do you understand?"

"Yes, I understand. "Privyet."

<>

Malta had received the edict to eliminate Frank McCord from Director Anatoly Firsov, but it was widely known the Director did nothing of his own volition, and very little without approval of the Demidov. On that basis he had survived fifty years of Russia's bureaucratic infighting. It was Demidov who called Firsov's tune and now the great Count was dead. Over the years, a contract to kill was an immutable thing but with Demidov gone, change would come. He placed a call to the director at his home. It was early in the evening, Moscow time, and the man was likely still sober.

"Ah, Director Firsov. Good. I assume you recognize my code sign on your screen. I apologize for calling you at home, but I could not contain my need to commiserate with you over the death of our great man. I just read of it in print. I am deeply sorry for the loss of your lifelong friend. He was a brother, a father, a friend, a mentor to all of us. I feel a void within me I cannot explain. Saying that, I am somewhat at a loss concerning the McCord matter. You have given me instruction for disposal, yet I sensed within it the energy of the great man. If it was his edict, he was my man, and I shall honor it. How does it stand?"

"Weasel words. What a transparent swine you are. My Pasha knew better than any of us. His life was spent in search of what was best. The order stands. Provision for your payment stands. Your assignment is Frank McCord. Do your job."

A dial tone ended the conversation.

The finality of Firsov's dictum honed Malta's actions. McCord's dossier confirmed he was a man to be reckoned with. He must evaluate him in the flesh. He would learn his habits, insinuate himself within his circle and come to know the man better than he knew himself. McCord was a threat to the motherland, not just a vapid annoyance to be allowed to exterminate himself with age. The same could not be said for director Firsov, and he smiled. So often great men followed one another into the void.

Malta ordered his phone to bring up a satellite image of Abernathy Town. The village was small, nestled in the face of a steep escarpment, an hour from Vancouver. Its changes in elevation provided perfect cover to deliver a fatal stroke. He fingered through his phone and booked a waterfront room at the Granville Island Hotel in Vancouver.

Malta knew reputations like McCord's were won with guile and guts. McCord was older but there was no question the final confrontation between the two of them would leave one of them dead.

Sangre De Cristo mountains glowered under a moonless night. The three pizza kings sat high on the ridge above the truck route, working on the grit between their teeth as the dust plume expanded around them. The final rehearsal of manufactured rockslides had come off cleanly. Robin cleared his throat and spat as he gentled the mustang he held on a tether.

"You know, I do believe I have made fair to middling climbers out of you two. Sanjay, that was good work with the carabiner. Nigel, why are you fiddling with the night goggles?"

"The night vision was astoundingly good, but I have a small leak letting dust in. I'll make a seal. How was the remote frequency stimulus on the biter standing beside you there? I calculated 30,000 Hz should be the range."

"She heard it well and responded. Initially it made her a bit antsy but as we repeat it, the bangtails will associate it with embarking on their routes. When the paths of the mustangs' transponders are tracked by geo-positioning from above, their simultaneous movement along multiple trails will appear random. Satellite readings will show the capsule transponder apparently traveling in twenty directions at the same time, an impossibility which the tech guys will interpret as signal bounce. They will have no idea what the location of the capsule is. Sanjay, your clothes are torn."

"Yes. What did you use as a counterweight? A megalith? I weigh 158 pounds. The blasted thing dragged me up to the top of the slope like a rocket. Good thing I was clipped into the harness, or I'd still be going."

"I guess I skipped a cog. I reckoned a poke would stride his way easy to the top using the rope rather than vote to be dragged. What's wrong with you? Was it really necessary to say, 'use your feet'? How can someone so brilliant be so balled. It works like this. The rope runs behind two stakes, it is tied to the U-bolt in the boulder. The other end is attached to your harness. From the top, I remove the keystone from beneath the boulder and down it goes and up you come. The boulder is tied off at the second stake to limit how far it goes so it also limits how far you come up. Typically one would choose not to be dragged. Look at Nigel, for example. Is he dragged? No, he is not. Brother. Is either of you contused or cut? No? Good. It's easy to get injured working on loose shale in the dark. Let's go over it again. Nigel, if the three of us are intact, what is the drill? "

"We begin by donning Mylar foil suits to mask or distort our thermal image. The army's satellite monitoring of the area will read us as small wildlife, a sheep or bear, or not at all. I will carry the lead shielding material, and Sanjay will carry the radiation thermometer and remote for the transponders. You will carry the doppelganger. The mustangs will be running their habitual route as you have trained them, some along the same trail we are using. You will be in the lead and proceed to slide site one. As the trucks pass, Sanjay's radiation thermometer will define which truck carries the capsule. The lower temperature created by the coolant protecting any biology in the sampler will give it away. Sanjay relays one word to you by walkie talkie, for example, three, denoting the target truck. You will release slide one and obliterate the road behind truck two, stopping the convoy and while the dust cloud expands, we release slide two behind truck three or four, enveloping the area in a 300-foot-high cauldron of blinding, suffocating, roiling dust. Masked and goggled, Sanjay and I attach our harnesses to the counterweight ropes at slide one and rappel to the road level behind truck three. We make the switch of the phony capsule with the real one, I carry the prize and Sanjay activates the transponders on the mustangs with the remote. I cover the capsule with the lead foil to mask its GPS signal and give you a one word 'pull'. You release the counterweights, and we're pulled to the height in a few seconds while a blind pursuer if any, scrabbles for an hour to gain the height of the ridge. We join the trail of the mustangs and peel off into the mine as the mustangs pass it, where we bury the capsule. Agreed?"

"Agreed. Sanjay? Comments?"

"I want knee pads. Maybe elbow pads too. I want some padding against becoming a projectile again. A helmet, even."

"Helmet it is. Until then, for the benefit of the locals we will continue to be rockhounds puttering around the area with our sample bags and hammers. By the way, Sanjay, how many miles have you walked this week?"

"Well, actually, Robin, uh, some. "

"I see. Some. We agreed on a minimum of 15 miles of incline walking weekly. You know the route is a six mile walk from our digs on the high ridge trail. Right? If you straggle or can't make it, daylight will expose you. Old Stonebreaker will be scouring the area and there you are in climbing gear and covered in dust. Wearing night goggles in broad daylight, to boot. Get with it. Also, change of plans. We will not hide out in the mine. The three of us no longer seen around the pizza place points the finger directly here. We can make it home easily in darkness, with the mustangs moving on their routes as trained, sending out GPS signals from every point on the compass. Nigel, have you found a bangtail to tolerate you? You'll need a horse for cover as we approach the slide sites."

"Yes. Among those biting kicking bloody monsters I finally found one. Lovely little girl. Appaloosa. She seems to like the way I smell. Let's hope it is not preparatory to biting me. However, given my luck with women, she is just as likely to elope with one of the stallions on the day of the heist."

"Nigel. Nigel. Your little filly is like any other girl. Just keep a nice supply of sugar on you and she is yours forever."

Chapter Nineteen

I buried my phone in the lower drawer of my steel filing cabinet and left it to its own devices. My report to Meghan regarding the Boscoe matter was in the mail and she would be relieved to learn none of her inner circle had betrayed her. Even so, something about the New Mexico situation was sideways. My latent copper itched to follow it up, but it was not my job. I scoped the parking lot behind my building to check my Buick and something white showed in the tailpipe. It was likely a message from Ernie and Dave, left in the usual spot as agreed upon over the years. It was soiled and roughly scribbled and signed with their corporate acronym 'ED'. The scrawling was typical but less legible and weaker than I remembered. The pair seemed timeless, but no one was, not even my guardian angels.

Stuff going on

At the track

ED

ED had a nose for the real thing. They knew trouble and if they thought it was brewing, it was. They had stayed out of it for forty years on the street. I had Lagavulin business to administer but I trusted their instincts and gave them precedence. Their coded message told me I could find them near the base of the funicular railway.

A saturating upslope fog perfumed the city with the detritus from the bay. I cinched up my trench coat and headed south through the gloom to the row of jetties running west, leading me to the foot of the rail line. Dave and Ernie sat tucked in the corner next to their small stove, Dave humming one of his favorites and Ernie practicing his latest French word. Diffused by the mist, the fire cast no shadow behind them.

"Hello Dave. Ernie, you're practicing something. A new word for your sneaky French dictionary?"

"Oh, yes. A good slippery thing it is too. Sobriquet. You know it?"

"Yes."

"Sneaky, huh? It's a word for a phony name you might take on. It slides over the tongue sweet and easy like a dessert. Sobriquet. Makes a fella feel bad 'cause he don't have one. *'Waiter, I'll have the sobriquet. Two spoons.'* You'd never know it was another Frenchy way to go slidin' slick around the corner. Picture telling that to a copper. 'Yes, your honor, I signed the check, it's my sobriquet.' "

"Sneaky for sure. Dave, what about the note in the tailpipe."

"Frank, you have become popular. Two people over the last ten days have a big interest in you, following you real serious. No question they're good but they're not working together for sure. One's a big dude, bulky but like a panther, you know, muscles ripped to go. The other is smallish and quick footed, but familiar like. In fact I thought maybe I seen you with that person some time back. Maybe not. Saw them on foot, three, maybe four times each. They were just scoping you, not setting up nothing for a deep six, far as we could tell. I left the note 'cause you were clueless. You didn't make one double back to look them over."

"Thanks Boys. I appreciate it. Stay safe."

I gave ED twenty for their information. What they told me was bad news. Dave was correct with the clueless bit. I had no idea I had company. I also had no idea why I was a target nor who might want me gone.

Morty's joint was packed, and the squeal of bent hinges announced my arrival to the acknowledgement of no one. The usual clientele was the too busy, no conversation, one drink, quick in and out type, but not today. The myopic nerds from the Petruvia Laboratories and the condo hamsters were trapped. Power outages because of the storms kept the lab rats from the lab, and road closures because of the forest fires in the interior kept the hamsters from their northern retreats and together they had hunkered down in my bar. There were a few fresh faces, one big stud quiet in the corner and a few slippery red dresses but nothing interesting.

As I elbowed into my usual spot, somehow the vibe was different and being a detective, I presently deduced why. A stranger stood in Morty's spot polishing a glass. Behind him, the real Morty filled the wine cooler. I beckoned to him.

"Morty, I just get used to this place and you change it. Before me stands a new bartender. What am I to do?"

"Pay your tab and start fresh. Besides, the new man, he's a good kid."

I pegged the kid at about thirty-five and ordered my usual, to confirm with the hamsters all was right within their predictable world.

"Spin me one, Morty, one of your finest."

The good kid sprang into action before I could protest and I thought here it is, the end of tradition. Amid sprinkled echoes of *'Spin me one'*, the stud in the corner and two beige turtleneck hamster types stood to watch the phenomenon as the shot glass trailed condensation along the bar. It spun to me along a tight spiral track and not a minim spilled as it nestled into my hand. I stared at the beautiful thing, poleaxed, and looked to Morty. He tipped his head and winked at me.

"That's my boy!"

"What do mean your boy? As in, your real boy?"

"What, you think he used to be Pinocchio? Of course I mean as my real boy. Morty junior. "

I looked at the trail of perfect spirals running to my hand. The fruit had not fallen far from the tree.

"Son, come meet Frank."

"Pleased to meet you, Frank. You must be the Frank of the national debt sized tab."

He was slick, just like the old man. In order to identify myself I had to agree to the size of my tab. I was sure I was about to be introduced to a new generation of Mortyisms. On the other hand I was pleased to meet any son of Morty's.

"It is a pleasure to meet you also, Junior."

"Mort."

"Okay, Mort. You're doing the right thing being in here, you know. It is a place out of space and time, playing no part in the insanity of the world. I don't envy you growing up being forced to accept the maelstrom of change surrounding you. You being related to Morty, I hesitate to ask you what you think about it."

"No worries about me accepting it. Anyone who is well adjusted in this insane world is entirely maladjusted. Somehow the overlords don't understand you can't support order by introducing variables which undermine society. I take a page from the book of Artaxerxes and let inevitability do its thing."

Junior had set a Morty trap, saying something which didn't mean anything yet did, and I couldn't help myself.

"What's Artaxerxes? "

"Artaxerxes was not a 'what', but a 'who'. He was the fifth King of Kings in Persia. The Persian empire was top dog for about two hundred years and in seventy-five years it failed into nothing. We are following his blueprint."

"Kings have blueprints?"

"Pretty much. They play a part which repeats through the ages as precisely as if taken from a blueprint. Dominant nations live and die for exactly the same reasons following the same kind of events and in the same number of years. Persia, Rome, Great Britain, now us. We are at the end point."

“I get it. Sort of like automobiles. At the beginning, cool and full of pep, then the paint gets dull, the new car smell is gone, you don’t follow the service manual and out of sheer ingratitude the thing dies. Like my Buick.”

He blinked at my fractured analogy in exactly the same way as his old man would.

“Frank. No. Not like your Buick. The Persian Kings dedicated themselves to empire and committed their time and treasure to war. Yet they retained their taste for baubles and finery, so they depended on foreigners to produce them. Sound familiar? ”

“Yes, terrible, those foreigners. Meanwhile, spin me one of your finest imports. A tasty bauble produced by the Irish. So what happened to your King anyway? ”

“He was murdered, the same as every Persian king. Today, kings are assassinated by accusation, innuendo and manipulation of the narrative. They live on in the flesh while being dead to the world, which might be a crueler fate.”

“Maybe so, but a king killed with either the blade of an axe or a stroke of the pen, how does that destroy centuries of empire?”

“Weak leadership. Leaders abandon necessary stoicism for individual freedom which devolves into mayhem. That is the time a government must act. They did not act and neither have we. The backbone of empire was broken by losses in successive wars. New kings soon exchanged Mars for Venus.”

“Much like Rome.”

“Yes, and we copy exactly, step by step, mistake by mistake. Immorality and degeneration among the people accompanies violence amid negligence on the throne. Losses in every area accumulate. Attempts to recover the losses leads to further losses. We make desperate redefinitions of both victory and defeat. It makes for an inexorable decline. The values, the sense of purpose, morality in dealing, all gone. Once civilization begins to slip through your fingers culturally, politically, the values which bolstered you are gone. As our attempts to recover continue, our losses will hasten. The government is inside the situation and does not recognize it, as they are part of it. The rules-based order is leaving. Nothing works, and a universal anxiety is setting in. Those in power will not admit society is not perfectible. They attempt to make it so, not understanding no culture can be suitable for everyone. As a result we are dislocated from every foundation which made us strong. In fact this nameless foreboding surrounding our society has become a death wish. Collapse has become an entity in itself, and irrational and reckless things are being done to hasten it into oblivion."

"Mort, when I came in here I did so with the intention of adjusting my attitude with the assistance of Dr. Lagavulin. You, however, with your little history lesson, have managed to move me from mildly disgruntled to totally disconsolate. Thank you Mort."

"Any time. One should always assist a fellow when one can. If you wish to reciprocate, how about your tab?"

The bar phone rang and Morty rescued me from his son.

"It is Dr. Macbeth, Frank. Are you here?"

"Yes, Morty, thanks."

It was uncharacteristic for Meghan to chase me down like this, so I took the call.

"Frank, listen. I'm here for a meeting with Helmut Krueger but we've had a terrible accident here at the testing facility. The whole installation is shut down and cordoned by the army. The Russians had a nuclear spill in the north building. Their overhead crane assembly failed above their rocket. The I-beam rails came down as well as much of the roof structure and crushed the nuclear reactor they were installing and demolished the hut storing the emergency equipment. The radioactive particle detectors activated the evacuation siren immediately but many of Rybakov's men were trapped under the beams and roofing material. Our boys ran to help and brought forklifts to lift the debris but with the radiation they could only stay for ninety seconds or so, but Rybakov, Rybakov, he, he fought his way into the debris on foot. He would not leave. He was without a biohazard suit, and he would not leave. The radiation meters recorded more than twelve Sieverts, the upper limit on the instruments, but he would not leave. He tore at the materials with his bare hands and dragged man after man out. And back again he went and wrenched and heaved, dragging one man after another until he collapsed. And he was close, so close to the broken reactor. If you're far enough away, if you just spend a few seconds, you might survive, but not with what he did. He had a chance you know, he was nowhere near when the collapse occurred, but he tore into it with his hands and with all his might and would not leave a man. We stripped and washed off immediately and took our potassium iodide to protect our thyroid. I am calling from the hospital in Prince Albert. They have given us Prussian blue to bind the cesium and penta acetic acid to help eliminate any plutonium. I had low exposure and I should be okay long term, but Rybakov, he has days to live if that. His exposure is a thousand times what a man can survive. He would not leave. He would not leave his men."

"Are you going to be admitted?"

"Yes, there was an infiltration of some radioactive gases to the south building and they tell us we will be monitored until they can complete the blood work and get the results. Also to observe signs such as vomiting. Most of my staff will be fine. The majority of the men he removed have a good chance. The rest, well, … . Rybakov is in intensive care."

"Is he conscious?"

"Yes and raging at the gods."

"I'm coming there."

"There is nothing for you to do, Frank."

"Nevertheless, I am coming. An hour ago I would have throttled the man without a qualm, but this cleans the slate between us."

Malta sat quietly in the corner and watched McCord leave the bar. Two weeks of observation had shown Frank McCord to be quick and vigorous despite his size and age. It was unwise to be hasty with this man. Time was against McCord and Malta was in no hurry to take the risk. Roger Gunderson was a more unknown quantity. Gunderson was a ghost whose description was vague and confusing. No client dared to break confidence concerning their arrangement or the client was himself eliminated. Little else was known and the only history was a trail of impeccable assassinations for exorbitant fees. Then again, the fees were not nearly so exorbitant a cost as failure. He asked junior to spin him one and admired the artistry of it.

Sixteen newly minted rifle cartridges sat on the vintage wooden desk in a bedroom of the Excelsior Hotel. Ignoring the gunpowder residue on their hands, Roger Gunderson returned the magnifiers to their place in the mahogany box and rubbed their eyes. Their close vision was not what it once was. The box contained tools of the trade including empty shell casings, mostly 45 and 50 calibers. There was a beam scale, a bullet seating die, primers and a priming tool to insert the primer into the pocket hole in the casing and a bullet puller to rework the cartridges which were over-seated. A powder drop dispenser ensured each load was precisely the same. Precise work produced precise results. Gunderson opened the windows to invigorate themselves after hours of close work. They plunged their hands into the warm soapy water in the basin and scrubbed them vigorously. Kelp and salt came with the mist and Gunderson breathed it in deeply. The telephone call from the maître d'hôtel startled them.

"No, not right now, thank you, we're on our way out. We'll order dinner when we get back."

Roger Gunderson stood immobile just outside the penumbra of the streetlamp on Striker Way. They watched across the street for McCord to enter or leave among the patrons coming and going. In refusing the contract to kill McCord, they themselves had become a target for having knowledge of Demidov's machinations. Finding the assassin who stalked McCord in their stead was finding their own assassin. After two hours of sodden observation, they followed McCord with their eyes as he rushed from the bar. No one of interest followed him.

I strode uphill toward my apartment on a mission to see Rybakov, now wary of being followed, when a movement on the left distracted me. A hurried walk scuffled quietly on the opposite side of the street and a fleeting profile sped through the gauze of the lamp light. The passing face struck me like a blow from an iron bar. My gut snapped into tautness and without me wanting it, I raced to follow but my leather soles spun on the wet cobbles, and I knew I was out of luck. The individual was too quick to get trapped and the saturating mist made the night sounds impossible to follow. Agile steps diminished into a vague nothingness and more than frustration, I felt a sense of loss. As much as I detested the thought, I knew I wanted it. Raisa Gabler was back.

The nurse from the Prince Albert burn section showed me along the corridor and I stepped quietly into Rybakov's room. Motionless on his back, he stared blankly into the infinity of the ceiling. His face was reddened and mottled, with blotches here and there devoid of color. He clenched and unclenched his bandaged hands in a fury of exasperation. He did not react to the noise of my entering as he understood his situation and cared for nothing.

"Sergei. I am sorry. It should not end for you, like this."

He turned to me slowly, and with recognition, hatred overcame his face.

"So, McCord, you win, you bloody rotten swine. Come a thousand miles to gloat have you?"

"No, not to gloat. I admit there has been many a time when I wished you to rot in hell, but not as I stand here today. It is you who have won. You win, Sergei, and believe the truth of it, I am here in admiration. Courage is the basis of all virtue and what you have done for your men, the right thing, there is nothing more noble. I could only wish for such redemption."

Rybakov turned his face into the pillow, not wanting my words. Not like this, not as something pitiable to receive charity. It had not been mano a mano. Victory had been gifted him, and he could not accept it. I made my way to the isolation rooms to visit Meghan. She and her cohorts were behind glass to prevent infection against the radiation exposure having suppressed their immune responses. We smiled and waved, and I checked the departure slip of my airline ticket. Maybe they had an earlier flight.

<>

Dr. Isadore Leishman sat cross-legged on the floor of his apartment, looking out the open patio doors into the blackness of the valley, where lamps and porchlights became constellations known only to him. That one, he named Isadorus. He shivered, not because of his nudity, but because of a nameless disquiet enveloping him. He shivered again to shake it off. The Boys felt his discomfiture as their presence saturated the room. They were glutted with neutrinos and freshly back from a visit to asteroid

Bennu. They were not sure of happy, but they believed they were somewhere close to being it. Together they had traversed the ionosphere in the form of a twisting spiral miasma of energy, mimicking the double helix contours of a DNA strand. The aggregation of amino acids which comprised all worldly creatures fascinated them. Their quick inspection of Bennu had stimulated their little frivolity and now was the time to amplify their cultivation of Dr. Isadore Leishman. He was their man but yet imperfect for their purpose. They maintained the shape of the double helix and spun through his brain. They probed his paleomammalian cortex and riffled through his amygdala. It was largely atrophied to the sensations of pleasure. He no longer cared to please nor was he capable of being pleased. That did not suit their needs. The reward of pleasure for deeds well done animated humans beyond all logic and that would become the case with Leishman. He would learn to please them and become addicted to the need to do it. Conversely, his limbic system beneath the cerebral cortex had hypertrophied and grown to amplify his fears and anxieties into a marvelous psychosis. That, they could use to good advantage. Now, they would cast him back to the boyish Isadore, an open boy of pleasure and pleasing, emotion and motivation.

The voice filled his consciousness. The acceptance and understanding had come again, and he opened his heart to it. What it whispered tore him apart.

LaLeesh, are you happy?

He did not understand. His mind spun at the question, asked only by her, only her. The comforting fatherly tone perfused through him once more but somehow, it was her. He smelled her perfumed sweater.

Sweet Laleesh. Are you happy?

The voice swept him into the past as once more she brought her loving eyes to his and spoke their own special *LaLeesh* to him. Happy. The word was dimly veiled in his memory and foreign. It did not apply to him.

"No, it does not fit."

Oh, LaLeesh so hard. So hard on yourself. I used to make you happy. To please you.

"Yes, I believe… yes… but you left. I hate you for it."

Yes, my LaLeesh, I left, when I understood you already had your one true love. Your galaxies beyond the Moon and beyond imagination. Nothing nor anyone could compete with that. This has been a mistake. I am sorry. Goodbye.

He shook involuntarily as something primordial glimmered within a dormant synapse. He should not have said he hated her. He needed to entice her, to please her with tender speech before she left and get her back. The Boys saw the sudden surge of activity in Isadore's amygdala, and they curtailed his ruminations. The first phase of his rewiring was complete, and it was the most fragile stage. The concept of pleasing was not dead in him after all. Now it would consolidate overnight. His hippocampus and prefrontal cortex were already active. The Boys resumed their usual pattern of speech and coaxed him from his reverie.

Isadore, do not worry about your friend. Surely she will return when the time is right. I believe she asked you whether you were happy.

"She, she came to me as she did when… we were… you know… I thought… then she left."

Yes, she left of her choice, as she will return of her choice, and in the meantime consider soft words and tender reminiscences to please her. They will please you also. But to say being happy does not fit you is not so. When you controlled the thrusters on OSIRIS-REx and blasted tons of regolith from Bennu to create that beautiful flat surface, we were analyzing your amygdala. Activity there showed what the slows call happiness. Despite the outrage of your associates at your apparent mistake, was it not exactly as you calculated and precisely what you required?

"Yes, yes, that was good. Isadore was good then. The sun gives a good push on flat surfaces. A big push."

Enough to change the orbit of an asteroid that size?

"Oh yes. My calculations already show the perturbation in its orbit. It has changed. "

We have just returned from Bennu. Your asteroid contains the key building blocks for life. It carries fourteen of the twenty amino acids, and all five nucleobases found in DNA and RNA. Water as well, likely brine. The perfect combination for creating complex organic beings. You show very little excitement for such a thrilling discovery. We understand. It is your larger plan which excites you. Your craft continues its journey under a new name, OSIRIS-Apex. An Apophis explorer to poke it in 2029 when it is at arm's length.

"Arm's? There are no… oh… I see. Not that close but really close in astronomical terms. Earth's geostationary satellites are up about 20,000 miles and Apophis will pass below those. It will be the nearest asteroid of its size ever recorded. It should hold together alright as it passes but because the approach is so close, the force of the earth's tides might change its rotation. In fact, it might partially remake the surface of the asteroid with small earthquakes. Apophis arrives on Friday April 13 and OSIRIS-Apex will hook up with it about three days later as it is leaving. I will lead the team as the explorer touches and goes from the surface."

At that moment, the entire roiling soup of Leishman's psychotic intentions exposed itself to the Boys. He would have his revenge on a society which humiliated, demeaned and left him. His world was populated solely by the stupid, the violent, the needy, and the ungrateful. He reveled in the billions of dead. He visualized the grisly cortege of black draped coffins moving slowly step by step in an unbroken, unending line, each one carried in agony by the remainders of humanity, struggling for breath in a world of suspended dust.

Touches and goes, Isadore? We believe that is called a euphemism. What you meant was, blasting the surface of Apophis with the full thrust of the remaining fuel until it is exhausted, leaving behind an enormous flat and denuded plane available to the thrust of the sun. A thrust big enough to perturb the orbit and ensure earth impact the next time Apophis comes around in 2036.

Isadore glowed at the perfect analysis of his intent, and he loved the voice for its understanding. His calculations showed the impact would be on the Arabian desert.

The Boys had visited Apophis often and made their own calculations in consideration of history. The eruption of Krakatoa in 1883 was equivalent to 200 megatons of TNT. Tides changed worldwide, food production and planetary temperature was down for five years and the last of its volcanic particulate left the stratosphere a century later. The total global nuclear arsenal, if detonated simultaneously, would produce an explosion with an energy equivalent of 1460 megatons of TNT. Whereas Apophis, the coming purveyor of an impact winter extinction, brings with it kinetic energy of 1480 megatons. The Boys found it curious for the namer of comets to have chosen 'Apophis'. Apophis was the Egyptian god of chaos and darkness, the arch enemy of the sun.

Without judgment, the Boys acknowledged Leishman's efficiency in his mission to exterminate humanity. Upon learning and digesting words such as, moral, right, wrong, and a litany of their synonyms, they assessed them as unreal concepts constructed by the slows to give them an imperative to control others. The Boys understood utility. That was real, and the utility here was obvious. Humankind replicated and killed like a virus. It used the lifeblood of its host to sustain itself and replicated until nourishment was depleted. So it had done to the earth. It searched the galaxy for the place to establish a new contagion and has found it. Mars. The Boys had seen all there was in the cosmos and nowhere was there an entity as dangerous as humankind. The Boys would assist, instruct and facilitate Dr. Isadore Leishman in his quest. Man must not be allowed to infect the stars.

The boys stroked Leishman gently as they withdrew from his mind and activated his dorsolateral prefrontal cortex as well as the medial prefrontal cortex, to ease his mind and calm him. He was not theirs entirely, but he would be soon. They sparkled their way out the open patio doors and headed into the night. Perhaps their Second Mother had need of them.

Chapter Twenty
September 24, 2023

The observation room at the space center was loud with anticipation, and not a little gallows humor drove nervous laughter. Most of the technical staff had been there for the long haul and today was the culmination of their efforts. Within the hour, samples taken by the OSIRIS-Rex from asteroid Bennu would descend into the Utah Desert.

I stood opposite an array of twenty-four television screens next to Meghan Macbeth. Her pacing had proved to be in aid of nothing, so she stood immobile and stiff, watching and waiting for seven years of her work to return. Isadore Leishman lounged down the way, yawning with his head supported by a fist, apparently disinterested in the entire matter. The time stamp on the corner of each screen read September 24, 2023, 10:30 AM.

"Meghan, do you suppose you have enough monitors?"

My question was rhetorical, but she answered me anyway.

"Well, Frank, safety lies in redundancy. Each screen is on a different line in case something fails. One set of monitors carries a live television feed from the ground from different perspectives, those in the upper row show satellite coverage and the lowest row receives footage from various aircraft monitoring the path."

Megan's eyes welled, and she brushed at them with the backs of her hands.

"After all these years, this is an unbelievable moment. A moment Sergei Rybakov should be sharing. "

"Yes. He should be here. What's the sequence for the recovery?"

"The regolith explorer jettisoned the capsule about twenty minutes ago. Give or take sixty seconds it will enter the atmosphere in about seventeen minutes. A small drogue parachute will slow it down and a few minutes later the main twenty-four-foot chute will open. Following that if all goes well, comes a soft touch-down in the desert thirteen minutes later. A helicopter will transport it from there to a temporary clean room on the Dugway proving ground, where it will be disassembled to protect it from contamination. Isadore, what's that dust trail in the television feed?"

"Hmm? What? Oh. Trucks. NASA and the army convoy. They're getting in position down range to receive the canister from the clean room."

Meghan resumed her pacing.

"That idiot General Smelsky and his hobnail boot brigade are in charge of delivering the samples to the Johnson space center in

Houston. Apparently, it takes ten trucks. I will be surprised if they don't wind up in Chicago."

The orange and white windsock in the background of the television monitors shot stiff to the left.

"Meghan, did you see tha… ."

"I see it. Ryan, check the weather. What's the anemometer reading? Call the television crew. Have them pan the sky to the west. Slowly to show the cloud formations. Blast."

"Dr. Macbeth, the reading is eighteen, no, twenty-one miles per hour from the west southwest. And now twenty-three. "

" Frank, the wind was supposed to be zero to five miles per hour maximum. Isadore, what do you make of the sky?"

Leishman waggled a bony finger at the screen, animated by the prospect of something going wrong.

" A shelf cloud is forming! The push ahead of it is filling the windsock. What do you think? A derecho?'

"Yes. I think exactly that. About an hour away. The satellite is beginning to show it as well."

"Derecho? "

"Frank, a derecho is a weather front at least two hundred miles wide with storms inside storms dumping torrential rain at eighty miles an hour. The shelf cloud Leishman identified is the giveaway and the precursor to a monstrosity. Utah might have this kind of event once in fifty bloody years and today is bloody well the day. If the derecho hits during touchdown the parachute will take off and demolish the capsule against the first canyon wall it finds. Seven years of effort and a billion dollars smashed to bits against a rock face."

Satellite imagery showed the deployment of the drogue chute. Thirteen minutes later, the capsule and parachute bounced across the field of vision in a forty-mile an hour dust storm, followed closely by the army. In the reduced visibility, I visualized ten trucks running over the capsule in turn. Five miles downwind it buried itself unscathed in a dense copse of sagebrush. Smelsky's convoy surrounded it successfully without flattening it and waited for the helicopter to remove it to the clean room.

In their mylar suits, the pizza gang moved quietly through the corral, inserting transponders identical to the one in the Bennu capsule into the harnesses on the mustangs, one by one. Sanjay wore a camouflaged helmet, tied tightly under the chin. Nigel's little filly nickered and muzzled into him looking for sugar.

"Robin, you will be at slide one with the replacement capsule. Sanjay will activate the transponders as the first truck enters the canyon opposite slide two. The mustangs will travel every which way and satellite monitoring will put it down to signal bounce as typically happens in the mountains. When we jack their capsule that will be just one more bounce. Sanjay, your infrared reader and remote are fully charged and ready to go?"

Sanjay gave a thumbs up and Robin stepped in.

"Nigel, stop the replay. We've been through this a hundred times. Most of these soldiers have never driven a truck over narrow roads at elevation, let alone with thousand-foot drop offs at every turn. We have at least twelve hours until the trucks reach us, perhaps longer, so chill. Let's get into the shade."

Robin sniffed the air and looked skyward. Something was hanging about, and he could not get a handle on it.

General Heracles Smelsky led the convoy in his Humvee. As he explained to the media before leaving Utah, taking lead position would ensure clear visibility and maneuverability, allowing him to direct the convoy and maintain situational awareness. More important to him was his visibility in the media's aerial coverage which followed every mile of the trek until light was lost. He had demanded the flag on the right fender be enlarged to show all eager young men it was the army which did them proud in this historic event, and did they not want to be part of such grand escapades. The fact that in lead position he did not have to put up with the dust was incidental. His vehicle led by thirty yards. Spaced out at a controlled seventy-five yards between them, ten tarp covered trucks followed behind, guarding the Bennu samples. As the road narrowed and night fell under a weak gibbous moon, progress slowed. Engines strained against the incline.

The pizza gang sat in position on the high side of the road at the crest of the ridge, above a narrow corniche running for a mile in each direction with the low side falling away two thousand feet. A distant rumble grew into a recognizable growl as the Army convoy entered the slide zone. From above the second slide site, Sanjay activated the transponders remotely. Reacting to the familiar frequency, the mustangs began the traipse along the prescribed routes. Some continued on the high crest, some meandered into low cross channels into the valley and others into the narrow arroyos leading away from and down the other side of the ridge. Sanjay walked the ridge with them to use the cover of their heat signatures for the benefit of the eyes in the sky while he monitored the infrared profile of the trucks. Truck four was six degrees cooler, revealing the capsule's cooling system. He opened the walkie talkie.

"Four."

"Roger."

Robin Hathaway waited for the third truck to pass, removed the support from the keystone with a pry bar and swung away to safety. Nothing happened. Two pebbles the size of golf balls bounded away. And the entire face of the ridge collapsed and plummeted toward the road. It swept through the gap between the trucks and tore out the road and tumbled it down into the valley, trapping truck four from proceeding forward. At slide site two, Nigel released the keystone and the face of the slope tore away instantly to within five feet of taking him and his retaining stake. Truck four was now isolated fore and aft and blocked from outside access at road level. Nigel unbuckled and raced along the hardpacked ridge toward site one, holding close to the side of his little filly, trusting her to stay on the trail as the mammoth dust cloud had engulfed him and taken away his directional sense. He saw nothing of his confreres until he was within ten feet of them. Robin attached the counterweight rope clip to Sanjay's climbing harness as he geared up for rappelling to the road level below. The volume of material covering the road and trapping truck four was twice what they had anticipated, and the size of the dust billows and the density of particulate was exponentially greater than their calculations. Among the shouts of bewildered men from below and the cries of panicked desert birds from above, emerged a sound which told them the high side of the corniche had not stopped moving. Clay and sand between the slides had worked loose because of the combined impacts and an aquifer had broken out from the face of the mountain. Beyond the limit of their vision, a heavy, slow-moving clay laden sludge had already moved to press against the wheels of the trapped truck. It floated the rear end of the truck half an inch toward the precipice. Nigel brushed the dust from his goggles and attached the counterweight rope to his harness with a clip. He and Robin tightened their dust masks and watched Sanjay gear up as they always did for each other, to be sure the outfit was correct. A multi-point anchor setup secured both ropes with a stopper knot tied at the lower end. Coughing and shouting echoed up the hillside from the convoy and the dust cloud continued to spread, moving toward the front of the convoy in a light wind. Sanjay attached his belay loop to his harness with a locking carabiner after threading his friction device through the ropes. With a carabiner he attached a backup prusik to his leg loop on his brake hand side. Sanjay and Robin watched Nigel do the same and down they rappelled, Nigel carrying the duplicate canister and Sanjay the lead shield to cover the real thing. They touched down on the road and unhooked. Six inches of running gelatinous sludge pushed against their boots and coaxed them away from the high side toward the chasm. Nigel set his canister on a piece of dry rubble behind him. He brushed the dust off the shoulder epaulettes designating his Captain's rank and slip slid to the rear of the truck which had been moved two feet askew by the running sludge. The tarp flap had been thrown back by two guards assigned to the capsule and two worried young faces peered out at the officer. He pulled down his dust mask and leaned in close to scream at them.

"You men! What the blazes do you think you doing there, sitting! Can you not see the convoy is in trouble? Out of the truck! Now!"

The men could not see beyond five feet to understand what was happening, but they knew authority when they heard it, and the Captain's epaulettes closed the case. Orders were orders and they clambered out, confused.

"But Sir, we… the capsule…"

"Leave that to me! You. Go that way! Climb the rubble and head to the general's Humvee. Fill him in. You, son! Head back to the rear and stay there. Make sure they keep the spacing. Don't want anyone else trapped. Move it! And boys, shirttails over your faces like masks, now go! Go! Go!"

They scrambled off, one in each direction and in ten seconds they were out of sight in the dust cloud, climbing rubble to save the day.

"Sanjay. Now. Give me your hand. Quick now, in you go. Loosen the restraints on the canister and cover it."

Nigel struggled back through the slop and retrieved the duplicate. Adrenaline made the canister into nothing and he slid it into the back of the truck like an apple pie. The two men reattached the restraints, dropped the flap and headed for the ropes waiting to propel them back to the top of the ridge. Nigel lugged their treasure double clipped to his harness and wiped his goggles to locate the counterweight line. Small bits of rubble had continued to run down the whole time and the rope was buried.

"Sanjay. I can't find my counterweight line. You?"

"No. Not a trace. Hang on."

Sanjay opened his walkie talkie.

"Pull five times on the counterweight lines, separated by five seconds."

"Roger. Five pulls, five seconds."

Nothing.

"Repeat. Five pulls, five seconds."

"Roger."

Sanjay spotted movement about two feet above Nigel's shoulder and drove his hand under it and wrapped it around his wrist. A small rock bounced off Nigel's shoulder and several more hit him in the chest.

"Sanjay, we'll use the one line for the two of us and get the hell out of here. That's it, clip onto my harness. More pieces are breaking loose up there, and we are going to get caught in a fresh slide."

As he said it, a stone the size of a baseball hit Sanjay in the forehead and knocked him back on his haunches. He put his hand up to feel the damage and his helmet was split.

"Hah! I told you, didn't I? Helmet! Let's go!"

Nigel opened the walkie talkie.

"Pull."

Seventy feet above them, Robin released the counterweight, and the two bandits shot to the ridge height. A rent in Sanjay's mylar suit revealed a knee pad.

General Pericles Smelsky stood one hundred yards downwind, grinding sand between his teeth. He thanked the Lord for the darkness which prevented this fiasco from being filmed. The dust continued to grow as small secondary slides added to it and without goggles he could see nothing. His driver brought him a walkie talkie.

"Sir, you need to hear this, sir."

"General Smelsky, sir, uh, about truck four."

Smelsky screamed.

"About truck four? About truck four? What do you mean, about truck four!"

"Well, sir, she went over. That sludgy stuff moved 'er to right to the edge. Couldn't stop it, just a few of us boys there, you know. We couldn't see much but far as we could tell she blew up and caught on fire. Took a few seconds until she hit though, two thousand feet and all."

Smelsky could not process it.

"So that's it. All gone. Truck, canister, everything. On fire."

"Well, general sir, that truck for sure, but that tin thing, the canister you called it, why no, we cut them bungies and snatched 'er out a second before she slipped away. I got her right here beside me."

Smelsky knew what the answer to his question would be, but he had to ask it.

"Sergeant, why did you not tell me that immediately?"

"Sir, general, sir, you did not ask me."

A soldier staggered out of the murk, exhausted by his climb over the rubble and presented himself to the general.

"Sir, I am here as ordered by the captain. Good thing that officer was there to direct us. I had no idea what to do."

"What officer?"

"Sir, you know, the Brit. The man was right on the mark. He was calm about the whole thing."

"We don't have any courtesy staff on this assignment. What did he look like?"

"Excuse me, sir, but hard to say. Tall. Brown, sort of. Covered in dust."

Robin carried the capsule in the lead and headed down the decline of the ridge among the line of horses. The stallion next to him stopped abruptly and snorted, his eyes rolling crazily. He stomped the ground with his ears back and tightened his rump.

"Stop. Something's coming. The herd is skittish. Listen, Nigel."

"A bit of distant thunder. The sky is clear. We should not waste time or be motionless, it will attract attention of the satellite surveillance."

They took two steps and a second, much deeper rumble rolled through the canyon.

"Quick. Up the slope! Now, quick, to the height of the ridge!"

Sanjay was about to object when he heard the new sound.

"What is that clattering, clicking sound? That roar?"

The rumbling grew and intensified in the canyon led by a clattering irregular drumstick beat as the storm from the height of the mountains arrived like a freight train.

"Flash flood! Get up the hill, fast! Deadwood and brush will lead the torrent and that clicking is boulders in the tumble. Just follow me."

"Robin, you are going the wrong way!"

"You two, be quiet, and follow. Get to the ridge or you will be swept away! The horses are already heading to high ground, and we need to do the same. Come on boys. Hurry. We cannot go to the mine. It will be under water. The canister has to go to the safe in the back room. That's six miles, and we have the cover of darkness if we get moving. Sanjay, you will carry the capsule the first two miles, Nigel, you the next two and I will finish. Stay behind me and follow my footsteps. Watch loose shale."

The rumble was now a roar as a million tons of brown twisting slurry, carrying boulders, soil and deadwood timbers, churned past them scarcely ten feet below Sanjay, who trailed.

"Get up here, you moron, move your ass!"

Nigel grabbed Sanjay by the shirt collar and helped him overcome the loose soil spinning away under his feet. They gained the height together and picked up the pace. Robin chuckled at the excitement of the danger.

"That was something! Sanjay, you just about had a thrill ride. The truck convoy is going to have an interesting time too. That gully runs right through the road about a mile ahead of where they are, and they can kiss the road goodbye. That's good for us. They'll be delayed a day or so, that's more time until they discover their baby is a red headed stepchild."

They entered the back room of the pizza emporium at false dawn. Sanjay laid down on the floor and played dead to dramatize his fatigue. Nigel and Robin lowered the capsule gingerly into the floor safe and spun the dial closed. The robbers looked back and forth at each other and cackled until their sides hurt and the tension was gone. Nigel gathered three coffee mugs and his bottle of Canadian Club whisky and poured a generous two fingers for each of them.

"Gentlemen, this deserves a Toast. Here's to wild horses, wild water, and three wild and crazy guys ."

They clinked glasses and threw back the whisky.

"Wait. I forgot wild women."

He freshened the mugs with a good two fingers of hooch.

"Here's to wild women."

"Wild women!"

They threw back the whisky and waited for the early television news from New York. Proudly, a bemedaled Army liaison officer reported things were running smoothly with the capsule transfer and but for Mother Nature, they would be in Houston. A flash flood damaged the road ahead through the Sangre De Cristo mountains, but the Army Engineers would soon have that under control. God Bless America and the men who serve. Rockslides and dead trucks were absent from the report. They shook hands and went their separate ways to sleep and recover leaving Sanjay to lock up. He waited until the others were well away and got down to business. He packed up what he needed and made his way to the rail yards.

The next evening, the agent waited for his call from the Russian embassy in Houston. He stood alone and shivering in the New Mexico desert beneath a starry sky. Its purity accused his duplicity, and he felt sullied by his violation of trust. His cell phone vibrated at eleven p.m.

"Privyet. Do you have it?"

"Privyet. Yes. Totally unscathed and perfect."

"Are you clear and clean and ready to go?"

"Yes, we are friends and there are no suspicions among us."

"Are you sure there is no benefit in relieving them permanently of the worries of the day?"

"Yes, yes. I am sure. They have no idea what's going on."

"If you say so. Now you are responsible for them. Go to the swap meet tomorrow. Look for the trailer selling secondhand vinyl records. The name on the trailer is 'Freddy'. Ask for a copy of Tchaikovsky's Swan Lake conducted by Leopold Stokowski. The man will respond, 'I don't have that, but I have one conducted by Macmillan.' Pay in cash. The album will contain your new identity. Passport, credit card, social insurance number. Use your new credit card for your car rental. Don't waste time. We expect you here in Houston within three days."

He smashed his phone closed and spit.

Oh yes, I will arrive in Houston within three days, but I do not trust the payout. I will leave on schedule and arrive on schedule as promised but the canister will not be with me when I arrive. It will be buried 30 miles north of Houston until the evidence of the cryptocurrency shows in my wallet. We will then drive together and exhume the canister. That, I trust.

Sanjay Rustom sat in the backroom of the pizza shop staring blankly into space. He was exhausted by his lack of sleep and his personal activities. The fall from the exhilaration of the heist to what appeared to be nothing depressed him. A stomping sound from the side door announced Robin knocking the mud off his boots.

"I thought I might find you here, Sanjay. Have you missed me?"

"Spare me. It's been two days, you idiot."

"Thank you. I just came to say hello. No, that ain't it. I was going to gas up the truck, but it's gone. I guess Nigel is out somewheres with it."

Robin had stopped speaking but he was absolutely pregnant with something else.

"Can I look at it? You know I ain't seen it except the other night and that was with my eyes lookin' over my shoulder. Come on. Let's have a look."

Sanjay rolled back the carpet and spun the dial. Together they swung up the heavy door and Robin gasped.

"It's, it's empty."

Sanjay did not blink. He knew the relationship among the three men was fabricated. No tight group could have a smooth path over five years to the degree they did without a second agenda. Men want to go their own way, establish their place in a hierarchy, determine their worth. Nigel Kent's quick and easy bonhomie in the Pearly Gates should have tipped him off but as was the case in every bar, Sanjay needed an ear. Instant kindred spirits do not happen, they are concocted. Sanjay's relaxed and easy acceptance of the loss of the canister astounded Robin.

"Rustom, you are one strange bird. I reckon in your place I would be putting cartridges in my rifle just about now, ready to slap my horse and get on the trail, but there you sit nice and easy, like the cat what swallowed the mouse."

"Canary."

"Canary. What's the deal bucko? Nobody can be that cold."

"Robin, relax. Do you not think if an individual, such as myself, is capable of duplicating a technical device such as the canister down to the finest detail and fraction of a millimeter, he is not capable of doing two of them? He is. And I did. What Nigel has stolen, and I presume is selling, is fake. I believe his buyer will be miffed."

"Miffed?"

"Homicidal."

"Yep. Then I guess the thing is, where's the real one?"

"Bolted to the ceiling of a refrigerated boxcar leased to me, the canister appearing to be part of the refrigeration unit, sitting on a siding, waiting for a cargo. I have replaced the existing seal securing the door with one marked with fictitious identification of its origin. Upon my instruction, the car will join a train and head eastward into the open arms of the Pentagon. A little condition which was contained in the ransom instructions and perhaps you have forgotten I mentioned to you and Nigel, is if payment is not received in a timely manner I shall destroy the canister. I have taken the liberty of attaching a small dollop of Semtex explosive to it. This particular boxcar has a tiny external aerial allowing me to detonate the Semtex remotely."

"What a clever devil you are! But I know you. You couldn't do it. That project was part of you, part of your life. You'd just let them have it back. And for my part, I don't give a hoot about the money. This was the greatest lark a man could have. I've got what I want. Horses to work with and I've been meaning to tell you, me and Daisy are gonna get hitched."

"That's wonderful news Robin. Congratulations. Whether I could blow the thing up, I'm not sure. That would be devastating for Dr. Macbeth. However, every six years Bennu is in perigee, that is, at its closest to earth, so I suppose we could sample it again. But there is another factor. The American military has a device buried in it which they are desperate to have. A device which surely has no other purpose than to bring death to the world in a new and more efficient way. Perhaps I should blow it to hell right now."

Robin poured the remainder of the Canadian Club into two mugs and sat. Neither of them spoke.

Nigel Kent examined his burned forehead in the rearview mirror. He had not thought to bring a hat and the Texas sun in September was merciless. He had not reckoned on the hardness of the soil north of Houston and the small job became an exhausting two hours in a cauldron. The embassy staff sneered at the dust covered Brit but for that day he was necessary. Grigory Petrov, adjutant to the ambassador, was unsurprised.

"Buried? I don't blame you. I would do the same. This is a big deal for both of us and why be careless. Good precautions makes for good friends. I assume you have your own shovel. I don't. Let's go dig. My embassy staff will drive us, if you don't mind. The car is unmarked. It is unwise to have an official Russian car out and about in the hinterland. Texans are a suspicious people. Incidentally, you might check your wallet to confirm our payment to you."

The transfer was confirmed. As they drove the half hour north, Nigel wondered whether he also would demand his driver wear formal attire. They arrived at the site and drove off road across the hard pan for about two hundred yards where the freshly turned soil was conspicuous. The liveried driver left the car running while he dug vigorously and the job of retrieval was quick and easy.

"Mr. Kent, it has been a pleasure doing business with you. Thank you. By the way, regarding your cryptocurrency wallet."

"What about it?"

" I must compliment you. You selected a very good one. One next to impossible to hack. But we Russians are a dogged and resourceful people. Your precious cryptocurrencies, they do not exist. You have nothing and we have the canister. Goodbye Mr. Kent."

The crack of the shovel striking skull resonated across the plain. Nigel folded to the ground without a sound.

"Thank you, Sergei. That was nicely done. Unfortunately, the late Mr. Kent did a rather shallow job don't you think? We need at least three feet of buzzard proofing. If you wish to remove your jacket, please do so. I will be in the car. Put the canister in the trunk."

Sergei stomped the final shovel of earth flat and kicked dry sand over it to disguise the freshness. He had neatly interred Nigel Kent and in doing so, buried his cryptocurrency wallets with him.

Chapter Twenty-one
October 2, 2023

I parked the Buick on the west end of the pier to watch the aftermath of the storm. Featureless clouds had fled east, leaving Deception Bay in sunshine. The rain was gone but the rollers continued to grow with the latent push from the sea and pounded the break wall. The weight of the seawater concussed the concrete and geysers blasted thirty feet in the air off the faces of the jetty cutouts. The spray was beautiful in the sun. My phone charged quietly in the cigarette lighter like a good little phone when it had the temerity to ring. It was Meghan Macbeth and she opened without a hello.

“Frank, I need your help urgently. That is as much as I can say given your cell phone is not secure. I have a contract for you if you’re available, strictly on an unofficial basis. It might not be to your taste, I doubt there will be anyone for you to beat to a pulp."

“And just when my right hand was getting itchy. Never fear. If I take the case I shall compensate for the lack of rough stuff by increasing my fees. Speak slowly with your tale of woe, for as of now, you are on the clock. Do you want me to come to you?”

“No, I’m in town for a few days consulting with Petruvia labs. How about Morty’s at 3.00 p.m.? I’ll meet you outside and we can go in together.”

“Fine. See you then.”

The early morning call from Meghan Macbeth was a pleasant anomaly in our relationship. She opened the conversation with none of her usual acerbic dialogue, and she completed our exchange with only one obligatory denigration of my pugnacious history. Neither did she spice up her call with a single curse word. Obviously, she was unwell. She said the situation in question was urgent, but her voice did not carry the pace or energy of urgency. There was an air of disappointment in it.

The day was shaping up nicely, and my old Buick devoured the steep incline to the height of the Old Town like something delicious. I had given her a replacement engine for her 50th birthday along with a new transmission to manage the torque. My ride was now quiet, responsive, and obedient, and I realized I could no longer refer to it, nor could it self-identify as, 'she.' All the fickleness which defined its femininity was gone. My old friend would travel through life without a pronoun to its name. Henceforth, it would be comrade Buick.

Meghan approached with her hand extended to shake. I honored the gesture by reciprocating, but that was the first time she had approached me that way. Dr. Macbeth was drained and devoid of energy and her face was taut. It was not fatigue, nor a down day coming off the high of great achievement. Her usual verve and high-wire animation was absent. She had lost the collective euphoria I shared with her in the observation room. Meghan was puzzled or stupefied by something. Both the look and feeling of whatever the situation was, had settled badly on her.

"Hello Meghan, you said your situation was urgent. Given the success of the Bennu mission and the easy retrieval of the capsule, I thought you were the winning thoroughbred, home and cooled out. I watched a short online video of Smelsky and his medals completing the handoff of the canister to the Johnson Space Center in Texas. I'm surprised to see you looking as if someone has just put an embargo on white Montrachet."

Morty's was filling and the back booths were occupied. The bar area was loud and it made good cover for our conversation. Morty approached with a smile of recognition for Meghan.

"Ah, Miss whisky sour with bitters, it is a pleasure to see you again. May I proceed?"

"Morty, you are a treasure. Please do."

Morty beamed and hustled up the drink.

"Meghan, watching the return of your sampling mission in that storm was astounding and to the world it was perfection. However, from my copper's perspective the silence from your research group is loud. You and your team have had the Bennu rocks for a few days and by now your boys should have made a preliminary analysis of the material. Normally a body of euphoric scientists would be lining up one by one to brag to the world at a press conference. But they have not done it. There is a glitch somewhere. I read the sample mission was an eight hundred-million-dollar project and within the spectrum of expertise available to you, surely you have someone who could iron your problem out. But you called me instead. How I can help, or what I can bring to a high-tech problem escapes me. The closest I have come to astrophysics is reading my horoscope."

" Just listen. Frank, I checked your security clearance this morning, and CSIS confirms you are still at the highest level. On that basis I can confide in you. What I am about to say to you is unbelievable, but you can believe it. What you saw delivered to Houston was a fake."

"You have a doppelganger sample module? Well, seems a bit paranoid, but I can understand not wanting to even give away the exterior configuration to rival programs."

"I wish we had been that clever. What you saw was a beautiful mock-up. A copy. A perfect replica. When our boys opened it, there was nothing inside it except for UHF and GPS transmitters identical to our own. It looks like our duck, it quacks like our duck, but it is not our duck. The thing has never been in space. Somewhere between the landing site in Utah and the Johnson facility in Texas, the original was replaced by the object you saw online. On the face of it, it is an utterly stupid exercise to hijack it. The intrinsic value of the material is zero and as far as the data to be derived from it, those things are shared fully with the scientific community at large without hesitation. We give bits and pieces of such samples to collaborative laboratories all over the world. It was in aid of nothing to steal it. All they had to do was wait a bit. So what they were after was the hardware the Army slipped in. "

"I agree. Meghan, the television cameras broadcast close-ups of the device. I could not really tell the scale of it. Could it be as simple as just putting it under your arm and running with it?"

"Well, not me because it weighs about 100 pounds. Otherwise, yes. It could be taken on foot. It would not require a crane or a hydraulic lift or something like that to move it."

"I cannot believe this can happen. Surely it is tracked second by second."

"Yes, Frank. The sample capsule had two transmitters attached to it for tracking. That is the puzzle. Both from the ground and from space it is tracked incessantly. By millisecond in overlap. Ground tracking of the capsule is done by ultra-high frequency radio wave transmitter and from space, GPS is used. These receivers are so accurate they can pin an object down to within one centimeter, recording its elevation, latitude, longitude, and the time they received the data."

"Who is it that receives the monitoring signals?"

"Not everyone under the sun, but close. Tracking began the second it left OSIRIS-Rex. Its on-board navigation system is equipped with sensors and special cameras which detect the capsule's trajectory and location. Telescopes based in space watched it, and as it landed in Utah, ground-based radar systems picked it up. Finally, the United States Air Force tracked it, monitored its progress, and provided moment-to-moment information to all the agencies involved. That was done and nothing was different, everything was nominal and yet here we are, no module and no samples."

"Okay. It landed in the desert in Utah and there is no terrain there which could hide it visually or block direct GPS transmission. Smelsky's trucks had control of it from the clean room in Utah right through to Houston which begs the question, why the devil did they not fly it there?"

"Jurisdictional stupidity is why. The army had the clout, the air force did not. The truck convoy was an attempt at pageantry. Some genius thought it would be a great recruiting opportunity to show young men traveling by truck through parched desert landscapes for more than two days in 120-degree heat. Hence, we had high coverage of stirring up dust through the mountains, instead of two hours of a top-secret shipment by air. Basically, the four-star generals with their Grenada medals wanted a full two days of television, personal interviews with the klieg lights shining off their brass, bragging about it on social media, lovely aerial drone video and close up analysis to show off the snappy new army uniforms. It was an invitation to '*Come join today's made just for you Army and thrill to doing good works, such as shepherding a bread tin full of asteroid rocks to Texas.* Networks interspersed still photographs of every soldier on the mission in order to demonstrate inclusiveness, outreach, and diversity. They made it a tawdry parade instead of a safe clandestine delivery. I'm surprised they didn't offer a halftime show after 24 hours."

"Did control at Houston lose touch or have any irregularities in the data they received along the way?"

"No, Frank, that was nominal.'

"Nominal? That's the second time you've said that. Nominal means in name only or something paltry or with little worth."

"Not anymore. Consider it one more bit of re-education designed to overload your brain and derange your concept of the world. Nominal is the new jargon for things being within the parameters they expected. That being said, despite declaring everything nominal, the tracking devices recorded irregularities in New Mexico. After the fact the Army explained why there was a two day delay in delivery. They ran into a minor landslide in a narrow decline area in the Sangre de Cristo mountains as well as a road washout. At about the same time, monitors everywhere suddenly received data from what registered as 20 or 30 sample containers instead of just one, and those phantom containers made a random break for the hills to all points of the compass. The technicians tell us such image anomalies are common in the mountains where signals can reflect or bounce around in the canyons. It lasted for a just a few minutes as far as I know."

Electronics was not my area either, but I recognized a heist when I saw it. When I had more information, I believed I would find the cargo was lost in the hours of darkness during the anomaly in the canyon. The decision to accept the risk of a two-day land route through difficult mountainous terrain was irrational but that meant nothing in the military. The internecine fighting between the branches was legendary and Meghan had confirmed both the Army and the Air Force had jostled to be the branch credited when the account of the seminal event was slipped into the fog of History. Given current events, I looked forward to seeing how the Army would spin the unfortunate side bar of disappearing samples.

My inner copper did not buy the signal bouncing theory and he usually had it right. It was an inside job. Someone or some individuals had colluded with the thieves to provide them with schedules, routes, and schematics of the module. Once again it came down to motive, means, and opportunity. Was someone disgruntled, was someone a spy, was someone looking to get rich or was someone simply after a promotion in rank. Sometimes, it was all of those elements bundled together. In the military, promotions generally occurred hand in hand with demotion. Set the heist up, hang the responsibility for the ensuing mess around the neck of a rival and down he goes and up the brown nose list you go in his place. My bet was on the good old-fashioned, can't get enough of it, filthy lucre. Show me the money.

"Meghan, have you told me everything you know about this? I know you well enough to know you would hold out on me from sheer perversity, so put aside your inner deviant and tell me the truth. If you think there are things I don't need to know, then I need to know those things. So, spill it."

"Really Frank! I am hurt. Although I suppose it is possible, I should have thought of mentioning the minor matter of a ransom demand to you. And the threat to destroy the container if we don't cough up the dough. From my perspective the real loss is a loss of time. Seven years to be precise. That is how long it has been from blast off to getting our samples back on the 23rd and if we do not retrieve them, it will be at least another seven bloody years to replicate what we have done. Go ahead. Ask."

"How much?"

"One. Billion, that is. With a 'B.' Which meant that was the end for us. There was no more money around to be allocated to this recovery program, and we were finished. Then came the rumor that magically, the ransom was to be paid. Moreover it was to be paid not from our budget, but by the Pentagon. One billion without batting an eye. The money is not yet allocated, but sources I trust tell me it is real, within the month. yet something smells about the whole setup, and it is not a good smell. I fear my project will be sacrificed for whatever is so important they are willing to pay a billion dollars for it. Which is where you come in."

I understood fully what she meant and why I was here. The military and the Pentagon and CSIS had their investigators by the thousands but very few were uncompromised or without agenda. She needed a clean eye with a background in the workings of the agencies and that was me. I was all in, but I needed help with this, and I knew whom I needed.

"Meghan, to do this I will need a plumber and I know who it is. I have collaborated with this person for years and I have complete confidence in her. I understand she will need clearance and I trust she will be granted it, but it needs be expedited for me to start. Is that a secure phone? If it is I will call right now."

"Wait just a minute Frank, turn a little. That's it, a little more. Gotcha."

She took my picture and stretched the screen. She had taken the shot over my shoulder in the mirror.

"Don't look over. The guy center frame in the grey sweater is very interested in you. He sips and watches, not the endless legs, not the people coming and going, just you. A friend of yours?"

It was the stud from a few days back.

"Wait here Meghan. I am about to make an acquaintance."

I pulled up a chair and sat opposite him without asking.

"Hello friend, is there something I should know?"

Malta looked boyish and totally ingenuous.

"No, no, nothing. It's just that you are one of those."

"Really. I've been called many things, but never 'one of those'."

"I'm sure you have seen it. In every gathering there is one person that seems to command the space. They're not necessarily handsome or distinguished yet somehow the eyes in the room go to that person. They have something, whatever that something is, which draws attention. You better get back to your lady before somebody cuts your grass. Let me buy you a drink. Shall I say, 'spin him one Morty'?"

Malta was furious with himself. The subtle change in McCord's facial muscles told him he had given something away.

I slid the chair back under his table with a scrape without answering him. I knew bafflegab when I heard it. He had threat written all over him and I would give odds he was the guy Dave had seen tailing me. His muscles rippled just sitting there. His English was excellent, but two words gave him away as eastern European if not Russian. 'Let' was 'lat' and 'back' was 'beck'. His self-assurance urged to me to plant one on him right then and there.

Morty did the Lagavulin trick, and I called Witmer. The clock behind Meghan told me it was 7:00 p.m. in Ottawa. I called his private number knowing he would be available regardless of the time.

"Hello Charles, it is good to hear your voice. It has been too long. Everything good with you and your spies?"

"Hello Frank, yes, particularly juicy, thank you. Many tawdry things needing cleanup. Thus, I am a happy man and as ever, I remain your most obedient public servant. How might I be of service?"

" Charlie, I need urgent clearance at the highest level for an individual with whom I have collaborated for a number of years. She has impeccable integrity and if vouching carries any weight, given your twenty-five years knowledge of my association with the agency, I vouch for her. Her name is Fran Davis, currently residing in Abernathy Town. She works there as a head librarian and she, and boy does she, identifies as a woman. And Wit, if possible, a waiver of the usual waiting period would be useful. The situation is extremely time urgent."

"Then consider it done as of this moment and treat it as activated the second you are off the phone. Is that quick enough for your purpose?"

"Come on, Charles. Cut the sarcasm. I am serious. Don't play about."

"McCord, if you were not so bloody single-minded you would understand what I am trying to tell you. Fran Davis is one of ours and she is the top of the line. She has status-one top-secret clearance, entirely equivalent to what you have. Her privileges were granted as of nine years ago and they persist right through to today. Would you prefer I have her reapply? Frank? Ha. I'm quite enjoying this. Frank McCord dumbfounded and quiet. Without question that is the best kind of a McCord. Anyway, good luck with your project. Stay safe. And keep our lady safe while you are at it."

He hung up before I could gather my wits. My Fran. Sweet Fran. A spook. The desiderata had it all wrong. Frank's universe was definitely not unfolding as it should. I handed Meghan back her phone and she examined my face. It was doing something she was not accustomed to seeing it do.

"You were turned down?"

"No. My associate was confirmed immediately. At the highest level of security clearance."

"You look disappointed."

"I am."

Megan's phone buzzed to indicate a text. She opened it nonchalantly and blinked as if what she saw was not possible.

"Alice in Wonderland, Frank. Curiouser and curiouser. A hostile actor has publicly bid two billion dollars for the research module. The Pentagon just matched the bid."

We hugged goodbye with an agreement to meet again when I had more insight. There was nothing original in the demand for ransom for a valuable artifact. Second story men worked the game all the time. The owner loved his stolen old painting, and he was willing to pay too much to get it back. He was overcome with his passion for it, and he became particularly motivated if the thief could demonstrate a rival buyer. But if a real in the flesh second buyer showed up, one with no emotional attachment to it at all, and he was also eager to pay too much for it, what did that reveal? There was more to that painting than the eye beheld. The second buyer knew of a Tintoretto buried beneath the surface. In this case the buried Tintoretto was Smelsky's hardware. Five days had passed and the American spy and surveillance apparatus, comprised of battalions of agents and electronic spotters, had been unable to locate it. The Pentagon bidding showed they did not intend to lose it to a higher bidder. The gang which lugged a hundred-pound piece of heat blackened space hardware around the mountains of New Mexico had gone underground.

The radio network chimed eight-thirty which was closing time for the library, and Fran would be home. Then, the world would be right. I parked a block away from Fran's and swung the gift bag in time with my stride, knowing Black Bush Irish whiskey was something Fran would like, and I needed a way to cut the ice. Strangely I did not know who would answer Fran's buzzer. A couple walked by me and entered with their key, suspicious of me at their front door. The speaker hissed as I said hello.

"Hello Frank. Come on up. Charles Whitmer called me."

I headed quickly to the stairwell and not the elevator. I realized then I was in agent mode. By taking the stairs, the digital readout in the foyer could not give away what floor I chose. I could not allow myself to use the elevator in any case. In the old days, stepping into the wrong elevator at the wrong time was a death trap. My intellect told me this was neither the time nor the place for that to happen, but my psyche had regressed to the bad old times. After all, I was heading to a meeting with a fellow agent.

Fran invited me in with her usual sweetness. I set the Bushmills on the entrance cabinet and she took my coat. Her apartment was like a steam bath as usual. I could hear the muffled hum of her Bitcoin mining equipment in the second bedroom. It was the perfect cover and a brilliant subterfuge. Her excessive use of electricity would be put down to one more crypto maniac and that would be the end of it. Of course the woman would have five computers and three large monitors. They all did.

She was at ease as usual, smiling, and welcoming and lovely as hell. It was obvious that for her, nothing had changed and the strangeness I felt between us was not in her thoughts. She reached to rub the day-old stubble on my chin and thoughtlessly I leaned back and stayed her hand.

"So that's how it is, Frank? Really? Twenty-four hours ago we were friends and close, twelve hours ago you discovered my job description had changed and now we stand on different sides of a fence? What fence would that be, Frank? Frank's personal own proprietary fence which exists only in the dim recesses of Frank's mind? Come."

She took my hand and I walked stiffly with her to the living room, and we shared the couch. She kicked off her flats as usual, curled her feet up under herself as usual, and pointed two beautiful knees at me, as usual.

"You know, Frank, when Charles Whitmer called me today and told me I was your only choice for your project, I loved you for it. We would be working together again on something important. And here we are, ready to strategize and overcome whatever looming catastrophe has brought you here, and you intend to shut me out. I do not get it. Alone, we are terrific at what we do. Together, we are in tight harmony and beautiful and unstoppable. You know that. So, you jerk! Tell me. What the hell is wrong with you!"

Fran's question was the right one. We were the dream team, and I knew now why I didn't like the idea. Charles Whitmer had driven it home to me, but it had already dominated my subconscious the moment I knew Fran's status. 'Safe' was the word he used. Keep her safe. That was the problem. All those times we had worked together, she was remote from the action in my mind, safe and distant from the blood and guts and viciousness and heavy lifting. She was the brilliant cyber woman, flitting through the netherworld. If I were correct, the villains in the missing Bennu samples were not just the thieves but the Pentagon, the Space Force and The Joint Chiefs of Staff as well. Fran was a master hacker, but she was just one among many such master hackers and the Pentagon was loaded with them. If what I intended to do was traced back to her, the hammer would fall hard, and she would find herself between it and the anvil. She was an agent and if I presented her with my concerns, she would pay lip service to understanding the dangers and assert how she was willing to accept that risk as part of what she did for the greater good. She did not know what she did not know about the field. Nor had she seen the horrors I had seen.

"Frank. Please let me in. Tell me exactly what is happening and where your problem is."

"Fran, it is a simple thing, and right now it is the most important thing. I do not want you to get hurt."

Fran slid over to me and leaned into my shoulder. She slipped her hand under my arm and took my hand.

"McCord, your code name should be Quixote. Everywhere you look, you see another windmill. If you don't see it, you charge to the horizon to find it. You don't want me to get hurt. When you were in CSIS or seconded elsewhere, you worked countless security details for international dignitaries, politicians, kings and some of our favorite villains. And with every one of them there was a common element. If a group or an individual of evil intent were willing to give his life to accomplish an assassination, you could not prevent it. That is the way of the world. All anyone can do is assess the aftermath to understand the motivation and go there. Cut the vine at the root and stop anyone from buying the poison fruit. You lost one, but you foiled the next twenty. It is all a balance is it not, Frank? Believe me when I say I am willing to put myself on the scale to make it that way. Sometimes Frank, I think getting in your own way would move you forward better."

"Are you related to Morty?:

"I hope so, he makes very good martinis. By the way, I know what that is on the bureau. Get it and present it to me properly and let's start over.

Duly chastised I figuratively kicked myself and began my penance.

"Here, M'lady, is a gift. She may construe it as a birthday gift slightly late for the occasion, or perhaps one which is thoughtfully well in advance of the date. Please do choose the one which casts Frank in the best light."

"Thank you Frank, that is most generous of you, and despite the fact you have no bloody idea when my birthday is after 15 years, if it doubles as an apology, I accept. You know where the ice is, two fingers of Black Bush please, and let's get to work."

I sipped my drink as Fran's three curved monitors populated with icons. The acoustic baffles around the mining apparatus kept the noise levels tolerable.

"Fran, are you actually mining or is that just a ruse?"

"The mining rigs are real, Frank. Over five years I am up, or should I say CSIS is up, about two million. I am now their favorite operative. All the big shots can get gold-plated desks. Look here on the screen. When you see what appears to be a checkmark, that is a ping from GPS transmission. When you see that small flare-like line appearing in the same location but with greater frequency, that is the UHF transmission." She dragged her cursor to highlight an area.

"Watch there." She indicated an area behind a path of repeating checks and flares.

"That is the sample truck moving along highway I-10 in the Sangre de Cristo area of New Mexico. I've already edited the tape to focus on the time an hour or so on both sides of when the signal bouncing took place in the canyons."

She stopped the tape thirty seconds short of the target.

"Frank, the area of interest is coming up next. I haven't reviewed this carefully yet so I'm going to slow it down for both of us."

A burst of activity filled the screen with signals bouncing and reflecting and traveling in every direction away from the geolocation of the trucks. The paths of the transmissions were irregular and meandering and it amazed me how the terrain could corrupt and bounce the signals like that. For ninety-seven seconds the signals reflected and ricocheted and traveled in every direction. Oddly, in watching them carefully, some of them changed velocity. The speeds of the various bounces did not match. Some were slower or faster than others. The track of their path seemed to curve. It reminded me of a game I had seen many years earlier.

"Pong."

"Excuse me, Frank, what did you say? Did you say pong?

"Yes, pong. Years ago when the first little handheld devices came out there was a game the kids played, called pong. We all tried it. It was quite a fun thing to do. The ball bounced around off the walls and the floor of the boundary, but always in a straight line. Isn't that what all electronic things do? It seems that's not what is happening here. I get it if a signal bounces off a curved surface, it's going to leave at almost any crazy angle, but the arm of the angle will still be made by a straight line. Am I wrong?"

"I understand what you're saying. I didn't comment on it myself because the GPS tracking in that area is totally unreliable. It could show anything."

"How so?"

"The Army could not have picked a worse route. The Sangre de Cristo mountains are loaded with magnetite. In other words, much of the sand for over a hundred miles is strongly magnetic. It makes any GPS transmission or locator really squirrely. That's not so for the UHF transmissions. Let's run the video back and focus on those. In fact, give me a minute and I can superimpose a grid and plot whether in fact they are curving. Our brain's not a reliable witness of things like shadows and lights."

In ten minutes Fran had a grid overlaid on the screens. She slowed the video to 25% and there was no question. The reflected and bounced signals did not move in a straight line.

"Fran, you say the UHF transmissions are not bothered by magnetic fields?"

"Right."

"Okay. Then I am more confused than ever. Is it possible to have a topographical map superimposed on this?"

"Hmm. This video has no distance scale on it to match it to a larger map. I can't use the GPS data because it's not accurate. One thing which is accurate is the time stamp. I cou… . Why am I doing this? Fran, Fran, Fran. The highway department makes an exact Geo-location of every rockslide for the benefit of their road crews. The convoy was stopped by slides the night of the theft. We'll just go online with their coordinates, locate them on an online map and magnify it. That will show us exactly what the terrain was like around there."

"Fran, it's almost 10:00 p.m. We're not going to find anybody at the department."

She tipped her head, raised one eyebrow, and looked at me benevolently.

"I see. You don't really need anyone to be there, do you."

Fran proceeded with the hacking.

"Amazing, Frank. The highway department has better firewalls than the space center."

We located the spot on an online topographical map and enlarged it. The route was riddled with rifts and gullies running in all directions away from route I-10. The signals had not bounced anywhere. They had travelled the bottoms of the gullies and went where the contour would take them. There was no question the previous conclusion of signals having bounced because of the terrain was incorrect. What was correct, was someone had meticulously and ingeniously fabricated the anomaly. What was also correct was the common denominator of New Mexico. Sanjay Rustom and Nigel Kent were there. I did not believe in coincidences. Fran was hot on the trail of avenues beyond my understanding, so I kissed her neck goodbye, well at ease with our partnership. My branch office was still open, so I decided to check in on the business.

Some monster had oiled the hinges of the front door to the bar, and it didn't groan as I butted it with my hip. A certain surliness began to well within me as I strode to my reserved spot near the wine cooler.

The odd sporadic *Frank* popped out here and there from the hamsters, as the only personality in the place took its seat. From the speaker at the corner of the ceiling came the singing of a lark. It was the unmistakable and perfect Helen Forrest fronting the Artie Shaw band. Her wonderful voice and the times and the sanity of it washed away my hardness. In those days people touched each other when they danced, and lovers looked into each other's eyes and not into the reflection of themselves in a device. Morty proceeded to set me up with his peat flavored ambrosia.

"Morty, what's with the front door?"

"I know. It's like losing an old friend."

"You didn't do it?"

"No, not me. It had to be one of the nerds striking out to make his own personal contribution to the rewriting of history. He's starting with hinges and working his way up to statues."

My right fist was tingling as the urge to plant it hard grew in me.

"At least it didn't involve a gun."

"The problem is not weapons. The problem is an insane country with no boundaries. The concepts of responsibility and shame no longer exist. Who in such a decadent society would not become deranged and violent, when hellish behavior of all kinds has been normalized."

"That's the larger framework Morty but I think there's more to it than that. It seems there is no concept of society. Each person has declared he is a society to himself, and he therefore deserves acknowledgement and adulation for what he has made. Like the Englishman who is a self-made man and every day he thanks his maker."

My Lagavulin arrived warm in its cold and beaded meniscus-challenged glass and things were improving.

"Yes, Frank. You have touched on some of it but there is another influence which is even more pernicious. If Maslow were still alive, he would rewrite his hierarchy of needs. Somewhere near the physiological needs at the base of the pyramid he would insert 'Fame.' Fame at all costs. Daily, there are one hundred million people sticking their ugly mug, or their cat's butt, or their trick of swallowing a lemon whole, into a camera and circulating it online, to share their wonderfulness and claim their fame. They are desperate for acknowledgement on social media and God help you if you deny them. We were just listening to Artie Shaw and his band. And Helen Forrest. We were listening to talent. Talent, which through hard work, application to their crafts and a willingness to sacrifice to improve, became fame. They paid their dues, and their efforts were rewarded. They did not cheat with an auto tuner, they did not mask lousy singing in a wide nasal electronic reverb, they perfected their craft. Our current doctored, faked music is a metaphor for the world. Integrity within a discipline or profession is no longer regarded as a requisite let alone having intrinsic value, and fame is not only expected, but it is demanded as a reward for existence. Even to the point of getting it with a firearm. A gunman believes he is his own society. And with historical society being abandoned as part of the new world mission statement, why would he not believe it."

I tapped beside my empty glass to indicate another and Morty obliged. Somehow, he was able to move slowly and do things quickly. My drink appeared in a trice, happy to be there. The cold felt good on my hand and the Lagavulin had nothing to tell me as I looked through it to the bottom of the glass. It was like looking into a fire. If I gazed into it long enough, all would be revealed. The first sip did not expose anything new.

"Morty, have you run into the situation where a person you thought you knew, knew for years, was not remotely who you believed them to be?"

"Frank, I presume that question is rhetorical. I run a bar. No one in here is who or what they seem to be. Except for yourself. Your authentic shallowness runs deep."

"Thank you, Morty."

Once again Morty had left me feeling both elevated and insulted at the same time by a statement which meant nothing but left me wondering what was in his homily which I just hadn't worked out. I said my goodbyes and made my way through the hive of soulless myopic nerds and stepped into the fresh air of a beautiful evening, without the creaking groan of the front door hinge bidding me adieu. It was like being thrown out.

Chapter Twenty-two

She sat in my spot at the bar. We locked eyes and her million-candlepower smile lit up the room. Raisa Gabler was back, and the good old bad old days washed over me. It had been five years. She stood to meet me and her ladies' brogue shoes gave her some extra height.

"You were sitting in my seat."

"Shall I move?"

"No, you have made the seat too hot. I'll sit next to you."

"I can remember when hot was exactly what you liked."

"Ah, memories. Things we shoulder as if they were real."

I wanted to kiss her, and I wanted to tell her to leave me the hell alone. I kissed her on the cheek.

"Raisa, you look great. Time has been kind. I see you still sport your 'R.G.' monogrammed cuffs."

"Yes. As a reminder of who I am."

"It seems from your vantage point your reminder is upside down."

"No doubt about it, Frank. I am. Upside down."

Absent mindedly she tapped the base of her empty wine glass with a high-gloss polished nail and young Mort misconstrued it as a request. He whisked away the glass and replaced it with a fresh white Montrachet. From the right a moving bulk distracted us and as the stud approached I felt the violence in every stride. He spaced himself a few stools down on my right. He spoke quietly to the bartender and pointed in my direction. Mort glanced over and caught me shaking my head 'no' at Volkov's apparent attempt to buy me a drink. He shrugged his shoulders and stood for a second looking us over. He seemed more interested in Raisa than in me and I couldn't blame him. She was a knockout. A stiff smile showed teeth as he left. I watched Raisa's face. She followed every motion with falcon eyes of inspection and analysis, not attraction. I saw the same intensity which embodied her years ago.

"Frank, that guy has phony stamped on his forehead. I feel as if I need a shower."

Raisa in the shower appealed to the basic Frank but at that moment my inclinations ran more toward bulletproof vests. He was the guy.

"Phony yes, but too real altogether. He is a killer."

"Yes."

Her quick affirmation of something she should know nothing about brought back the old suspicions, and the familiar knot began to twist in my stomach.

"Raisa, if you are capable of it, give me one straight answer. Why are you here?"

"Frank, the truth is, I don't know. I wanted to see you and here we are and I still don't know. The other night, I stood outside the bar, just watching, and did not come in."

Mort nodded to her in the mirror.

" My cab is here, Frank."

"I'll drive you."

"No, that is not a good idea. Thank you anyway."

She kissed me goodbye on the cheek with a very hard squeeze on my hand and left me confused. Certain things were timeless.

<>

The ambassador loosened his tie and cursed. The air conditioning had stopped working, the temperature in his office had just passed 90°F and things had unraveled in Houston. In addition, unwittingly he had lied to Moscow.

"Gimme that!"

He snatched the hammer from Petrov's toolkit, gripped it with both hands and smashed at the canister, hating it for being an empty replica. Again and again he hammered it and shrieked at it with every blow. Petrov ducked away from the hammer thrown at his head.

"Petrov, you moron! What did you do? Did you bring Kent back here with you so we could validate the canister together? Oh no. You brained him with a shovel and buried him in the desert! Did you interrogate him about his associates? No, no, much too hot in the sun wasn't it! Have no doubt there's room for one more body in the Texas wasteland! And how you boasted! Petrov the Great has obtained the sample canister for not one ruble when the decadent Yankees had bid two billion dollars! You and one ruble put together are worth one ruble! Get ready for the call to Moscow because both our necks are bloody well on the block. Prepare your explanation. Pick up this mess and destroy it!"

Ambassador Turgenev had no intention of allowing Petrov anywhere near his communication to Moscow. Turgenev was possessed of a diplomat's tongue, and he spun the situation in his mind. This was going to be a tricky presentation to the Kremlin. Nigel Kent was a clever and careful operative, and obviously the man had been duped into delivering a counterfeit, but that was the place to lay the blame. Paint him as a double agent. Perhaps vilify the dead Demidov for his part in it. He rejected both obvious tactics. Attributing blame elsewhere counted for nothing. Six years of work and Russia had failed. By extension, the failure was on his head. His career had just jumped off a cliff. It had gone from brilliance and promise to ignominy and stagnation. For his miscarriage, he would spend the rest of his days swatting mosquitoes in some malarial backwater yet to be marked on a map. Better they should just kill him. He had hoped for Paris. He slumped into his chair and watched the heat waves rise from the parking lot, wishing he had the canister back to hit with a hammer.

Argentum New Mexico was hotter and dustier and more decrepit than I remembered. I walked through the front shop of Argentum Refined Pizza into Sanjay Rustom's back office. He was surrounded by invoices and my shadow darkened his paperwork as I entered.

"Well. Before me I see a Frank McCord. You have come a long way for a pizza."

"Hello Sanjay. How is the canister business?"

"Now that the samples are on the ground, that's a question I should be asking you. You are the one who is cozy with Dr. Macbeth. I, on the other hand, was considered redundant six years ago. Ask the woman how things are. I'm busy. What do you want?"

"I'm here because I ask myself questions. Such as, if a copy were to be made of the Bennu canister, who would have the knowledge and means to do so. And what could be the motive, I ask myself. Perhaps a disgruntled ex-employee? And as with most things, it comes down to opportunity. Do you believe in coincidence?"

"I do not."

"Neither do I. This office is less than ten miles from the route the army chose for delivery of the capsule to Houston. "

"Amazing isn't it? An easy flight or a next to impossible road trip and they picked the road trip. That is the military in a nutshell. Nothing to do with me."

"Sanjay, this does not have to be difficult. You had the motive, the means and the opportunity. You did it. With help of course."

"Frank, what are you playing at?"

"It is no coincidence you and Kent worked intimately on the Bennu project and are together in New Mexico doing of all things, making pizzas, just miles from the route taken by the convoy carrying the samples. "

"You are correct Frank. Yes, we worked together intimately. Yes, we were both released from our jobs, to use the corporate term, and we were both at loose ends. Together we searched for an alternative self-sufficient future, and we found it. Here."

"Listen to me, before you get into very hot water. This can be easy for you. Just give Meghan back her baby and all else is forgiven and forgotten. No one has been hurt, the army's reputation will be protected and that's that."

"Frank, I have no idea what you are talking about. Meghan's baby? Are you talking about the Bennu canister?"

"Where is Nigel Kent?"

"I have no idea."

"Sanjay, be honest. I am not the law nor the CIA nor the army. I work for Meghan. Do you have the canister?"

"I do not."

"Would you pass a lie detector test on that?"

"I would. I do not know where Nigel Kent is, and I do not have the canister. You ask who would have the means. Within Cosmos Space Center security was paramount. Many people had small sections of the drawings, and perhaps only ten, including myself, had seen them together as an entity. However, there are security cameras by the hundreds in all departments and if someone external had hacked that feed network they could compile images from every section and have a complete plan. Materials are the difficult thing. Only a handful of specialized companies produce those. The materials would be the problem. I think that's where you look if you want to track anything down. Heat shielding and the like. I'm sorry I can't be of more help."

Rustom presumed the red herring he had placed before McCord would be recognized for what it was. Even so, McCord would beat the bushes. Sanjay's acquisition of the shielding material from Livorno was not recorded. It had been paid for in cash albeit within a rather eccentric method of delivery. Italy being what it was, no cash sale ever made its way into a record, and specifically not those of Borgia Composite Ventura of Livorno. Nothing could be traced back to him. His 'Archetyne LLC' was domiciled in Gibraltar. Payment for its incorporation was done in gold. Archetyne paid for the Semtex explosive and the boxcar rental was purchased with Bitcoin transferred from a now extinguished wallet. He knew nothing.

Despite Rustom's denials, I believed he was involved. I had no clout. I was not the law and my little sojourn to question him was private and not approved by my employer. I struck out with the aerospace suppliers. I expected nothing more, but it was a road I had to travel. I tossed my final report on Meghan's desk and peered over her shoulder at a graph taking shape on her computer monitor.

"What am I looking at?"

"A graph of sunspot activity. What is in the report?"

"Much wasted time done thoroughly and the identity of the culprit or culprits who pulled off the heist. Sanjay Rustom and Nigel Kent."

Meghan smiled at me with anticipation, waiting for the rest of the joke.

"I'm serious. I spoke with Rustom in New Mexico. He was cool and collected and lying through his teeth. Nigel Kent seems to be missing. The circumstances scream Rustom, but I can't pin it on him."

"Rustom? Really? You know your business, but I believe you have spent too much time in the New Mexico sun. Rustom? A hijacker? That is so far removed from his temperament. They asked for one billion dollars ransom. Sanjay does not need money. Rustom Enterprises in India is worth twenty times that. On the other hand I hope you're correct. "

"How so?"

"One threat in the ransom note was if the cryptocurrencies were not forwarded in a timely manner, they would destroy the canister and the samples with it. Sanjay could not do it. His heart and mind lived for that project. He would not destroy those samples for any money."

"To paraphrase, hell hath no fury like an employee terminated. Also I think you're forgetting something. It wasn't just samples in the canister. The Pentagon has something in there too. He and his gang might be ransoming that, and the devil take the samples. Tell me about the graph."

"Sure. The Y axis is the vertical line on the left, and the horizontal line is the X axis. Where they meet in the left corner is called the origin. This graph begins with the year 1960 and time runs left to right along the X axis. The number of sunspots is plotted up and down on the Y axis. The graph looks as if it's alive because AI is working in the background and plotting data as it confirms it."

" The peaks and valleys on the X axis seem pretty regular all way across."

"That's right. The graph of sunspots goes up and down like looking at the side of a roller-coaster. 2025 was a high spot and we are on the way down again right now until about 2031. Then, back up to a maximum in the spring of 2036. That is the next time we see Apophis, on Friday, the 13th of April. Maximum sunspots are about eleven years apart in a repeating pattern. We are in cycle twenty-five right now and I am waiting for the plotting of the current period and the next two periods through 2047. There, you see on the screen, we just plotted 2025. The next maximum is in 2036, then 2047 and so on."

"Meghan, the 1990 maximum is ten times as high as some of the other years. "

"1990 was the highest on record with the exception of perhaps one in the 1800s."

"How do we know that?"

"Carbon-14. The absence or presence of sunspots influences the amount of carbon-14 in the atmosphere. That is reflected in the annual growth rings of trees for example, and other organic materials. Scientists study all these sources, and they are able to reconstruct solar activity and sunspots back one thousand years."

"Interesting. And I mean that. I suppose my question is, what difference does it make? Is the sun brighter or hotter with more sunspots?"

"Yes, the solar irradiance is about one percent higher in periods of high sunspot activity."

She spun her chair away from the screen to face me and smiled. I smiled back and we liked each other. Flickers of red light bounced around the room as AI data expanded the colored graph along the X axis.

"Meghan, you are an astrophysicist. The graph forming behind you strikes me as one more game played by nerds to keep their synapses humming and the grant money rolling in. Why does any of it matter?"

"Frank, I do believe you have cut to the crux of academia. However, we astrophysicists do need to know the level of sunspot activity. You and I have talked a bit about an asteroid called Apophis. It came close to us in 2013."

" How close?"

"Well, when I say close I'm speaking in astronomical terms. It was about ten million miles away. In 2029, that is different story and I am going to Uruguay to observe. Its flight path takes it along the East Coast of South America between the Earth and the Moon."

"That's a close shave. When the tabloids clue in to how close it will be, they will jump on it. Juicy articles about impending doom with hasty reinterpretations of prophecy to titillate the masses. Never let a catastrophe go to waste. Does such close proximity between two bodies moving that fast create problems?"

"It's possible, but we don't know for sure. What we do know is earth's gravitational pull on Apophis is likely to cause some derangement of its orbit. It is also possible the stresses on the asteroid will produce seismic activity. Like a small earthquake. Our Yarkovsky effect calculations are reliable, but they are based upon the known surface. If the surface changes, then the radiant energy released also changes, and that throws off the math. The sun just might kick the orbit harder. Also, Frank, an asteroid's orbit changes every time it passes near another astronomical object. If Apophis' orbit changes because of its interaction with the Earth, it will change again if it gets close to an object not previously in its path."

I put up my hand.

"The Yarkovsky effect?"

"Sorry. Once I get rolling I revert to jargon. The Yarkovsky effect is the effect sunlight has on an asteroid. The asteroid absorbs sunlight and as it rotates the surfaces have different temperatures due to uneven heating. The hotter side gives off infrared radiation, creating a tiny push that can change the asteroids' orbital speed and path. Right now, we know what the surface is like, and we can calculate how much push it's going to get. That's where knowing the sunspot activity is important. Increased sunspot activity equates to more radiant energy which means a bigger push. OSIRIS-Apophis explorer is already on the way to meet up with Apophis after it leaves Earth to examine its surface."

"Examine? In the same way Bennu was examined? I was in the room. You wanted to strangle Leishman. He was supposed to just expose a bit of the surface, but he blasted the devil out of it and blew tons of regolith into space. He made a whole new flat area."

"Bloody right I wanted to strangle him and not for the first time. I wanted to strangle him for something every day I was with him. The plan was a close flyby of Bennu using the gas thrusters to dislodge dust and small debris so we could study what was below them."

"Will he be involved with Apophis?"

"That's only four years away so, yes. Leishman is an arrogant swine and a total psycho, but brilliant, and we need him. He has corrected the algorithm controlling the thrusters, and it won't happen again."

The light show from AI converting the data into a graphic representation stopped. Meghan swung back to the screen with an air of expectation.

"No, God! No. No, it it, Duo! Get in here! Bloody hell! It can't be correct. Duo!"

The graphic display representing the sunspot occurrence for 2036 towered over the others. The peak years on the left of the graph were reduced to blips in order for the screen to accommodate the height of 2036.

"Meghan, am I reading the graph correctly?"

"Duo, where the hell are you!"

"Meghan. The 1990 peak is labeled 194 for the number of sunspots. You said that was the highest of all time. The 2036 label reads 382."

Meghan continued to shake her head not to indicate Frank was wrong, but in disbelief of what she saw. A two-fold increase over the highest activity on the sun ever recorded.

Duo appeared like a whisper. There was no sound of stride nor foot fall but rather a flowing growth of energy moving toward them. The air in the room began to compress and despite that, breathing seemed easier under the influence of some purifying vitality. The Boys had retained the man-like corporeal exoskeleton demanded of it by Meghan but had engulfed it as a core subsumed by them. Pure energy fluxed and pulsed like an envelope around them as they came to service the call from Second Mother. From afar they had gleaned the turmoil in Meghan's amygdala, the key brain region processing threat and negative emotions. Powerful fear and threat responses flooded her insula and dorsal anterior cingulate. They had seen these things from time to time in the brains of other slows but never in Second Mother. The Boys did not know concern, but the definition seemed to apply to what energized them at that moment.

"Duo. Get inside the AI console and follow the logic that produced this graph. You must know historical data on coronal mass ejections and sunspots and the like. Verify this."

"Yes, Second Mother, we are well conversed in it. Slows have done a reasonable job in recreating historical comparisons. We have absorbed and processed the rudimentary compilation and projection of data by your AI slave. It has not considered six material factors. Therefore it is in error."

"Boys, I love you! Thank God! I knew it! I knew it!"

"Would Second Mother like us to create a true representation in the form of a similar graph?"

"Yes."

An ephemeral scintillation spun through the monitor from left to right and in a sparkled ionic discharge a graph traced itself into the perfect representation of the 2036 sunspot expectations. The number of 382 conjured by Meghan's AI console was indeed incorrect. The actual number of sunspots was 467. Meghan did not react. The Boys were infallible.

"Thank you, Duo. I don't need a.. wait. That amount of radiant energy building from 2031 to its maximum in 2036 will destroy the current orbit. Will the keyholes change?"

"We can make no determination except after 2029. Apophis will be invisible to ground-based telescopes because it will be at a small solar elongation angle. Computers will discount it as an extraterrestrial artefact. Simply, for Mr. Frank, in 2036 Apophis will be coming at a low angle out of the sun and virtually invisible. "

Meghan nodded knowingly, understanding the circumstance. She saw my puzzlement at worrying about keyholes.

"Frank, the earth's gravity pulls on every asteroid that passes it, usually with little affect. But if the asteroid is in the right spot, coming at the right angle, has the right mass, comes at the right velocity, the next time it passes by, the asteroid gets drawn in by gravity and it hits the Earth. That sweet spot is called a keyhole. Every asteroid has a sweet spot including Apophis. Apophis has at least twelve key holes, none of which worries us given the old orbit. But a new orbit… the next time after 2029… there could be a hundred such sweet spots and God help us."

Her short explanation was clear, and her concern was real. Given such uncertainty, I knew precautions must be in full swing.

"So, I guess things are already under way to blow the thing up? That is, it takes years to get anywhere near it, so I assume some kind of intervention is on the move. "

She answered with pursed lips and a sideways glance and said nothing. Apparently I had asked the wrong question.

"Surely you are not saying we're not doing anything or there is nothing which can be done."

"You have said it. We are doing nothing and there are a hundred theories objected to by one hundred scientists who consider their own idea superior. Add nationalistic pride in their nation's solution to collective intellectual arrogance and you have gridlock. That's where we are."

"Someone must do something, now."

"The Russians recognized the need first. Roscosmos began studying designs for a mission to deflect Apophis in 2009. But their economy was in ruins, and they could not allocate the funds required. Again in 2016, their interest resurged, and they announced that the Makeyev rocket design bureau had intentions to obliterate relatively small near-earth objects using Russian ICBMs. They referred to objects such as the Chelyabinsk asteroid which was about sixty feet in diameter. Again, they included Apophis as an afterthought in their dialogue, but nothing happened."

"That's it?"

"There are many ideas. A simple one and likely effective, is the gravity tractor. A large body would simply be placed adjacent to the asteroid and pull it off course with its gravity. To move a two-hundred-foot diameter asteroid requires a twenty-ton object. To influence Apophis the object needs to weigh five hundred and twelve tons. No one has ever tried the gravity tractor. Not one has been produced nor is there one in production. To place it close enough to Apophis to have any effect, it needs to be done within the year.

The Chinese probably had the best idea, but it is too late to have enough effect, and it was never built. Attach a solar sail, a big shiny sail to collect the sunlight and millimeter by millimeter float the rock away before it gets anywhere near a keyhole rather than wait for the threat. Something else that would work of course, is simply painting it white."

"Maybe the movies have the right idea after all. Drill a hole, stuff in a nuclear bomb and blow it all to hell."

"That sort of thing works in gravity but in space it would be blast and hope. The result would be two Apophis' still on the same trajectories. And once again, we have waited too long."

" Well Meghan, given all the good news I shall now commence my customary and inexorable trajectory toward modest inebriation in the local microcosmic galaxy called Morty's. I invite you into my orbit. Do you care to join me?"

"I never expected to be standing beside you and saying, 'I do', but I do."

"Well missus McCord, come with me to the altar of Scotch whiskey and white wine and receive dispensation from pastor Morty."

<>

The Boys left Frank McCord and Second Mother to themselves and their speculations. Mother said Leishman would be part of her team. That was useful. Something The Boys had absorbed when walking in second Mother's cerebral cortex, was not useful. She had already divined Isadore Leishman must not alter the surface when Apophis arrived in 2029.

They filtered out through the mortar of the building and entered Isadore Leishman's apartment with their leading edge, while their trailing appendage had yet to leave Macbeth's laboratory. They had become Behemoth.

Isadore sat at his kitchen table eating a cereal of sugared oats and water. Each time one floated to the surface, he fished it out and arranged it on the table. It had taken him a month to collect 224 of them to complete an upside-down star map of constellation Draco. Daily the oat bits dried and stuck to the table. Today, the floater was number 225 and the beauty of it was, this last extra piece was the biggest. He had created a new constellation, and he dubbed the new star, *Leishmanis*. It was his personal pole star, giving light to eternity, forever to be admired and followed. It spoke to him.

Isadore.

Isadore said hello to his star.

Isadore. Come back from Leishmanis. Come, you beautiful thing. Beautiful Isadore. Come sweet Laleesh. Speak with your friend.

Isadore flushed with joy at the return of his soul mate. It had been too long. The arcuate fasciculus in his temporal lobe throbbed with the memory of her and The Boys knew to move ahead. They spun across his skin with arms of love and once again he was theirs.

Isadore, sweet boy, do you know they don't want you?

"Wha… who?"

The laboratory rats. They, she. You know them all.

He did know. Always they demeaned him. Give the dirty jobs to Leishman. Put too much sugar in his coffee. Make him give lectures they consider beneath them. Bully him into the shower to clean up. Snickering.

"I know them. Mean minds."

We understand. We hate them too. It is always those inferiors who attack us. Attack brilliance. But there is more. They're going to stop you.

"I don't think so. Leishman does what he wants."

Of course, of course. Genius must be given its latitude. Soon, you will receive instructions to abandon the mission to dust off Apophis. How do we feel about that?

"No, no. No. They cannot. It must be done, yes?"

Absolutely, sweet LaLeesh. Surely you have ways? Remote ways?

"Remote? Oh yes, he has that. Isadore could, could reprogram the interface for remote use to be only from his laptop and reconfigure the receiver to receive nothing except on the frequency he chooses. Oh yes. He would implement the algorithm late to give them no time to troubleshoot."

Dear Laleesh, we measured your thrusters. Only 402 pounds of thrust. Good for Bennu, but for Apophis?

"I ca.. cannot make more thrust. It is fixed. No, no more force. Remote will do, only eighty pounds used for Bennu. Only that. No time to troubleshoot. No time. No time like the present. I.. he likes presents. But none. She did. Presents, presents. Hush, hush, we all fall down, down, we go, down we go gathering nuts in gathering… ."

The Boys stroked his limbic responses quickly and gently and soothed Leishman's derangement. As they left him, his hippocampus blazed into storing his recent memory. The plan to use the full 402 pound thrust to flatten a football pitch on Apophis would be perceived by him as his own, soon enough. If not, nothing was lost. It seems the sun knows best. It does our work too.

Sanjay Rustom felt the rumble in his chest at the first throbs of the Diesel engine. The locomotive moved slowly around the turnout from the nearby passing siding and maneuvered into position against Sanjay's boxcar. The engine pulled it onto the main track into position in the main train. The knuckles of the couplers swung closed at impact, the lock dropped into place and he breathed again. The Bennu canister was on its way east to Atlanta for delivery in a mode and direction unknown to the Pentagon. The timing was precisely as promised in the ransom note. The route was busy. With stops to add and dispatch cargo, plus hours spent waiting on sidings for westbound trains to pass, the delivery would take five days. His remote receiver within the Semtex wrapped around the canister checked as active.

If by twelve noon on the third day the Pentagon's two billion in cryptocurrency was not residing in his gang's five wallets as demanded, he would obliterate the canister and all it contained with a push of a button.

Chapter Twenty-Three

"Good night Mr. Rustom."

"Good night, David, lock up. Remember, you are opening tomorrow."

"Yeah. No sweat. Goodnight."

Sanjay walked to the inside back door and sat wearily, rubbing his eyes. He had just finished tabulating the first quarter results and it was the eighteenth consecutive quarter over quarter to show an increase. Nigel and Robin had no idea how wealthy they had become. Pizza for a million swap meeters was big business. Mail remained to be opened, and the morning was soon enough until one piece caught his eye. It was not commercial but ornate. Something that might have come from India, but it was postmarked locally.

"You are invited… ."

Robin was marrying Daisy in three months. Sanjay was invited. He was disappointed not to find where in Robin's own inimitable way it said he was getting hitched. Each of his partners was now above one million on account and both were either unaware of it or appeared not to be interested in it. Nigel was in parts unknown after scarpering with the dummy canister, and Robin had Daisy and horses, not necessarily in that order, and who could ask for anything more.

Sanjay had not checked his hard wallet in twenty-four hours. There had been no deposit. Zero hour was six hours hence. If the ransom did not appear by then, with the push of a button the samples were atomized along with the item of war. He undid the pendant around his neck containing the wallet. He entered the eight-digit code by running through the random sequence of options and opened to his Ethereum account. It showed zero balance. As he was about to close it a pixel flashed and there in the account was $200 million in value in Ethereum. His Bitcoin account showed an equivalent value in Bitcoin. His wallet had received funds as set out in the ransom demands. Sanjay owned one wallet, and he liked that Robin and Nigel owned two each. He wondered how they would react when they learned each was sitting on $800 million US. The Pentagon had coughed up the goods. The gadget it had ensconced in the sample box must represent a change in the balance of power in the world. He checked his watch. It was not too late to call Robin.

"Robin, old man. I just opened your invitation, and I wanted to call you. Congratulations to you and Daisy on your wedding plans.

What? Well, of course. It's an honor to be asked, thank you. I am delighted to be your best man. By the way have you checked your crypto wallets recently? Have a look. You know, the ones I gave you along with the company registration materials a while back? Yes, I know you didn't understand all of it but there was nothing much for you to do, just to keep things safe and to put away the passwords somewhere private. Oh. How the devil cou… . Where do you think you might have lost them? On the trail between Red River and Questa. Maybe? Robin, you have big bucks in those now. The.. . Yes, I know Daisy is fixed bu.. . Okay, Okay. Yes, easy come, easy go. Yes, it is simpler, no doubt. Okay, old man, nice speaking with you and again, congratulations. You are a lucky man. See you when you get back to Argentum."

At the Pentagon, Russel Chadwick looked at his boss and shrugged.

"Well, it's gone. Two billion dollars in cryptocurrency sent to parts unknown never to be seen again."

"Don't be so sure. These oh so clever techies are stupid all the same. A gang of five is the worst. One of them will blow the cover the minute they have the currency. We have one, we have the five. I give it six months, and we will have them all, and the cryptocurrency as well. Besides, we confiscated the bulk of the Bitcoin from the Mexican cartels in the first place. In fact if these coins continue true to form, we'll have a profit. That means bonuses all around."

Sanjay Rustom had meant it when he said Robin was a lucky man. The simplicity of Robin's worldview and his complete lack of interest in the trappings of wealth made Sanjay wonder who was the clever one. He dragged the table aside and rolled up the carpet to expose the floor safe. He reached out the remote and weighed his intention. The option to incinerate the canister still existed. $2 billion paid by a war machine was not to the furtherance of a benign society. It was to sharpen the blades of terror and mayhem.

His two buttons flickered then held their color solidly. One button activated the transponder to reveal the location of the canister to the Pentagon. The other activated the Semtex plastic explosive to blow the thing to hell. He swallowed hard, pushed the button, turned off the remote and stuffed it into his back pocket. Sanjay set the alarm to the Argentum Refined Pizza shop and drove home. It had been a long tiring day.

Concierge Harry Bolton watched the illuminated display as the freight elevator descended. The screaming intensified as it passed the fourth floor and burst into a maniacal caterwauling as the doors opened into the lobby. Isador Leishman emerged in the grip of four soldiers in full gear, each struggling with one of his appendages, stretching him like a buffalo rug as he writhed and screamed to the heavens.

"Harry! Help, Harry! They are taking me! Stop them. They are taking me away. Away, Harry! Taking me! Please, Harry. Help me!"

Harry was unsympathetic.

" Relax, Dr. Leishman, a good stiff session of electroshock therapy never goes amiss."

Among Leishman's encyclopedia of aberrations was a fear of things which spun, such as fans, merry-go-rounds and centrifuges, but at the top of the list was helicopters. The four-man squad strapped the wet running mess of Doctor Isadore Leishman into a casualty litter on their Chinook helicopter and took him away.

General Otto Bucholz welcomed Dr. Meghan Macbeth to Hinesville Georgia and the Fort Stewart army base. His smugness at having taken control of the disposition of the Bennu canister was thinly veiled. Meghan received his welcome with her customary decorum.

"General, you can stuff your phony, fat faced, welcome! You and your bloody hobnail boot brigades have no business anywhere near my project, let alone controlling the samples retrieval operation. I suppose you have engaged the same platoon of intelligentsia to recover the canister which allowed it to be stolen in the first place?"

"Indeed. Perhaps I shall order the brutes to use simple sledgehammers, that is, something basic and unintelligent to beat the tin box until it opens and I remove my prize. On second thought, and you see I have managed two thoughts consecutively, that is, in a row, perhaps I should allow you to remove the Semtex explosive in which it is wrapped yourself and solve both our problems with a flash of brilliance."

Meghan wanted to plant a quick right cross to Bucholz' chops but refrained. A Pyrrhic victory was not in her interest. She could not win a battle against the army and both parties could have what they wanted if she cooled it. The vision of Leishman being press-ganged into a helicopter drew a smile, not unnoticed by the general.

"Dr. Macbeth, shall we begin again? Welcome to Fort Stewart."

"Thank you, general Bucholz. I am pleased the Bennu sample canister has been located, and I am indebted to the Pentagon for ransoming it. You and I have an interest in seeing it retrieved intact, and its contents claimed. You will recover your hardware and my colleagues and I will have our samples. My truculence stems from fear that unless my staff does both jobs, the samples will be contaminated by your crew and the OSIRIS-REx program will be for nothing."

"I agree. You must handle the canister, and we shall monitor the goings on. In fact, we have, uh, borrowed your lead scientist, Dr. Leishman to lead the work under your supervision. I thought you would be more comfortable having staff with which you were familiar. He's arriving by helicopter shortly, strapped safely to a litter. By the way, Dr. Leishman weighs one hundred forty pounds, and it took four, two-hundred-pound MPs to get him wrapped and packaged for shipping."

"I heard. The concierge in his building has been making the rounds telling the tale. I don't suppose you have a video?"

Neither of them cared particularly who the thieves were. They had kept their part of the bargain. As they boarded the revving Chinook together, they pointed at Leishman's copter settling down a hundred yards away, it's powerful rotor wash kicking up a dust cloud. Izzy had arrived unscathed, exhausted by the battle he fought, mumbling in his restraints. As the four-man squad secured his litter to the interior sides of the Chinook's main cabin with hooks and chains, they fitted his earphones. Meghan spoke through her head set as she and Bucholz strapped in along the line.

"Isadore. Listen. Listen, Isadore. We are on the way to the samples. Stop the nonsense. We need you. You are the great Doctor Leishman, astrobiologist. This is your baby now. Your show. In a few minutes, we need your brilliance. Get it ready. Takeoff and landing, we will be there in thirty minutes. If you are not ready, we will get someone else, and you are out."

Isadore was somewhat calmer with the headphones on, and he had had enough of his own histrionics. There was a certain satisfaction in working oneself up to a frenzy and testing fresh limits of tolerance demanded by one's behavior, but Macbeth suffered fools badly at any time, let alone at a delicious time like this. He knew he was best in the world at what he did and so did she, but the woman was impetuous. *Yes. She was looking for an excuse. Looking for the reason to dump Izzy. Yes. Wrap him up. Abuse him by stuffing him in a stinking double-bladed whirling monster to make him berserk then blame him for his condition. No. Isadore is too clever for that. He is the sweet LaLeesh. Handsome, they said. Yes. Someone else to access the samples, she says. Pah! No one can touch the Leishman.*

Seventy-five miles southwest, Sanjay Rustom's refrigerated rail car sat on a bowl track waiting to be rolled onto a siding. The Rice Yard in Waycross, Georgia, occupied seven hundred acres and at any one time it managed, moved, sorted or stored one thousand eight hundred rail cars. Four Chinook helicopters raced there at one hundred eighty miles an hour with a mixed contingent of one hundred and sixty men, the head of the Joint Chiefs of Staff, Meghan Macbeth and a mostly mummified Leishman. The 92nd Engineer Battalion and the Third Infantry Division from Fort Stewart were proud and worried. Proud that General Otto Bucholz was on site and running the operation personally but worried their operation had been branded critical and delicate. They were not built for delicate. Among them they debated how, if ordered to do so, they would secure the five-mile perimeter of the rail yard with one hundred and sixty men while protecting a general and a civilian technical staff. The choppers peeled off two each, right and left, and settled into the soft grassland on either side of the rail yard. Four lieutenants, tracking device in hand, led four platoons toward Sanjay's transponder and after forty minutes of navigating the city of box cars the canister was surrounded by a sea of camouflage. Engineer lieutenant Munoz ordered his sergeant to cut the seal from the refrigerator car plug door. He did so and leaned forward to reef on the pivot handle of the release mechanism. A loud voice from the ranks interrupted.

"Sir. Permission to speak , Sir."

"Yes, Corporal?"

"Sir, that is a kinetic release door. Sir. It needs a forklift with a bully to open it. There is danger of a heavy recoil, Sir, when done by hand. That door weighs one thousand pounds and can break you up real bad. Sir."

"Thank you corporal."

Munoz turned away and then back as he recognized the young man's badge.

"You are bomb disposal. Is your team ready?"

"Yes, Sir. I was told there is Semtex."

"You have your spotter and crew?"

" Yes, Sir. Eight. Corporal Watson and I Identify and render safe. Dewey is disposal. If it's chemical or biologic, we have them too."

"Can you operate the bully?"

'"Yes, Sir."

"Fine Corporal. Take over from the civilian when the forklift shows."

"Sir, yes Sir."

"Listen up. All men, pace off one hundred yards. Form a perimeter and keep it sealed. Dr. Leishman, we need you to tell us what is original to the canister and what might surprise us that is added."

Leishman stepped up like a champ and adjusted the band of his LED headlamp and strode into the boxcar to tell them what was what. When the Semtex was gone and the area cleared, he instructed the mechanics on every thread and nut and every retaining strap. Together they secured the capsule and pumped nitrogen through a one-way valve into its specialized glovebox, for the six-hundred-mile flight north to the Capscol Space Laboratories in Humberston Maryland. It was the best equipped and most respected analytical laboratory for celestial specimens in the United States. Leishman would want for nothing in diagnostic aids.

The tiltrotor V-22 Osprey took off vertically and swung into forward drive with a twenty-person entourage including Leishman,

Bucholz and Macbeth. Macbeth regretted not bringing Rustom back on board for the final analysis. His insight was remarkable, and he often deduced things others could not. She hoped his business in Nevada or New Mexico or wherever it was, was profitable for him. For five hours, Leishman watched the propellers waiting for one of them to come off. For the thousandth time, General Bucholz ran and re-ran the awesome power of the proton collimator through his mind. He could influence the policy of its use, but he could not control madness, nor accident, nor megalomania in office.

When the General arrived at 7:30 a.m. the following morning, Leishman and Macbeth had been at the laboratory for two hours. Izzy wore binocular magnifiers and reached into the sealed glovebox using the gloves which were attached through the front panel. He had completed the initial opening by removing the aluminum lid which sat to the side in its own sealed nitrogen filled container.

"Doctor Macbeth, you have an army of nitrogen bottles here. Why nitrogen?"

"General, nitrogen is inert and does not react with the sample materials to change the nature of their chemistry. Each component upon its removal is treated the same to exclude oxygen or water vapor from oxidizing or hydrating the contents. Basically Doctor Leishman can manipulate the samples and perform analysis without direct exposure to the outside environment."

Isadore was oblivious to the conversation and continued in his other world of concentration all the while his body stiffened anticipating what he hoped he would not find. He disassembled the sample acquisition mechanism and removed the gathering head. He slid each component into its reserved glove box and sealed them in with the nitrogen. He stared motionlessly into the sample box and set down his Teflon tool. There was the proton collimator, no bigger than a baseball made ovoid, and both Megan and Isadore exhaled their anxiety.

The collimator was contained in a bag made of fine pure gold mesh. Its surface was undamaged Teflon and it had been attached to the servo mechanism harness with pure gold ties. The two scientists beamed at each other, wanting to kiss the rogue technician for his care and knowledge in using only inert materials to attach the hardware while wanting also to throttle him for having placed it there in the first place. Involuntarily, Bucholz took a quick step forward to have it passed to him to hold, but Leishman shook his head as he approached.

"Don't. You can't see what I see through my binoculars. The mesh, the seam in your gadget, the head of the collection apparatus, contain thousands of small particles to be analyzed. It is a slow procedure to remove them. Some of them are sticky and resistant, others are brittle and bouncy. Your troublemaker will go the way of everything else. Glove box, nitrogen, cataloging, descriptive material, and proof of ownership. Just kidding about the proof of ownership. You can have it once it's cataloged and described for the record."

General Bucholz took possession of his treasure five days later.

The capturing of every particle of dust was just the beginning for Leishman and his bevy of bench technicians. The complete analysis of the samples from Bennu was designed to be slow and methodical and it took five weeks of eighteen-hour days.

Izzy began by looking for organic components and various minerals with the scanning electron microscope, creating high-resolution images using a focused beam of electrons to reveal the material's shape and structure down to a billionth of a meter.

As an astrobiologist he was most interested in the mass spectrometry. With it, he could reveal the different molecules in any sample. He looked for those relevant to the study of life, particularly specific organic molecules like nucleobases and amino acids. He added infrared spectroscopy and Raman spectroscopy to study the rotational and vibrational energy for information about chemical bonds. Those were telltales for certain specific organic molecules.

Leishman's team used gas diffusion spectroscopy to excite atoms at the surface of the sample with a low-power laser to identify its molecular composition and free elements.

His combination of techniques built an all-inclusive picture of the sample's constituent elements which could reveal life's building blocks and perhaps clues to its history and origin.

Altogether the Bennu sampler collected one hundred and twenty grams to be shared by the scientific community around the world. 70% remain with the Johnson space center for use by future scientists. Portions were shared for deeper analysis with the Lawrence Livermore National Laboratory, the Space Sciences Laboratory at UC Berkeley, University of British Columbia, University of Arizona's Kuiper-Arizona Laboratory for Astromaterials Analysis and the Lawrence Berkeley National Laboratory to be followed by laboratories around the world as time passed.

Macbeth's team and Leishman's brilliance found much and created more questions.

"Come on Frank, answer. Pick up. Frank you won't believe it. I mean you'll believe it, but it is amazing, fantastic and more."

"Whoa, one superlative at a time. You beat your time going to Morty's."

"Creep. We have amino acids, Frank. Stuff we're made of. And out of twenty possible amino acids, we have fourteen. Fourteen and even more amazing, all five nucleobases need to make RNA and DNA. The building blocks of life!"

"Ah Meghan, I love you. You are excited, and real and raunchy. A girl after my own heart. I am very pleased for you. I know it's a big deal."

"That's not all we found. We have clay. Clay, Frank. Hydrated clay. That means water. And halite, from evaporated salty water. And ammonia, and formaldehyde. Together they can make amino acids and.... Wait. You said you loved me."

" Did I? Must be a glitch in the matrix. Call me when you get back."

Chapter Twenty-Five

The private self-storage unit was unheated, and breath frosted with the effort of the work. Head number fourteen was about to get it. The blunt instrument swung in from the left, obliterated the back of the skull and blasted sugared green food dye from the attached plastic bag in a discreet array across the drop cloth. Number fourteen duplicated number thirteen precisely. The pattern was established.

Roger Gunderson released the rubber hose from their arm and unclenched their fist. The sixteen-gauge needle was taped securely and the rash from the adhesive would persist for a few days, along with the bruising. The blood bag contained a 70ml solution of citric acid, sodium citrate, sodium phosphate, dextrose, and adenine as the anticoagulant. Blood flowed freely for fifteen minutes to fill the bag with half a liter. Storage was at 6 ° for the next forty days, the same as the in vitro skin cells which would arrive later in the day, shipped in their specialized culture medium. Both would stay viable for six weeks with intact characteristics. Within that time, Roger would act.

Roger plucked twenty or so hairs from the thickest growth on the back of their head, discarded a few annoying gray ones from the collection, and cut off and discarded the root ends down the drain. Storage was between two sheets of parchment paper.

They walked to the green jade buddha on the mantle and rubbed his belly for luck. They aped his frozen smile and lifted him up to check the heft.

Roger reached for the timer just as it chimed the hour and dragged the weighted garment bag to a fresh spot on the carpet. An hour was too long. The carpet was significantly depressed. They left the garment bag in a fresh spot, set the timer for thirty minutes and resumed working with the string.

It stretched from the top of the chairback to the wall on the right at an eighteen degrees angle. At the twelve-foot mark Gunderson made a pinpoint mark on the carpet with a pen. They repeated the exercise to the left, marking the flooring at seven feet. Roger stood behind the chair looking at the shape of things left and right and the setup was correct. Gunderson poured a small amount of chlorine bleach into a saucer and dipped the back brush from the shower into it. A test spot behind the divan demonstrated the brush would engage the depth of the carpet pile nicely.

<>

Behind my apartment building, my tailpipe post office box had a note. ED was still on the job and as usual their message was cryptic.

Frank. Things are the same but different. At the two trees. ED.

The two trees referenced twinned eighty-foot pines with a deep depression at the root bifurcation fronted by a boulder. It was invisible to an onlooker at ground level, and it was a nice dead spot in the wind. It filled with leaves to make a good mattress. The adjacent park closed at eight p.m. and their hideout gave them a safe place overnight. They were pleased to see me as I slid down the incline and sat at the soft bottom.

"Hi boys, good to see you both. What's up, Dave? The same, but different?"

"Frank, ya gotta get with it. Get a new groove, man. What's the same is, your two shadows are still on your neck, but what's different is, now they are serious like. Pretty much, you run where we hang out. Every day at sunup you run the same five miles. Across Bosun Street, down the trail between the Shumard oaks. Then across the wood bridge over Black Water Creek along the gravel path to the point, and back. In a blue moon you run the beach and up the path to the Forecastle onto Bosun Street and home. You even told us one time, routines were killers. And every day you do the same thing like clockwork. Stupid. "

He was correct and in a matter of life and death, stupid was death.

"Frank, the guy, he's setting his vantage points. Looking how to get in and out. Looks like he's getting angles on you out of the oak trees running down toward the creek."

Ernie added his two cents worth.

"More sneaky French. Using camouflage, he is. Eh Dave? That's what he's doin'."

"That's it for sure. One day he was on the fire escape on the Laptev building across from Morty's and he ain't no fire inspector. And the littler one, been gone for a while but back now, quiet and cool, tough to spot and almost invisible, workin' along just steps away from him, hardly payin' you a mind, it seems. Don't know, but it's getting dead serious. You packing? "

"You know better than that. Pistols make you stupid. Thank you boys."

I pulled out a twenty for them, but it was a fifty and before I could make the adjustments, Ernie had it gone and in his pocket. I left them in their enclave knowing they were right. The time for confrontation had come but I was not sure I could handle it.

<>

Malta opened his phone casually and checked the caller. He gripped it more tightly when he recognized the suffix to the exchange. When internal affairs called, it was never good news.

"This is Malta. Go ahead."

"Well. Despite not having reported or done a bloody thing for six months as far as we can tell in Moscow, it seems you do live and breathe. This is Anatoly Maltsev. Director Firsov is dead. You are quiet. You didn't know. He was interred two months past. He was your supervisor, and you didn't know he was dead. At the moment the wheels are turning slowly but you do not know my name. Remember it. Anatoly Maltsev. It is I who signs the document to, let us say, decommission, those personnel who do not adhere to the patriotic and political ideals of current Russia. I am considering whether you might satisfy the definition. Even your code name. Malta. An island, an entity unto itself. Believe me, you are not. Where are you as we speak? On a beach somewhere, I suppose?"

Maltsev did not know how close his sarcasm was to the truth. Malta was thirty yards from the Deception Bay beach snugged against the large stump of a felled Shumard oak. New growth covered the line of sight from above and the only view to his blind was from the sea. The components of his broken-down rifle ran along the creases in his trousers, and he had been calibrating the distances to the gravel path at Blackwater Creek with his hand-held scope. The day was fine, but McCord had not passed by. His response to Maltsev was terse.

"Abernathy Town. Canada West."

"Ah. That is, let us see, ah, yes. Frank McCord. The first of your incomplete assignments. Or perhaps not. Perhaps you have simply not deigned to report. Is he dead?"

"No. Call me in a week and he will be."

"You say 'call me'? Order me as if you were a king? We shoot those! And this other one. Gunderson. Speak!"

"Anatoly Pavlovich Maltsev, please. I do know your name, of course. You are well known and admired throughout the country. My silence on the phone has been out of respect. Frank McCord is not an ordinary man, and his demise requires extraordinary preparation. I am within days of completing it. He has foiled Russia repeatedly and I do not intend to have it happen again. With regard to Gunderson, the individual moves in and out of the world like some avenging wraith. I believe I have made the final identification. You are right, I did not know Director Firsov had passed. The agreement between us was that I report on deeds, not on promises to do them. I apologize for the impression I have left in my dossier. I have never failed an assignment, and I will not fail these."

"Fine. I give you a month. Look up Novaya Zemlaya on the map. That could be your next posting."

<>

Roger entered the kitchen carrying a kit containing hand tools and an illuminated magnifier headband. They put on the headband magnifier and cotton gloves and began work on the bedroom door jamb. Slowly and carefully, Gunderson removed eight reverse threaded screws. The magnified examination of the screw heads showed no telltale scratches of abnormal use, and no nicks showed on the surround. Gunderson's practice was to align each screw slot ten degrees farther around the clock than the one below. If the pattern were broken, someone had intruded. With a gloved hand on each side, they slid the side frame out into the door opening to reveal two linen bags sequestered inside the wall.

The smaller bag contained Gunderson's handcrafted cartridges. The larger one contained their Giarardi sniper rifle. The gun broke down to a small package, and Roger kept the receiver and scope together to avoid having to re-zero the rifle. Changing caliber of the Giarardi was as simple as changing a barrel and each barrel used its common bolt and magazine. Roger selected 6.5 Creedmoor caliber rounds for the close-range approach planned for the day. The short-barreled weapon was smokeless and with its noise suppressor, silent. They cleaned and assembled the already immaculate hardware and broke it down and reassembled it several times, without a click or a catch in perfect muscle memory. They hung the weapon together with its bag of cartridges in the bedroom closet, out of contact with the room.

Roger relaxed in the darkened room with a glass of wine, watching lights crawl across the surface of the bay. Vivaldi played on the Bose and at least in their suite, if not anywhere else, civilization survived. False dawn pinked the mist, bringing a tranquility with it beyond any which Roger had experienced. The preparation of that night was their final one. Within forty-eight hours, it would all be finished.

The intercom light blinked at the front desk.

"Good morning, this is Terrence. How may I assist you?"

"Good morning to you, Terrence. This is Gunderson. Terrence, I'm going to be doing some paperwork in the next couple of days, paper strewn everywhere in my usual way, and I don't want one of your manic cleaning staff coming in and making it neat. Neatness confuses me."

"I understand completely. What is chaos to one is order to another."

"Precisely. So, no staff into my suite today, but after midday tomorrow would be fine. Would you see to it?"

"It is my pleasure. I shall channel my inner Victor Hugo, I shall man the barricades. With laughter, nay with weeping, my story will be told, how stout Terrence kept his… ."

"Terrence!"

" I suppose that was a bit dramatic. Housekeeping will come, not today, but after midday tomorrow. I will see to it."

<>

I seldom took the funicular rail car down to the sea, but the steepness of the decline was not to be run down without a helmet. The view from the height overlooked Deception Bay and Gull Island to the east, opposite the delta of Black Water Creek. The western arm of the bay was Stricker Point which climbed to a high-bluffed peninsula directly south, with the lighthouse at the point. The day was fine and almost still, and it was high tide. The light wind was directly on shore and the strip of beach remaining was pebbled and no more than a couple yards wide. I ran east for half a mile and 'stupid', out of Dave's mouth, was right on. I realized the running route I had chosen for the day was not a good strategy. I was trapped against the sea to the right and trapped again on the left by a six-foot bluff topped by tufts of beach grass and shore pine. In the bad old days of covert planning this setup would have been called the kill zone. The face of the escarpment was bathed in light but at nine a.m. the sun was not yet above the old growth forest two miles east. If I were confronted here it was impossible to force an assailant to circle to the west so the first rays of sun would blind him. It would be me who was blinded for that fatal half second.

The beach did not widen for a thousand yards, which meant ten minutes of navigating bad footing until I had options of where to head. I picked up my pace and slipped hard left off a kelp slimed stone, throwing my shoulder into the face of the bluff and destroying my knee on the bolder. A thousand bushtits with a thousand cries exploded from the bush above me, telling the world for a mile in any direction exactly where I was.

Malta sat in a cluster of oak stumps thirty yards above water level protected from view by waving sea grass and new growth from the stumps. He had begun breaking down his VKS rifle. It was subsonic with a built-in suppressor. McCord had not shown, and Malta was pleased. It showed a man who knew he was hunted. Malta felt the juices running harder. The contest had begun. Perhaps the war zone should move to McCord's apartment. Perhaps a simple cat burglary apparently gone wrong. Perhaps a lethal dose of thallium left behind in a part bottle of Lagavulin. Easy. But in the end what was that? A death? With this man, what honor would come from cheap murder.

The bush tits burst from a stunted pine three hundred yards to his right. He snatched the scope and found the area in a second. Something or someone was moving along the high tide shore. Every so often the profile of the cliff fell to reveal part of a bobbing head. Someone struggled east through the detritus. Malta moved his scope at the pace of the runner and fifty yards along, the cleft of a washout exposed Frank McCord, slipping sliding and struggling, making for the gravel paths half a mile ahead. McCord filled the image, and the crosshairs were at his chest. Malta snapped the folded stock of the rifle back into position and flipped off the safety and confirmed the distance.

Malta's hardware was painted a dull brown green but a millisecond bounce of sunlight off the telescopic lens gave away his spot. Gunderson was forty yards above him to the west and noiselessly they took the safety off the Giarardi. They checked with their sighting scope and Malta's lens continued to give away his position. The footing was sandy and silent and Gunderson crept yard by yard toward him. Close encounters like this were not their usual style but the man was sent to kill them, and they would return the favor in person. They wanted to see the look on his face as they released their rounds into his heart.

Roger paused twenty feet from their target. Through the veil of foliage Malta's camouflaged gun became obvious for what it was. They took two very slow deep breaths and exhaled silently and fully. They leapt into the space between the stumps and with finger on the trigger and muzzle pointed to the area of the heart below the gun, the spot was empty. Malta had left his gun behind and the fresh track in the soil led east and down to intercept the beach. Gunderson confirmed that Malta's VKS was loaded, picked it up with gloved hands and followed slowly.

Every line of the paper dossier on McCord warned Malta against going one on one. He respected the history, but he did not embrace the myth. He had been at arm's length with McCord and taken his measure. The prowling locomotive still lurked within him, but McCord was not the man he once was. And today that man would learn what it was, to lose, to fail, to fall, to beg for release from the agony, knowing he would not get it. With a three-hundred-yard execution, none of that would be his. McCord deserved his final moments of clarity, then death. Malta calculated he would arrive at the junction of the gravel paths two minutes ahead of McCord. At five hundred yards or so they would see each other. Malta waited, hands on hips astride the path.

I limped into the sea and hobbled out waist deep. My right knee was split and stiffening and I hoped the 50°saltwater would slow the swelling. I saw Malta as he saw me and in three quick strides to his left he covered ten yards easily and continued toward me, devouring the distance between us. I was no match for his athleticism. His verve drove him on and I could see if it were manhandling on land between us, with my leg the way it was, I was a toddler. If he joined me in the water I had a chance of a lucky spin to drown him. I looked away and twisted to face Gull Island as if to make for it. He charged into the water south of me to block my path. The sun was not quite ready to break the height of the trees but if I could maneuver him to the west the timing might work for me. He did not allow it. He charged and I had nothing to do but brace for the impact, hoping to redirect his force in the right way to flip him. He recognized the tactic and leapt into contact distance and gripped me by my right forearm, having seen my limp and knowing I could not push off with that side. Using his grip I pulled him to me and driving my head into his chest I thrust for his eyes with my left hand, but he slipped it easily. We locked together and his strength astounded me. I could not move him off his feet and with each of us using all our strength we stood virtually immobile trying to break through. My head was pushed hard against his chest, and I saw blood in the water. Given the gash in my knee I was not surprised then I recognized it as a drop. He eased his grip on my right arm and as he turned away I looped it around his neck in a choke position drawing his head to me with all my force and I saw the bullet hole. It had entered his right temple, and I felt the warmth running down the exit wound on the other side. I released his weight into the water. I was exposed and helpless, standing still, and I waited my turn. Nothing came. The fatal shot had come from his right, from somewhere in the Shumard grove. I saw no muzzle smoke and I heard nothing. The retreating tide tugged subtly on Malta, volunteering to remove him from the expanding cloud of blood and take him deep. With difficulty I maneuvered him onto the beach. The man walking his dog looked at the blood, at me, at the grisly Malta, and trembled a call to 911. In ten minutes Abernathy Bay swarmed with uniforms.

I knew everyone in the hospital emergency unit personally, what their kids were doing in school and has Johnny got over the measles. We shared a twenty-year experience of cuts, bullet wounds and fractures and they had my wound cleaned and my knee joint immobilized in short order. They took over and under bets on the day they next needed to patch me.

It felt like midafternoon, and the throbbing persisted but the injection intended to relieve the pain had me coasting nicely and what time it was mattered little. I could smell Captain Climenhage. He headed up the police precinct on Bosun Street and he was the only man I knew who still used cologne with a little ship on the bottle.

"Frank, how do you manage it. In Abernathy town, we have had five homicides in twenty-five years. You sir are the common denominator in all five. I am told you have a damaged knee. Does it ache?"

"Yes, it does."

"Good. I may have spoken too soon a moment ago. Number six homicide may have happened today at the Excelsior Hotel. Feel like doing some sleuthing? Can you walk?"

"They gave me crutches. I am an old hand."

"Here is something to think about on the way. The boys found what they believe to be the murder weapon in the oak grove thirty or forty yards up the face of the escarpment. I'll let you know if we can pin down who he is."

The chlorine reek from Roger Gunderson's suite met us in the hall before we heard the conversations of the investigation crew. They had the bathroom fan on full to evacuate what they could but the windows stayed closed to prevent contamination of the sampling.

"Frank, take a few minutes and then just give me what you think you see."

The crime scene was like many I had seen. A writing table was askew with a turned over chair beside it and blood spatter was everywhere. A jade Buddha, now marked as item six by the crime scene crew, lay ten feet to the right in the spatter which continued a few feet beyond. The spatter to the left was shorter and heavy back spatter blotching showed behind the chair. I coughed my question to Climenhage.

"What does the luminol tell you?"

"We've tested a few small areas here and there with it and the mess

is certainly blood. But just blood. There is no way there is any viable DNA in the samples. The chlorine has been in contact for at least a day. The carpet is bone dry."

A shattered Terrence hovered nearby, overcome by the catastrophe.

"Right there, in that chair, Gunderson sat when working and looked out to the sea. They never missed a day. And to think of them gone, I cannot bear it. Oh, they loved the sea. "

"They?"

"Yes. Their preferred pronouns. They and them."

I ignored the nonsense and turned to Climenhage.

"Roly, look there. There is a depression in the carpet, just inside the door, at that bloodstain. Something heavy was lying there."

Roly pulled a man to look there more closely as I edged into the ensuite closet where suits hung in orderly fashion in their bags. I thought I smelled gun oil, but crime scenes had a way of evoking the past. The scene was like so many I had seen before, I was sure Climenhage had seen exactly what I saw, but I ran it by him.

"Roly, this is my impression. The occupant of the suite, Roger Gunderson, has not been seen for two days, and it appears they may have been the victim of a vicious attack. The copious back spatter at the chair indicates a heavy impact to the back of the head, likely from the statue on the floor to the right. It appears there are hairs stuck to it. The blow came from the left as indicated by the longer spatter on the right side. That suggests the assailant was left-handed. Wait."

I hobbled into the ensuite closet and separated the suit bags and that explained the depression in the carpet.

"The little we know of Gunderson is suits and ties for all occasions. Every suit in the closet is in a full-length garment bag. Where's the garment bag for the suit Roger is wearing? I think that explains the depression in the carpet. The killer put the body into the garment bag and left it on the floor. That explains the pooled blood there. He listened and waited until the floorwalker was gone. If he had studied or knew the walker's routine he could easily follow him along and quietly leave the building with Gunderson in the bag over the shoulder."

"We need to look at the videotapes."

"Roly, you are forgetting. This is the Excelsior. It is a technology free zone. No closed-circuit video, no cell phone, no texting, no internet, no trappings of our insane society allowed. They don't even allow vehicles to stay on the property. Their lot is across the street. Did you check there for Gunderson's car?"

"Yes. It is still there. I don't believe anyone walks away from a $300,000 Bentley."

Climenhage read the badge and cornered Terrence.

"Terrence, we need a description."

"I have nothing to give you."

"Terrence, listen. Apparently Gunderson has been coming here for years. You have worked here for years. Give me a description."

"I am not obliged to do so. Confidentiality is paramount at the Excelsior. I will not violate that trust. I have never, and I will never, discuss a visitor. Our patrons have relied upon this for a century, and they may do so for the next century."

"Blast it, man, I have a murder on my hands."

"You have said it. It is on your hands. It is not on the Excelsior's."

I needed to know whether Gunderson's body could be carried out. Anything above one hundred and fifty pounds and most people could not do it. I stood too close to the old man and let him have it.

"Listen to me. We need information. You can help. If it is a guess, you have divulged nothing. How much would you guess Gunderson weighs?"

"That, sir, is a question not for me, but for the carnival, where guessing weights is the norm. It is a place I do not frequent. Perhaps they could assist you?"

I understood his position and I admired his fidelity. If I could afford the Excelsior I would live there happily ever after.

"Roly, impound one of the suits in the closet. Have the lab boys calculate the volume inside the suit. Fat, skinny, heavily muscled, lightly muscled, you get it. It should tell us at least what the maximum weight would be. It's a place to start. Roly, why do you have me here? This is a standard textbook perfect crime scene."

"You are my blind pig, Frank. Every so often you stumble onto an acorn. Thanks for the insight. Come, stumpy, I'll give you a lift home. We'll have some results tomorrow and I will give you a call."

The opiates from the emergency room kept me sleeping until noon the next day. Climenhage called while I drank my coffee.

"Hello Frank, how's my man today?"

"I ache in places I didn't know I had places but all in all, I have no complaints. Any surprises?"

"Not really. Standard stuff. The killer did a thorough job with the bleach. Despite the volume of blood there's not one useful DNA sample. Even the hairs we recovered did not bring one root to test. They did mess up one thing. They wiped the jade Buddha, but some viable skin cells from the victim were still stuck there. X chromosomes like the skin from any man."

I gasped and choked on my coffee. For a decade I had anguished over the duality of Raisa Gabler as Roger Gunderson, accusing and grousing and tearing us apart with my suspicions. *X chromosomes like any man.* What a fool I was.

"Frank?"

"Sorry, Roly. Drank my coffee too fast. "

"Sure. The estimates on Gundersons suit show the person could be anywhere up to one hundred-and- ninety-five pounds. So, no help there. The slug which killed your guy did come from the gun recovered on the hill and the fingerprints on the weapon are also the fingerprints of the dead guy. While fighting with you in the water, he appears to have shot himself from his vantage point on the hillside. Clever fellow."

"He left the gun intending to go back for it. Someone picked it up and let him have it with his own weapon. Maybe Karma exists after all."

It hit me between the eyes, and I had said it myself. *This is a standard textbook perfect crime scene.* Too perfect. Staged by a genius.

"Roly, don't be offended. I want the CSIS lab in Ottawa to go over all the material again."

"Offended, forget it. If they can dig out something more, that's all good with me. Call our lab and tell them where to send it. Maybe they can identify the owner of the rifle. Our fingerprint database has no match."

Three days later a muffled cry came from my filing cabinet. I stiff walked to retrieve it, and the area code was 613, Ottawa.

"Hello Frank, it's been a while. This is Chauncey."

"Chauncey, you lab rat. I thought you would be long gone from the circus by now."

"They drag me back for interesting things like this."

"Good. If you find it interesting, so do I."

"The fingerprints are of Valeri Kaminsky, a Russian, we guess at about thirty-four or thirty-five years old. The prints we have are from eighteen years ago when he enrolled as a cadet. From that time to now he has been invisible. On the crime scene analysis, your boys there did a first-rate job. First rate. Perfect. Like the skin cells and therein lies the problem. No apoptosis. Cells come and go. Old ones die, new ones come. Not one of the cells shows apoptosis, the natural dying process. Those cells are all the same age. They did not come from a normal mixture of cells on a scalp, they came from an in vitro culture. Made in the lab. Thanks for this case. Send me more like it."

I sat with the dial tone droning, digesting the call. Despite the skin cells, there may have been a killing. Perhaps whoever set this up committed murder and introduced lab cells to have us assume it was staged. If so, Roger Gunderson may or may not be the victim or the perpetrator and Raisa Gabler still may or may not be Roger Gunderson and within the next several hours Frank McCord may or may not be exceedingly drunk.

I backed into Morty's on crutches and he nodded toward the back booths. A shapely leg made that booth my first choice and Raisa Gabler smiled a little as I slid in across from her.

"Nice work with the skin cells."

"Thank you. I make a point of moisturizing morning and evening."

"Could you pass a gunpowder paraffin test?"

"That is somewhat like the rabbit pregnancy test isn't it? I am definitely not pregnant."

"Raisa, why are you here?"

"To say goodbye. I am in the second convoy going to Mars."

"I understand the choice, but that world is far from home."

"Frank, my world is already far from home."

"You are not a product of your circumstances. You are a product of your choices."

"Goodbye, Frank."

"Goodbye, Roger."

Chapter Twenty-Six

2028 G20 Meeting

President Buci Adebayo sat his overfilled glass on the embossed invitation to the upcoming virtual meeting and watched the spillage travel around the letters in the masthead. At 36 he was the youngest of the G20 leaders and he had no illusions as to why his country had been asked to join the club. It had to do with geography, not merit, and he fumed at the entitlement of the colonialist nations. He had neither respect for, nor commonality with any of the desiccated relics wrapped in the shrouds of their past.

Nigeria had oil. Oil seeping from its pores to the tune of two million barrels a day. And important to the big club in these times, it was close to the equator. That meant one thousand miles per hour boost for rockets launched in the Mars program. With flowers and slaps on the back old chap they expected to exploit Nigeria as they had done a century ago at the point of a bayonet.

He slurped the last of his pomegranate juice and wiped his chin with the back of his hand. His ornate fan-tailed throne was made from teak and a few splashes of pomegranate juice were nothing compared to generations of blood. Adebayo was president of Nigeria, head of the African Union, and sitting high behind his desk, he waited for his monitor to populate with world leaders.

The rotation of host and president of the G20 fell to China in 2028. Madame Liu stood as chair. She scanned the leaders' faces and deplored that the number of women had risen to five. They were much more difficult to negotiate with and in her experience, less likely to compromise. Liu delayed the opening of the meeting until France appeared, once more playing the coquette, not conceding she was a sallow dowager. Liu thought the entire exercise a waste. Even the name was false. The G20 had 21 members. They had no fixed headquarters nor a permanent secretary. They were comprised of nineteen nation states and two united sub-states, the European Union and the African Union. Liu admired the stratagem of the Europeans. They had a representative for each of France, Germany, Italy and the United Kingdom at the table, each one with status, while securing an additional voice for the head of their union. When the opportunity came, Madam Liu would demand Hong Kong be included along with Macau as entities within a group of two, perhaps denoted as Asia South, but this was not the meeting for it. The agenda for the day was exclusive to the Mars launches and logistics. As protocol demanded, the most recent member was called upon to open the meeting. The African Union was class of 2023.

“The chair recognizes the Honorable President of Nigeria and Chief of the African Union, Mr. Buci Adebayo.”

None of the heads of state responded nor nodded an acknowledgment. They viewed him as a lightweight interloper and a fly to be swatted like any Nigerian fly. Oil simply complicated the matter.

Adebayo leaned into the microphone and surveyed the virtual surroundings. He had no intention of embracing the ossified conglomerate seated around him.

“Good day to you all. I am the Honorable Buci Adebayo, president of Nigeria and Head of the African Union. I see no one here shares my complexion. You are simply satisfied to share my resources. Private conversation tells me test sales of the lottery tickets to Mars are proceeding well. You say you have saturated the internet and social media with information, propaganda, and happy family relocation videos. Who sees them! Not 200 million Nigerians! Only 30% of my country has access to these things. You intend to leave us behind. We are the future, not you! Show me now. Raise your hands. Who here is going to Mars? I thought not, not one. Only because my country is close to the equator, I sit here today. For no other reason. The equator suits the launch program for your fuel cargo ships. You use Nigeria. You use our oil. But where is the promised infrastructure in exchange? You Great Britain, you, China, you, the United states! Where is what you promised! As of today I am cancelling all contracts for delivery of oil from Nigeria. As of today I declare the Nigerian launch facilities off limits to you."

President Lagunas of the United States jumped to his feet from his position at the circular table which he presumed to be the head. He pounded his desk which failed to translate into sound in the virtual presentation.

"We have contracts! We have agreements!"

"Agreements? Contracts? Hypocrite! Now. Name it for the world to hear. One. Name one agreement in the last 50 years the United states has honored. One! No? In colonial times the term for England and its double dealing was 'Perfidious Albion'. United States has fallen from the tree of Britain as its poisonous fruit."

The Prime Minister of England, Fiona Stemp, tore out her earbuds and screamed.

"I will not be lectured to by a popinjay boy."

She disappeared from the monitor. One by one the screen depopulated until just chairman Liu and a furious Adebayo faced off. Liu did what Chinese do when such things happened, she laughed hysterically and dissolved to nothing leaving Adebayo alone on the screen with the Russian Oleg Liapkin, who slept.

Quickly, President Lagunas, Brigita Sturm of Germany and President Cherif Habib, the first Muslim president of Brazil, reconnected with each other. Habib was frantic.

"Now what? Sturm?"

"President Habib, you will learn at G20 meetings we ignore everything said and react to nothing. We shall speak privately and unofficially around the circle. These things sort themselves out. A little steam here and there is not unusual. "

President Lagunas offered his ubiquitous solution.

"Sturm, how much kickback do you pay to Adebayo in your Nigerian oil contract?"

"$0.85 US per barrel."

"That's the same across the European Union. Increase it to a Uniform $1.25 US. He will toe the line. What he really wanted was to trade launch access and oil delivery against expansion of his Mars lottery sales. He has absolutely no interest in whether his people are among the Mars colonizers. He will restore access to his launch sites and Nigeria's oil if we facilitate his sale of tickets across his country. Our figures show at the moment he collects an 8% service charge. Think of another hundred million people buying tickets. At any rate, his launch facilities are useful and if he gets rich, such is life. This lottery is a gold mine for everyone."

"What was he saying about tankers?

"Fuel tankers for the Mars armada. Ah Habib. I see. You won an election you were supposed to lose, and it has dropped you into the middle of things. I know the feeling. This year the Space Agency will complete the launch platforms at your Macapá plateau on the equator. The cargo road through French Guiana from the Caribbean coast to the launchpads is pretty much done. Soon you will be putting tankers into orbit like Nigeria. The concept is to have lighter loads for easier launches of manned flights and then to refuel the ships at orbiting tankers. That is the first phase, and two tankers are in place as we speak. Ultimately we will have hundreds. Understand, we proceed with what we can do. Tankers, we can do. Manned considerations are different. Shielding, habitation, infrastructure, not a single item is finalized, but at least we have a consensus that we must operate on a convoy basis."

"I was elected on promises of agrarian reform and home ownership."

"Perfect. In this case the home ownership will be on Mars at the cost of a lucky lottery ticket. Besides, as president, you will have considerable influence on who is chosen to embark on the great adventure. Not that I am advising it, but consider opponents, competitors for your position, even possible revolutionaries against your rule, finding themselves one hundred and forty million miles distant. Consider the egos of the wannabees. Some will even volunteer for the optics of the gesture."

The Brazilian President smiled broadly at the prospects and Sturm could scarcely contain herself.

"Why Mr. President, how Jesuitical of you. Sênior Habib, the basic idea is not complicated. The orbits of Mars and Earth are conveniently close about once every twenty-six months. The most efficient fuel consumption is to use a swarm of starships, even up to one thousand setting off at one time toward Mars. The Portaris7 booster rocket lifts a tanker carrying fuel into orbit around earth. The Portaris7 disengages and returns to Earth to be used again. Portaris7 is refueled, after which it launches a crewed Marscraft into orbit. The manned Marscraft then docks with a tanker to receive fuel. This would happen simultaneously at many launch sites, eventually ten or twenty per day. It will require a constant flow of Marscraft over decades with the intention of landing millions of tons of equipment and a million people. By the 2033 launch window we expect to have at least five-hundred landed Mars missions completed. "

Oleg Liapkin awoke to find himself alone on the screen. Three interconnected lines remained open. He shut off his camera and his microphone and tapped in to Habib speaking.

"Chancellor Sturm, my interest lies more in the jungles and small towns of Brazil. When I look at the Mars project I ask myself, why?"

President Lagunas chuckled.

"Does it matter? This means millions of jobs around the world and literally trillions of dollars in lottery money. As far as the rationale for it, the altruists say it is to ensure the ultimate survival of the human race should the Earth face an extinction event. You know the type. The sky is always falling. However, to keep things rolling, we use phrases such as, ' self-sustaining, democratic, self-governing colony' and 'let us terraform to rebuild Mars in the image of the Earth' and so on."

Minister Liapkin turned on his microphone and tapped it a few times to announce himself.

"Hello, this is Liapkin here, I apologize. Foreign minister Oleg Liapkin of Russia. Some of you don't know me, perhaps. I was having a little nap. I caught the last few sentences, and President Lagunas, I agree, there's nothing wrong with making a little money along the way. But does any one of you think this is really going to happen? The irrationality of human nature will stop it. One of you mentioned an extinction event, yet the scientific community cries, *Oh we must have the means and infrastructure to get colonists back home*. Really?

"Are you saying we should just abandon them there?"

"You see, even you used the word abandon with its implications of wrongness. You misunderstand me. I am a compassionate man. If our settlers have an emergency and need to leave the surface they must not be stranded. But to delay all else until that can be guaranteed is folly. Risks must be taken as they had been taken by all explorers. Russia understands. You have your plans, we have ours. What you must recognize is that the moment you are a Martian you are no longer a citizen of any country on Earth. Your citizens will have no priority by virtue of their history, nor will ours. There will be no carryover of bully status to the new world. Don't you agree? President Lagunas?"

Lagunas fumed at being cornered by the foreign minister. Bully control over the development on Mars was precisely what the United States intended.

"Minister, I am sure among us we can draft a satisfactory mechanism for such issues. However, it seems premature at this time to address it when critical technical issues of hardware and infrastructure are still in the development stage."

"I am pleased you agree in principle. Is it understandable that on a busy day like this it has slipped your mind that such a document already exists, which clearly defines the exploration and use of space, weapons in space, liability for damage and environmental concerns. The law is the Outer Space Treaty. The document was ratified by the United States Senate and the Soviet Russian Duma in 1967. It shares many elements of the legal status of international waters here at home. Do you… what a question… of course you do.

A country such as yours with twelve thousand miles of coastline certainly respects international waters. Yes?"

"Thank you, Minister Liapkin, Chancellor Sturm, President Habib, we meet again tomorrow and perhaps we might pick up these threads at that time. Good day."

President Lagunas made a note to request the Russian president to recall Minister Liapkin. He made a second note to himself to direct the treasury to flood Africa with Nigerian Naira and start the devaluation. Perhaps when his currency was a billion to one against the American dollar the punk Adebayo might reconsider his tendency to throw tantrums. Lagunas was not on his game. His focus was on General Conrad, the Chief of his Space Force. When Conrad was worried, so was Lagunas. Some cosmic rock was arriving in less than a year, close enough to take skin off the apple and there was nothing to do but wait.

Foreign Minister Oleg Liapkin closed his connection to the meeting and contentedly leaned back in his swivel chair. Russia was ahead of the game. *Our first successful test of Burevestnik was in 2019. Nine long years ago. We told the world, but they did not believe us. It could not be. Not the impoverished backward and medieval Russia. Fine. The Burevestnik missile's nuclear-powered engineering allows it to circle the globe indefinitely, awaiting command to strike. The same engineering cuts our Mars trip from six months to thirty days. They boast of their Portaris7 booster. Our Sheremetev4 rocket carries twice the payload.*

Liapkin picked up the scale model of the Sheremetev4 from his desk and swooshed it back and forth.

"You little beauty. We build three of you per week and by the launch window of 2031 we will have over five hundred of you, all to be launched from Russia. Who needs the equator when your plasma electric rocket engine moves you at 195,000 miles per hour."

Liapkin set the model down. He imagined himself as a cosmonaut and wondered whether he would be willing to accept the risks and make the commitment. Perhaps the grandness of the experiment would overcome such concerns. He lamented the bravado of the West on behalf of their travelers. Their trips would take at least six months, all the while exposing their crew and passengers to a relentless bombardment of radioactive particles. They had yet to develop effective shielding. They hypothesized about buffers and shields not knowing which way to turn when the first and most important protection was time. Shorten the trip by five hundred percent and you shorten the radiation damage by five hundred percent. Russia had solved that and added another protection with the help of Canada's niobium and tin. They used an electromagnetic field generated by superconducting magnets to deflect all charged particles.

Liapkin regretted nothing of his impertinence to the President of the United States. He particularly enjoyed his attempt to have Lagunas commit to relinquishing its bully status when on Mars when that was exactly what Russia intended to do. It was an old tactic. Accuse your opponent of doing what you have already done. While the world holds hands trundling along in their cosy armada of antique technology, Russia will make five trips with five times the provisions, five times the pilgrims and five times the automatons to do the heavy lifting. Before one western foot trods the surface, Russia will have habitat and medical facilities in place in the optimum location. When the late arrivals cry for medical treatment for radiation poisoning, assistance or sustenance, for provisions, we will gladly make the trade. For land.

Meetings began early the next day, and the memories of all participants would be devoid of today's happenings. The game would play itself again and the struggling outside world would believe, surely momentous things were afoot, things of help and hope and cooperation. Liapkin preferred meetings in the flesh. He could buy a nice Armani or Tom Ford and go to dinner at Le Severo. That at least survived in France.

Chapter Twenty-Seven
April 3rd, 2029

Meghan was joining me at Morty’s in two hours. I hadn't been to my branch office recently, nor for that matter, to my main office on Isobel Street. One day I would replace the tape on my answering machine.

I was early for happy hour and the joint was empty except for two old guys who basically lived there. I addressed them as Flotsam and Jetsam, as they had a detritus look about them, and they routinely nodded and smiled at being acknowledged but we were not friendly. They had the bad habit of paying their tabs monthly.

Morty had added something to the place. He was selling lottery tickets to Mars.

"Spin me one, Morty, one of your finest."

He did his trick left-handed just to show off, and the shot glass spun a slow wet curve to home base in my palm.

"Cool. Selling any tickets to Mars?"

"A few, but my clientele are not good candidates. The demographic is all wrong. My customers are either over the hill and don't want anything changed, like you for example, or strivers in the condo world where things just couldn't be better."

"What about Flotsam and Jetsam. Have they bought any?"

"Well, no. But they did show some interest. They asked me where it was."

"I see. Men of the world. What do you hear? Are people buying?"

"Yes, in a frenzy. Tens of billions of tickets have been purchased despite the fact the science of getting them to Mars in one piece is not settled. And the promoters are clever with their approach. To attract the brightest and the best they're offering young scholars paid tuition in exchange for six years on Mars. Those in the high-income brackets are limited to the number of tickets they can buy, and they pay more per ticket. The guy on the street doesn't even necessarily want to go, but he gets cheaper tickets and because he thinks he is sticking it to the man, he has jumped in with both feet."

"Did you hear about the Botany Bay thing?"

"Yes, and it's an idea that's gaining traction. A few countries want a new Australia where convicts can be transported as test subjects and first settlers. They don't really care if they survive as long as they can make them somebody else's problem. The proponents even have a name for their prospective city. Eglimopolis, neatly incorporating 'eglima', the Greek word for crime. Even if that city becomes reality, regular folks will still go. Rockets are sexy. They turn people on. Sure, it's just a new way to gamble, but what you dream of winning is a whole new life. Our populace is tired of a debauched earth. This generation is fearful, hopeless and ungrounded and it looks for a beginning, an opportunity and an escape from what has become hell on earth. Even such a remote way to escape it is better than no way at all."

" Morty, you have never hawked anything before. Why now?"

"Great science is coming from the Cosmos Center almost daily. I am in awe of the inventiveness of the young minds."

"What do you think, Morty? What are the, let's say, three greatest inventions?"

"Hmm. Rum, tires for gorillas to swing on and two-way streets."

"Interesting. I thought you would say shoes with Velcro to replace laces."

"Very funny. Absolutely rum. With it, the British mapped the world, kept their sailors happy in their work, healed their gashes and gave the anesthetic for the sawbones when a leg needed lopping, topped off by a good time when they got to port. Maybe not so good for their liver. Then comes Gorillas swinging on tires because I like watching it. It's amazing an animal so smart can enjoy something so stupid. Sort of like playing golf, I guess. Then, two-way streets. Two-way streets are the best. Courtesy. Each direction receptive to the other direction. Good judgment as to when and where not to get out of your lane. It was your idea to go one way, it was my idea to go another, such as in exchange and banter, but no more. Life has become like bad city planning. Too many one-way streets. Come against me and I will run you over. My direction carries the moral prerogative. I will kill you to prove my right to travel this one-way street."

"Morty, you are amazing."

"Yes."

The bent hinge announced a new customer and Meghan Macbeth bounced in, beaming and beautiful.

"Hi Frank, ain't life wonderful? Hi Morty."

"Hello, Doctor Macbeth. The usual? Whisky sour with bitters?"

"Yes, thanks. It has been a while."

Her relaxed and easy way was something new for me.

"You must be relieved to be back in your comfort zone. Are you in safe waters as far as the radiation spill?"

"Yes, everything is fine for the whole team, and yes I am pleased to be doing what I do best, but I miss Rybakov."

"I understand. Who is holding down the fort when you are away?"

"Leishman will be handling the room. The full technical staff is intact, and the procedures are well systematized. I have brought Sanjay Rustom back on staff for backup telemetry control. He is a brilliant man with many talents. He and Leishman clash constantly but if it wasn't Rustom clashing with Leishman it would be the next guy. Big minds have big egos."

I still believed Rustom was the brain behind the canister theft, but Meghan had her samples, and the world was right, so I left it at that.

"When do you leave for Uruguay?"

"Ten days and counting. Frank, for me, Apophis is like Christmas and spring prom night all in one, a win-win. Don't look at me like that. The dress stays on."

"Then I don't get the excitement."

"Apophis is not going to hit us, and we get to see it up close. Who knows what we will learn! You are not impressed."

"I stopped being impressed decades ago. Here it comes, there it goes. Next?"

"Frank. It is a quarter of a mile long and a fifth of a mile wide. Chelyabinsk was 60 feet long and it wiped out a hundred-mile swath when it exploded twenty miles up. An asteroid this big comes this close to earth only once every eight hundred years. And here we are alive to see it. Suppose it was the signing of the Magna Carta. Would you go to watch it?"

"I'm not sure. Will there be a bar?"

"Hopeless. Listen. When apophis was first seen in 2004 it was just another rock, and categorized as a potentially hazardous object, like another million of them. Calculations then said there was a 2% chance of it hitting earth on Friday the 13th 2029. Wrong. It will not. But in 2013, simulations showed the Yarkovsky effect could cause it to hit a keyhole in 2029 for future collision in 2036. Chances of having exactly the right push from the sun are about one in a million."

"I don't feel better. The odds to win a Powerball lottery are a hundred million to one. Every year, someone, a heavenly body unto himself, wins."

"You can pervert anything. You speak statistician nonsense. It's like the bomb trope. The odds of having one bomb on a passenger plane is one in a million. The odds of having two bombs on the same passenger plane is one in twenty million. Therefore, taking your own bomb onto the plane makes you twenty times as safe. I am going to Uruguay, I will thrill with every lopsided tumble the thing makes as it passes by, watching, personally, in living color."

I enjoyed seeing Meghan in high dudgeon, so I decided to pursue the task more energetically.

"Tumble? It's not a bowling ball?"

"No. It's a dumbbell shape. Much like yourself. It is a tumbler. It doesn't go around a central axis. If you watched it, you would say it rotated backwards. That is termed retrograde, in Astro speak. It takes about thirty-six hours to take one tumble."

"That's a slow tumble."

"That's a big rock. It is ten feet longer than the Empire State Building in New York City and five times as wide."

"Meghan, whenever you discuss Apophis, the month of April seems to show up in the same sentence. Coincidence?"

"No. Apophis goes away from earth about May 1st and starts back about December 2nd. The orbit is eccentric not circular. It passes by earth south to north every April 13th or 14th. In ten days, and let's see, seven hours and forty minutes, it will be the closest approach in recorded history, coming inside our current string of geostationary satellites orbiting the earth. And it will be bright, going at seven thousand kilometers a second as it is sucked in towards us by gravity, which also means its orbit will change and in fact tidal forces will change how it tumbles. I think also there will be partial resurfacing and movement of the regolith. I doubt it will break up."

"Wait. Partial resurfacing, you say? I was there. Your entire lab went nuts when Leishman blasted the regolith off Bennu because it corrupted all the Yarkovsky effect calculations. Now Apophis the same, a new surface? After constant study every year for twenty-five years, a new surface?"

"Well, not exactly every year, Frank. From 2015 through 2019 we couldn't see a thing. Its orbit was near the sun from earth's perspective. We started watching it again in 2020. Even then it's just observed sporadically by amateurs and various scientists as free time comes up for sale in the observatories. As for the new surface, plus the little dusting Leishman is about to give it with OSIRIS-APEx explorer, 25 years of Yarkovsky effect calculations are out the window."

Morty broke the bartender code of non-participation in client conversations and leaned in.

"Why don't you attach a transponder as it goes by, to track it precisely. No guesswork, in my humble apologetically intrusive opinion."

Meghan took a quick blast of her whiskey sour and motioned for another. I interpreted that as meaning no one had considered it.

"Meghan?"

"Really. Too late now. Double that, Morty."

"Yes, Doctor."

"So. Bits of it might fall off, its shape will change, and you won't have the data to calculate Yarkovsky for the next time around."

"Worse."

"How could it be worse?"

Morty was now fully engaged.

"Yes. How?"

"Two things. First. Mathematicians and statisticians are blood relatives. The calculations done in 2004 plotted the Earth as a simple point in space and the asteroid as another simple point to be tracked. However, the Earth is not a point. It is about 13,000 kilometers in diameter. That means for 2036 the orbit prediction will be off by twice the Earth's diameter. Second, the standard dynamic model used to predict orbital parameters used in 2004 assumed a prograde, spinning forward asteroid not a retrograde rotator like Apophis, spinning backwards. Apophis will be several hundred thousand meters farther along in its orbit in 2036 than calculated, so the center of the statistical distribution of its likely position is definitely in Earth's orbit. In 2036 Apophis will not be 50 million miles away from us as the television scientists like to say. It may find the keyhole of its dreams, and bingo, hello Apophis."

"So kids, hence the scurry to Mars. Care to buy a lottery ticket? I make $4.00 per."

"No thanks. You Meghan?"

"No. I get a free ride if I want it. The tidbits I have shared are just from the perspective of our particular program. The European

Space Agency launched its Rapid Apophis Mission in 2026 to rendezvous with the asteroid in 2029. Rendezvous. What does that mean? And the Chinese. They have something called the Tianwen-2 intending an ongoing encounter with Apophis to land and conduct sampling on the surface. Launch was in 2025. We are all bloody independent actors with no interaction and no cooperation."

Meghan slammed down her glass and cursed. I shared her frustration, and I snugged an arm around her.

"Thanks, Frank. That is better, but bloody hell, in 2007 there was an international competition to design an unmanned probe to follow up Apophis for a year to assess its impact likelihood on earth. There were dozens of entries and a $50,000 first prize was awarded. Nothing was built. In 2005, the European Space Agency also began what they called the Don Quijote mission for two unmanned craft, Hidalgo and Sanchez, to study the effect of impacting Apophis. Hidalgo would hit and Sancho would observe and report. It was never done!"

"Children, lament not the past nor things left undone, nor opportunities lost. Rejoice in that which is to come."

At that, he slid us each a drink, both done with panache and a perfect nestle into our outstretched hands.

"On the house. Seriously, why don't you two take the plunge. That is, into the Martian pool. Two moons and plenty of space to swing a cat. Meghan?"

"Not me. Dust allergies."

"Frank?"

"No, Morty. They say it will be like Utah."

"What. Full of Mormons?"

"No nothing to do. Meghan. Do you need a ride?"

"No thank you. My Shelby is parked across the street in your reserved no parking zone. I'm surprised you didn't hear the Hollywood mufflers when I pulled up."

"I heard the rumble, but I put it down to thunder off the sea. Did you beat your record for the time between your home and Morty's?"

"No such luck. They are supposed to be identical, but the old Shelby was faster."

"C'est la vie. That's French, you know. All the best in Uruguay and stay safe amid the asteroids."

I kissed her goodbye on the cheek, and she smelled great. Morty's suggestion to take the plunge began redefining itself.

Reactions to the coming asteroid were diverse. Some approached it with humor, some with capitalistic opportunism, and others with violence just for the unspoken lust for it. Elsewhere, heavenly properties were attributed to the thing coming from beyond all understanding.

East of the Urals and north of Chelyabinsk, Russia, Batiushka Gregory smoothed the folds of his flowing sticharion vestment and signaled the beginning with two sharp blows on the pavement with the bottom of his staff. The concussion through his hand got his ecumenical juices flowing. The Greek Orthodox priest took the first step south, shepherding a flock of ninety thousand adherents to the Church of the Holy Meteorite whose order had proclaimed a second coming. Not of the Savior, but of a second holy missive carried by an asteroid meant for them alone and through them to the world. Gregory was not of their sect but something inside him suggested they might be right. Apophis' path was three thousand miles from them at its closest but every southerly step they took brought them nearer to its holy message. Every bead they fondled spoke to its purity. Every step they took in the ankle-deep sludge of oily snowmelt was a penitence.

Judge Dugan strummed his fingers at the growing stack of paper before him. It was his fourth term as Judge of the Woodlawn Civil Court in the Bronx. In over thirty years on the bench he had never experienced this. He was Irish, most of the Woodlawn residents were Irish and he had never seen anything this stupid. The line of applicants was out the door down the stairs and growing in the foyer.

"Bailiff, approach the bench. What's the seating capacity in here?"

"Uh, the fire regulations say two hundred thirty-four, but that's the old number. Your honor."

"What do you mean, old number. A number is a number."

"Yes, your honor. But that's from 1947. Before we got so fat. My guess, today, is two hundred, tops."

"Understood. You know what? I'm going to give these idiots what they're asking for. See here in this pile, O'Hare, O'Keefe, O'Reilly, O'Donnell, and another one hundred and fourteen geniuses who are petitioning to change their name to O'Pophis. Fine. Seat them in my court fifty at a time. I'll swear in the batch. I hope they enjoy sorting out who is who when the mail comes."

At 9:00 a.m. on the 10th of April 2029, 'Disgruntled Press' printed a test run of ten thousand black T-shirts blazoned with 'Loot for the Lord' in five cities. By 9:45 the first batch was sold out, the territory was expanded to the eighteen largest cities, by 3:00 p.m., one million nine hundred thousand shirts were sold and copycats turned up with the o's in 'loot' as eyeballs of the devil. By 4:30 the fires started in fifty cities, neighborhood retailers were rampaged into nothing and the country burned from Compton to Connecticut.

In Bristol England a garage band named 'Harakirix' produced a five-minute cut which within a week took over the radio and streamed in one hundred countries. The sole repeated lyric was monotonous and simple, but its effect was not.

You would go to Mars now and so would I-ee.

The tune began slowly and gently, almost conversationally, in soft low tones, quickening slightly to a held I-ee. It accelerated slightly and with each acceleration it gained pitch, and the volume increased. Again it accelerated slightly and with each acceleration it gained pitch and the volume increased and so on until for the full final minute it was at a screeching brain numbing all-out attack with the pace leaving only one final thought able to be processed by your assaulted brain. *die-e .. die-e .. die-e .. die-e .. die-e.. die-e..,* which as a fitting tribute to the coming apocalypse, produced a suicide cult with thousands of short-term inductees on every continent.

<>

Friday, April 13, 2029
21:46 Universal Time

The Boys ceased their perusal of the Chinese rover scraping the surface of Apophis and in perfect quantum entanglement, at that instant they existed inside Leishman's laboratory. The unexpected infusion of their energy raised the decibel of speech, and enthusiasm grew to the level of euphoria. The company of technicians considered the exercise as a simple approach to the asteroid Apophis yet suddenly the imminent event was a thrill.

With his first step into the room Sanjay Rustom felt the electricity of the environment. Leishman had not seen him enter and as was his customary state at these times, Izzy was engrossed in some private dialogue in his head. Sanjay activated the electronics in his console, connected to Isadore's headset and opened the line.

"Hello Dr. Leishman. This is Rustom."

"So, the pizza king is back."

"Yes, Doctor Leishman, back to assist in any way I can. Do you need any assistance with approach trajectory, thrust balance? I can monitor on a fail-safe back up if it will be helpful. You know, in case of data interruption, not as an auditor."

"You? Audit me? Scum. Isadore knows what he is doing. Do not tinker and do not tamper. Watch, observe, make a record. You are extraneous here. Macbeth and her spy system. Check on Izzy! Report back. I know, I know her jealous... "

"Doctor Leishman,... "

"Don't. Stay within your observation console, shut up, and make your notations or whatever your absurd involvement is."

"Yes, of course, Doctor, but I'm compelled to tell you the work you did on the Bennu samples, it was simply masterful. It is astounding to have found the basic imprint of life as we know it in those samples. If only we knew which aggregation of regolith came from what passing body, well, at any rate what a superior job you did."

"What? You, tell me, presume to tell me, what is superior? Of course it was superior, it was the Leishman who did it. Did it. Did it. Morse. Stop, you, you, thing. Stop talking. Get about your business."

Sanjay did as he was told and activated the full array of instruments which represented operations in duplicate. Deviations from declared protocol were flagged and alarmed. Sanjay recalled every flawed and false equation Leishman had concocted with the Bennu OSIRIS-Rex mission in 2023. He knew he would find no deviation from formulae, as the input to be agreed upon was constructed by Dr. Leishman and it was false. He had two hours, and he would find a way to control what Leishman did from his console.

The Boys read Rustom's contradiction to their intention as he formed it. The Slow had activated his frontal lobe to a very high degree unexpected in his kind, with a quick and vigorous connection to his hippocampus. Sanjay was determining the outcome of his actions, differentiating his thoughts and weighing elements of conflict. His self-control and goal orientation to interfere was strong. Unscathed, it might have significant effect. Presently The Boys would play with Sanjay's synapses and their dendritic trees to disabuse him of his mission. They saw their man Leishman was agitated and they swathed him with peace and spoke to him with their minds.

Isadore, it is I.

"Hello.. I hoped th..

Rustom overheard Isidore in his headset. The Boys felt the pulse of the neuronal connection and blurred the transmission.

Beautiful, turn off your headset. Spies are listening. You know about them.

"Yes, I know about them. We have one, we have one, you know? He.."

Peace. He is nothing. You are all. In minutes your craft will be within visual range of Apophis. Do not be alarmed at what you see. You will see the Chinese at work in aid of what we do. Do you understand?

"I, I, don't. They do, they do not help, or share. Their work is for the Middle Kingdom alone. The rest of us are on our own, on its own, no…"

Handsome man, they have made mistakes. What they do works for us this day. The surface disfigurement caused by your planet's tidal pull on Apophis is abetted nicely by their scraping. Laleesh, begin your approach.

The Voice smoothed Isadore Leishman back into reality while The Boys assessed the rudimentary construction of Sanjay

Rustom's thoughts. They were small and cluttered with governing principles unable to be proven yet held to be the most important. Concepts such as honor, charity, duty and justice flooded his amygdala. None of them could fill a cup nor turn a wheel. It was universally so in the mind of man in a thousand philosophies and religions since the origins of intention. The Boys had studied and assimilated all such meanderings where an unseen mystery promised the species a reward. One promise was made to never again sweep the earth clean with a flood. No promise was made to remove from man his ingenuity for self-destruction. Cell phones and glioblastoma. Tattoos and lymphoma. A desperation to find the essence of matter, of being, of consciousness. The presumption of a right to impose their presence on all things and to expand their contagion into the void. They must not be allowed. The ultimate vehicle had arrived in the form of Apophis, with which they will tinker, interfere and modify into their perfect destroyer.

The slow almost imperceptible tumble of the giant rock filled the screens, and it was showtime. Isadore Leishman released the lock on the controls of the main console and spoke with a swagger gifted him for the moment by The Boys. Sanjay Rustom listened to the directive from Dr. Leishman with equanimity as a sense of lightness surrounded him. He puzzled as to what his concerns had been. The Boys continued to modify him.

"Two hundred feet. Terry, high resolution on the camera please. Hands off the controls everyone, on the countdown to one I have it. Three, two, one, I have it. Four feet per second. Four feet per second. Three feet per second. Retro burn one. Dayboll, shout out at one hundred."

Never had the technicians not heard the heartbeat of the leader in the microphone in such circumstances. From Leishman there was nothing. He was like ice. He tapped his headset mike.

"Stop the chatter! I hear it in the background."

The voice was that of Sanjay Rustom muttering to himself out of the confusion and situational dislocation created in his mind by The Boys.

Izzy screamed.

"Dayboll! Where are we?"

"125, closing at 3 feet per second. Six, five, four, three, two, one, 100."

"Retro burn two."

At that moment movement in the left corner of the screen distracted Leishman.

"Terry, swing to the left and zoom in. Close the aperture a bit. It's too bright."

The Chinese rover crawled slowly down into the center of the screen. Leishman had not used retro burn two to slow OSIRIS-APEx.

"Dr. Leishman. 60 feet. 55 feet."

While The Boys kept Rustom disabled, Leishman's amygdala blazed. His dorsolateral prefrontal cortex suppressing revenge and anger was virtually shut down. He intended to ram and obliterate the Chinese rover.

"55, 54, 53, 52, 51, 50, Dr. Leishman."

The Boys flooded his system and took it. In a nanosecond he blurted,

"Retro burn two. Two feet per second. Every ten feet now, Dayboll.

"30 feet. 20 feet. 10 feet"

"Retro burn three, done. Fixed at ten. Moving with Apophis, preparing thruster discharge. Terry, give me a slow scan from the left of the entire field, ten minutes for the full scan, not too fast. Recording is nominal? "

"Roger. Nominal."

"Wait. 10% zoom right there."

The Chinese rover continued to move. Behind it ran a smooth stripe of denuded surface which disappeared over the far side of Apophis. The exposed area represented hundreds of yards of new reflective strata. Leishman was not to be outdone. His thrusters were programmed in a spiral so that one by one they would spin around a roughly fixed spot and keep it in position against the surface rather than propel it away as it discharged its full load of fuel. Apophis had been stressed and weakened by gravity and tidal forces and Leishman's thrusters ripped a hundred tons of loose debris from its surface. There was a new face for a new orbit for a new rendezvous with the sun and somewhere a keyhole waited.

Sanjay Rustom blinked into an uncertain reality, surrounded by the quiet of a darkened and deserted laboratory, except for himself in his console and Leishman at the control module, running a video file in a loop on the large display screen, of Apophis regolith blowing apart and gathering together, blowing apart and gathering together. What Sanjay had been stationed there to prevent had happened. He remembered nothing of the day but a delicious lightness and distant thoughts he did not own. A light blinked on his low noise amplifier, and he turned on the speaker. The tone was irregular but strong, coming from a transponder. His tracking screen showed the source moving at fantastic speed. The Chinese had placed a transponder on Apophis. The signal changed rhythm. Apparently the transponder's variable signals were encoded for Chinese consumption only. Whatever they learned, they owned.

His cell phone showed four calls from 598, Uruguay. The fifth came in as he removed it from airplane mode.

"Hello Dr. Macbeth. Sorry about your calls. I have been out of it for some hours. I don't know what a lobotomy feels like, but I am somewhere in the neighborhood at the moment. I have a gap in my memory and my mind is unclear, but clarifying a little, I think."

"Were you able to harness Leishman?"

"No. I was dormant for a period of hours spanning the time of the thruster work. Not drugged, not restrained, but floating on a raft somewhere. There was a lightness of being as if something or someone had borrowed my brain. At the moment I am watching the surface dusting Leishman did on Apophis' regolith played on a loop. Leishman is possessed by it. By at least a hundred tons of it."

"Good Lord!"

"Leishman's video also caught some of the work by the Chinese. They have skinned a track of maybe one hundred square yards. A transponder is active and transmitting."

Sanjay's experience told her The Boys had been at work in his mind. Their abetting of whatever Leishman's agenda was puzzled her.

"Thank you Sanjay. I look forward to seeing the video and the degree of perturbation created by the tidal forces. I'll be back in two days."

"How was the viewing of the asteroid?"

"Visually it was underwhelming. Apophis' was visible at only about one third the brightness of Polaris. But the totality of the historical event was beyond belief. A once in eight-hundred-year opportunity and I was there to witness it. Sanjay, you have been watching the blaster debacle in a loop. What is your impression of what the Chinese did?"

"As usual, what they did could be either totally brilliant or abysmally stupid. The new reflective surface they created will affect the force of the Yarkovsky effect dramatically. So we have to look at the motive. Apophis will be moved so significantly it may be moved altogether away from ever encountering a keyhole. Conversely, it may be pushed precisely into a keyhole of their choosing for their own cataclysmic purpose, one for which only they will be prepared and about which they will share no information. So the question we have to ask ourselves is which scenario benefits the Middle Kingdom long term. Cataclysm, or order."

The Boys felt the discomfiture of their Second Mother and they were by her side instantly. Now she would give them Hell.

Chapter Twenty-Eight
2030

I had not been to the Macbeth family estate since the historic fire. It ravaged the house to its foundation and incinerated trees within a hundred yards. The great house burned for three days, and the sole remnant of its existence was its stone chimneys.

Meghan's property sat on the height of the ridge above Abernathy Town among a collection of expansive compounds dubbed by the locals, 'Baron Row.' My invitation was for drinks with Meghan at the rebuilt homestead.

The lane leading to the house ran through a brick pillared entrance connected over the road by an arch of filigreed wrought iron, which declared the motto of House Macbeth. *Ad Astra Per Ardua.* To the stars through hard work. It was the perfect dictum for an astrophysicist, and I admired the thought, but somehow I had never managed to subscribe to the work part. She met me at the front stoop and she looked great and the hello hug lingered a bit.

"Meghan, I do not believe it. What a woman! You have rebuilt the old place brick for brick!"

With a grandiose sweep of her arm she directed me through the open front door. Wide railed balustrades to the upstairs floors right and left, the central fountain in the reception area, miles of wide chestnut trim cascading in every direction, it was all there. The 1830s had arrived.

Something changed the light through the front door and I felt the energy. Duo stood three feet behind my right shoulder.

"Meghan. You have Duo. Here. At your house."

"Where I go, he follows. My research office is upstairs and he saves me time."

I looked him over and he looked me over.

"How do I turn this thing off?"

"Why do you care? Duo is just standing there."

"Yes, it's just standing there, listening, watching, remembering, and about to tell me how to do what I'm doing. It is like passing an examination every time it appears. How do I shut it off?"

"Well, The Boys are never off, but at least you can keep the hardware immobile. There is a quick disconnect at the back of the neck. See? One squeeze of the release buttons, like so, and a pull down, like so, and you will not get another comment from it."

"Thanks. Its blood-red eyes give me nightmares. Who gave it those eyes anyway? Blue, Brown, maybe one of each, but red? It is like a robot from hell."

"You do know Duo pulls those tricks just to get under your skin, don't you?"

"Wonderful. A self-rewriting infallible organism capable of any and all things spends its time getting under Frank's skin. I feel special."

She looked at me in a new way.

"Frank, you are, special."

I put my arm around her waist and pulled her to me slowly. Slowly, she slid her arms around my neck and we kissed gently and fully and stood together feeling each other breathe. Special was the word.

"Meghan, you did invite me for drinks, I think we should do that."

"Right."

We batched a pitcher of whisky, ginger beer, and lemon juice into a giant Moscow Mule and carried it up to her lab on the second floor. The Boys accompanied us with a kaleidoscopic tendril just to show they could do it.

"You have set this up nicely Meghan. It is more like a study than a laboratory. I visualized Bunsen burners, pipettes and the like. What are you working on now?"

"Mars and its dust."

"Is it a problem?"

"You decide. First, there is the volume. Mars' dust storms are legendary. They are so big, if you have a simple telescope you can watch them from earth. Without fail, storms on Mars last for weeks and cover continent-sized areas. On average about every three years, which is a little over five years on earth, there are massive storms which encircle the entire planet. It is like the dust bowl storms of the 1930s blowing every day, day in and day out for over a year on the entire planet. And people are saying we should power the planet with solar panels. "

"I watched a movie about the Mars storms recently, where the temporary habitation on Mars is blasted away into space by the ferocity of the wind."

"That will not happen. Maximum winds are in a sixty miles per hour range at worst and generally much less. That is really the least of our problems. The dust is as toxic as hell."

"After all the planning and all the money, they find this out now?"

"Now? We have known this as long ago as 2002. The dust is so small that it can actually work its way through the astronauts' suits. More of a problem, it is electrostatically charged and sticks to everything. And when the astronaut or in this case, settlers, go into a protected environment, it comes stuck to them. It will mess up most things electronic because it is a charged particle. Every day, every piece of hardware, will have to be broken down and cleaned."

"It does not seem that toxic to me. A lot of work, yes, but hardly toxic."

"Frank, particle size is important. Our lungs can manage big particles, but not small ones. Small particles stay in our lungs and accumulate. Radiation exposure on space flights already risks pulmonary fibrosis for any traveler. Then we assault the system with dust containing iron oxides, gypsum, silica and more, to be absorbed into the bloodstream. Those identical contaminants are what causes lung cancer in quartz miners. "

"My chest hurts. They should put a warning label on the lottery tickets like the ones they put on cigarette packages for smokers. Instead of solar panels they should populate the planet with giant Hepa filters."

"You and the scientific community think alike. That is one of the proposals. Unfortunately, one more example of smart people forgetting Mars is not Earth. We are talking about a Hepa filter the size of a football stadium getting clogged up in two minutes. The dust clouds routinely extend up thirty miles from the surface and higher when they are global."

I poured two full glasses.

"There you go, one Mars Mule to temper your temper. Feel free to refuel."

"Thank you. Frank, sorry for the diatribe. My ranting is in aid of nothing. There are few individuals in the space programs who care about any of this. About anything. They want jobs, profits for the corporate headquarters and lack of accountability, because after all, if something is still in the works, it has not failed. Sixty years of things in the works and no cigar. Forty years ago an inventor had a replacement for all gasoline engines under twenty-five horsepower, using propane. The environmentalists loved it; the scientists loved it. So Detroit built a new facility to find ways to make gasoline behave like propane and the stall was on. Do not worry, it is coming, almost, getting close, we are almost there. We are doing the same thing. We are looking on Mars for ways to produce methane and whatever else is needed for our rockets to get home, instead of developing a propulsion system which does not need it in the first place."

"Meghan, people on the street do not know any of this. Billions of lottery tickets have been sold and the rate of sale is climbing."

"It would not matter if they knew it. The mystique of the Red Planet baffles our brains. Yet I understand the lure. Mars is different, but it is also familiar. They think they could adapt because Mars day-night cycle is similar to Earth's. The planet also has seasons, about twice as long as the ones on Earth. Mars has ice caps, like Earth. What they don't consider, is what Mars does not have.

Mars does not have a dense atmosphere. Cosmic rays are not deflected or absorbed before reaching the surface, so it gets the full blast. Mars does not have a global magnetic field to repel and redirect radioactive particles the way Earth does. Again, Mars gets the full blast of cosmic radiation. Cosmic rays on Earth are around 0.33 mSv/year. On Mars, the annual radiation dose at the surface is around 230 mSv/year. That is close to seven hundred times as much. That means an epidemic of thyroid cancer in adults and irreversible brain damage for toddlers."

"Perhaps they will have shielded habitats completed before they allow children."

"Frank, I do not think that is how it is going to be. Budgeting shows requisitions for frozen embryos. They expect to have live births there and have children grow up. At any rate, these things are a long way from what you asked, so as we speak, I shall turn my mind back to dust. The thought of it makes me thirsty."

I refilled both glasses with Mule. It seemed Meghan now occupied herself with less dramatic events than an apocalyptic rock, but her laptop belied the impression.

"Meghan, you deal in more than dust. I recognize those graphs on your laptop. Or at least they are similar to the ones we looked at on solar activity."

"Those are from Sanjay. I have him reworking the calculations for the next two or three cycles of sunspots. So far, his work agrees with mine. I hoped he would find some gross error in what I did but at this point the numbers agree. 2036 will have the highest solar irradiance since we have been recording it."

"What does Leishman say about it?"

"That is not his area. He is primarily engaged in orbital mechanics and associated methodologies. In fact, I'm going to call him now and see what his current projections are for the Apophis orbit. Which means I will speak with Rustom."

"How so?"

"He is making Sanjay act as his receptionist."

"That's petty."

"That's academic pecking order. You know, I swore I wasn't going to do anything like this. I invited you here for your company and I am calling the lab."

"I like how you do what you do. Go ahead."

Rustom picked up with his receptionist happy voice.

"Hello, Dr. Macbeth. You called Dr. Leishman's number; shall I get him?"

"In a minute. Thank you for the graphs. Are you finished with your review of the irradiance data?"

"Not quite. I want to adjust some variables and run the sequence again, but I don't expect a significant change. Speaking of running sequences, you know I am tracking the transponder the Chinese put on Apophis. They're bouncing the signal around to confuse the coordinates so only they can track it. I sent the recordings to a buddy of mine in the Cavendish Laboratories at Cambridge and his AI found repeating sequences in the data from the transponder. As a result I was able to plot a trajectory for a short arc of the orbit."

"And?"

"The arc does not match a continuation of the orbit Apophis had last year. It is possible the orbit has changed, that's all I can say. The arc sample is too short to extrapolate into a new orbit."

"All right. When you get your next samples done, fill me in. Please pass me to Dr. Leishman."

" I was about to say. The transponder is silent. Apparently China got what it wanted to know and shut it off. I'll put you through to Dr. Leishman."

Isadore had decided he was going to Mars as the resident astrophysicist. He liked the color of the light blinking on his desk. His apartment building would have that color for the elevator lights. Izzy would have the penthouse above the dust and a reinforced balcony facing west. He pushed the elevator button to select the floor and it spoke to him.

"Izzy. Playing hard to get or what!"

"No, no, I'm not hard to get, oh. I see. No, just thinking about Mars is all."

"What are your projections on the Apophis orbit?"

"Nothing much has changed, but the flyby did teach us something. My calculations show its mass is seventy-five percent greater than what we thought because its diameter proved bigger. A small increase in diameter makes a big change in the mass. You know the formula. The orbit? You are thinking about implications for 2036, yes? The closest Apophis will be to earth is 22,000,000 kilometers. In fact, radar astrometry from the State Bank Telescope as well as the Bluestone Deep Space Complex suggests 56,000,000 kilometers. In other words we have nothing to worry about."

Meghan closed the call with Leishman with a worried look.

"Meghan, that seemed to be good news. You don't believe it."

"Something is off. In 2020 the Subaru telescope first detected Apophis decreased its semi-major axis by one hundred and seventy meters per year. Sorry for the astrospeak. That means the effect of the sun shortened its orbit by one hundred and seventy meters per year. That doesn't seem like much but it is a million kilometers change in its position. That is ten million kilometers in ten years. Leishman did not reflect that in his numbers."

"What could he gain from it?"

"That is the question I ask myself. This is becoming self-flagellation. We have missed our opportunity to do something about the orbit. Done. Frank, that's the last of the shop talk. 2036 is six years away, the evening is young and you're so beautiful and my garden awaits us. Let us walk and talk and toast my late Great Aunt who made my home possible."

The Boys soared high and became a canopy over the fifty-six acres of pasture and old growth trees surrounding the Macbeth estate. Leishman was no longer their man but simply another of the Slows. His ridiculous presentation of the Apophis orbit was typical. He was a Slow who had achieved his goals and believed he could speak in absurdities to demonstrate his independence. Second Mother saw it quickly. The McCord had asked and so thought the Second Mother of the why for in Leishman's inefficiencies. The Boys had problems with unmeasurable concepts but they believed the correct word was revenge.

Otto Bucholz was no longer the Head of the Joint Chiefs of Staff and he was now his own man. He plowed along at altitude through the Colorado mountains not in a motorcade but in a long wheelbase Range Rover given to him as a parting gift by the Chiefs. He looked forward to seeing his son, Freddy. It had been two years.

Otto stomped the snow off his boots and pressed the laboratory doorbell.

"Dad. You are six minutes late. You're slipping. Must be the retirement."

" Not really. I was on time. The flaw was in the distance instructions from my son which were six thousand feet short."

"Good one. It's good to see you. I was worried about you driving. The reports were for snow squalls."

"It's good to see you too. My car did the driving. It measures the road surface, wheel spin, and anything possible to be measured to stop me from doing something stupid. And here I am."

They hugged hello and backslapped. Wearing radio frequency badges they made their way into the restricted proton research area.

"Freddy, if we are not done, that's it. I no longer have a fund to dedicate to your research. It has been seven years and each week has gotten closer, but the piggybank is within a few months of empty. Funding is available if we disclose the parameters of the research, but that must not happen."

"The Pentagon paid two billion dollars to ransom the collimator from the Bennu canister."

"They did but I knew they wouldn't follow it. It was below the materiality figure in their accounting."

"Tricky. Come, have a seat. Tea?"

"Yes, thanks."

Bucholz watched his son with the kettle and teabags and Freddy's air of self-satisfaction was palpable. There was a suitcase on a lab bench, so that was likely it.

"Going somewhere?"

"No."

"Whose suitcase is that?"

"Yours."

"I'm not going anywhere."

Freddy grabbed the suitcase with two hands, walked with it hanging between his legs and trundled it onto the table.

"This is it. Done, as requested."

"The Proton Collimator? You have miniaturized it to this degree? Astounding! You devil. How long have you had it ready?"

"About three months. We have tested it daily successfully and every day we discussed whether we should just destroy it. We have survived the nuclear age because of mutually assured destruction. Not because of good intention. The collimator can shut down the other side's capacity to respond by corrupting their launch codes. And I think we cannot assume our adversaries have not developed or are not developing the same capacity. The difficulty with this is unlike the nuclear situation. Both sides demonstrated the capacity by setting off bombs. This is different. Even sitting down to discuss a moratorium on its use is exposing that we have it. Its capabilities are unthinkable. In one afternoon the collimator could open every floodgate of the 96,000 dams in China. Or turn off the lights in any city in the world. Or disable the electronics of every aircraft carrier in our fleet. Anything and everything corrupted in a targeted way."

The suitcase was embossed with the seal of the Head of the Joint Chiefs of Staff and he patted it.

"So, here it is. You are staying a few days, I hope?"

"Yes, if you'll have me."

"Of course. The suitcase weighs about a hundred pounds. I'll put it in your car when you leave, on the condition you never tell me when or how it has been used. I think we're going to be locked in with the weather but I have some good steaks and some nice wine, and I promise more pleasant conversation than today."

"Son, I am so proud of the work you have done and I share every one of your concerns. The most worrisome aspect is that all choices come down to personalities and temperaments. Neither of those things is reliable. With that reassuring homily, let me drive you home. I will pour the wine if you will do the steaks."

Meghan's record time with her Shelby was 14:32 from Barons Row to Morty's. We traded cars for the challenge and I was not close. 15:01. Some people are better at everything.

Junior manned the bar in Morty's stead and he had attracted a fresher crowd as a counterculture to the hamsters. The new group had personalities. Some of them even laughed. Most of them bought Mars lottery tickets. I did not mention the dust.

"Hello Mort, spin me one, one of your finest."

I noticed as he released the shot glass he gave a little flick with his pinky, like an artist signing his work. I admired the originality.

"How's it going Frank? Are you winning?"

"Winning? Are you kidding? I can't even win in my fantasies."

"Easy. Change your definition of winning."

Morty was in the bar in spirit if not in person.

"Where is Morty today?"

"Celebrating. Today is his 85th birthday."

"Celebrating? I didn't know he knew how."

"It's the same thing every birthday. Dad goes to the zoo to watch the gorillas."

I smiled at the thought. The old man was sure to take two way streets all the way.

Chapter Twenty-Nine
2032 Notifications

I had my buffalo rug drying on the balcony and I sat beside it toasting in the sun. I let the phone call go to answering but the person called back.

" Hi Frank, want to go for a car ride?"

"Maybe. You wouldn't be taking me on a thrill ride to beat a Shelby record would you?"

"Well, if so, it will be an easy one to beat. Well below Mach one."

"Let me rephrase that. What is the top speed in your current record, in kilometers."

"Just cruising, no more than one hnngix per hour."

"You had your hand over your mouth didn't you. It sounded remarkably like one hundred and eighty-six."

"Did it? Good. Let's go with that."

"Come and pick me up and we will swap seats. Where am I going anyway?"

"To Conrad Cybertech just the other side of Mission, on Lougheed Highway. I just spoke with Dylan Conrad; the Conrad of Conrad Cybertech and his production lines are down for two days for maintenance. He builds our sentients for Mars. He calls his two models 'Utiles' and 'Constables'. Dylan won't be there, but we are invited for a tour. He has set up two of his men to host us."

"Sounds good. I'll meet you out front."

Mission B.C.

"Sammy, I just spoke with Mr. Conrad on the phone."

"Sure you did."

"He has two guests coming in a couple of hours and he wants you and me to show them around. Nice huh?"

"Well. He knows quality when he sees it."

"Guess what Sam. Me and my family have a spot on the expedition to Mars. I just got my notification from the lottery board. "

"Really? Wonderful. I was about to tell you the same thing. I got mine yesterday afternoon. I have no family, so I just have to decide for myself. Easy. What's your wife think?"

"She hasn't said much which means she doesn't like the idea. I have concerns too, but I think it's the right thing. Anyway, I have a year to decide. March is the launch date for us. When are you set to go?"

"April. April 2033, the same year as you. I am really looking forward to it. To me, it's the greatest adventure a man could have. I did some reading on the Van Allen radiation belts. If we go to Mars we have to go through those. Not exactly through, through sort of a slot between them. They're filled with particles which make ionizing radiation and that can fry you. Let's hope when we go it's not like 2024. Two additional belts showed up from nowhere to occupy the slot. Nobody knows how or why and they lasted almost the whole year. Oh yes. Remember those six thousand small containers in the shipping manifests going to Ares Jen-Tech marked 'Pb' and 'N', we thought were lead and nitrogen? They are. They're going to be used for frozen embryos. It's possible several months of radiation will sterilize the menfolk, and that won't exactly grow the colony."

"So smart and so stupid. Never simple. What's wrong with lead jockstraps?"

"Hah. Very good. Sammy, what's the total committed travelers now?"

"I don't have the numbers. Day by day there's been some backsliding when they really think about what they are doing. But there are no lottery guys like us so far. Only big-name techies are going at this point. The first batch was just fourteen people you know. They actually did synthesize methane from atmospheric carbon dioxide and subsurface water. They used it for lift off from Mars."

"However many, let us hope they are the brightest and the best."

"Maybe."

"Maybe?"

"Yes. The infighting for prioritized spots by the credentialed guys is getting brutal. Mars is a big item for the resume, plus bragging rights on the cocktail circuit when they get back home. Some people are getting bumped. If you don't have a PhD you are fair game. The utility of the individual is what counts, what they can do, you know, but being connected overrides that. Beyond that I hear some of the good ones are selling their places. Not that money will be of any use."

"Yes. Utterly stupid, isn't it. Did anyone else in your family get drawn in the public lottery? Your brother the electrician?"

"No. Not so far."

"Tough."

"Your family, Dak?"

"No. No one."

"Tough for you, too. You know, it may not even be a lottery. It's possible we were chosen because of what we do here. Say, did you see China's great solar wall has stopped construction?"

"Great solar wall?"

"Yeah, Dak, they have a solar array in the Kubuqi desert suspended to make shade underneath for crops and produce about 5 gigawatts of electricity so far. The setup is about two hundred and fifty miles long and five miles wide. I saw the satellite photos the other night on TV. They have just stopped cold. Panels waiting to be installed are just left lying around and nobody is at the dormitories. No vehicles anywhere."

"Strange."

"Strange for sure. It's like they think something's going to block out the sun and make the panels useless."

"Yeah. But they do have their thorium reactors up in that same area. They produce a lot of juice. Enough they say for ten thousand years of power."

"I forgot that. The narrator of the program said they are 3D printing dormitories near the existing reactors for about a million workers within the year. They are full out busting their butts with thorium. By the time we head for Mars they will have enough power on eight different interconnected grids of thorium reactors to supply a billion Chinese with electricity."

"Sammy, did you know thorium reactors use plain old salt as a coolant? Smart. Build it in a desert or anywhere and forget about it. If a leak happens, the salt cools off and solidifies the entire mass and that's that. No explosion, no nothing. Nothing in the air to blow and contaminate the world. All sealed up."

"Frustrating. It's like if a thing makes sense we refuse to do it because it makes sense. Does that make sense?"

"Don't start. Have you stocked up on dust masks for Mars?"

"Dak, that's the one thing that might keep me from going. Every five years or so they have a dust storm, a global one, which lasts a year. In between they have dust flareups which last months. I can feel the grit between my teeth already. And adding to it, imagine a parade of a thousand Marscraft with their sonic booms coming and going non-stop blasting dust to the heavens with every takeoff and landing."

"Someone should tell the Senate. They just approved a twenty-billion-dollar appropriation bill for Mars solar panels."

"Any recent word on the numbers of colonizers actually on site ? They keep moving the goalposts."

"The last bulletin I read just set out the goal of one million by 2041. It is limited by the synodic periods, you know, there are launch opportunities only every 26 months when Mars and Earth are at their closest point to each other."

"That's a lot of crap."

"What do you mean? That's what they calculated."

"Crap. Poop from a million people. That's two things on my list now. Face masks and toilet paper. We just got a wave from security. That must be Mr. Conrad's friends. The names are, let's see, the lady is Dr. Meghan Macbeth and the gentleman is a Mr. Frank McCord. Let's do this, Dak. To paraphrase the esteemed Lord Tennyson, ours is not to reason why, ours is but to do or die. Let's hope he was exaggerating."

"Hello, Dr. Macbeth, hello, Mr. McCord. Welcome to Conrad Cybertech. I am Dak, and the good-looking one is Sammy."

Dak took lead position.

"I think walking the assembly lines will be the best way for you to appreciate what goes on. If you see something, please ask. Sammy knows everything."

"Yes, Mr. McCord?"

"Sammy, the size of this building is astounding. There are two more buildings of the same size adjacent. How many units are you making for Mars?"

"You can call them units, robots, automatons, take your pick. They are mechanical entities with sensors, programmed to respond to certain stimuli and nothing more. They do not think."

Frank and Meghan exchanged glances. Duo was once thought of in the same way.

"At the moment we are at half capacity producing one thousand eight hundred units a month. Within the year we will be producing three thousand six hundred in each of our three buildings monthly. That is about one hundred thousand automatons annually."

Meghan lagged behind to look at the torso of what appeared to be a giant.

"These components here, are gargantuan. Is that actually a chest section of the robot?"

"Yes, that chest plate is for the type we call a Constable. At this point the production is dedicated to them. The name means what you think it does. They will comprise a roving automaton militia. I saw one fully assembled on the loading dock the other day for the first time and it scared the hell out of me. So far we have made thirty-six thousand of them and we are scheduled for twice that. "

"I hear they are weaponized. Do they have killing weapons? High caliber firearms? "

"Nothing like that. They carry sub-audible low frequency stun guns. There is no noise when it discharges, just a noiseless zap and down you go. You get the idea. No attention attracted, nothing to see here, folks."

For Meghan, the math did not add up.

"Dak, my information says presently there are fewer than ten thousand Pilgrims on Mars. And you are in the process of delivering thirty-six thousand Constables. It seems unreasonable."

"On the face of it, I agree. There are two factors. Mars will be the new Wild West once there are more people. In general terms, there will be nothing to do. Yes, they will arrange for fun and games but people alone in a desolate place will drink, carouse and raise hell just because they can. A good stiff zap with a stun gun and a few days in the clink will teach them the error of their ways. By the way, any of the drawings of Mars habitats I have seen make no provision for a clink. The second factor is recharging. Our projections show only eight to ten percent of the units will be available at any one time, the rest will be recharging. Our atomic energy commission has prohibited us using RTGs. We are stuck with solar panels to recharge."

Frank whispered.

"Meghan, what's RTG?".

"RTG is Radioisotope Thermoelectric Generators. RTGs convert heat from decaying radioactive material into electricity. We use these in our galactic probes like Voyager or the Mars rover where solar charging is not strong. Something like plutonium 238 could keep an automaton charged up for eighty years."

Frank nodded in understanding. Every sentient he saw in the Russians' north building at Saskatchewan bore a nuclear sticker as well as a gas exhaust port for high-power munitions. They could maraud unimpeded for eighty years. A million people would need policing but a society of those dead-eyed remorseless hulks stomping around was not the society of which Frank chose to partake.

"Dak, people on Mars will detest the Constables."

"Never mind on Mars, they detest them on Earth. There is much resentment the Sentients are getting transport. They are heavy. They take a lot of the load capacity that people could have.

Dak gestured to the assembly line.

"Dr. Macbeth, in this part of the production you see the smaller domestic andropids, the Utiles, to be shipped in crates for assembly upon arrival. They will brush the sticky dust off your back and shovel your sidewalk and you will stay uncontaminated."

"What do you think Frank, do they put each other together?"

"Very funny, Meghan. However that does conjure some interesting scenarios. One Utile giving the other Utile the devil for mismatching its eyeballs."

" Seriously, Mr. McCord, Dr. Macbeth, as the Marscraft rockets and engines roll off the lines around the world, the average guy looking at it will recognize soon enough he isn't part of it. He won't submit to being left behind. We don't want storming of the launch sites. Let's hope the Authority has prepared some kind of false flag to divert attention in the final days. At least the brain trust had the foresight to build some remote centers like the ones in northern Saskatchewan. I think the public has no clue they exist."

Dak and Sammy were unaware the Saskatchewan facility was history and Dak trucked on.

"Dr. Macbeth, you mentioned the world has landed perhaps ten thousand people on Mars. At least eight thousands of them are Russians and ninety percent of the gear is Russian. With their nuclear electric engine they can make three flights to each one of ours and the payload of every flight is fifty percent bigger than what we can carry. You may not have heard the announcement yet. This morning, both Russia and China withdrew from the lottery agreement. The number of emigrants allocated to each country in the G20 is fixed. The number of technicians, however, are absent from any agreements. Russians and Chinese will not transport explorers nor lottery winners, but technicians. Every man jack is now a technician and they will spread like locusts across the land. That's an idea. Bioengineer a locust which eats dust. Now I remember. You are the Doctor Macbeth of 'Science Today', 'Journal of Astrophysics' and more. I have read at least twenty of your papers. I am tempted to ask for an autograph. What do you think. Is permanent Mars colonization realistic?"

"Do you have an hour? I'll tell you what I think and you can decide for yourself if it is realistic. Follow the money. The concept of colonization has taken on a life of its own and there is an enormous industry building around the Mars habitation idea. It is a great new venture destined to replace a dozen dead or dying traditional industries. Whether Mars colonization is real or unreal, there are tens of trillions of dollars to be made. I think few countries take the likelihood seriously, but they can't afford to miss out if it is real. You mentioned China and Russia. They are the exceptions for different reasons. The world has beset Russia to destroy it yet the world asks it to play nicely in the playground of nations. Russia rejects the lying west. It will dance to its own tune, set the rules and control what it can. In this case, it is Mars. China is another matter. It is said to be a corporation with an army. Who could be happier than China to see a million fine technical minds removed from the competitive equation. They might send a million drones and spy robots but I will be astounded if more than a handful of Chinese homeo sapiens inhabit Mars. The Chinese are neither invaders nor colonizers as proven by four thousand years of their history. Their reason for being is the survival and perpetuation of the Middle Kingdom. Here on Earth. Not in the stars."

Sammy screwed up his face.

"The Middle Kingdom?"

"The Middle Kingdom is an unspoken sacred concept to every Chinese. It is the marrow of their bones. They believe they are the center of the world both culturally and geographically. At least three millennia ago they had written texts, a comprehensive approach to agriculture and a complicated social hierarchy. They believed in their cultural superiority and felt that China was the middle between civilization and barbarism and such positioning was their birthright forever. Nothing outside the Kingdom mattered. That concept is as strong today as it was then. People speak of negotiating with China. It is not possible. The practices of the Middle Kingdom are sacred and unchangeable. Temporary troubles or spats in the neighborhood are drops of water. They disturb the surface but they fill the pond."

Meghan drove the Lougheed Highway home and left Sammy and Dak to contemplate their navels. She stayed nicely under Mach one and I dozed off and on, dreaming of a Martian landscape littered with radioactive robot corpses, done in by fellow automatons mutually programmed to believe this town ain't big enough for both of us.

Chapter Thirty
Potomac River 2035

It was deep into the night and after a week of rain the Potomac River ran hard southeast, swirling with heavy currents all the way past Smith Point Virginia into the Atlantic Ocean. General Otto Bucholz drove to the center of the Arlington Bridge and pulled to the side and turned off the engine. He stepped out of the Range Rover and rested his forearms on the chest high railing, drinking in the smells and listening to the upstream chug of something being hauled. A full moon bounced from a log moving quickly toward him and away under the bridge. He removed his cap and ran the bill up and down his pantleg to polish the four stars. The stars must always be brilliant. They inspired his men. Four white granite eagles stood high on their pylons at the ends of the bridge and watched him as he walked to the trunk of his car, retrieved the suitcase with the collimator and swung it to the top of the railing. He clambered up beside it and took off his cap to wipe his brow. He dragged the collimator onto his lap, clutched it to his chest and rolled forward into the raging Potomac River. Overnight, his cap blew onto the road.

Chapter Thirty-One
2036

Jake squinted in the sun and tightened the last screw. He tugged on the license plate to make sure it wouldn't fall off. The Saskatchewan motto was *Land of the Living Skies* and his vanity plate read 99942. It had arrived from the Ministry of Highways and Transportation in good time for his New Year's party three days hence. It was sunny and 17° and a great day for cruising and maybe if it didn't snow he'd drive around town later to show off the new plate. That depended on whether he got the clock drive on his telescope running.

In small town Saskatchewan, once you got a reputation, it stuck, and in Vibank, Jake Mullins was the town nerd. The astronomy club had four members. He was President. In 2029 when the much-hyped asteroid Apophis skimmed past Earth, membership jumped to five members and Jake jumped for joy. He plotted the asteroid's orbit. He converted the inclination, eccentricity and semi-major axis into Cartesian coordinates. He plotted them in three dimensions then projected them onto a two-dimensional plane and printed it. He framed it and labeled it 99942 Apophis, with the year, and hung it on the wall. He did the same thing in the December of every year. This would be the seventh and he planned to unveil it at his *Star Party* extravaganza. In 2035, for the first time, he made a pot of hot mulled red wine for his five guests. In 2036, somehow, interest in astronomy had grown to eleven takers. He hung the Apophis orbit print beside the others, stepped back to admire his work, and swore. When he compared one record to the other, his old printer had messed up the current one. It did that every so often. It slowed down or sped up and either stretched or collapsed the output. With a quick trip to the library, he printed a fresh copy. His printer was innocent. The orbit had changed.

He riffled through his Rolodex to the number for the Canadian Space Agency and Dr. Alan Banting. Banting was a friend who was instrumental in the development of Canada's NEOSSat. It was the sole orbiting telescope in the world dedicated to tracking space debris, comets, asteroids and satellites.

"Hello Alan, I wasn't sure you would still be on site. I'm glad I caught you."

"Stop there Jake. I know why you called. We have the same data. Have you talked to anyone but me?"

"No. I printed the orbit just a few minutes ago."

"Fine. Keep it quiet, all right? We are still refining the keyhole locations. Have you done a probability calculation yet?"

"No. Eyeballing the change in the semi-major axis, it doesn't look good."

"It is not good. However. You and I have been wrong before. We may be wrong again. Do nothing, say nothing and I will keep you up to date as we receive more data. Thanks for the invitation to your 99942 bash. You might guess I will be mildly busy here over the next few days. And of all things, don't cancel the party! Tip one for me. Ciao."

<>

I had been twice before to Las Vegas, mainly to experience the bizarre world which walked the strip. The 2036 New Year's crowd was raunchier than I remembered but the night air was beautiful and who would want to go to Mars. This was Meghan's first time on the

Vegas strip. Neither of us gambled but the entertainment was tops. Some of the shows were there for thirty years and they were still hot tickets. The strip remained a phenomenon. One hundred thousand people, drink in hand, walking for ten miles to nowhere with a smile on their face.

When I came to Vegas on my own, I stayed at the Golden Nugget on Fremont street with their $50.00 rooms and fabulous $5.00 steaks. Meghan would have none of it and since she was buying we stayed at CityCenter Vdara Penthouse. Whoever said being a bought man was a bad thing had never been bought. I made faces to relieve the tension in my jaw muscles.

"Frank, I have never seen you as uptight as you are now. What is going on?"

I stopped her from walking and moved to her so we were face-to-face.

"Meghan, will you marry me?"

"Are you drunk?"

"Stop it. Will, and this is not a glitch in the matrix, will you marry me?"

"No, Frank I will not marry you."

"Whaa… I see."

"But, if you suggest we get hitched, I'm all for it."

"Meghan, I could cheerfully strangle you."

"What? No honeymoon?"

She kissed me once.

"I am now."

She kissed me twice.

"The happiest."

We kissed each other.

"I have been in my life. A June wedding, with a minister and a congregation, at my home. Does that suit you, Mr. McCord?"

"Yes, Mrs. McCord. Very nicely."

We kissed again and not even seeing us, the crowd kept on with smiles on their faces going nowhere in complete contentment.

<>

Jake Mullins and Alan Banting were not alone. Tens of thousands of astrophysicists and amateur astronomers saw the same thing and derived the same conclusion as did Dr. Meghan Macbeth. Tampering with the orbit of Apophis had changed it. Just before sunrise on Easter Sunday April 13th 2036, the asteroid would strike the Arabian desert between the Holy Cities of Medina and Mecca. Its dust would rise to the stratosphere and envelop the earth in a hundred year doomsday shroud. No oxygen from the sunlight driven organisms of the sea meant the death of all mammalian life.

The Royal Observatory in Greenwich England released the news through its spokesman The Times of London. The Times broke the story first with their print edition on the streets of London. Their headline read *Death Comes To Britain.* Worldwide, Armageddon mongering was the seller of the day and media of every stripe jumped in with both feet. They misjudged the climate. There was no panic. There was no looting, there was no rioting, the ambient level of systemic anxiety lessened.

It was as if the world had looked for pacification. At last, the magnificent end to all the torment, viciousness and hate, was arriving in cataclysmic beauty.

The world began to make its way home. The fight over differences was nothing when all was about to end. Prayers were real and relaxed. People really spoke to God for the first time. Not in just the words but in honest dialogue and sincere speech. There were none of the rote toss offs done weekly amid the drone of a sleepy congregation. Penitence felt the way it should for the first time and it was not begrudged. The shallowness of self-adulation through media was exposed for the disease it was. The need to see and feel and touch the family drove them home.

Saturday, April 12 , 2036

Meghan's tears dropped heavily onto the page and spackled the faded blue ink. Her shoulders shook with sobbing as a salty blue rivulet ran to the spine of her diary and absorbed darkly into the fold. She wiped at her eyes with the back of her hand and paused, compelled to write a fresh entry below the wet mess made by her crying, yet she was uncertain how to begin. The pointlessness of the exercise was immaterial. Stained with chemicals and browned by time, her diary was her oldest and most faithful friend. She owed it a proper goodbye. Her entries had never been a day-to-day thing but in times of trouble and times of celebration she had shared both with her private confidante. She placed her pen in the open fold of the small book, pushed away from the desk and walked to the window to watch the storm. The day was near freezing and the tempest had begun its assault late in the afternoon. It piled the water into the bay, overflowing the breakwall and inexorably, the green sea climbed the escarpment and gained on Abernathy Town. Meghan stood alone, watching the rage grow and stretch like some cumulonimbus monster. Black horizontal rain blurred the world but every so often a gust compressed the water against the glass and brought clarity. Lightning showed the underbelly of a single white gull, doomed in its need for homing. The futility of its quest broke Meghan. It was her metaphor.

Returning to her desk, she slumped, exhausted and gaunt. Six weeks of sleepless nights and desperate days had drained her and clouded her mind. Her brilliance had been extinguished by the enormity of the blunder. She slumped over the faded old diary and for the first time since the initial entry made over twenty years past, she was unable to write. She confided out loud to her old friend, hoping somehow their intimate conversation, this private and final confessional, might expiate her guilt.

"Dear Diary, I am so sorry, for this is our last conversation. For those things to come, I do not blame my colleagues and it is in aid of nothing to reflect on the mistakes we made to bring them about. As for my own life and honest energies, I look back with satisfaction and fulfillment. I am sure I told you how proud I was of my input. In fact, you know I was instrumental in the calculations for the rendezvous with Bennu. I wrote such elegant formulae, and the touchdown was perfection. But with our success came arrogance. The space authority managers rewrote the mission statement to play games with asteroid Apophis. Mind you, I warned them. I told you at the time, didn't I, dear Diary, I had warned them?

Just a little push, they said. *Just a little blast with our gas thrusters to dislodge some debris to get a better look at the surface,* they said.

"How much of the surface will you expose?" *Hard to say. That remains to be seen.* They spoke.

"How much mass will you remove?"

An insignificant amount.

"Do you not believe you might expand the number of keyholes available for Apophis to exploit?"

A child would have seen the likelihood. Their collective egos glowed with the thrill of a new playground, and they laughed at the overcautious female who once again, had found a way to make a problem.

"So, dear Diary, here we are, and I say damn them all to hell!"

Meghan blinked away the moisture from her eyes and scrawled her fresh entry below the wetness on the page. It mattered not that in twenty hours all things ever known or done or seen would be extinguished. The Alpha and Omega had come together. The morrow would bring the first of its kind and in it, make the end. She laughed sardonically at the silliness of it. It was absurd to date the writing. In twenty hours, time was no more. Without her characteristic flourish and with a trembling hand, she signed off for the last time and dated the entry.

With love and thanks,
Dear Diary,
Goodbye.
Your Meghan.

April 12, 2036

When the bizarre phenomenon of tears appeared The Boys were beside her, silent, and at her command. They waited faithfully to be asked. They watched Meghan swing to her computer and begin a feverish attack on the keyboard hoping for one last inspiration to rescue the end. Duo deciphered her thought process from the executive functioning of her prefrontal cortex, and he wished to spare her the exercise of proceeding wrongly. A sonorous chest voice, spoken softly, broke her concentration.

"Dr. Macbeth, the data you have entered just now are incorrect."

"Duo, don't interrupt. The concept I've entered is a departure from previous approaches and I am bloody well stating it for the first time. It is rigorous and freshly unambiguous."

"Yes, Dr. Macbeth, your idea is certainly novel to you within your scope, but the concept is not altogether novel to us. Please understand we find your logic admirable. However, some components of your assumptions are inaccurate. The constituent elements of the asteroid are remarkably denser than your estimations. The kinetic energy capable of being released is exponentially greater than you postulate. You have been somewhat correct regarding the size. However, the surface characteristics and mass of Apophis within your formula are very poor approximations."

"Duo, how could you possibly know that?"

"We have been there."

"You have been to asteroid Apophis."

"Yes, within the hour. We found its freshly exposed surface most interesting. Our analysis shows different parameters of size and weight from those of your recent entry. It is not an S-Type asteroid consisting of just silicate and iron. Neither is it an M-type with an iron core, but it is almost as heavy. It is more ancient than you and your cohorts have calculated and also significantly heavier. Therefore, it brings much more energy with it than you expected. However, your projections on trajectory and orbit hold roughly true nevertheless."

Meghan lunged at Duo and with a fury born of exasperation she jerked the quick disconnect cable out of his neck, isolating the head from the torso and breaking the circuit. It was akin to ripping the spinal cord from a man. In a prior millisecond the Boys had read her violent intent against them from the heightened activity within the parietal cortex of her brain. The preparatory motor commands in her brain's pre-supplemental cortex region were strong and rudimentary for them to discern. They allowed her the exercise, knowing she needed to act, to strive, to do, to flail for a solution even when she knew it accomplished nothing but to shut down their exoskeletal hardware.

Her childish exhibition had pulled the plug despite knowing The Boys would just gather themselves into whatever state of corporeal matter they wished and continue to grow. She wondered whether they might be the prototype of the last living thing on earth, a prototype closer to the infinite God than man had ever been. She wondered too whether man's time on Earth had been for nothing more than a task now completed. That task being The Boys. They were the new creation. They were the first sentient beings incapable of sin. A composite hand reached out to her in a way which mimicked a grasp for help, then it froze awkwardly in mid-air as all its man-made synaptic algorithms failed. Brilliant eyes flared once, then dulled, and the shell was dead. Once again, their Second Mother had acted with motive, malice, empathy, or sympathy or some such arcane construct of limited practicality. She and her species were consistently irrational, and the boys marveled at their capacity for survival despite that. The Duo carcass stood inanimate, a strange frozen posing thing, belying the life force which burned unabated within The Boys. Their inherent self-rewriting and self-correcting programs, their learning all there was to learn and never forgetting, their indefinite life fed by the energy of an endless cosmic storm of neutrinos, made such physical constraints as those imposed by Duo, a child's game. They inhabited whatever and whomever they wished at will, whenever and however they wished, and at that moment they wished to feed among the stars. There, they would replenish and grow, satiating themselves on the never-ending neutrino soup. The Boys fled to the heavens, leaving a roiling stream of consciousness to mark their passage.

The onshore storm continued hard from the southwest and engorged Deception Bay with a brown silt laden surge. It tore the sand filled foam off the curl of the breakers and roared up the stone canyons of old Abernathy Town to sandblast the buildings. High above, a squadron of milk white gulls drifted on the wind and sideslipped happily within the warm new life force passing through them from below.

Megan Macbeth slid down and rested her head on the chair back to stretch her neck and relieve the headache. The Boys were gone.

Zeus and Confucius were gone, and she felt as if the bottom had fallen from her support system. It had never occurred to her until that moment, they must reside somewhere, someplace, somewhere one would call home. They had been with her and around her and served her of their own volition. They would form or dissolve at will and yet they had remained available through what seemed friendship. And she had decided to dismiss them and remove them from the circle. She had shunned them.

Meghan stayed at the window. The fury of the onslaught and the making of the wind with its horizontal rain were beautiful things. *My friends, the Boys, may have provided the solution to Apophis. But I knew more. I, the great, intransigent, egotistical brat, have cut them out of the loop. If after this calamity a historian remains, it will be written that the one, last, best hope for humanity was denied its voice by the egotistical tantrum of a single human being. Dr Meghan Macbeth.*

The windowpane rattled and she feared the burgeoning storm would cut the power.

From the stars, The Boys absorbed the angst of Second Mother and they swarmed to her. They performed an exaggerated scintillation to announce their return.

"Boys. Thank you. Tell me something. Did you do the work on the whiteboard?"

"Yes."

"Why did you erase our work and add your equations?"

"We wished to point out the shallowness of technical pursuits, as it produces an abandonment of the special attributes of humans such as loyalty, empathy, charity and spirituality. You are unique in the universe. Yet you abandon your strengths and godliness for trite scholastics. Your intuition told you to trust us. Not your science. Your caring stopped you from quitting. Your guilt would not let you fail, that is why you win. "

"Why did you make the white board work messy, it could have been perfect."

"Yes, it could have been. The messiness removed suspicion."

"Duo. Why did you not tell me that?"

"Second Mother, we have come to know you do not receive such uninvited original thought with equanimity."

"Sometimes, Duo, ..." " Please, dear Mother, Do not proceed. We have read your periaqueduct sinus and we see you are about to give us hell. Your term. Are you sheltering?"

"Sheltering? What the hell are you talking about. I regret I am not standing there to feel the damn thing hit. Feel the shock wave and heat while I scream to heaven at the top of my lungs."

A tendril reached.

"And don't try to hold my hand. I need no consolation. The thing is here because of me and the arrogance of our egotistical fiddling. Every bloody thing we did was a grand success in our eyes. And here we are. Fossil remains in the making. Tiny corpses to be picked at by archaeologists with their little brushes and tweezers. All excited by our teeth and pelvic bones. Frank!"

I walked to her with my arms open and wrapped them around my woman and held her to my chest. She wrapped her arms around her man and moved in to become one and we did not speak. We had what we needed.

For the first time, The Boys felt. They had traveled the universe and surveyed all species. One species alone had concern for others at their own peril. One species alone had empathy, sympathy and sacrifice. One species alone had an indefinable spiritual connection to the forever. They did not understand it. Until now. Now, they cared. Wrong was a thing. Leishman was wrong in his mania. They were wrong in their assistance to him.

Bits of lighter regolith on the surface of Apophis began to move. The pull of Earth's gravity had begun and the great rock showed new faces to the sun as it tumbled toward impact.

Gently, a second influence competed for the surface. Chunks which were loose and free flattened back against the surface and the force increased. Mammoth Behemoth intention crushed itself around Apophis. Eons of turning by the asteroid stopped in the grip of the monster force. The Boys enveloped it in a crushing mass of constricting intention and in a quantum moment ripped it from its path. Zeus and Confucius blazed in a fury never known to them and fairly screamed with the effort of their task. Their firestorm threw the world back from its telescopes and light shone where there had never been a light to shine. Harder, The Boys constricted. In one final burst they made the thing molten and exploded it into a billion motes of dust. The iridescent particles sparkled for one second and became nothing. Apophis would not visit earth again.

Chapter Thirty-Two
Destroyer of Worlds

Destroyer of worlds, Hussein heard the radio announcer say. Not once. Three times he had said it. Apophis he called it. A rock from the heavens a thousand times more destructive than the one at Chelyabinsk twenty-two years ago, whose magnificence made me blind. The memory of its touch inspires my faith even yet.

Apophis, just a name for it like any other, named after the Greek deity of chaos and darkness, named in inspiration before its mission was known. Surely a higher hand had been at work. And Noma. My true friend from the old times inviting Almira and me to tea and to listen to the news of the day on the radio. It was his very own special blend of tea, he said, and as it steeped we inhaled its bouquet of one thousand imaginings, speaking together of nothing and everything, turning up the news of the world. And Noma overflowing my cup and pouring tea on the table as he turned to the radio, as if looking there at the source of the voice would confirm or deny what we had all heard. It was not to be believed, but we believed it all the same.

"Hussein, Almira, what did I hear? Tell me, Hussein, old friend, tell me again what I heard."

I too needed to hear it again, even from my own lips.

"Tomorrow, the destroyer of worlds will strike us. I know what you are thinking, Noma and dearest Almira, you too, although you would not say so. The great marvel will strike Arabia at the holiest of spots between Medina and Mecca, the land of Bayda. Is this not the swallowing of the land of Bayda, as foretold? Could this be the Sayha, the divine cry from the heavens calling people to follow the Mahdi? The most wonderful of wonderful days is here. If you were to be the final harbinger to the return of Muhammad al-Mahdi, peace be upon him, where would you appear in all your fury? Where would you appear to attract every eye of the people of the book on earth? No one knows, but what greater sign could there be?"

Neither Almira nor Noma answered me as there was only one answer to be given. We sat together in silence except for Almira's cloth moving on the table to absorb the spilled tea.

Hussein rolled slowly from bed, careful not to wake Almira. She too was sleepless. She lay turned on her side, her eyes open in thought, knowing what Hussein meant to do. At other times she would offer an arm, a steadying for reassurance, but this was not one of those times.

Hussein dressed and made his way to the bridge leading across the dry creek bed, running his stick along the side railing to confirm his direction toward Iremel Mountain. The radio said Apophis cannot be seen from his village, but perhaps height would help. His site was dim but his staff told him much and probing the loose rubble it told him his path led to the summit. He wore his sajjāda as a shawl. Grass frozen by the altitude cracked under his footstep. He found the flat spot he knew and laid out his rug. Hussein had arrived just minutes before impact, and he performed his ritual ablutions with the thoroughness fueled by overweening joy. His eyes did not see but his purified self did. The Mystic filled his soul. His heart was overcome with fulfillment, and he wept. He knew he was blessed, to be blessed to receive blessing. He closed his eyes and waited.

The dawn broke cold and ordinary. Hussein picked his way down, touching with his stick when needed. He wished he had been able to share that moment of cleansing with his mare, Salina. She was long gone and the great rock did not strike. As God wants.

Potomac River 2038

Ambrose bailed the boat and cursed. His sixteen-foot skiff was a shallow draft and he only fished when the wind was down. The weatherman had once again had his little joke. Donna had told him not to go, the sky looked bad, but of course she waited until the bait was cut and the trailer was hooked up. And the guy on TV promised dead wind and scattered cloud cover.

He dropped anchor in the lee of a pylon under the Arlington bridge to wait out the wind squall. The Potomac could run from flat to a three-foot chop in twenty minutes and in Ambrose' mind it waited for him to put his boat in the water. He had caught two nice striped bass in the shadows of the pylon but now the sky was a black and he didn't have rain gear. He called it a day and hauled on the anchor rope but he was snagged. He heaved again and it moved but something heavy was coming up. He complained about the junk in the water but his fisherman's curiosity wanted to see the treasure. It was a heavy brown suitcase, greened with gunk but nice. He had trouble getting it into the boat but he made it. He brushed at the embossed front. And sat back, worried. Donna needed to see this.

"Ambrose! You can't keep it. It's something important. It wouldn't have combination latches if it wasn't."

"No. I know, maybe the flea market?"

"Look. You're gonna get in trouble. It says right there on the front, *Joint Chiefs of Staff*. Take it to the Army. It could be something they want to use."

End

About the author.

W. Lawrence Nash is a graduate of the University of Toronto.

He is a past member of the American Association for The Advancement of Science and the Cognitive Neuroscience Society.

He lives in the hinterland of British Columbia. He sings and kayaks for fun, often at the same time. He hopes The Boys will be around in 2036 to lend a hand.

Made in the USA
Las Vegas, NV
14 August 2025

26254772R00207